A New Beginning

I realize that it's possible that I am having a midlife crisis, although I am loath to use that expression since it means that I only expect to live to be eighty-four. (But, honestly, who really wants to live that long anyway, unless you're fabulous like Jessica Tandy or Ruby Dee?) But the plain truth is that I am going through *something*, whether it's a midlife crisis or early menopause or simply crushing boredom. At some point between being a good wife and a good mother and always doing the right thing, I have lost *me.* So, instead of taking Zoloft, as half of the women in the PTA do, or succumbing to twice-weekly couch sessions with the local shrink, I am going to take matters into my own hands. I am going to renew myself. I am going to recapture my former babe status. I am going to do something for *me.* Something that has nothing to do with my children, whom I adore, or my husband, whom I do love. Something that is solely about Ellen Ivers.

Something New

Janis Thomas

BERKLEY BOOKS, NEW YORK

THE BERKLEY PUBLISHING GROUP
Published by the Penguin Group
Penguin Group (USA) Inc.
375 Hudson Street, New York, New York 10014, USA
Penguin Group (Canada), 90 Eglinton Avenue East, Suite 700, Toronto, Ontario M4P 2Y3, Canada
(a division of Pearson Penguin Canada Inc.) • Penguin Books Ltd., 80 Strand, London WC2R 0RL,
England • Penguin Group Ireland, 25 St. Stephen's Green, Dublin 2, Ireland (a division of Penguin
Books Ltd.) • Penguin Group (Australia), 250 Camberwell Road, Camberwell, Victoria 3124, Australia
(a division of Pearson Australia Group Pty. Ltd.) • Penguin Books India Pvt. Ltd., 11 Community
Centre, Panchsheel Park, New Delhi—110 017, India • Penguin Group (NZ), 67 Apollo Drive,
Rosedale, Auckland 0632, New Zealand (a division of Pearson New Zealand Ltd.) • Penguin Books
(South Africa) (Pty.) Ltd., 24 Sturdee Avenue, Rosebank, Johannesburg 2196, South Africa

Penguin Books Ltd., Registered Offices: 80 Strand, London WC2R 0RL, England

This is a work of fiction. Names, characters, places, and incidents either are the product of the author's
imagination or are used fictitiously, and any resemblance to actual persons, living or dead, business
establishments, events, or locales is entirely coincidental. Further, the publisher does not have any
control over and does not assume any responsibility for author or third-party websites or their content.

This book is an original publication of The Berkley Publishing Group.

PUBLISHING HISTORY
Berkley trade paperback edition / November 2012

Library of Congress Cataloging-in-Publication Data

Thomas, Janis.
Something new / Janis Thomas.
p.   cm.
ISBN 978-0-425-25769-2
1. Housewives—Fiction.   2. Midlife crisis—Fiction   3. Blogs—Fiction.   I. Title.
PS3620.H62796S66 2012
813'.6—dc23   2011052124

PRINTED IN THE UNITED STATES OF AMERICA

10 9 8 7 6 5 4 3 2 1

All my heart, Mom.

Acknowledgments

Writing a book is a solitary process, but publishing a book, like raising a child, takes a village. Thank you to Wendy Sherman, my fantastic agent, for your belief in my work and your many talents, and to the staff at Wendy Sherman Associates. Thanks to Jackie Cantor at Berkley for taking a chance on me, for your keen eye, and your love of laughter. To Amanda Ng for your patience in answering my many questions, and to Berkley Books for welcoming me into your fold.

I have been blessed with an amazing family, too many members to name here, but you are all special to me. Thanks, Dad, for your unfailing generosity and support and your writer's empathy. I love our debates, even though I know I drive you crazy! Thanks to my brothers, Mark and Craig, and to my niece Jacqueline for donating your time and energy and paper and ink. Thanks to my sister Sharilyn for the music, for your infectious enthusiasm, and for lovingly taking care of my kids whenever I needed some quiet time to write. And, of course, Mom, thank you for everything.

To Linda Coler-Fields, you are as essential to my life as the nose on my face. Thank you for your constancy and counsel. Thanks to Super-Penny Thiedemann, for your love, your Virgoan attention to detail, and your brainstorming techniques

Acknowledgments

(read: martinis). A big Thank-You to my Aunt Hilary, my cousins, and the Friends of Fiction (and Sometimes Non) Book Club who so generously read *Something New* fresh from my computer, and who gave me the confidence to send it out into the world. You guys are my lucky charm! Thanks to Michael Steven Gregory and the Southern California Writers Conference for providing a safe haven for us lunatics—uh—writers. You work tirelessly to support us and help us achieve success. Thanks, also, to Monique High, for setting this all in motion.

Finally, thanks to my husband, Alex, for your love and for your patience during those times when I was so consumed with my work, I was only *pretending* to listen to you. And to my kids, A.J. and Elle. You won't be able to read my books for decades, but you inspire me every single day, and I love you both more than words can say.

Something New

One

I am not a desperate housewife. *Desperate* is far too dramatic a word for someone who lives in a twenty-three-hundred-square-foot house in a bucolic suburb like Garden Hills. *Malcontent* is also an overly strident description, better suited to furtive, angry rebels meeting in the basement of some dilapidated tenement, putting the finishing touches on their blueprints for how they are going to overthrow "the Man." So, it is fair to say that I am neither desperate nor malcontent. I am bored.

Boredom is a common occurrence in matrimonial suburbia, insidious in the way it can masquerade as complacency. A lot of my peers suffer from it, and the ways in which they deal with it are as varied as their cars. (A myriad of styles, colors, and makes, but each of them worth enough to feed a third-world country.) Bridget Lowell joined a modern-day EST group that provides her with numerous opportunities to "live with dignity," one of which is to compile a list of all the things she's done wrong in her life and attempt to make them right. Given what I know about Bridget, she'll be at it till hell freezes over. Jim Lampert bought a Harley Davidson and has taken to zipping off on weekends sans wife, children, and minivan. Laurie Hanson has had every line between her neck and her hairline injected with Botox. She may no longer *be* bored, but she sure as hell *looks* bored, since she can't muster up a single expression of emotion on her placid face.

I thought I was immune to the midlife boredom routine. After all, I am married to a great guy who makes a great living selling office supplies, have three point five children (the point five is our dog, Sally), live in a great neighborhood in Southern California, and have all the creature comforts I desire. Sure, I gave up my career, but I manage to keep busy with the whole motherhood thing and find it quite rewarding—most of the time. I throw dinner parties, wowing my friends with my culinary skills (learned from the Food Network), and throw parties for my kids, wowing their friends with cool, completely off-the-wall cakes (also learned from the Food Network). I race here and there in my silver Ford Flex, dropping the kids at school, sports, ballet, junior guards. I make the appropriate noises when one of them gets the Principal's Award, or when my husband wins a new account. I do all the shopping and cooking, and most of the cleaning (except twice a month when Delmy shows up with her SUV of a vacuum). I help with homework and belong to a book club with six of my friends. (I try not to make pretentious selections like a few of the other members seem to do. I mean, *Atlas Shrugged*?) I volunteer at the school. I am an avid recycler. I give the occasional blow job to my husband when he's feeling stressed out. So, all in all, my days are pretty full.

But my forty-third birthday approaches—a day that will

signal that I am no longer a hair's breadth away from my thirties, but firmly entrenched in my forties. And I find that I am feeling wistful about my life. And bored. I am looking at things differently. I am looking at myself differently.

I have begun to gaze in the mirror for longer periods of time now. In the mornings, before my children wake up, and at night, after they have surrendered to sleep. There I stand, down the hall from my little progenies, staring at my reflection and wondering just who the hell it is staring back at me. I trace the wrinkles around my eyes with my index finger, lines that can be called *laugh lines* in your twenties and thirties, but in your forties must be labeled *crow's feet*. I run my hands through my reddish-brown hair, noting that ten years of Miss Clairol have stripped it of its luster and bounce. I pull my shirt up and spy the harsh effect gravity has had on my breasts, the havoc that childbirth has wreaked on my abdomen. And I think, *Wow, Ellen. Look what you've become.*

I was considered a babe once, sometime around the Clinton administration. But that time has long since passed. I have become a suburban cliché. The kind of woman lambasted ferociously by a certain chauvinistic shock jock on talk radio. The kind of woman who was once hot but has let herself go. I wasn't aware of the slide; I had simply changed my focus. I mean, who has time to pluck her eyebrows or shave her legs when she has three children to feed, clothe, and ferry to school?

And worse still, my husband, Jonah, is the kind of man who doesn't even see bushy eyebrows or hairy legs. He no longer loves me for how I look (which he did when we were first together, telling me that I made him hard every time I flashed my baby blues at him). He loves me for *who I am*. This may come across as a compliment, like he is the very best kind of unconditionally loving person, and he is. But when no one demands that you keep yourself in shape and properly groomed, well, you just don't keep yourself in shape and properly groomed. Whenever I complain about my flabby stomach, Jonah lovingly slips his arms around my middle and tells me that I grew three perfect babies *in there* and I should be proud of that fact. This little nugget used to reassure me. Now, it makes me want to punch him in the face.

I know I sound ungrateful, and I know there are millions of women out there who would kill for a man who loves them despite the mushroom cap spilling over the waistband of their favorite pair of jeans. My friend Mia, for one. Her husband has taken to making not-so-subtle comments about the size of her thighs and has even gone so far as to place Jenny Craig coupons on the refrigerator door. (I told her that if Jonah ever did that to me, I would beer-batter and fry up the coupons and force-feed them to him with Tabasco sauce.) My cousin Jill complains that her husband, Greg, never compliments her like he did when they were dating and that he rarely initiates sex. Jonah compliments me all the time, but lately I have come to mistrust these ministrations from him. "You look wonderful," he says in his most sincere voice, but I question whether he really *sees* me anymore. And when we make love, which we do at least once a month or more, as scheduling and children allow, I can't help but wonder whether he is replacing me in his mind with one of his attractive work colleagues, or an acquaintance at the club, or this particular checker at the grocery store who looks exactly like a porn star. Not that I blame him, really. I mean, if I weren't so busy trying to figure out who he's mentally fucking, I'd probably be fantasizing about someone else too.

I have started to suspect that the term *perfect marriage* is an oxymoron. I have started to wonder whether all marriages, even good ones like mine, harbor lies of omission and petty resentments and secret longings. Whether all husbands and wives sink into a quagmire of ambivalence, which they ignore in order to preserve the sanctity of their union. I have even begun to question whether human beings are truly meant to commit to one single person for the entirety of their lifetimes. The divorce rate being what it is, apparently I am not the only person to raise such questions.

I realize that it's possible that I am having a midlife crisis, although I am loath to use that expression since it means that I only expect to live to be eighty-four. (Although, honestly, who wants to live that long anyway, unless you're fabulous like Jessica Tandy or Ruby Dee?) But the plain truth is that I am going through *something*, whether it's a midlife crisis or early menopause or simply crushing boredom. At some point between being a good wife and a good mother and always doing the right thing, I have lost *me*. So, instead of taking Zoloft, as half of the women in the PTA do, or succumbing to twice-weekly couch sessions with the local shrink, I am going to take matters into my own hands. I am going to renew myself. I am going to recapture my former babe status. I am going to do something for *me*. Something that has nothing to do with my children or my husband. Something that is solely about Ellen Ivers.

I've decided to start with an area of my life over which I have a modicum of control: my outside. I am going to start working out again and eating right, like I used to do. I am going to invest in some beauty products that target the skin of "women of a certain age" (*my* age). Because I know that when you feel good about yourself, when you are confident in how you look, you open yourself up to a world of possibilities. And possibilities can lead to adventures, both large and small.

I feel better for having made this resolution, even though I have no idea what kind of adventure might be headed my way. I only know that reinvention is the mother of satisfaction. And I could use a little of that. Couldn't we all?

· Two ·

Of course, resolutions are easily made, but without inspiration and motivation, they are nearly impossible to keep. I realize this on the fourth day of my supposed renaissance when I bypass the treadmill and head straight for my son Connor's Pop-Tarts, which are calling to me from the kitchen counter where he left them. I'd been diligent for three days, jogging a total of six miles, sweating my saggy boobs off, my heart thumping alarmingly in my chest, cursing with every seemingly endless minute on the torturous machine. But by Thursday, my resolve has been whittled down to nothing, as I wonder just what the hell I am doing this for. Or, more to the point, *for whom*? When you have a husband who loves you no matter how you look, why put yourself through this hideous, organ-jarring exercise? For the endorphins? Please. I can get just as high on sugar and caffeine with a fraction of the effort.

I have also given up on the gaggle of wrinkle creams and

rejuvenating tonics and facial scrubs and moisturizers that I purchased at Target Monday morning. It's not that I am suddenly accepting of the trails that time has blazed on my forehead. It's more a matter of perseverance. By the time I've finished the dishes, checked homework, herded my children to bed, folded laundry, and answered my e-mails, I barely have enough energy reserved for washing my face and scrubbing my teeth before I fall, exhausted, onto my pillow. And I have discovered that beauty regimens are pretty grueling. You need a degree in anti-aging just to master the process. Seriously, universities ought to offer a course. Lines-Be-Gone 101. First comes the scrub, then comes the toner, then the undereye cream, which must be applied before the targeted wrinkle erase, which is followed by the all-over age-defying serum, and finally comes the moisturizer. I was in labor for less time than it takes to apply this shit.

And besides, who is going to care if my wrinkles suddenly seem to fade? Who is going to notice that my stomach is flatter than it's been since the birth of my last child? Perhaps hearing that Hugh Jackman is coming to Garden Hills for a little fun in the sun would produce the inspiration I need. But Hugh is too busy promoting his films. Besides, he has better places to recreate, like San Tropez or Fiji or Monte Carlo. So here I am at ten A.M. eating the last strawberry-frosted Pop-Tart in the box, knowing that Connor will be really irked when he finds I've pilfered his goods (even though I buy them). As I finish it off, I wonder how I am going to fill the hour I've just acquired by not doing the treadmill, and I get annoyed with myself for losing my steam so easily.

After I swallow down the last of the crumbs, I give my cousin Jill a call to see what she's up to. She promptly tells me that I must be telepathic because she was just about to call me. And I should come over *immediately*. She says this as though there is something of vital importance that I must see or hear, but I know Jill too well. Most likely, she can't wait to show me the color she chose for her toenails at her mani-pedi this morning. But since I have nothing better to do, I agree, telling her I'll be there in five minutes.

Jill lives about a mile away, and since I have no reason to apply makeup or earrings, or even brush my hair, I make it to her place in four. As I pull to the curb in front of her ranch-style home, I notice a moving van in the driveway of the house next door and several young guys hauling furniture into the house. I can tell by their bronzed (and bulging) biceps that they are surfers and/or sun worshippers—and probably students as well, earning extra cash to support their extracurricular activities. They are the kind of strapping youths who cause even the most happily married women to simultaneously clamp their thighs together and drop their jaws. I watch as two of them effortlessly pull a floral sofa from the van's rear end and, instantly, I think about my own rear end, which is currently encased in a tattered pair of gray sweats that may or may not have a hole revealing my left butt cheek.

Let me take a moment to dispel any notion that I am some kind of hag or that I look like a vagrant who just stepped out from under a cardboard box. I'm not, and I don't. I am a moderately attractive, almost-forty-three-year-old woman who manages to look more than presentable at PTA functions and cocktail parties. I do all the requisite primping when I need to, so as not to embarrass my children or my husband. I fit into a size ten, although nowadays I prefer that my waistbands have elastic. I own two pairs of Ferragamo pumps (which Jill talked me into because they were on sale) and a great Versace dress that I wore to Jonah's firm's Christmas party last year. But I prefer sweats or jeans and T-shirts for my everyday ensemble and cannot be bothered to apply makeup regularly. But as I stare, gape-mouthed, at the four studly twenty-somethings hefting chairs and tables and lamps and boxes across the lawn, I wish I had taken thirty seconds to drag a brush through my hair. And put on a pair of pants that I was certain didn't have a goddamn hole in the butt.

I reach for the sweatshirt I keep in the back of my Flex for emergencies. As I squirm and gyrate in order to tie it around my waist, hoping that it will cover the alleged hole, Jill appears at the front door.

"Come on, come on!" she calls, drawing the attention of the boys next door. She glances over at them and gives them a coy wave reminiscent of a beauty queen.

Jill is not classically beautiful, but she has that fresh-faced, youthful quality that brings to mind those Ivory Girl commercials from the eighties. Originally from the South, she is the epitome of a Georgia peach, with a rosy complexion and a bubbly personality to match. She is two years older than me and looks thirty-five. (Bitch!) And she is always perfectly coiffed and well groomed. (Yes, she manages to find time to shave and pluck despite the fact that she has three children.) At the hands of her menacing African American trainer, Buick, she keeps herself fit and trim. (Buick, like the car, though he more closely resembles a Hummer.) And she has the loveliest green eyes I've ever seen. Why her husband, Greg, won't touch her anymore is one of the great mysteries of life, equal to the current resting place of Jimmy Hoffa.

Jill flashes the movers a smile, and I notice that the two carrying a computer desk up the porch look like they might drop it on their feet. I alight from the car and head up the flagstone path, where Jill meets me halfway. She drapes her arm around me and giggles.

"A little eye candy to keep you going all day."

I laugh, but I can feel all of the boys' eyes on the two of us and can almost hear their thoughts as they consider us: The Beauty (Jill) and the Beast (who else?). Well, at least the sweatshirt is covering the hole on my ass.

She guides me up to her front door, takes one last look at the testosterone fest, then ushers me inside.

Like Jill herself, her house is neat and orderly, bright and cheerful. No piles of stuff lying on surfaces, which I find mystifying since she has three boys. (Four, if you count Greg.) She tells me that she allows her sons freedom in their own rooms; she doesn't care if their personal dwellings look like they've been hit by a monsoon as long as they keep the rest of the house neat. (I tried this edict at home, but to no avail. My children, God love them, are themselves little monsoons who regularly leave a trail of destruction in their wakes. I hustle after them like FEMA, and with about as much success.)

As I enter the kitchen, I detect the aroma of freshly brewed coffee. Jill has set two mugs on the granite counter and goes about filling them from the Braun all-in-one she got for Mother's Day.

"What's the matter?" she asks with an uncharacteristic frown. Frowning and Jill's face do not go together, which is why she has never needed—and probably will never need—Botox. I, on the other hand, am a frowner of the first order and would require at least three vials of dead botulism cells for the furrow between my brows alone.

"What do you mean?" I counter, stirring two teaspoons of sugar into my mug.

"You look . . . I don't know. Bummed out."

Jill knows me better than anyone, even my own sister. And she has a way of getting me to talk about things I'd prefer not to talk about. She has an intuitive side that always emerges when I'm around. I consider just how much I should reveal to her, what she'll make of all my inner musings. I wonder if I should tell her about my failed attempt at reinvention and, consequentially, my inevitable obsoletion.

"Is *obsoletion* a word?" I ask aloud.

She looks at me, almost cross-eyed with puzzlement. "What the h-e-l-l does that mean?"

Jill has been spelling out swear words for so long that it's become a habit. She does so even when her children aren't around, and ironically, all of her children can now spell. I am suddenly reminded of a conversation I bore witness to about three months back when Jonah had taken the kids to a ball game and I'd stayed at Jill's for dinner. She, cooking her old standby, chicken with peanut sauce and rice, burned her hand on the electric range and had blurted out a shrill f-u-c-k!

Her son Decatur, thirteen going on forty-seven, had given her an award-winning eye roll. "Jeez, Mom. Why don't you just say *fuck*?"

Jill had promptly ordered Decatur to wash his mouth out with soap, to which he replied, "I will if you will. Just because you spelled it out doesn't mean you weren't *thinking* it."

At which point, Denver, nine years old (and no, I don't know why my cousin named her boys after cities starting with the letter *D*—another great mystery) chimed in with, "Pastor McInerny says that the *thought* is as bad as the *deed*."

"Pastor McInerny is an a-s-s," replied Decatur.

"Who's an ass?" came the voice of six-year-old Deet (short for—wait for it—Detroit) as he walked into the kitchen to grab a juice box from the fridge.

"Well, d-a-m-n!" Jill had said, throwing up her arms in surrender, then proceeded to drink three quarters of a bottle of white zinfandel before pronouncing herself s-h-i-t-faced.

"What's so funny?" she asks me now, noting the smirk that is pasted to my face.

"Nothing. Not a d-a-m-n thing."

"Ha ha ha." She takes a sip of her coffee and eyes me over the rim. "You're bummed, right?"

"I am most definitely *not* bummed." I refuse to be described by a phrase that lost all popularity by the year 1991. "You asked *me* over, remember?" I hazard a glance at her long acrylic nails as they tap a staccato rhythm on the countertop. Jill usually chooses a color with one of those cutesy names like Just Peachy or Everything's Coming Up Rosy. Today they appear to be Out Damn Spot Red. I lower my eyes to my own fingers, which are currently clutching my coffee mug. My nails are short and unembellished, as usual, and I think, *Balefully Boring.*

"Yes, I did." She nods thoughtfully. "I saw something at the salon this morning that made me think of you."

I remain silent, waiting, thinking, what could it possibly be? UFO? Machete-wielding madwoman? Hugh Jackman naked, streaking across Vale Street? (That would definitely be *something.*)

She reaches into the drawer behind her and withdraws a magazine, and I can't help but think of all the magazines decorating nearly every flat surface in my house, from the living room coffee table to the backs of all three toilets. Who carefully places magazines in a drawer in the kitchen except for a completely anal-retentive neat freak? That's my cousin Jill. And I both love and resent her for it.

"I saw this article," she says, pointing to a headline on the right side of the cover. I am able to read the boldly printed name of the magazine, *Ladies Living-Well Journal*, but, my eyesight being what it has become, I cannot read the title of the article. It's just as well, I think. It's probably about how to spice up your sex life or how to cleanse your body of unwanted toxins. Or maybe it's about how cleansing your body of unwanted toxins can spice up your sex life.

"It's a writing competition," Jill declares, barely keeping her excitement under wraps. "The best blog wins ten thousand dollars!"

"I don't even know what a blog is," I reply. In truth, I have a vague notion, since all three of my kids are required to blog for school. But theirs are the only ones I've read, and since the subject of their blogs ranges from the age-old debate of lunch boxes versus paper sacks to why PF Flyers are the absolute bomb and no other shoe should ever be worn, I sort of zone out when I fulfill my parental duty by skimming through them.

I realize that Jill is talking and I try my best to do what I always ask my children to do: to give her my full attention and listen with both my ears.

"Now, the deadline to enter is next Friday, and you have to post once a day for two weeks," she says, "but you can write your blog posts in advance if you want. The magazine gives you all the info you need to get started."

"Blogs are losing popularity," I tell her. "I heard it on the news." Actually, Connor told me, but hearing it on the news sounds more authoritative.

"Only with kids," she counters knowingly. "Blogs are still the rage with middle-agers."

"Who are you calling middle-aged?"

"Stay on point, will you? You'd be a great blogger!"

I take a deep breath and blow it out on a sigh. Then I snort. Now, I know that snorting is not the most attractive habit, but it is a very effective way to convey derision.

"Don't do that!" Jill complains. "I'm serious, Ellen. This is perfect for you."

At one time I was a mildly successful journalist. I wrote freelance for a variety of magazines and newspapers and had garnered a reputation for being fast, funny, and philosophical. I'd even begun a novel, just before meeting Jonah. Needless to say, the first eight chapters of said novel are, at this moment, lying in the bottom of a box on the uppermost shelf of my attic, collecting dust and feeding mice.

"I haven't written anything since Connor was born," I say.

"I know. And I just can't understand why."

"I'm busy!" Defensiveness creeps into my tone because I know what Jill is thinking. She's thinking exactly what I'm thinking. Busy with *what*?

"Look, when your kids were little, yeah, okay. But they're all in school now. I know you can carve out some time for this. A few hours a day is all you'd need."

"I'm busy reinventing myself," I blurt out before I can slap my hand over my mouth.

Jill is silent for a full ten seconds, regarding me as though I am a new and interesting species of insect—fascinating to look at for a moment, but almost certainly about to be squashed.

"And what, pray tell, does that mean?" she asks.

I shrug noncommittally. "I'm just taking some time to reassess my life and make some positive changes."

"Like wearing T-shirts that don't have stains on them?"

I look down at my white peace-sign shirt. Sure enough, there is a tear-shaped drop of strawberry-colored goo just above my right breast. Perhaps I should have put the sweatshirt on instead of wrapping it around my waist. But then, what would I have done about the hole? I guess I could have walked *backward* into Jill's house.

"Yeah. Like that," I say, folding my arms across my chest.

"Pop-Tarts?" she asks, and I nod. "Frosted or unfrosted?"

"Frosted," I reply, and it's her turn to nod.

"So, how's this reinvention thing working out so far?"

I agree to take the *Ladies Living-Well Journal* with me because I know that Jill will pout and moan if I don't. She basks in small victories, and I haven't the heart to deprive her of this one. I tell her that I will think about it, to which she replies that I really ought to do more than *think* about it. I am a wonderful writer, she tells me. And getting back to the computer will fit right in with my resolution to improve myself. This is something just for me, she says. Perhaps she is right. And I will look at the article. If not today, then tomorrow. Or over the weekend, between soccer and T-ball. Or between Jessie's costume fitting for the school play and Matthew's science project. Or after I finish the ten thousand other chores I've racked up. Oh, who am I kidding? I might as well dump the magazine in Jill's recycling bin on the way to my car.

But I don't. I cheerfully hug my cousin and make my way down the path to my Flex. As I shove the key into the door lock, I see movement in my peripheral vision and automatically assume that it's one of the movers. But when I look up, I see a handsome man dressed in faded jeans and a white T-shirt heading in my direction. He waves and smiles, and

I see the laugh lines etched into the corners of his eyes—because men, no matter what their age, have laugh lines, not crow's feet (totally unfair, but what can you do?)—and a smattering of gray hair in his closely cropped sideburns.

"Hey there," he says.

"Hi." I pull open the door, toss the magazine onto the passenger seat, then internally argue with myself as to what to do next. Jump into the car and speed off like a wheel man for a bank job, or just stand there like an idiot with the car door open? And as I struggle to make this decision, I realize that I haven't had a conversation with an attractive stranger in a very long time. And as this realization dawns, I am suddenly frantic to hide the Pop-Tart stain on my shirt.

"I'm Ben Campbell," he offers, sidling up to my Flex. "My family just moved in next door."

"Oh," I say. I desperately want to cross my arms over my chest, but I don't want to come across as closed off or aloof, which, according to Dr. Phil, is exactly the impression that this particular gesture suggests.

"Yeah," he says. "It seems like a great neighborhood."

I notice that his eyes are the warm hue of melting chocolate. His hair is a shade lighter. His face is angular but not harsh; his smile gives him the ingratiating look of a faithful puppy. Oh, and his body ain't bad either. He's probably in his midforties, but there doesn't appear to be an ounce of flab on him, and the tight white tee he's sporting leaves little to the imagination. His six-pack abs are practically bursting through the fabric.

Perhaps I should feel guilty for doing something that is so closely related to outright, drool-dripping ogling, but I have been married for thirteen years, and during that time I have never strayed. And let me tell you that any married woman who claims she doesn't assess members of the opposite sex is either blind, a liar, or a closeted lesbian who is using her unknowing husband as a beard.

I suddenly wonder how awkward it would look for me to remove the sweatshirt from my waist and tie it around my shoulders, like Ally Sheedy did with all of her sweaters in *St. Elmo's Fire*. And a split second later I am truly ashamed of myself for giving thought to such a ridiculous idea. Besides, who in the new millennium even remembers bad 80s Brat Pack movies, no matter how iconic they were at the time?

"I saw your car here when we signed the escrow papers last week," he explains. "I figured you must be a friend of the family."

"Cousin," I reply. I usually don't speak in clipped, one-word sentences, but I am irrationally worried that Ben Campbell will see the stain on my shirt and immediately put his new house on the market in order to find a home with more suitable neighbors, or at least neighbors who don't have relatives who are part of the unwashed masses.

I am perplexed by the visceral reaction I am experiencing just by having this conversation. I assume it is because, at my age, thrills are hard to come by, and talking to a fine man clad in ass-hugging Levi's certainly counts as a thrill.

"Cousin, ah," he says and nods. His eyes dart to my shirt and he sees the strawberry goo. How could he not? It's right there, just above my right nipple; in fact it's exactly where my right nipple *would* be if I were twenty-three.

"I hear the school system is terrific," he suggests.

"The best." At least I have now graduated to two-word sentences. Yay for me.

"Well." He sighs good-naturedly. "I guess I'll see you around."

"Definitely," I reply. Okay, so I've reverted back to one-word sentences. At least this particular word has four syllables. And I can be proud of myself for not stammering or stuttering like a schoolgirl, or breaking out in a cold sweat. And I'm pretty sure I didn't flinch when I saw him notice the stain. So there's that.

I give Ben Campbell props for not looking at me as though I am some kind of mentally challenged nut job. He does quite the opposite, in fact. He flashes me that easygoing smile and gives me a two-finger salute, then strides back toward his property. The four moving guys have emerged from the house empty-handed and Ben Campbell stands for a moment shooting the breeze with them. I pray he is not telling them about the wacko he just had the displeasure of meeting, the one with the bright red stain on her boob who also happens to be conversationally challenged. But I will never find out. Because I hop into my car with as much agility as an almost-forty-three-year-old woman can muster, crank the key into the ignition, and speed away with my composure, if not my dignity, intact.

· Three ·

Thursdays for the Ivers children are jam-packed with activities, and adhering to their schedule requires tactical and strategic planning worthy of a SWAT team. From the moment school ends at two thirty, it becomes a mad dash to get all three of them where they need to be, on time and appropriately dressed. Connor, who is twelve, has baseball at three fifteen. Matthew has soccer at three thirty. Jessie also has ballet at three thirty, and because her dour-faced Russian ballet coach informed me that it is "dire zat she be here *on time!*" I have to drop Matthew on the field at three twenty and leave him in the care of the other soccer moms while I race to the far end of town to get Jessie to the studio. At four thirty, Connor has karate, Matthew has Wilderness Scouts (held at the local Y, which has acres of concrete—the only sign of "wilderness" is a five-foot-square, balding patch of yellow grass), and Jessie has rehearsal for the elementary school musical. This year, they are doing *Charlie and the*

Chocolate Factory and Jessie is delighted to have been chosen to play an Oompa-Loompa, not realizing that every child who auditioned got to be an Oompa-Loompa.

As a mother, I am duty bound to be at all of these activities at the same time, but until cloning becomes mainstream for humans, I must alternate on a weekly basis. Today I am sitting in the bleachers adjacent to the soccer field, having dropped Jessie off at ballet and returned in time to watch twenty minutes of Matthew's practice before I have to pick Connor up at baseball (which is mercifully nearby) and race back across town to pick Jessie up, then watch in the rearview mirror as all three of my children struggle to change clothes in the car while their safety belts are firmly locked in place.

Matthew does his best to kick the ball toward the opposing goal, and I find myself thanking God that he makes it all the way down the field without tripping over his own feet. At ten, my second son is in the middle of a painful and somewhat awkward growth spurt. His feet are two sizes larger than the norm for his age, and he hasn't managed to synchronize them with the rest of his body. It is almost as if they have little brains of their own, which are constantly firing opposing synapses to the ones shooting from the brain in his skull. It is painful for a mother to watch, and I try to be sympathetic to his plight. But I am hard-pressed to say the right thing to him to make him feel better. When I make light of his situation, he gives me a lower-lip quiver like he's about to burst into tears. And when I make supportive statements, as in "You're going to tower over your peers in six months," he merely shrugs disbelievingly and tells me that six months is *forever*. So mostly, I just say nothing. I applaud his successes (like now, when he's gone ten whole minutes without falling on his face) and overlook his failures (like when his left foot got caught in his bicycle spokes and he took a major header onto our driveway). They say that the key to success-ful motherhood is choosing your battles. In my opinion, the key to successful motherhood is knowing when to shut the fuck up.

As my attention wanders from the soccer field to the group of onlookers, I am once again struck by the way in which my fellow parents interact. There are clear demarca-tion lines drawn around the small groups of moms, and I think that no matter how far we advance as a species, so-cially, human beings never really evolve beyond high school. The cliques for thirty- and forty-somethings are as powerful as they were in our teens. I remember my Grandma Phyllis, who spent the final ten years of her life in a seniors' commu-nity, telling me that even octogenarians have cliques. (She was proud of the fact that she belonged to the group of "easy ladies" who claimed that sexual intercourse was the best pos-sible way to pass the time while you were waiting to die. To this day, I can't pass the Rolling Hills complex without thinking of my Nana having sex. Ewww!)

I see Nina Montrose, most likely homecoming queen of her alma mater, relay some juicy tidbit of information to Glo-ria Gisler and Jenna McCray, and I assume it has something to do with her recently enhanced, gravity-defying breasts. Gloria touches a finger to her collagen-inflated lower lip and Jenna conjures an expression of surprise and delight while placing her hands on a waist so tiny it would make Scarlett O'Hara seethe with jealousy. Meanwhile, on the bottom bench of the bleachers, I overhear Tina Sinclair and Maddy Holmes try to carry on a conversation about the virtues of composting while their toddlers takes turns sliming each other with their half-eaten yogurt pops. On the far side of the field, Weight Watchers compatriots Lily Reyburn and JoAnne Malloy watch practice from their beach chairs and surreptitiously binge on their sons' bite-sized Nutter Butter sandwich cookies.

Still, I far prefer the soccer moms to the baseball parents who take the whole sport so seriously you'd think they were watching the majors. Those people are ferocious! The Beach Cities League (yes, Garden Hills is a beach town, despite its incongruous name) is well known around Southern California for the number of professional baseball players it produces. Therefore, all of the parents take the process very seriously, and there is a certain tension that permeates the practices and games (even though ninety-five percent of the kids are taking part in the sport merely as a hobby or a way to get out of afternoon chores). Most of the moms and dads stand along the fence line shouting encouragement or, more to the point, yelling criticisms, at their children; erupting into fits of hysterics when their child hits a home run; and falling into vociferous despair when one of the kids, God forbid, makes an error. I once heard a T-ball mom offer her son twenty dollars if he hit the ball past second base. Twenty dollars! To a five-year-old. The mother was inconsolable when her little boy's hit made it only as far as the shortstop, at which point her husband told her she should have offered him a puppy.

Today, I am sitting next to Rita Halpern, who is the maternal grandmother of Peter, a classmate and pseudo-friend of Matthew. Rita took Peter in and will serve as his guardian until his mother's stint in rehab is complete. Apparently, Roberta became a slave to OxyContin and had even gone so far as to set up an online "companionship" service for the Garden Hills male population in order to support her habit. I find myself inexplicably envious of her. It's not that I condone excessive drug use or that I am a staunch supporter of prostitution. But Roberta certainly can never complain that her life is boring. Criminal activity, arrests, convictions, and the county lockup followed by withdrawal tremors and group therapy—her life can be compared to a gigantic roller coaster. Dangerous and frightening, yes, but definitely not dull. And now, she gets the added benefit of not having to sit through seven tedious hours a week watching her children attempt to play sports.

On the surface, Rita has a cavalier attitude about most things, including her daughter's plight, but I sense that deep down, she feels things very intensely and uses humor to hide it. Right now, she is joking about one of the kids on the field (thankfully not Matthew) who is struggling to catch his breath and has to keep going to the sidelines to puff on his inhaler.

"Jiminy Cricket, someone get that kid an oxygen tank!" she says in her usual strident tone.

"Rita, he's asthmatic," I tell her.

"Well, Jesus, Mary, and Joseph, then why the heck is he playing soccer? Is his mother writing a book? *My Life in the ER*? For God's sake. Take him home and put him in front of the TV!"

I laugh. I can't help it. Rita is one of those people who says whatever she is thinking, consequences be damned. I like to think it's because she has reached an age where she no longer cares what other people think. I myself will never reach that age, of course.

"And look at that chunky kid," she continues, ignoring the sharp look that Maddy Holmes casts in our direction. "Couldn't they find a uniform that fits him?"

It's true, Lionel Malloy's shorts constantly ride up, exposing his generous thighs to the world. He pulls them down every few minutes, then proceeds to yank his underwear free of his crack in one violent motion. It is an ongoing display, and I often wonder if JoAnne even sees it happen or if she's too busy pilfering his snacks to notice. Maybe someone ought to write her a note: *Get Lionel some new shorts!*

"You shouldn't joke about it, Rita," Maddy admonishes sweetly. "Lionel has a problem with his thyroid."

"He has a problem with *Cheetos*, more likely," Rita fires back, then cackles with glee. Maddy promptly turns around and continues her discussion of banana peels and apple cores and this wonderful new product she found that keeps the compost stink to a minimum.

"Peter's playing well today," I venture, and Rita gives me a sideways glance.

"Honey, the only time Peter touches the ball is when he gets hit with it. But it's nice of you to say so." She nods to herself. "I noticed that Matthew hasn't tripped at all today."

"Not yet," I say, and immediately feel guilty for having been so insensitive. But Rita just cackles.

"You're a good mom, Ellen," she says. "You recognize and accept your children's limitations."

By putting it that way, I am able to absolve myself of guilt. But I wonder if she's right. I love my children fiercely, and I do accept them for who they are. And although I strive not to draw comparisons, sometimes I cannot help it. All three of Jill's kids, for example, are all-around hyperachieving kids. No matter what they are playing at, they succeed. Now, Connor is great at baseball and water polo, but karate and ice hockey, not so much. And Matthew struggles with both soccer and baseball (which I choose to blame on his feet). And he's absolute crap (if I have to be completely impartial) at Wilderness Scouts, having earned only three badges so far while the rest of the scouts in his troop have at least seven apiece. He does excel at putting models together (since that has absolutely nothing to do with his feet) and has shown an aptitude for science. Jessie plays tennis and has a mean fore-hand for an eight-year-old. She's also a terrific swimmer. But she wants to be the next Hannah Montana, and unfortunately she cannot carry a tune in a bucket.

I am concerned that none of my children will achieve greatness. I am concerned that they will all be forced to settle for mediocrity and it will somehow be my fault. I am concerned that I am not pushing them hard enough, that I am not nurturing their dreams or supporting their aspirations. Or perhaps I am merely projecting onto them my own feelings of complacency, inadequacy, and mediocrity. God. My poor kids.

And then, like an apparition out of a nightmare—like the one where you are naked in the middle of a crowded room, or you're uncontrollably urinating in a pool full of people—I see Ben Campbell sauntering across the parking lot toward the soccer field, with a fair-haired boy of about ten in tow. As I watch the father and son approach one of the coaches, I am silently thankful that I altered my appearance since our meeting this morning. I traded my holey sweats—which are currently lining a trash bin in the garage—for a pair of jeans, and my peace shirt for a collared rose-colored blouse that complements my figure to the degree that any article of clothing can. I have also applied a smattering of makeup and a pair of earrings. I don't know why I took even a small amount of care with my appearance this afternoon. (At the time, I didn't correlate my embarrassing dialogue with Mr. Handsome-Next-Door-Neighbor to my wanting to look halfway decent.) But I am awfully glad I did.

The coach nods and shakes the boy's hand. Then the boy shrugs shyly and trots onto the field with the coach as introductions are made all around.

"Oh my," Rita says, and I assume she is talking about Ben

Campbell, who is wearing a pair of Levi's—these look slightly less faded than the ones he wore earlier, although how I remember that, I cannot tell you—and a blue V-neck cotton sweater. But when I turn to her, I see that she is concentrating on a spot on one of the lower bleachers and hasn't even noticed Ben Campbell.

"That bran muffin is working like Roto-Rooter on my intestines."

She eases herself down to the lawn and makes a beeline for the bathrooms on the far side of the field. Meanwhile, Ben Campbell has meandered over to the bleachers. When his chocolate eyes find me, I expect him to execute a swift about-face and hightail it for the other side of the field. But instead, he smiles a greeting at the moms on the lower level of the bleachers, then begins to climb toward my seat.

What is the matter with this guy? I think, wondering if he has a soft spot for stray dogs, orphaned children, and unsettled middle-aged women.

"Hi," he says warmly, pretending I am normal, pretending that I did not make the most unspeakably pathetic impression on him only hours ago.

"Hi." Uh-oh. Another one-word sentence. Not a good way to reverse his impression.

"Mind if I sit here?"

"Not at all." I breathe a sigh of relief. Three words. I'm on a roll.

He lowers his delectable bottom onto the wooden bench and smiles. "It's Ben."

"I know. Ben Campbell," I say, as if to prove that although I have difficulty constructing complex sentences, I have no problem with recall.

"I didn't catch your name earlier," he says.

"It's Ellen. Ellen Ivers."

"Well," he says. "Nice to meet you . . . again."

"Yeah. You too." I take a breath and blow it out. "I'm sorry if I, uh, seemed a little standoffish this morning."

He gives me a grin. "I thought maybe I was offensive."

I look over at him with surprise. He has to be one of the most inoffensive men I've ever met. "You're kidding. You were very nice."

"I meant sweaty and smelly offensive. After all the furniture-lugging, my wife wouldn't get near me until I showered. I figured you were reacting to my rankness."

"No," I say, laughing. "I think I was just having a little aneurysm."

"Ah. That explains it, then."

We share a moment of companionable silence. I notice that Maddy and Tina are constantly glancing back at us with curiosity, and a part of me is pleased by this. It's that "little thrill" thing at work again. Of all the moms present, this particular piece of fresh meat chose to sit next to me. (Who cares that he probably did so initially because he felt sorry for me or was planning to offer me the business card of his therapist?) This moment will fuel me for at least the rest of the day, and I allow myself to bask in it.

The slight breeze carries the scent of his aftershave to my nostrils. I try to ignore the effect that it's having on me.

"Is your son out there?" he asks, then shakes his head. "Dumb question, right?"

"Not at all," I reply with a straight face. "I could be one of those weirdos who watches kids' sports for the sheer enjoyment of it."

"That *would* be weird," he agrees, grinning broadly.

I chuckle, then point at my son. "Number six. That's my Matthew."

He nods. "My son's Liam. He just turned ten."

I watch as Liam makes a charge toward the goal, weaving through the other players effortlessly, the ball like an extension of his own (normal-sized) feet.

"He's good," I comment.

"Yeah, he's pretty coordinated for his age."

Of course, Matthew chooses that moment to fall on his butt, becoming a tangled mass of prepubescent limbs flailing on a sea of green grass. In my peripheral vision, I can see that Ben is stifling what would surely be an expression of amusement.

"He gets that from his dad," I say.

He looks at me and unchains the smile. "Of course."

It occurs to me that I have reverted to the confident, intelligent woman I used to be. Then it occurs to me that in the two conversations I've had with the man beside me, I've gone from social misfit to gregarious funny gal. Ben Campbell is probably thinking that I'm schizophrenic. But what the hell?

"Where did you move from?" I ask, my eyes still on the field. Matthew has now gotten to his feet and is attempting to steal the ball from Liam. He doesn't have a prayer in hell.

"L.A. area," Ben tells me.

"So, not far."

"Well, no. But in terms of my job, it's a lot different down here."

Talk about a leading statement. I ask the next logical question. "What do you do?"

"I'm a cop," he says matter-of-factly. "Detective."

"Wow. Keeping the world safe for humankind, huh?"

He laughs. "I try."

I process this information, looking at him from a new perspective. He's like the superhero of dads. His kids probably can't wait to bring him to Daddy Career Day. (My kids are still confused about what Jonah actually does.) I fleetingly wonder what it would be like to be married to a cop instead of an office supplier. I mean, Jonah's work is important (how would people do business if their companies didn't have the proper equipment?), and sometimes it's dangerous (he handles a whole line of very sharp letter openers), but let's face it, we are not talking about someone who is trained to use a gun and probably saves lives on a daily basis.

Ben is talking, so I tune him back in. "My wife, Linda—you'll meet her—she's an environmental lawyer. She lowered her caseload when we had the kids, you know, pro bono work mostly, but she just got an offer from a firm down here to go back to work full time. So I put in for a transfer. The timing was good."

Wow. An environmental lawyer. I'm impressed. She actually does something important, something that makes a difference in the world. (I know, I know, motherhood is supposed to be the most important job, but you can't really put it on a résumé, now can you?) I suddenly feel inadequate. What have I been doing to make the world a better place? I mean, recycling only goes so far. I still use too much water in the shower, I leave the lights on all the time, and I've never donated a single dollar to any "save the wildlife" charity, ever. Bambi would probably take one look at me and pee on my shoes. I tell myself that Linda the Lawyer is probably a lousy cook, and she probably looks like Madeleine Albright on a really bad day, and no matter how immature it sounds, these thoughts make me feel better.

"What?" asks Ben. "You have a funny look on your face."

"You've only just met me," I say lightly. "Maybe that's just the way my face is naturally."

"Oh," he says skeptically. "Well, you kind of reminded me of the little Tattoo guy from *Fantasy Island* for a minute."

I am so shocked by his words that I burst into laughter.

Maddy and Tina simultaneously glare at me, most likely annoyed that they are not privy to our amusing repartee. If I were fifteen, I would stick my tongue out at them, but instead I merely smirk.

"You're saying I look like Hervé Villechaize?" I exclaim.

"No, no," he says, laughing with me. "It was just the evil grin. You're a lot better looking than Hervé Villechaize."

"Wow," I say. "Thanks so much."

Both of us still smiling, our eyes meet. And for an instant, I cannot feel any of my limbs, cannot detect my heartbeat, cannot draw in a breath. I am certain that Ben is not experiencing the same set of bizarre symptoms I am, but that fact does not diminish the effect his direct gaze is having on me. I quickly make a show of glancing at my watch and see that practice is due to conclude in two minutes. I stand up suddenly, almost lose my balance, barely avoid tumbling down the bleachers (firmly dispelling the myth that Matthew gets his klutziness from his dad), and feel Ben's firm grip on my forearm, steadying me. In that split second, I notice that his fingers are long and hairless and his nails are clipped short.

"Thanks," I say, feeling my cheeks flush. "I've got to get moving. Still three more extracurricular activities to get to."

He releases his hold on my arm. "Three more?" he asks with surprise. "Today?"

"Three kids, twelve thousand activities," I joke, and he smiles.

"Wow. I'm glad I stopped at two kids."

I feel that I should say something other than *See you around* or *Welcome to the area*, but I can't think of anything pithy or humorous, so I just give him a little halfhearted wave as I climb down the bleachers. I pass Maddy and Tina and feel their speculative stares boring into the back of my head as I clamber over to the field to collect my son. Matthew is talking to Liam about something of apparent grave importance, gesticulating madly, and as they approach, I catch the word *Transformer*. Liam's big brown eyes are wide as Matthew explains something to him about regeneration or transmutation or whatever it is that Transformers do. I call to Matthew, trying to hustle him along, and receive a furrowed-brow look that tells me he's in the middle of a very important discussion that cannot be rushed. I check my watch again, then put a hand to my hip.

"Matthew. *Now.*"

"Looks like Liam and Matthew are already thick as thieves."

I turn to Ben, who is suddenly standing next to me. I nod. "Yeah. Transformers."

"Maybe we can get them together for, you know, a play date or something."

I glance at him and unsuccessfully suppress a grin. "They're ten. You don't call them play dates at ten."

He shrugs in a self-deprecating fashion. "What do you call them, then? I mean, I should probably get familiar with the current lingo."

"Just 'hanging out' is sufficient."

"I'll remember that. I don't want to be the uncool dad."

As if that *would ever be possible.*

"Matthew," I say again with a fraction more urgency in my tone. Ben comes to my assistance and calls to Liam, who immediately obeys and marches over to his dad. Matthew follows. Introductions are made all around, and I'm impressed by Liam's manners as he politely puts his hand out to shake mine and tells me that it's very nice to meet me. (I am happy if my kids manage to utter *Hi* instead of just grunting self-consciously when meeting new people.) I compliment Liam on his soccer skills and earn a toothy, sideways smile.

Ben affectionately ruffles Liam's hair, and we all move toward the parking lot, the boys shuffling ahead and resuming their debate about which is the most awesome Transformer.

We reach my Flex, and Matthew and Liam do a quick knuckle bump before Matthew jumps into the backseat.

"Good luck with the rest of your day," Ben calls to me, then shifts his attention to his son. I get behind the wheel and start the car, watching through the windshield as father and son head for their own car. I think of Ben Campbell's hand on my arm. Those strong, lean fingers. I shake my head as if to clear it, take a deep breath, then peel out of the parking lot as the next phase of Operation: Thursday Afternoon gets underway.

Four

On "Mad Dash" evenings, Jonah has the good grace to alleviate me of dinner duty, picking up takeout on the way home. Tonight he has opted for Dragon King, the local Chinese place that makes the best scallion pancakes within a hundred miles. Usually, I lay waste to at least four of the eight pancakes, but tonight, the first one I pull from the carton sits uneaten on my plate. I am currently trying to estimate the amount of calories and saturated fat contained in a single wedge of the deep-fried disk. My kids happily munch on their egg rolls (at their age, fat and calorie counting is an alien concept), and I have to remind them, for the four-thousandth time, to chew with their mouths closed. Jonah has reached his scallion pancake quota and is now shoveling chicken lo mein onto his plate with enthusiasm. He offers me the ravaged carton and I shake my head, garnering a look of puzzlement.

"You okay?" he asks.

I nod and smile reassuringly. "I grabbed a snack at the Y," I lie.

I am not in the habit of deceiving my husband, but a little fib like this seems harmless. It goes to the greater good. In marriages—mine, anyway—I have found that it is problematic for one party to engage in self-improvement tactics when the other is not. It shifts the balance of power too much. Like the time Jonah did Atkins. I was so envious of his sudden fitness that I consciously whipped up his favorite carb-rich dishes at dinner just to punish him. Or the time I joined a yoga studio at Jill's insistence and started going to classes before breakfast. Suddenly, Jonah was besieged with early-morning client meetings and vendor emergencies that had to be solved at the crack of dawn, so that I could barely make it to half the weekly sessions. Ultimately, I had to let my membership lapse. I will admit that I was secretly relieved to have an excuse to give up yoga, as the only position I truly enjoyed making—and was moderately successful at—was Corpse. But still.

"You forgot to eat lunch, didn't you?"

I nod and smile again, thinking of the Pop-Tarts. For some reason, I have gotten back on track with my whole resolution, reclaiming-my-former-babe-status thing. The Pop-Tart transgression was merely a setback. (And if I do the treadmill after dinner, I can erase those two or three hundred calories in forty minutes.) For the rest of the day I only chose healthy fuel for my body—a salad at lunch and a protein bar in the late afternoon to keep me from turning into Low-Blood-Sugar Monster Mom. I am now opting for the tofu with mixed vegetables instead of the lo mein and scallion pancakes.

At this time, I am not drawing a correlation between my renewed desire to lose weight and my acquaintance with Ben

Campbell. He hasn't entered my mind at all over the past few hours. Really, he hasn't. Okay, this isn't quite true. He has. But only his hands, which have intermittently come to mind since our bleacher encounter. I tell myself that it is only natural to revisit the touch of a man other than your husband, regardless of how inconsequential or innocent said touch was. I am certainly not thinking of Ben sexually—this is the truth. I can appreciate his good looks, in the same way that I appreciate, say, Brad Pitt's appeal. And Ben is definitely one of those all-around great guys to whom women can't help but be attracted. But he is also, clearly, happily married, with a terrific family life. And so am I. So am I.

However, tonight, I find myself looking at Jonah more critically than usual. The way his blue-gray eyes—which are beautiful and expressive—disappear when he smiles. Normally, I find this endearing, but tonight it inexplicably irks me. And the way he purposely lets a noodle hang down over his chin so that he can noisily slurp it into his mouth for the amusement of our children. I always laugh along with the kids, but tonight, this humorous display disgusts me. And how he sniffs at the wine in his glass before he takes a sip, as though his nose will reveal to him a bounty of secrets about the Beaujolais he is about to imbibe. Tonight, this action seems as pretentious as it is absurd. Jonah guzzles any and all kinds of wine set before him, including ones that taste like jet fuel.

Still, when he slides his hand across the table and intertwines his fingers with mine, I don't think of Ben Campbell. I think of Jonah. My husband. With whom I have spent the last fourteen plus years of my life, and with whom I will spend the next forty or so. He is as solid a man as they come. His family comes first and without exception. He is a true "the glass is half full" kind of guy, always looking on the bright side of things (sometimes to the degree that I want to smack him). He may not be the best listener in the world—his eyes start to glaze over whenever I get philosophical, or when one of the kids takes too long telling a story—but he is always there for us. And he never complains when I ask him to pick up tampons on his way home.

I give his fingers a squeeze, then make a point of planting a kiss on his cheek before I get up to clear the paper plates from the table. Sally, our lab mix, eyes me from her dog bed just inside the kitchen. When I say *lab mix* I am only referring to what the gal from the shelter wrote on the adoption form when we brought her home. I'm certain she does have some lab in her. Along with a bit of every breed of dog known to man. Perhaps some noncanine breeds as well—when she rolls around in the mud in our backyard, she often closely resembles a shaggy elephant seal. She is large and hairy, and she has a tail that could bring down a pillar of solid stone when she gets excited. (I have the bruised calves to prove it.) Her eyes are brown and look like they have been tattooed with eyeliner, her ears flop like a bloodhound on steroids, and when she shakes herself dry, she hurls wads of saliva, dousing any and all innocent bystanders with a veritable geyser of dog slobber. But she is sweet tempered and affectionate, although not the most efficient home protector. In fact, as a guard dog, she stinks. When the doorbell rings, she races up the stairs and tries to bury all ninety-eight pounds of herself in the six-inch crawl space under Jessie's canopy bed, probably hoping against hope that my eight-year-old daughter will protect *her*.

Surreptitiously, I bend over and place the scallion pancake just in front of Sally's nose. She sniffs it once, then rolls over and shows me her belly, as if to say, *I'm watching my weight, too.* But the second I turn away from her, I hear a slurp of epic proportions, and when I turn back around, the pancake has vanished.

Now that we've finished dinner, there is no longer anything to keep my children's mouths busy, thus the pre-dessert conversation begins. While I clean up, Jessie regales her brothers and her father with her exploits at rehearsal, gesturing wildly for dramatic effect as she talks about one particular Oompa-Loompa who doesn't know his right foot from his left and cannot, *just cannot*, learn the steps for their first big number. Jessie, who excels at ballet and is an avid fan of the Wii dancing game, is intolerant of such incompetence. I almost expect her to stand up and shout, "I cannot *vork* under zese conditions!" She does stand up, without any exclamations, and proceeds to perform the Oompa-Loompa dance number without making a single mistake. My husband and Matthew applaud her, causing her to beam with pride, but Connor just rolls his eyes.

"That is so easy!" he balks. "I could do that."

"Oh really?" Jonah fires back. "Let's see it, Baryshnikov."

"What? Now?" Connor's preteen cockiness wavers.

"Right now," Jonah replies with a knowing grin. As a father, Jonah is aces. He has the uncanny ability to reprimand without anger, to call our children on their transgressions without browbeating them. He uses humor to defuse situations like this rather than choosing humiliation techniques. He taps into their thought processes, inspiring them to really understand the implications and consequences of their behavior. I envy him. Even on my best day, I am more likely to yell and scream than sit them down for a soul-searching heart to heart. But as a mom, I don't have this luxury. Who has time for a behavioral postmortem when dinner needs to be cooked or homework reviewed or baseball/soccer/

karate/ballet/tennis uniforms laundered/stitched/patched/purchased? Screaming and yelling are quick and to the point, however fruitless they may be.

"Okay, fine." Connor has risen to the challenge, even though we all know what is about to happen. He takes one step, then another.

"Wrong," chirps Jessie.

"I don't know where the music starts," he says defensively.

"That's all right," Jonah says with a smile. "Jessie will sing while you dance. Go ahead, Jessie."

Jessie begins a rousing, if painfully out-of-tune, rendition of the Oompa-Loompa song. Connor executes the first few steps correctly.

"Oompa-Loompa Loompa di doo, I have another puzzle for you. Oompa-Loompa Loompa di di. If you are wise you'll listen to me."

By the end of the stanza, Connor begins to lose his place, fumbling around the dining room with no apparent direction while Jessie and Matthew giggle. He throws his hands in the air and smiles good-naturedly, then completes his performance with a combination moonwalk/robot move. Then he falls into his chair, defeated.

"Okay, it's not that easy," he concedes as his siblings and dad applaud his effort.

"I did like that last move," says Jonah. "They ought to think about using it in the play."

"Daddy, that's silly," Jessie says solemnly. "Oompa-Loompas don't *moonwalk*!"

"That would be cool, though," Matthew offers.

I arrive at the table with four dishes of Breyer's ice cream, and the conversation screeches to a halt as Jonah and the kids dig in. I walk away from the table and Jonah calls to me.

"You're not having dessert?"

I turn back to him and see that he is wearing a speculative look. I shake my head.

"Maybe later," I tell him. "When I'm not so full."

I manage to plod through two miles on the treadmill during the allotted hour of television my kids enjoy nightly. Jonah wanders in and out of the upstairs bonus room at regular intervals, tossing banal questions at me like, "Have you seen my gray-and-turquoise tie?" or "Were you able to pick up more deodorant soap?" or "Where is that copy of *Business Weekly* I brought home from the office?" I huff and puff and breathlessly sputter my answers. ("No." Gasp. "Yes." Gasp. "On the coffee table next to the coasters . . ." Gasp, gasp.)

When, thankfully, I finish, I guzzle down a glass of water and throw a towel over my shoulder, then walk downstairs on rubbery legs to the family room, where I find Matthew and Jessie playing tug-of-war with the remote. Jessie is like the TV police. When the kids' hour is up and the show is over, she feels that it is her obligation to officially bring the session to a close by turning off the television and the cable box. Her brothers always take issue with this, claiming that the hour isn't really over until the TiVo kicks back to live TV.

"I was watching that commercial!" shrieks Matthew. He has fifteen pounds on Jessie, and his hands are bigger, but I'm betting on my daughter for this round.

"Commercials are bad for your brain," she tells him righteously.

"But I wanted to *see* it!"

"That's enough."

Three sets of eyes turn to me and three mouths instantly start to laugh.

"Yo, Mom," Connor says around his smile. "Nice look."

"Are you okay, Mom?" Jessie asks, her concern smothered by her laughter.

"You look like you're gonna keel over," Matthew chimes in.

I catch sight of myself in the mirror over the piano and almost shriek myself. My hair is a sweaty, tangled mass, my face is as red as a lobster, and my eyes look as though they are about to pop out of my head. I break into a grin and regard my children.

"Well," I say. "We can't all be naturally beautiful, can we?"

They laugh some more, but their laughter turns to grumbling when I tell them it's time for bed. Connor gives me the least resistance, knowing that, as the eldest, he gets an extra half hour to read quietly in his room. He has recently discovered the J.R.R. Tolkien *Lord of the Rings* series and can't wait to get back to Frodo and his cronies. Matthew stamps his foot and informs me that he won't go to his room until he gets to watch the commercial that Jessie's remote-hoarding has deprived him of. I shake my head firmly and point to the stairs. Jessie looks up at me with her big blue doe eyes and insists that she needs a glass of milk to help her sleep. I shake my head again and jab a finger at the stairs. Reluctantly, she and Matthew trudge to the second floor, where they and their older brother hurry through their nightly ablutions while I supervise.

When at last all three are safely ensconced in their beds, I drag myself to the master bathroom to shower. I crank the water to hot and step beneath the spray, then stand unmoving for a full minute, allowing the hot stream to wash the profusion of sweat from my body. I reach for the soap and begin to lather myself, moving my hands over this body that has been mine, for better and for worse, for the past forty-two years.

I have always had a little extra meat on my bones. Frankly, after the births of each of my kids, a little extra meat turned into a couple of porterhouse steaks. But I do have occasional moments of appreciation for what nature has given me. I may never have been rail thin, but I have always been strong and healthy. I don't get winded easily, I have never been struck with serious illness, and I never need to ask my husband to lift heavy items. (Although I often do ask for his help in order to stroke his inner caveman.)

Perhaps it is my imagination, or just wishful thinking, but as I run the soap across my torso, I can feel the definition of my rib cage more clearly than I did a few days ago. And my stomach seems to be a little less shelflike in its protuberance. I am secretly pleased, although I know I still have a long way to go to reach my goal, which is to fit into my wedding dress (I have no idea where the damn thing is, probably stuffed in a bag, tucked away in the attic next to my unfinished novel). But it's a start, and I resolve to complete three miles on the treadmill tomorrow and promise myself that ne'er another Pop-Tart shall cross my lips.

I feel a cool waft of air swirl through the bathroom, and a moment later, the shower door slides open. Jonah stands on the other side of the stall, naked as the day he was born, smiling at me.

"Showering at night?" he asks slyly. "Want some company?"

He might as well have asked if I want to get laid. I can tell by the low, lascivious tone of his voice, his nakedness, and the fact that the head of his penis is pointing directly at me.

"Always," I say. Although, in truth, sex in the shower is not one of my favorite pastimes. Unless your partner is six-five and can support all of your weight during the act, the sheer logistics are next to impossible to work out. And forget about oral, unless you have an affinity for drowning. But, in the interests of pretending to be spontaneous and carefree, I take his hand and lead him under the hot spray.

He immediately palms my breast, a move I anticipate since it is always his first. His thumb slides over my areola, and I am surprised by the sudden heat that courses through me. This is the man I have been making love to for the past fourteen years, without exception, and it is difficult to believe that such a small, overused action can still arouse me. His hand slides down to my waist, coming to rest for just a moment on the spot where my torso begins to curve outward toward my hips. Then it continues its journey, around my hips and down to the top of my ass. Jonah grasps my left cheek and pulls me into him. I can feel his penis against my belly, hard and ready and twitching impatiently.

Sex with Jonah has always been satisfying. We met in our late twenties, so our coupling was never the animalistic, firework-inspiring romp that postpubescents boast about and that I myself have never had the occasion to experience. But from the beginning, he and I fit together well, physically and emotionally. He is not selfish but is concerned with my pleasure. No matter how turned on he is, or how close to the brink he gets, he dutifully holds himself back until I have climaxed before he allows himself to come, shuddering spasmodically and making that low, guttural noise that brings to mind the onset of food poisoning.

As in most relationships, the frequency of lovemaking in ours has lessened. During our courtship and our early married years, four or five times a week was the rule, and we enjoyed lazy sessions that stretched on for hours, occasionally requiring snack breaks to refuel our spent energy. Now, we carve out fifteen-minute tête-à-têtes when we can manage it, after the kids are down. I know this is merely the natural progression of a married person's sex life. And yet, for some reason, perhaps the fact that menopause is looming in my not-so-distant future and wreaking havoc on my hormone balance, I am suddenly overcome with a sense of loss. Even as my husband pushes himself inside me with his usual sharp intake of breath, I feel a quiet desperation, an anger at all of the unfulfilled promises and shattered illusions that saturate the lives of the middle-aged.

I am middle-aged. I know they say that forty is the new twenty-five. But *they* are full of shit. Forty is forty, and forty-two suddenly seems fucking *old*.

"Are you okay?" Jonah's voice is a hushed whisper. I look up to find him staring intently at me, his rhythmic thrusts temporarily suspended.

I nod and smile reassuringly, hoping that the hot water from the showerhead is camouflaging my tears. I reach my hands around his waist, noting that his has not expanded much over the past few years—well, at least not as much as mine has. Grabbing his ass, I pull him against me, forcing him deeper inside me, and the sudden pressure in my loins causes a grunt to escape my lips. That's all it takes. Jonah immediately returns to his task, the task of giving me pleasure. Eyes at half mast, his breath comes in ragged gasps as he presses me against the tile. Pumping into me, speaking into my ear about how much he loves me and how good I feel and how well we fit together.

I make all the right noises, but I just can't seem to give myself completely over to the act. It is as though my mind is detached from my body. My limbs are responding to the commands I give them: lift right leg and intertwine it with Jonah's (carefully, so as not to catch any of his hair in my ragged toenails); squeeze Jonah's buttocks with both hands (trying not to think about Charmin toilet paper); undulate like a belly dancer on PCP (does the local rec park offer classes?); moan lasciviously and say "Give it to me" and "Oh baby oh baby" and "Oh my god oh my god ohmygod" over and over again.

But I am merely an actor in a play, a bad actor at that, waiting for that blessed moment when I can exit stage left. I know that Jonah won't finish until I am sated, and I also know that a comet will crash into earth and wipe out mankind before I actually *will* come, so I pretend increasing fervor, forcefully hitching my breathing and sinking my fingernails into the soft flesh of Jonah's ass, gasping urgently as I nearly tear a chunk out of his earlobe with my teeth. I clench my thighs tightly around him and shudder spasmodically, crying out, "Yes yes YES!" All the while thinking that Meg Ryan deserved a fucking Oscar for the deli scene in *When Harry Met Sally*. I know it's pathetic that my thoughts are centered on a romantic comedy from 1989 while my husband is about to explode inside me. Yet I am relieved that this will all be over in about eight and a half seconds. And although I can't help but feel slightly guilty, I am well aware of one of the most basic truths known to wives the world over: A fake orgasm can be a woman's best friend.

Five

I have found that the only peace and quiet and absolute privacy I can get while my husband and children are awake and at home is when I'm in the bathroom. My kids learned early on that when Mommy is "making number two," she is not to be disturbed. And over the years since then, I have milked this edict for everything it's worth. Which is why I am on the toilet for the fourth time this morning, clutching the *Ladies Living-Well Journal* in my hands and pretending to go, yet again.

In the beginning, Jonah got so concerned about my colon that he insisted I see an internist.

"It's not normal," he said, looking at me like he'd just been sent over from the local hospice. "You know, to make . . . well, you know . . . to have a . . . you know . . . to *poop* so much."

I laughed so hard I almost *pooped* my pants. I assured him

that I was fine, but he remained unconvinced. I had to suffer through a week of his sidelong glances, which ranged from wistful to tremulous to downright panicked. It was then I realized that Jonah was terrified of losing me. Actually, he probably was less concerned about losing me than about being left alone with three kids under five whose greatest influences at the time were an annoying six-foot-tall purple dinosaur and an annoying two-foot-tall furry red Muppet named Elmo. (*La la la la, la la la la,* Jonah's *World!*) That would scare the *poop* out of anyone.

So I finally let him off the hook and explained to him that *le toilette* offered me a moment's reprieve from the demands of motherhood. To which he replied, "Why do you need a reprieve?" (At which I may have considered kicking him in the balls.)

By seven fifteen on this Friday morning, I have already endured three juvenile meltdowns and an uncharacteristic postcoital argument with my spouse. Jonah had awakened me with an insistent erection at five forty-five, which dutifully accepted despite my complete lack of interest. (A week has passed since our shower copulation and my impersonation of a sexual automaton, and although at the time I vowed never to have sex with my husband again, sometimes it's easier to just let them have a go.) This morning, I thought that I might actually get some pleasure out of the deal and that my dreamlike stupor would promote a happy ending for both of us, but I was wrong. I could not, for the life of me, become aroused enough to climax, and the more I tried, the further from orgasm I got. I was finally so chafed, physically *and* mentally, that I had to fake it again. Not that Jonah noticed. He came with a thunderous groan that I was sure would wake up the children, leaving me to wonder why my libido had suddenly taken a vaycay and whether I should investigate some kind of sexual therapy. Well, at least Jonah was satisfied.

I had been vertical for only ten minutes when the day went from bad to worse. It began before breakfast with Jessie's tirade about her beloved denim skirt that had not yet made it through the laundry cycle. The way she ranted and raved about my failings as a mother, I could have sworn my eight-year-old daughter was having her period. This was followed by Matthew's tearful proclamation that his Target boxer briefs were a "travesty" and "unacceptable" in the boys' locker room and that only Calvin Kleins would be suitable garments to encase his decidedly scrawny nether parts. Then Connor sent me over the edge by turning on the Wii before school, which I consider a mutinous and grievous act rooted in his tween obligation to rebel against his parents at any and every opportunity.

After threatening to disconnect the contraption, I regained a modicum of control only to be informed by my husband that he had a client dinner tonight which he had failed to mention earlier. "What's the big deal?" he asked when I complained. "It's not like you have some big Friday night planned."

"No, Jonah," I replied, attempting to keep my voice calm and steady. "I have book club tonight. It's on the calendar. You put it in your friggin' Outlook, for God's sake." I swear, Jonah would forget to pee without a reminder from his scheduling software.

"What am I supposed to do, cancel? This is the CEO of the Irvine Company. So you miss one book club."

He showed little or no remorse when I told him that six other people were counting on me, especially Jill. He merely rolled his eyes and revealed his blatant skepticism that book club has any intrinsic value whatsoever.

"You have no idea what book club is all about," I told him, seething. "It's a communal experience, a chance for us to connect and discuss topics outside our own limited lives. It's like church." Okay, maybe that was a bit much, but still. Jonah hasn't read a book since the Paleolithic era. He really has no concept of what books mean to me.

"Book club is an excuse for you and your friends to drink wine and gossip," he proclaimed, as if he were the King Poobah of Universal Wisdom. I really hate that tone of voice. So I clamped my mouth shut and escaped to the loo.

And here I sit, musing about the sorry state of my hemorrhoids as I flip through my cousin's magazine. I have managed to avoid reading it for more than a week now, but my excuses to Jill are starting to sound pathetic even to my own ears. ("No, I didn't look at the competition guidelines today, I had to clean my lint trap." "No, I didn't read the competition guidelines because I was busy realigning my fifth chakra.")

I am now twelve days into Operation Ellen, and feeling fine, but it has not been as cathartic as I thought it would. I still feel like me. Not that I expected to be transformed into some higher being, or Angelina Jolie or anything, but I thought I would somehow feel *different*. I have been eating right and exercising regularly and trying to have a positive, can-do attitude, and it's true that my skin is looking good and my waistbands are slightly looser and I have a slight bounce in my step, but I haven't yet reached transcendency. Perhaps I should have aimed lower with the whole reinvention thing.

I turn pages of the magazine mindlessly. I bypass the

article on spicing up your sex life, although after this morning, I could use some advice in that area. I briefly scan a two-page piece about a miracle cleanse that will scrub your intestines so clean you could eat off them and cause your colon to whistle "Zip-a-Dee-Doo-Dah." I'm not supportive of any diet or fast that erases wine from my daily consumption since, let's face it, wine is a housewife's heroin, and withdrawal symptoms include random crying jags over particularly sappy e-mails, littering the kitchen floor with every single pot and pan in the cupboard whilst screeching about how dinner is not going to cook itself, and beating the crap out of my kids—figuratively, of course. In my opinion, it's better to have dirty intestines and a nonwhistling colon.

A few pages later, I find myself staring down at the competition guidelines. *You could win $10,000 and write for our magazine!* the headline announces. *Create a blog at Ladieslivingwelljournal.com, write about what you know, and the blog that receives the most hits wins!*

I stare at the wall across from the toilet for a moment, searching through the cavernous recesses of my brain in an attempt to come up with at least one idea for a blog. The *write about what you know* part puts me at a disadvantage because I can't for the life of me come up with something interesting that I actually know about. I have spent the last thirteen years as a wife and mother and have done little else. I know how to change a diaper (though even that skill is a bit rusty now), I can make a cake in the shape of the Empire State Building (but who can't nowadays, thanks to the friggin' Ace of Cakes), and I can tell you the best places to go for a good bounce: the G-rated, inflatable, kid-kind of bounce, not the lascivious, consenting-adults kind of bounce. But who wants to read about such banal things? Don't people want to be informed and inspired, made to really think and ponder things, to find enlightenment, to be hit with an emotional impact that causes catharsis?

I know what my friend Mia would say. She'd say, "Girl, you are overestimating the intelligence of the inhabitants of planet earth. Most of these people have the IQ of a pork chop. They don't want to be enlightened. Not really. Oh, they might *say* they want that, to sound cool and all, but what they really want is to be entertained. Even the smart ones. For God's sake, my husband loved, and I mean *loved*, *Jackass 3D* and he went to Harvard!"

A tentative *tap-tap-tap* sounds at the bathroom door, followed by an even more tentative "Honey?" My husband. He did *not* go to Harvard. Although he, too, loved *Jackass 3D*.

"What?" I retort, glancing at my watch. I note with dismay that I have managed to get only three minutes and twenty-seven seconds of alone time before the cursed knock.

"I know you're probably in the middle of the mother of all poops." I can detect a note of derision in his voice, but he is doing his best to mask it, knows he ought to err on the side of not pissing me off any further. "Want me to take the kids to school?"

A conciliatory gesture. No dice, pal.

"Yup," I reply. Jonah hates it when I answer him with curt, one-syllable replies. Therefore, I do it whenever I know that he knows that I am displeased with him.

"Are you going to be okay about tonight?" he asks. He is making a concerted effort to pretend to care about my squashed plans.

"Yup." In truth I have no idea what I am going to do about book club, but I realize that it's not a crisis on the same level as, say, the polar ice caps melting.

"You sure?"

"Sure," I snap, rolling my eyes at him through the closed door.

He sighs. I can't hear the actual sigh, but I know Jonah. He always sighs. Another ten seconds go by. I count them down like Houston approaching liftoff. Just as I think, *Blastoff*, he says, "Okay, then. Have a good day."

"Fuck you." I whisper it so that he can't hear me. "Bye," I say, aloud, then return my attention to the magazine.

By the time I have finished reading all of the fine print of the competition, I am fairly certain that my house is empty. I am also fairly certain that there is no way in hell I can ever enter this blog contest. I mean, seriously. A blog post a day for fourteen days? That's *fourteen* ideas, and I can't even come up with *one*. And anyway, the deadline for the first blog post is today.

I know Jill will be disappointed, but she'll just have to get over it. As our Grandma Phyllis used to say, you cannot suck water from a stone.

I exit the bathroom, toss the magazine in the trash can, and wander down to the kitchen to find that Jonah has left me about a third of a cup of brown sludge in the bottom of the coffee carafe. I turn off the machine, let Sally out the back door, and head for the fridge. Then I pull out a low-fat raspberry yogurt that is about to reach its drop-dead date and head for the little alcove off the kitchen, where I boot up my computer. I know I have to call Jill and tell her I can't attend book club tonight because my husband is a fink, but I also know that she will go ballistic, so I put off making the call by going through my e-mails. As usual, I have a ton of spam, and several "special offers" from companies that I subscribed to in moments of weakness but from which I will never buy anything. I delete them all and am left with two PTA notifications, a short e-mail from my father that says "Hey girl" and nothing else, and a long e-mail from my sister, Lisa. She lives in Riverside and is conflicted about whether to have a tummy tuck and a boob lift, which her husband has offered to pay for. Lisa thinks that surgery is a cop-out and possibly a sin, but at a particular age, like, say, mine, or my sister's, who is eleven months younger than I am, a woman should take all the help she can get. In my opinion, *not* taking help is the sin. Gravity is a bitch. Metabolism slows to the pace of a snail on downers, and the imbalance of hormones causes women's bellies to bloat to barrel proportions. And once you pass a certain point, there is no going back, no matter how many fucking crunches you do.

I take a moment to reply that I think Lisa is crazy not to take Malcolm up on his offer and that if she doesn't, I will in her stead. Who gives a crap about cop-outs? I ask her. Sin-shmin! Anyone gives you a hard time, just tell them to go to hell, and then go get your new navel pierced!

Now, I love my sister, but she is very much influenced by her peers. And a large percentage of her peers belong to her church, which I call the Praise the Lord Church of the Word of God. I have nothing against good Christians, but the bulk of the women who attend Praise the Lord have made holy rites of quilting bees and bake sales and resembling giant pears, and they believe that anything a woman does that is not related to pleasing God is a sin punishable by ostracism. Taking care of yourself, applying makeup, and trying to look attractive is considered vanity with a capital *V*. Plastic surgery equals downright harlotry. I have told Lisa numerous times that she is still a vibrant woman who has the right to look and feel good. She is beautiful, I tell her. She just needs a little professional assistance to reach her potential. In my opinion, if God wanted people to be fat, He wouldn't have invented liposuction.

I know that she will suffer over this decision for another six months, and then will probably decide to embrace her inner Dom DeLuise and put on fifty pounds by consuming every unpurchased baked good left on the Praise the Lord banquet table at the church's holiday sale. She'll cry and be ashamed, but the church ladies will love her.

After sending off the e-mail, I skim over the PTA notices, which are in reality calls to action. "Spring Carnival is coming, ladies! We need everyone's help to make this the best carnival ever! Anyone who hasn't signed up to work the event needs to get on it!" What the e-mail doesn't say is that if you don't volunteer, Penelope Larson, the PTA prez, will hunt you down, trusty clipboard in hand, and publicly lambaste you into submission until you are begging her to let you—please, please, please—work the water-dunking booth. Last year I got dunked seven times before the next glassy-eyed PTA sucker—uh, volunteer—came to relieve me. And yes, four of the seven dunkings were at the hands of my own traitorous kids.

The second PTA blast is a too-long, preachy dissertation about the evils of candy in the classroom, written by Caroline Klum. Caroline fancies herself a wordsmith extraordinaire, seeing as how she is the editor in chief of the *Garden Hills Echo*, the free local handout that mostly gets used as liner for litter boxes, birdcages, and kennels of house-training pups. I find three errors in the first paragraph, and this gives me a certain smug satisfaction. I am not an editor in chief of anything. But I know that *i* comes before *e* except after *c*. Yay for me. Caroline does make some good arguments, though, about the blood sugar/hyperactivity connection. Candy equals frenetic and unruly behavior equals overwhelmed teachers equals nobody learns anything for the hour and a half after lunch. It makes me rethink the Jelly Bellies I put in my kids' lunch sacks this morning. Oh well, I think, unsympathetically. That's their teachers' problem, not mine. My bad mood is exacerbated by the fact that I'm screwed for book club, I'm not even an editor in chief of a stupid local home-printed newsletter, I'm an unhealthy influence on my children, and I can't think of one effing thing to write about in a blog. Even the teachers whose kids are high on crack candy have it better than I do.

The blog contest. Why am I still thinking about that? I'm not doing it. I'll fail terrifically. I'll be a loser not only in spirit, but in glorious megabyte-me reality.

As I scrape the last bit of raspberry yogurt from the container, I realize that my efforts at reinvention are on their way back to the crapper.

Twenty minutes later, I am on the treadmill, hoping against hope that the endorphins my body will release will drag me out of this self-pitying, self-flagellating place. I am sweating profusely to the sounds of Aretha Franklin's Greatest Hits. Slowly, I do start to feel better. I am burning calories. I am doing something good for me. I am a powerful entity in the universe. Okay, so doing the treadmill doesn't exactly elevate me to universal power status. Still. Two out of three ain't bad.

After close to an hour of this punishment, I walk on spaghetti legs to the phone and dial my cousin's number. I know I can't put it off any longer. Jill is hosting tonight's literary soiree and is counting on me to be her wingman. Or woman. As picture perfect as her house is, as anal-retentive as she is when it comes to plating appetizers or proffering stemware, she is completely insecure about having company. She rarely entertains because it is the one time when she second-guesses every single choice she makes, from the wine selection to the cocktail napkins to the damn hand towels adorning the vanity in the bathroom. One party will send her to her shrink twice a week for a month.

"I put out the *lily* hand towels last night, Doctor! Don't you see? Mona Emmerson's mother died seven months ago and her favorite flowers were lilies. Can you imagine how those hand towels must have made Mona feel? She'll never forgive me! And for God's sake, I served cocktail wieners! How could I? Liza Pierce's husband just lost his penis in a freak combine accident! Liza took one look at the wieners and burst into tears!"

I myself don't stress about throwing a party. My feeling is this: If there's a lot of alcohol and the food is delicious, no one will care that they have to dry their hands on a torn, mud-stained beach towel haphazardly slung over the shower stall in the bathroom. Give people enough booze and they wipe their hands on their own clothing, anyway.

"Are you bringing the cheese balls now or later?" My cousin doesn't bother with a hello. She knows it's me from her Caller ID and is getting right to the point.

"I've got some good news and some bad news," I tell her. "Which do you want first?"

She hesitates briefly. "It's not about the cheese balls, is it?"

"No," I assure her. "You'll have your cheese balls. You just won't have me."

"*What?*" she shrieks into the phone.

"I can't make book club tonight. Don't worry. I'll drop off the cheese balls later."

"No!" she cries. "You can't be serious! You are not missing book club, Ellen. You will be here tonight or I will disown you as my cousin, *forever!*"

"I can't! Jonah conveniently forgot about a *very impor-*

tant dinner with a *very important* client. It's too late to get a sitter."

I don't even suggest that I bring the kids to book club. One of the first rules the seven of us made when we started the club was that children were not allowed. No exceptions. Not even when Sandy Herman's husband got into a car accident that crushed his right leg thirty minutes before book club was to start. Sandy called up to explain what had happened and to ask if she could bring her son, Peter, because, of course, Ralph was in emergency surgery. (The fact that she even considered coming to book club instead of going to the hospital to be with her husband was discussed with great fervor during the first ten minutes of the meeting. Shock, surprise, and disdain were quickly replaced by complete understanding and acceptance when all of us realized that book club was as integral to our lives as caffeine. We agreed that we could go days without our husbands, but not a day without coffee.) But Sandy's request to bring Peter was categorically and unanimously denied. Sandy showed up forty-five minutes late, sans Peter, explaining that she'd left him with her mother-in-law at the hospital. When we asked her how Ralph was doing, she shrugged and gulped down three Chardonnays in two minutes flat in order to catch up with the rest of us.

"Okay," Jill says breathlessly, and I can tell she is starting to hyperventilate. "I'll call Karin."

"No, Jill. No. I am not having that girl watch my kids again. She's a Wiccan, for God's sake. She drew a pentagram on my kitchen floor with my one Chanel lip liner, made an altar out of my stepladder, and sacrificed a package of boneless chicken breasts on it! Do you have any idea how much boneless chicken breasts cost?"

"This is an emergency, Ellen. I *need* you here. So, she's a witch. So she wastes poultry. It's not like she's an axe murderer."

"No way, Jill. No." I hate putting my foot down, especially when I know Jill is in distress, but I hadn't mentioned to my cousin the seventeen piercings on Karin's various body parts and the gleam in Jessie's eyes when she saw them. I spent three hours the next day explaining to my daughter that when she was eighteen and not living at home she was welcome to pierce any part of her anatomy she so desired, to which she responded that I was nothing more than a warden in the prison of her life. Where do eight-year-olds come up with this stuff, anyway?

Jill is silent for so long that I think she has hung up on me. A moment later she says, "I'm going to call you back."

"Don't do anything rash," I tell her, "like putting your head in the oven."

"It's electric." Click.

Six

Trader Joe's is quiet on this Friday morning; only a hand-ful of shoppers grace its aisles. Right now, I am gazing at fourteen thousand kinds of cheese, wondering if I should branch out and try a crazy variety for the cheese balls I will not be able to eat since I cannot attend book club tonight. Jill still hasn't called me back. At least, I think she hasn't called me back. I can't really be sure since I left my cell phone on the kitchen counter. It's a bad habit, and it drives Jonah crazy. Every time I "forget" to bring the little evil device with me, or, God forbid, I haven't charged it and the battery is dead, my husband decides that he absolutely must get ahold of me *right this minute*. And when I finally do find the phone and see that I have thirteen messages from him and call him back, he rants and raves about how irresponsible it is of me, a mother of three and wife of one, to leave the cell phone, which he spent a fortune on by the way, at home/in the car/ on the floor of my closet/in my discarded purse. "What if

there's an earthquake or a tsunami? What will you do then?"
he shrieks. Most of the time, I just fake static and hang up.
That's the kind of gal I am. I fake static *and* orgasms.

"Hi."

I look up. It must be coincidence that just as the word
orgasms flashes through my brain, I am greeted by none
other than Ben Campbell. What this man is doing in the
cheese aisle of Trader Joe's at ten thirty on a Friday morning is a complete mystery to me. I should probably feel panicked, since panic is my go-to emotion when confronted with
an attractive man. But the endorphins from my time on the
treadmill are doing glorious things for my self-esteem, I am
freshly showered, and I am fairly confident that the black
capris I am wearing do not have a hole in the ass. Also, there
is no Pop-Tart goo on my shirt since I am currently abstain-
ing from Pop-Tarts.

"Lotta cheese," he says with a grin, turning his attention
to the refrigerated case.

"I was just thinking the same thing," I say. It's a lie. I was
thinking *orgasms*, but I can't really say that to my cousin's
sexy next-door neighbor, now, can I?

"You weren't at soccer practice yesterday."

He noticed I wasn't there. This inconsequential tidbit
gives me a tingle of pleasure. "Yesterday was Connor's day. I
was at his baseball practice. Miss me?" Did I really just say
that? I mentally slap my forehead.

"Like you can't believe," he says, not missing a beat. "This
gal named Tina gave me a lecture on recycling used toilet
paper."

"Sounds like Tina," I say with a smile. And because I just
can't help myself, I ask, "Aren't you supposed to be out chas-
ing bad guys or something?"

He squints at me, then smiles sheepishly. When he opens his mouth to speak, he sounds like Joe Friday. "Ordinarily, I would be, ma'am. Lots of bad guys to chase. Not so much in Trader Joe's, though."

I nod in agreement. "I love Trader Joe's. The bad guys don't know what they're missing."

"You got that right." We both chuckle companionably.

"I took some time off between the transfer," he explains. "For the move. My wife had to start work right away, so we thought it would be good for one of us to get the lay of the land, get familiar with the neighborhood."

"Good idea," I say, and pretend to continue perusing the cheese.

Ben reaches for some goat. And no, that is not a weird way of saying he just adjusted himself. He chooses the kind with an herb crust, inspects it, and returns it to the shelf. I grab some English Cheddar with Caramelized Onions, a package of Neufchatel, and a tub of Romano. Ben takes stock of my choices and gives me a speculative look.

"Cheese balls," I say.

"Back at you," he retorts, eyebrows raised. We both laugh again.

"I'm making cheese balls," I explain unnecessarily. Obviously, he knows what I meant. He's a detective, for Pete's sake.

He fixes me with a direct stare and says, "Let me ask you a question."

I feel something stirring in my belly at being the recipient of such an intense gaze, and although I am struggling to appear placid on the outside, my insides are turning to jelly. I chide myself for having this kind of reaction to him, even though I know that there isn't a damn thing I can do to change it. Body chemistry and hormones are what they are. You can't ignore them, just like you can't ignore gravity when you go bungee jumping.

Ben is now looking at me expectantly and I realize he has already asked the question but my mental machinations were so loud that I missed it.

"What?"

"Is that a dumb question?" he asks, a hint of embarrassment seeping into his voice. "It is, isn't it?"

I realize that he has mistaken my "What?" for a criticism of his question. I could save *myself* a lot of embarrassment and just let him continue to think that I find his question ridiculous and not worth answering. But then I'd never know what he asked. Better to make an ass of myself than to always wonder, *What was the question? What did he ask? Why was it dumb? What the HELL was it?* The unknown would keep me awake at night, tossing and turning and wondering, and for a woman fast approaching hot flashes, hormone surges, and night sweats, I really don't need anything else in my life that will deprive me of sleep.

"No, no. I wasn't listening with both my ears," I tell him. "I really didn't hear the question."

He looks relieved, and then his lips curl up with amusement. "You weren't listening with both your ears?" he mimics. "Okay. Well, it probably is a dumb question, anyway." He pauses, as if waiting for a drum roll. "If you were cheese, what kind would you be?"

I can feel my jaw drop to my chest, and a moment later, a deep rumble of laughter escapes me. I can think of only a few times in my life I have ever been truly surprised by a man, and this has to be one of them. This gorgeous, sexy hunk of a man with his liquid brown eyes and six-pack abs and super-hero job has an *inner geek*. I love it! He squints at me again, immediately assuming that I am ridiculing him with my giggle fit. I quickly stifle the guffaws, wipe the tears from my eyes, and shake my head to disabuse him of the idea.

Before I can stop myself, I reach out and place a hand on his arm. In all seriousness, I say, "I think that might be the best question I have heard in a decade."

Trader Joe's is a great market, and it's easy to linger for a while, but usually I am in and out in ten minutes flat. Not today. Ben Campbell and I peruse the aisles together as I play tour guide, pointing him in the right direction for each item written on the carefully itemized list his wife gave him this morning. He is an affable man, charming and self-effacing and unassuming, and once I have gotten past the fact that he is an out-and-out studmuffin, I find myself enjoying the easy banter we have fallen into.

As for cheese, he tells me that he would probably be Gouda. (He'd be *Gouda*, all right.) Tough, shiny, red skin on the outside with a mild, agreeable, if somewhat plain interior. I tell him I haven't known him all that long, but I think he'd be more of a Cambozola. He laughs and asks if that means I find him stinky. I laugh and reply that I find him unexpected. Me, I'm more of a Brie kind of gal, I say. Simple, dependable, and high in fat.

We come to the end of the frozen food and I catch a glimpse of the sample station, the place where customers can try some of the tasty food the store has to offer. No matter how short on time you are, you cannot do Trader Joe's without trying a sample. It's almost like there's some kind of electromagnetic force that pulls at you, and you have no choice but to succumb to it. I am desperately attempting to veer off course, since I don't want Ben to think I am weak and gluttonous, but I seem to have lost control of my cart. Two seconds later, Ben says something that fills me with relief.

"I love samples!"

Thirteen seconds later, I watch him stuff his face with turkey meat loaf and mashed potatoes, rice balls, and chocolate chip dunkers. I taste the turkey meat loaf and rice balls, think of my treadmill, and pass on the dunkers. Then we both chase the food with some pomegranate-cranberry iced tea. Ben sighs contentedly and drops his cup in the trash.

"I could've done without the rice balls," he states thoughtfully. "But those dunkers are the bomb." He gives me a sideways glance, then whispers, "Don't tell my wife about the cookies. She's keeping the family off wheat." He thinks for a moment. "And dairy. Red meat. Sugar."

All of the things that I love and adore, I think. "So what do you eat?"

He grimaces. "Tofu. Lots of tofu." He shudders emphatically. "But, hey. I'm on the job. If my partner is driving and he happens to choose McDonald's for lunch, what am I supposed to do?"

"Not tell your wife," I reply.

"You got that right."

"Is she a vegan?"

"No. She's American." He breaks into a smile. I smile back, praying that I don't have any turkey meat loaf stuck between my front teeth.

When we reach the checkout, he selects one lane and I select the opposing one, which causes us to occasionally brush our backsides against each other while the cashiers total our items. I'm going to blame my hormones again, but just the mere rustle of my capris against his Levi's is giving me the female equivalent of a woody. I know, *know*, for a fact that this man has no ulterior motives or salacious ideas in his head regarding Ellen Ivers. And I know that nothing will ever happen between the two of us. But I suddenly feel like I did when I was sixteen. Carefree, optimistic, my life full of possibilities, the world my oyster.

"Did you bring your own bag?" the cashier asks, dragging me back from my thoughts. Instantly, the warm fuzzies evaporate, quickly replaced by guilt and shame. I *do* have bags, green-friendly hemp jobs with the recycling logo stamped on the side. When I bought them, I was extremely proud of myself for being so environmentally friendly, such a champion for planet Earth. And yet, not once have I remembered to bring them to the store. I know exactly where they are: on the bottom shelf of my pantry next to the family-sized box of Cheez-Its.

I glance behind me and watch with horror as Ben withdraws a square of nylon fabric from his jeans pocket and proceeds to unfold it into a ginormous grocery sack. The blond cashier flashes him an appreciative, aren't-you-the-coolest-guy-in-the-world smile and begins to load his items into the bag.

I turn back to the cashier and give a curt shake of my head. "I forgot it."

The girl just shrugs and gives me a patient smile that seems to say, *That's okay. We get a lot of your kind*, and forcefully snaps open a paper sack.

Ben and I finish at the same time and push toward the sliding doors. As we head out into the sunlight, I glance over at his cart.

"Nice bag," I comment wryly.

"My wife's an environmental lawyer," he says. "What can I say?"

As we traverse the parking lot, I realize that my Flex is parked right next to his Volvo station wagon, and I let the coincidence roll right off my back. I glance at the bumper stickers adorning the rear end of the Volvo: *Obama/Biden '08*, *I Brake for Marsupials*, *Three-Mile-High Club/Sky's the Limit*.

I narrow my eyes at him as he pops the hatch open. He catches the look.

"What?"

I should keep my mouth shut. I know I should. Delving too deeply into the personal life of a married man probably is not something a married woman should be doing, especially a married woman who wants to reinvent herself for the better. I am not Catholic. I cannot go to confession and be absolved of my lustful, covetous thoughts. But I absolutely have no filter when it comes to blurting out questions I just need to have answered.

"Three-mile-high club?" I ask. "I didn't know they had bumper stickers for that one."

He shakes his head and laughs. "No, no, no. You're thinking of the *mile*-high club. It's not that." He gives a rueful smile. "Linda keeps telling me to scrape that one off, says I'm giving the wrong impression . . . which, obviously, I am. That's from the skydiving place." He says it casually, as if he got it at Jiffy Lube. "I won't scrape it off. I'm too damn proud of it."

"You jumped out of a plane?" I ask, incredulous. I know people do it all the time. People with death wishes or people with nothing and no one to live for. People who are deranged.

"Twice," he says. "It was awesome. I posted the video on Facebook. You should friend me . . . Or I'll friend you. You can check it out."

"I don't do Facebook." I feel like I am confessing a heinous sin, but Ben takes it in stride.

"Well, it was awesome. I mean, I look like I'm about to

throw up in the video, but . . . wow, your heart's pounding, your mind, totally blank. It was the greatest. I highly recommend it."

"But . . . but . . . why?" I can't wrap my mind around the "awesome" thing. I mean, how can hurtling toward earth at ninety miles an hour, wondering if your chute will open, knowing that if it doesn't, you're about to become a human pancake, be fun? "Why would you want to do that?" I ask again.

He shrugs. "I guess, I don't know, I've always felt it's good to try new things, especially if they scare the shit out of you." He loads his one super-sack into the back of the Volvo. "If you stop trying new things, you might as well just stop."

I stare at him for a long moment, thinking about his words. They are reverberating madly inside my brain. My synapses are firing at the recognition of important information, cathartic information, perhaps. Ben has no idea the impact his sentence is having on me. *If you stop trying new things, you might as well just stop.*

He finger-waves as he climbs behind the wheel of his car. I continue to stare at him as he slowly pulls the Volvo out of the parking slot. Before he drives away, the passenger window rolls down and I see him lean over. I bend at the waist to face him.

"This was fun," he says. "I can't say I've ever enjoyed grocery shopping as much."

I am completely at a loss for words, so I just smile. And stare at him until the Volvo is completely out of sight.

I am still pondering Ben's words as I move through my kitchen, assembling and preparing all of the ingredients for the cheese balls. For some reason, my thoughts keep drifting back to the *Ladies Living-Well Journal* and the blog competition. Am I actually afraid of entering the competition, afraid of failing miserably and looking like a jerk? If that's the case, then, according to Ben Campbell, I should just do it. It's not like I've never made a complete ass out of myself before. And the fact is, the blog competition is anonymous. Nobody would have to know how badly I failed.

If you stop trying new things, you might as well just stop.

Wait, when did I give Ben Campbell such power? The first time he gazed at me with those liquid brown eyes, that's when. I am not blind to the fact that I have developed a slight crush on my cousin's neighbor. It feels only slightly different than the crush I have on Hugh Jackman, and I would say that the *main* difference is the fact that I have actually breathed the same air as Ben Campbell. Yet both crushes would be categorized together in the same subfolder of *This could happen when pigs fly or when Republicans vote Jesse Jackson into the White House.* But the thought of Hugh makes me warm and tickly all over, and I find that thinking about Ben is having a similar effect.

I am almost forty-three. I think about the last time I tried something new that frightened me, and fitting into a new size of underwear doesn't count. As I grate the English Cheddar, I remember that six months ago, I tried a mojito at the Lancaster wedding. I am not afraid of alcohol, *obviously*, but I do fear the aftereffects of rum, so I am going to count that one. In fact, now that I think of it, I was so pleased to overcome my fear of a rum hangover, I drank three more. Or four. Five? Well, I lost track at four, but the important thing is that I tried something new.

Wow. Six months. Have I really tried nothing new in the last half year? I *will not* include laundry detergent or face cream because that would be downright pathetic, especially since I already counted the mojito. When was the last time I tried something new that actually inspired fear in me? I shake my head at the mound of grated Cheddar before me.

On my honeymoon I went jet-skiing for the first time; having had a childhood friend who died while riding one, I was deathly afraid of them. I remember now the terror I felt as I swung my leg over the seat, gripped the handlebars, and idled away from the dock. I recall how the terror quickly morphed into exhilaration as I got a feel for the machine and accelerated to full speed, the wind whipping through my hair, the spray of water splashing my face as I bounced over a wake, my heart pumping wildly in my chest. It was almost better than the honeymoon sex, if you want to know the truth. That was thirteen years ago, I realize now with something akin to horror. And before that? Parasailing in Florida with my ex. I was, what? Twenty-five? Eighteen years ago.

Jesus, I really need to get out and do something. As I grab the paprika from the spice rack and a mixing bowl from the cupboard, it hits me that this whole reinvention thing I have embarked upon is completely enmeshed with "trying something new." Exercising on the treadmill and avoiding Pop-Tarts are only a superficial Band-Aid. What I really need is to branch out, open myself up to the unexpected, take risks, embrace my fears. Clearly, these forty-two-year-old bones are not meant for some of the things I am afraid to do, like skydiving or surfing or anything else that puts excess amounts of pressure on any of my aged joints. But blogging?

I turn away from the mixing bowl and regard my computer. The monitor seems to be calling to me. I have the urge to drop what I'm doing and go over and plunk my fingers down on the keyboard. But alas, I must make the cheese balls. And there's also that little thing about my not knowing what to write about.

Before I gave up writing in favor of full-time subservience—I mean motherhood—I never lacked for subject matter. But I always gave myself a set amount of time to allow my brain to have a party. This was my preparation. I would do mindless tasks while my subconscious worked out the details of what would eventually end up on paper.

As I gaze at my tattered, almost illegible recipe, which I no longer need, I decide that I will let my subconscious take over while I make the cheese balls. I will allow the cooking to be a meditative experience that will unlock all kinds of fresh and wonderful ideas. Okay, I'm hoping for just *one* idea, but I'm trying to be positive. And I promise myself that when I am done with the cheese balls, I will sit down at the computer and enter the stupid fucking blog competition.

Damn that Ben Campbell, anyway.

Stay positive, I tell myself. *You can do it, Ellen. You're a writer. So, you've been on hiatus for a while. A long while. It's like riding a bike, right? Just go with this.*

I empty out the contents of all the containers into the mixing bowl, feeling the quiet energy of my ruminations as my mind begins to swirl with a vast array of inspired thoughts, tapping into the mysterious reserves of my untapped gray matter . . . and then the phone rings.

"It's all settled," Jill states adamantly, then proceeds to explain how she has made it possible for me to attend book club by pawning my children off on her husband.

"Greg hates my kids," I retort. "There's no way he is willing to watch them for the entire evening."

"He doesn't hate them," she says sternly. "He just thinks they're a challenge."

"Mentally challenged," I say. "He called them that the last time we all got together."

"He was drunk!" she cries. "You can't listen to him when

he's drunk! Trust me. Anyway, he offered to take them along with the *D*s. Bowling. Burgers. Boomers. They'll love it!"

Greg offering to take my kids for the night is akin to the Dalai Lama unleashing a hailstorm of bullets from an AK-47. I know Jill put him up to it, and I wonder just what she offered him in return. A night of sex with his buxom receptionist is my guess.

"He'll lose them, Jill. On purpose. I know that man. He'd lose his own kids if he thought he could get away with it."

"That's not fair. Greg's a great dad."

"Yes, Jill, he is," I say, acquiescing. Getting into an argument with Jill over Greg's questionable parenting skills is not worth the stress it will cause her, especially when she's already on the verge of a breakdown.

"Look, it won't just be Greg. Ralph Herman and Kevin Savant are going with their kids, too. Maybe Jonah can meet them at Boomers after his dinner."

I stare down at the stainless-steel bowl that is filled with Neufchatel, Romano, grated English Cheddar, eggs, and a plethora of spices. This is going to be a great batch of cheese balls; I can just feel it. The mother of all cheese balls. They will go perfectly with the organic red wine Jill always serves. A perfect compliment to the spanakopita and pastry puffs that always grace her buffet. Just the right precursor to the warm molten truffle bites that she buys from Bristol Farms but claims to have made herself.

It looks like I am going to book club tonight, even if it means having my children abducted from right under Greg's nose.

"Okay. They can go with Greg."

Jill's cacophonous sigh echoes over the phone line. "Thank you," she says sincerely. "I just can't do this without you."

"Yes you can," I argue. "But I'll be there." I let a few

seconds pass, then ask, "So, what's Greg getting out of the deal?"

She laughs without mirth. "I promised him oral."

Wow. Jill must really want me there tonight. She likes oral about as much as she likes natural childbirth. Have I mentioned that she screamed for an epidural as soon as her water broke during labor with her first child?

I hang up, wash my hands, then plunge them into the cheese goop. I breathe in through my nose, blow out through my mouth, hoping to recapture the meditative state I was in before Jill called. A wisp of an idea threads its way through my brain. I don't force it, just continue to mash the cheesy concoction with my fingers. I can almost grasp it . . . can almost touch it . . .

The phone rings, *again*. I curse, then glance at the Caller ID and see that it's Jonah. Perfect timing, as usual. I let the call go to voice mail, wash my hands thoroughly, *again*, being careful to scrape the cheese from under my nails, then call him back.

"Hey," he says. "You busy?"

"I'm making cheese balls for book club."

"I love your cheese balls."

"They're not for you," I tell him, and he chuckles into the phone. "What's so funny?" I ask.

"You're talking to me in full sentences. I guess you're not that mad any more?"

I am still mad, but my anger has lost its steam since the problem has been resolved. I explain to him what's happened, outline the plan for the evening, and quash his objection to Greg's being responsible for our children even for a short time.

"He's my cousin's husband," I say. "He's not going to let

anything happen to our kids. Grandma Phyllis would come back to haunt him, and you know how afraid he was of her."

"Bowling, burgers, and Boomers, huh?"

"You only have to be there for the Boomers portion. Consider yourself lucky."

He sighs. I am receiving a lot of phone sighs today.

"My dinner should be done by eight since the CEO is like a hundred," he says. "I'll meet them all at Boomers and bring the kids home."

"Thanks," I say. It is only one word, but it's full of gratitude, not venom. Jonah always comes through. "I appreciate it."

"I'm sorry for what I said about book club. I know it's important to you."

"You weren't wrong about the wine and gossip," I acknowledge. "But there is a bit more to it than that."

"I know," he says. But he doesn't mean it. I can tell. And he isn't really sorry. But at least he said it. When it comes to men, apologies are big even when insincere.

"I love you," he says, just as he always does before hanging up.

"You, too," I reply automatically. Then I hang up and head back to my cheese balls.

Four dozen perfectly golden-brown and highly aromatic cheese balls line the kitchen counter behind me. I sit in front of my computer, staring at the *Ladies Living-Well Journal* registration page, racking my brain for a decent username. I have tried several: *Forty-Something, Forty-Something-And-Fabulous, Forty-Something-And-Somewhat-Fabulous,* but all of those have been used. The problem is that the username is also the domain name for the blog, so my username has to be completely original and not something that has been used by any other person on the Web. Like I understand any of this.

I sigh and blow out a breath, determined not to be undermined by a lack of imagination. And suddenly, my fingers are flying over the keyboard, almost as if they have minds of their own. I glance at the flashing cursor and read the name I have typed into the rectangle. *SomethingNewAt42*. I like it. I send up a silent prayer as I hit the return key, then wait an interminable thirty seconds before I am rewarded with the legend: *Congratulations, SomethingNewAt42. You have successfully registered for the* Ladies Living-Well Journal *blog competition!*

Great. I have a username. Now all I need is an idea for a blog.

I browse through the blog templates and come to one that somehow speaks to me. I sift through the many background choices at my disposal and purposely pass over the ones I would ordinarily pick: the flowers, the smiley faces, the fruit bowls and wine. This blog is something new for me, after all, and I don't want the look of it to represent the old me. Settling for a sunset image across the top and no background image at all, I click the Save button, then go to my preferences. Once I have selected them, I am directed to my blog's home page, where I am instructed to write a brief description of the blog's theme or purpose. I purse my lips, stand up quickly, stretch my neck, and hear an alarming number of cracks. Then I sit back down and stare at the flashing cursor.

Okay. Here goes.

SomethingNewAt42

HOME PAGE

I have just popped my blog-writing cherry, everyone, so please be gentle with me. I had no intention of entering this competition in the first place—it was thrust upon me by a meddling and overeager relative who shall remain nameless until exposing her serves my purpose. The $10,000 prize is a fairly good motivator, although money alone cannot inspire a person to do something completely foreign, unnerving, and downright ridiculous. Actually, the catalyst for me dusting off my writing chops was a simple statement made to me earlier today that has been reverberating around in my brain:

If you stop trying new things, you might as well just stop.

Okay, so maybe it is a little clichéd, but the underlying truth of those words continues to haunt me hours later. Perhaps because of my current state of mind.

I am a forty-two-year-old wife and mother who has become trapped in a constant state of complacency. When I took on the roles of wife and mother so many years ago, it seems I stopped allowing myself to play any other part. I stopped playing me. I used to be spontaneous. I used to belt out "Why Don't We Do It in the Road" at the top of my lungs in the middle of a crowded shopping mall for no apparent reason. I used to do cartwheels, albeit bad ones, on my front lawn, right in front of the postman. I used to jog to the beach and jump into the ocean in the middle of winter, the cold water stinging every inch of my body, just to feel the wonder of being alive on the planet. I don't do any of those things any more. And today, for the first time in a long time, I actually recognized that fact and asked myself why.

That's not to say that I haven't enjoyed motherhood and wifedom. I am fairly confident that I have done an okay job in both categories; that is to say, my children won't need too much therapy and my husband hasn't left me yet for a young blond bimbo. But I don't necessarily want "wife" and "mother" to be the only two things that define me. If that sounds selfish, then so be it. After being a wife and mother for more than thirteen years, a little selfishness would definitely be something new.

What I guess I'm trying to say is that I'm writing this blog for me. I may suck at it. I'm not even exactly sure what I'm going to write. More than likely, my posts will be decidedly non-earth-shattering. I may not end up being defined by my blogging efforts, but at least it will be something new. And for a woman of my age and circumstances, something new sounds pretty fucking great.

Am I allowed to curse on this blog? There are no rules about swearing in the guidelines, and the *Ladies Living-Well Journal* isn't exactly the *Christian Science Monitor*, but still. It does seem a little on the conservative side. Well, fuck it, I decide. This is my blog, and if I want to curse like a sailor, I'll bloody well do it. Am I empowered now, or what?

My moment of self-satisfaction comes to a screeching halt when I realize that I still have no idea what to write for the actual blog itself. I take a deep breath. Exhale. Close my eyes. Breathe in again. Try to forget how much I despise failing. I open my eyes and place my fingers over the keys. I click the

New Post tab and watch as a blank text box appears on the screen. Shit.

I get up and pace around the kitchen, looking for things in my surroundings that will inspire me. Nothing. I drink a sixteen-ounce bottle of Evian in one long swallow and nearly heave it back up, then contemplate writing about the dangers of drinking too much water. That's crap. I absently pluck one of the cheese balls off the sheet pan, finding it cool to the touch, and take a bite, just for tasting purposes. Definitely the best batch I have ever made; sharp, zesty flavor, perfect mouthfeel. Still chewing, I return to the computer and let my hands rest over the keyboard. Without thinking, I begin to type. My fingers start to move, slowly at first, then picking up speed. And within a minute, I am completely immersed in the creation of my first blog post.

Oh, I have missed this, this creation thing. Writing was always therapy for me, whether or not I was being paid to do it. And now, I feel my juices simmering. The sensation is fantastic. I almost don't care if my blog is any good. Just to be writing again is . . . is . . . is . . .

I glance up at my title and hiccup with surprise. Oh well, I think. I don't need the ten grand anyway. This is for me. Fuck the rest of them. I keep on going.

. . . .

First Post: March 16, 2012
SomethingNewAt42

MEN ARE CHEESEBALLS

Heard that before? Of course you have. But if you think I'm trying to be funny, I'm not. I mean it in the literal sense. I actually believe the comparison has merit. And I should know. I just spent the last hour making cheese balls. Real ones with English Cheddar and Romano, and boy, are they good. *This* time.

Let me expound for a moment. About the cheese balls: You have a bunch of random ingredients. Some cheese balls are made with English Cheddar, some with Gouda. Roquefort or Camembert or any old kind of bleu you prefer. Some have a combination of two or three cheeses. But the cheese is the main thing, right? Men have a single main ingredient, too. Their *maleness*. It comes with the territory. (Okay, transvestites don't count.) Their maleness is the force that guides them and informs their entire makeup. It is their base, so to speak.

So, with cheese balls, along with the main ingredient, you have a plethora of spices to choose from. Salt and pepper sort of go without saying. I like to use paprika. Garlic, onion powder, maybe cumin or curry. Men have different spices, too. All kinds of spices. Like what they wear and the sports they watch and how much they drink or curse or pray, how careful they are with their grooming practices. Their good habits and bad. And, like the ingredients for cheese balls, all of the spices get mashed up with the main ingredient. There you have the dough. You roll the dough up into balls and put 'em in the oven, but you never really know what you're going to get until you pull your sheet pans out.

Sometimes they're crisp and golden, like the ones on my counter right now, and sometimes they are absolute duds. We're talking hockey-puck time. Men, too. Sometimes a man can have all the right ingredients, but when you cook him up, he just turns into ooze on the pan. Man ooze. And not the good kind, if you get my drift. And other times, you pop him in the oven and he comes out all hard and crusty. And just like cheese balls, sometimes you try the exact same recipe that came out perfectly the first time and it comes out completely inedible the second. Men are like that.

I really don't have any advice for you about how to choose a cheese ball recipe, or how to tell whether a particular man's ingredients will turn him into a golden-brown puff of heaven. I just thought I would point out the striking similarity between two such seemingly dissimilar things. But, hey. This comparison is not necessarily an insult. Some cheese balls come out perfectly, just right, delectable in every way. And so do some men. Though, for the most part, my money's on the cheese balls.

. . . .

I reread what I have written and wonder if there is any way I can unenter this goddamned competition. I mean, cheese balls? Come on! Then I read the post a second time and think, *Ah, what the hell.* And before I can stop myself, my index finger clicks the Publish button, and my post is sent into the digital universe.

Seven

Jill's house is even more immaculate than usual, all manner of dust, dirt, and grime having been eradicated by Isabella, her German/Irish/El Salvadorian cleaning woman. Isabella comes every Friday and spends an extra two hours on book club Fridays to make certain that every surface, including the tile and hardwood floors, is clean enough to eat off. I find this very comforting, especially since every now and then one of my cheese balls happens to roll off my plate and onto said floor, and I have no problem picking it up and popping it into my mouth without even so much as a cursory wipe.

My kids were more than excited about the prospect of hanging with their cousins and "Uncle Greg" tonight, since they know that he has a habit of letting his attention wander and they will pretty much be able to get away with anything. I gave Connor a stern talking to about keeping an eye on his younger siblings, and he managed to make it the whole way through my lecture without yawning once. I reminded them that their dad would be meeting them at Boomers to do his parental bit, and warned them to absolutely stay away from the gory, blood-spattering zombie-killing games that I insisted would give them all nightmares if they dared play them. Each of my three angels nodded solemnly. I can't be certain, but I have a sneaking suspicion that they were all crossing their fingers behind their backs.

Now I am working on my first glass of wine while I try to artfully arrange the food trays on the kitchen counter. I fan out the lovely gold-trimmed beverage naps—these do *not* have lilies on them—and set them between the ice bucket, in which a Chardonnay chills, and the bottle of organic red that is now open and "breathing."

Jill comes into the kitchen with a flourish, wearing a breezy peach-and-yellow blouse that beautifully complements her complexion, and a pair of white cotton slacks. She has applied just the right amount of makeup and her hair falls casually about her shoulders. Jill always looks smashing for book club, which fascinates me. We are, after all, meeting with our female friends. So unless she's hiding from me a girl-crush she has on one of the members, I just don't get the point. Oh, I know it's tied into her Southern roots and her need to be the perfect hostess. But still. Part of the reason I enjoy book club so much is that I don't have to look a certain way or try to impress anyone. Admittedly, I did take a few extra minutes this evening to assess my appearance. After all, you-know-who lives next door and should I run into him whilst taking out the trash, I want to be confident that I don't look like a homeless person rummaging through the bins.

"You look great," I tell Jill, and she beams.

"So do you. Wow." She reaches for her own wineglass and looks at me appraisingly. "You never wear makeup to book club. What's the occasion?"

"It's part of my reinvention thing."

She nods. "You've been doing the treadmill, too. It shows." I smile to myself but say nothing.

She is just pulling a batch of spanakopita out of the oven when the doorbell rings. It's only twenty to seven, and it is rare for anyone to show up this early, but perhaps one of our cohorts has had an exceptionally long week and is jonesing for a libation.

"Want me to get it?" I ask, knowing she will say no. A perfect hostess never lets another guest open the door. It would be *trés gauche*.

Jill shakes her head and slides the sheet pan my way, wordlessly asking me to plate the apps, then heads for the front door. The phyllo triangles burn my fingertips as I transfer them to the serving tray. I can just hear Jill's lilting voice wafting in from the foyer. A moment later, she appears in the kitchen followed by none other than Ben Campbell.

I jerk with surprise, sending the sheet pan and the half-dozen spanakopita I had yet to plate flailing through the air and onto the tile floor. The pan hits with a hearty *clang* and the spanakopita make no sound at all.

God, I am so glad I put on lipstick.

Ben grins. Really, what else can he do? "Hi," is all he says.

I collapse to the floor to gather the fallen appetizers, using a napkin to sweep up the phyllo crumbs. "Hi," I say, my focus firmly fixed on the tile.

"This is my new next-door neighbor, Ben Campbell," Jill says nonchalantly, as though my toppling over hors d'oeuvres happens all the time. To Ben she says, "And this is my cousin Ellen. Don't mind her. She's kind of a klutz."

Thanks a goddamn lot! I think.

"Good to see you again," Ben says as I haul myself to my feet. I throw the spanakopita away, despite the spanking-clean floor, and set the pan next to the sink. With nowhere else to look, I finally meet his eyes.

"You, too."

Jill cocks her head in my direction, and although I am not looking at her, I can feel her speculative gaze.

"We've actually met several times," Ben says.

"Ben's son, Liam? He's on Matt's soccer team," I explain.

He furrows his brow and looks at his watch. "What's it been, eight hours since our last rendezvous?"

"We ran into each other at Trader Joe's."

"Your cousin had the decency to show me around the store," he adds.

Jill nods and says, "Ah. Well, Ben just came over to give me his wife's regrets. I invited her to join tonight, but she can't make it."

"Duty calls," Ben says, then shrugs. "She's working on the wetlands suit."

I have no idea what he's talking about, but I see Jill's eyes go wide. "Wow. That's major!" she says, clearly impressed.

I guess I ought to brush up on local current events. Are the wetlands suing somebody, or is somebody suing the wetlands, and how would that work anyway? How does a piece of land instigate a lawsuit in the first place? Uh-oh. I need more wine.

"Well, I know you've got people coming," Ben says. "I'll get out of your way."

"No, no!" Jill exclaims. "The girls won't be here for another fifteen minutes, at least. Have a glass of wine."

He shakes his head regretfully. "The boys are waiting for me. Pizza night, you know." He turns toward the foyer, then glances back at me. "By the way. How'd the cheese balls come out?"

I smile modestly and let Jill do my bragging for me.

"They are the best she's ever made, Ben, really! Here. Try one." Using silver-plated tongs, she daintily and deftly lifts one of the golden orbs from the tray and places it on a napkin. (My Auntie Pam would be proud.) She then puts the napkin in his waiting hand. Without the reverence Jill so clearly thinks is due, he grabs it and tosses it into his mouth. I watch him as he chews, note his slight pause as the flavors hit his taste buds. He shakes his head, chewing more slowly now, as if savoring every second that my cheese ball graces his tongue.

Am I sweating? Very definitely.

"That is amazing," he finally proclaims, then gives me one of those direct gazes. And yes, it has the same impact this time as it had before. "You're good."

Must be the oven, I tell myself, resisting the urge to fan myself.

"Thanks. Secret family recipe."

"I better go before I steal the whole tray."

"Take another," Jill insists, tongs at the ready.

"No, really, thanks," he tells her, then shifts his focus to me. "But if you have any left over, you know where to find me."

"**What** the h-e-l-l was that?"

"What are you talking about?" I say, injecting as much innocence into my tone as I possibly can. Which isn't much, I'm afraid. I'm feeling too pleased with myself and my cheese balls. It wouldn't matter anyway because Jill is on to me.

"I'm talking about you and my hubba-hubba next-door neighbor. Since when are the two of you so chummy?"

"For God's sake, Jill, I just met him last week, in front of your house." Was it really only last week? I feel as if we've been "running into each other" for ages. "We talked a little at soccer practice, that's all. And I ran into him this morning at Trader Joe's."

She nods knowingly. "And?"

"And nothing!"

"I know that look, Ellen," she says, narrowing her eyes at me sharply. "You had that look on your face for two hours after we saw *Australia*."

All right, I admit, it was a terrible movie, but the scene where Hugh Jackman dumps a bucket of water over his torso kind of hit me hard.

"I do *not* have that look," I tell her. I couldn't possibly, since I've never seen Ben Campbell dump a bucket of water over his own torso, but I'm starting to conjure up a pretty good image in my brain just about now.

Stop, I tell myself. This will come to no good. I'll start comparing Ben's hypothetical wet torso to Jonah's nonhypothetical and very un-*Australia* wet torso, and then I won't ever be able to look at Jonah's naked body again, let alone allow it on top of me. Crap.

"He *likes* you," Jill says, and I suddenly feel like I'm in a Judy Blume novel.

"He does *not*!" I say.

"Look." Jill is suddenly serious, so I quickly take a large gulp of wine in preparation for what's about to come out of her mouth, because I know I won't like it. "I know you have this whole low self-esteem thing going—"

"I do not!"

"But you are a beautiful woman who only occasionally wears sweats with holes in them."

"Stop."

"And when you take the time to pluck your eyebrows—wow!"

"Shut up."

"Plus, you're very smart and witty—"

"Jill—"

"What I'm saying is—"

"Don't—"

"It is not completely out of the realm of possibility for a totally hot man to be attracted to you. Seriously, why wouldn't he be?"

Oh, let me count the reasons, I think.

"For one, he's married. To a totally brilliant environmental lawyer. For two, I'm married . . . to Jonah."

"Hey, Ellen, I'm not saying you should jump his bones or anything. But a little flirtation with someone whose name you do not share is never a bad thing. Trust me."

I look at her, totally agog. I have known Jill my whole life, and I have always known that she is a coquette of the first order, but she has always vehemently denied it, telling me that I confuse "flirting" with her intrinsic Southern charm (even though she left the South when she was still in diapers). This is the first time she has ever admitted this to me.

"Sometimes," she says, "a little extramarital flirtation is the only thing that gets me through the day."

I am about to delve further into the topic when the doorbell rings. Seven o'clock on the dot. The book club ladies have arrived.

———

Jill's living room is abuzz with the chatter of the seven of us as we partake of wine and appetizers and—yes, Jonah—gossip. The first hour of book club is *always* about mingling, catching up, and drinking wine. Right now, Mia Franklin is talking excitedly to Sandy Herman about this fabulous hair-straightening product she found at Nordstrom. I know for a fact that Mia's African American locks have been subjected to a pantheon of chemicals in order to smooth out their kinks, and I am surprised that she still has any hair left on her head. Regan Stillwater and Liza Pierce are giggling about the new produce guy at the local Vons. Regan has apparently taken to surreptitiously knocking over assorted fruit and vegetables just to watch him bend over and pick them up. Mona Emmerson is trailing Jill like a Sherpa, helping her transfer the platters from the kitchen to the coffee table, chirping about how much she *loves* the plain gold-trimmed napkins because they are *so* elegant.

I give Jill a wink and she covertly rolls her eyes at me while simultaneously thanking Mona for the compliment.

The seven women who make up this club, myself included, are very different, with varied life experiences and outlooks, but we all share the same love of books. And our differences are actually what make book club so entertaining. We have never all agreed on a book, not once. I think that's what keeps us coming back. We often joke that if we ever do, that will be a sign that book club is officially over.

Mona is older and comes across as a bit conservative, and she doesn't like any book that has expletives in it on principle, no matter the genre. She has three grown kids and four grandkids, volunteers for her church, makes quilts, and has been married to the same man for close to forty years.

Mia, on the other hand, is a brash former social worker

and current high school principal who tells it like it is and doesn't take shit from anyone. She and her husband Sidney have two kids, one boy and one girl, who are both out of the house already (because she started squeezing them out when she was twenty) and both of whom salute her like a drill sergeant whenever they come for a visit. (I should mention that the salute is *always* followed by a hug.)

Liza Pierce has lived in Garden Hills her whole life. In fact, if I'm not mistaken, she's never left the country. She has the full-time job of refereeing her four kids, whom she drives around in her metallic green Freestyle with the family-of-six decals in the back window, and a part-time job working for her husband, who cleans air ducts.

Sandy is in her late forties, with a husband and a teenage son. She works as a department manager at the local Kohl's and spends her days dealing with high-strung shoppers who bleat and screech and throw tantrums when their scratcher coupons reveal that they got the fifteen percent discount instead of thirty percent. (Though she says her *employee* discount makes it all worthwhile.)

Regan Stillwater is a sassy and cynical divorcée whose two kids live with her ex and his twenty-something wife in the Bay Area, leaving her to bask in her sizable alimony with various pool boys and, apparently, grocery store stock boys. She is outspoken and irreverent and may or may not have been a porn star in her youth. I totally love her.

And this is why I adore book club. Where else could you find such opposing personalities gathered together, all getting along and having a terrific time? The UN should take note. We have formed a sorority and everyone is allowed to express her opinion and disagree and debate. Sometimes voices are raised. One time, an argument almost came to blows. But at the end of the night, we all leave as friends.

A typical discussion about a particular book might go as follows:

Mona: "Why does the character have to say the F-word in every sentence?"

Mia: "Because he's from the fucking streets. This is not a fucking 'tea and crumpets' story."

Liza: "I can see Mona's point, but Mia's right about the character."

Jill: "The point is not that he says f-u-c-k every other word. The point is that he is a tortured soul who has never felt tenderness or affection in his entire life and who has no chance of ever finding true happiness because he carries around the excess baggage of his youth."

Sandy: "It's too bad he can't turn himself around. He does have the potential."

Regan: "Oh, who gives a crap? It was a crap novel anyway. Where's the wine?"

I tend to keep my mouth shut and listen for the better part of our meetings. I find the interaction fascinating. And I have to say that I have never met a book I didn't like. Wait, I'll amend that statement. I have never read a book in which I couldn't find some redeeming characteristic. Faults? Yes. Clunky language, certainly. But a book doesn't just happen. It is the blood, sweat, and tears of some masochistic, self-flagellating workaholic who has the fortitude and determination to actually finish something, no matter the price. It is hard for me to condemn a novel as rubbish. I like some more than others, and I dislike many things about some, but I honestly have never put a book down and not finished it. No matter how banal, I always want to know how it ends.

But I do love the debate.

Forty-five minutes later, we have moved on to that portion of the evening, and all of my cohorts are dissing the latest James Patterson novel, which was Sandy's choice. (Sandy likes murder mysteries. They're safe and dependable, just like she is.)

"Well, I think Mr. Patterson has just gotten too big for his britches," says Mia. "I mean, how masturbatory can you be?"

Mona flinches, Liza giggles, and Regan doesn't miss a beat. "Are you asking me personally?"

"I would never ask *you* about your self-love schedule, girl. Don't have that much time!"

"I liked his earlier books better," Sandy admits. "This one was hard to follow and I have to say that I didn't like any of the characters. They're all so removed."

"Assholes," Mia agrees.

Mona flinches again and takes a sip of wine. "Too much cursing."

"In the book or in this room?" Mia asks with a grin.

Mona grins back. "Both, if you want to know the truth."

That's the thing about Mona that makes her a welcome part of the group. She's not evangelical. She doesn't frown on anyone because they swear. She just doesn't do it herself. But I get the distinct feeling that nothing would give her greater pleasure than running down the middle of Main Street screaming *fuck* at everyone she passes.

"What do you think, Miz Thang?" Mia asks, turning her attention to me.

I shrug noncommittally. "It wasn't a total disaster, but the ending was kind of anticlimactic."

"I liked it," Liza says adamantly. "Patterson has switched things up, gotten out of his routine. He's trying something new."

My ears perk up at the last sentence and suddenly I am

thinking about my blog. I wonder whether anyone will read it, what they will think about it. Maybe I should peruse the other entries to see what my competitors are writing about, but that might undermine my confidence, which, frankly, after writing about cheese balls, is not very high anyway. No. I won't do that. But what should tomorrow's post be about? And the next day's? Oh, God, what if another idea doesn't come to me? What if the well is already dry? What if the *Men are Cheeseballs* post is the final literary accomplishment of Ellen Ivers? That would totally suck.

"Hello? Earth to Ellen!"

I look up and find six pairs of eyes staring at me expectantly. I feel myself blush, then turn to Jill, whose expression has turned suspicious.

I clear my throat and take a breath. "I have to agree with Liza," I say. "It's always good to try something new."

"So, what were you thinking about?"

I am not surprised that Jill has taken this long to bring it up. When it comes to having a pointed discussion, she is as organized as she is in every other aspect of her life. The ladies have long since left, Greg has already brought home the three *D*s and put them to bed, and the two of us are side by side at the sink, washing and drying the dishes.

"When?" I avoid her eyes as I take a dripping tray from her hands and gently wipe it with a towel.

"You know when. You were thinking about *him*, weren't you?" She uses a wineglass to gesture toward the house next door. Through the window in the family room, I can just make out the property fence and the beige stucco walls on the other side.

"I was not, Jill."

"Uh-huh." Her tone reveals that she doesn't believe me. "Then what? Come on. Give. You were off in Ellen-land, and you had this kind of smug smile on your face."

"I was thinking about my blog," I say casually, carefully placing the dry wineglass on the counter.

"Your *what*?" I turn to see her gaping at me in complete disbelief. "Did you say your *blog*?"

I nod and grab the crystal platter from her before she drops it in the sink.

"You mean for the *Ladies Living-Well Journal* competition?"

"What the hell other blog would I be talking about?" I snap.

"You did it!" she exclaims gleefully. "You really did it!"

"You're going to wake up the boys."

"I can't believe it!" she gushes, ignoring my comment. "This is so exciting! Why didn't you tell me?"

"I just did it today, for God's sake. Give me a break!"

"I am so proud of you, Ellen." Oh Jesus. Here we go. "You actually took the initiative and did something totally positive that's completely for you. You should never have given up writing, but that doesn't matter anymore, because you've finally gotten back to it. Don't you feel great? Aren't you just bursting with self-respect?"

Ordinarily, I bristle at Jill's patronizing tone. But she is so genuinely happy and filled with pride on my behalf that I just can't get mad at her.

"So, what's it about? I bet it's brilliant. It is, isn't it? I've never read anything you've written that wasn't absolutely amazing!"

"Hey, Jill, tone it down, okay? It's one blog post, it's not like I'm getting the Pulitzer." And *brilliant* is not the adjective I'd use to describe my man/cheeseball dissertation. In fact, looking at Jill's face, all lit up like that, I am certain that she is going to be more than a bit disappointed.

"Well, I can't help it. You're going to win, I know it." She shuts off the faucet with emphasis. "And I will be able to take credit for pushing you to do it! Oh. I can't wait to read it. I'm going to boot up my computer and I'll read it after you leave! What's your username?"

"Jill, I don't think your expectations should be quite so high," I tell her.

"Don't be silly," she chides me.

"No, seriously," I say. "And I don't want you telling anyone about this. Not a soul." Her expression falters. I know she is already thinking about how she'll comment about this on her Facebook wall. "And no Facebook posts."

"But I have five hundred and seventy-three friends! The more hits the better, right? All my friends will go to your blog and—"

"No." I am firm. "If you don't give me your word, I won't tell you my username."

Jill pouts. "I could just read all of the contest blogs and find you. I'd know which was yours."

"Yeah, but that would take a while."

She considers this for a moment. My cousin hates not getting her way, especially when it comes to me. But she can tell by my demeanor that I am not going to budge. She clenches her hands into fists and expels an exasperated breath. "Oh, all right! I won't tell anyone. I don't get it, but okay."

"Jill, I haven't written anything in a decade. I could make a complete ass out of myself. I really don't need an audience of people I know for that."

"See, there you go again," she admonishes. "Putting your-self down. Preparing for failure. You are too talented to fail. You're a great writer. And your blog is going to be fan-tastic, I just know it. It's going to be *brilliant*!"

Twenty minutes later, just as I'm putting the leftovers in my fridge, my cell phone rings. I don't want to answer it, knowing it's Jill, certain she is about to lay into me. But the house is blessedly asleep and I don't want to wake anyone up. I grab the phone out of my bag and punch the Talk button. Jill doesn't even give me time to say hello.

"*Cheeseballs?* Men are *cheeseballs?*"

"What can I say? I'm *brilliant*."

Eight

Saturday morning at eight forty-five finds me frantically stain-sticking Matthew's soccer uniform, which he left in a heap behind his bed after practice on Thursday. The white jersey sports a four-inch-long grass stain from a sliding header he took in an unsuccessful attempt to stop a goal. I wasn't there to witness the event, but Rita Halpern gave me a blow-by-blow description, including as much of a physical reenactment as her sixty-year-old body would allow, cackling bemusedly all the way through. I am now cursing myself vehemently for allowing Matthew to wear the jersey to practice in the first place.

He had insisted, and I'd firmly shaken my head and told him I wanted the jersey to stay fresh and clean for his first game. I then received the lower-lip tremble and was informed that he wouldn't feel like a real player unless he got to wear the jersey and that the rest of the team would be wearing them and, "Jeez, Mom, don't you want me to play well?" Well, shit. How do you argue with that? I mean, what was I supposed to say? "Matthew, sweetie, you fall down at every goddamn practice, and therefore there is a very high probability that you will stain your fucking jersey." That would've added another year to his future therapy, no doubt. Therapy that I will probably have to pay for because I'm convinced that Matthew is going to live at home until he's thirty-five.

Meanwhile, the stain is not coming out, even though I'm using my forty-dollar miracle stain remover that I ordered after drinking a little too much Merlot one night. The infomercial showed a guy rubbing a conglomeration of stain-causing substances on a white cotton shirt: ketchup, grass, grape jelly, red wine, mustard, motor oil, lipstick. And although I may have been drunk, I could swear he actually sliced his hand open so that he could drip his own blood onto the shirt. Then he rubbed this "miracle stick," which looks a lot like antiperspirant, on the stain, brushed the shirt with a scrub brush, ran it under hot water for thirty seconds, and presto. Stain gone! I am on round three of rubbing, brushing, and rinsing, and so far, the stain is winning. I fleetingly wonder if I should just use some Liquid Paper to cover the stain and call it a day.

"Mom," Jessie calls from the kitchen.

"In the garage," I reply.

"Can I stay over at McKenna's tonight?" she hollers in her typical eight-year-old "I can't manage to walk the ten steps it would take for me to talk to you in a normal tone of voice" way.

"I can't hear you!" I call back.

Instead of taking those mere ten steps, she ups her decibel level. *"CAN I STAY OVER AT MCKENNA'S TO-NIGHT?"*

"Jessie!" I holler, matching her volume. "If you want to speak to me, *COME HERE!*"

"Why are you yelling at the kids?" Jonah asks with a scowl as he comes through the side door that leads to the backyard.

I frown at him. "I am not yelling at the kids, I am yelling at *Jessie*."

"Oh, well, okay then," he jokes without humor. He is clad in shorts and a sweat-soaked, belly-hugging cotton tank top that reveals far too much of his underarm hair for my taste. Hugh Jackman might get away with the look. Ben Campbell, even. But Jonah just looks icky. To round out the ensemble, he has a surgical mask perched on top of his head, which he wears when he mows the lawn to keep the allergens out of his nose. Very manly, huh? He plucks the mask from his head and drops it into the trash, then starts to remove his shirt. I can smell him from six feet.

"You have no idea how you sound when you yell like that."

Yes, Jonah, I do, I think, looking down at the neon stain. *I sound like a woman on the edge.* If I don't get this shirt into the wash now, it will not be dry in time for the ten o'clock game, and even so, it's going to be close. Why the hell couldn't Matthew have been on a team with black jerseys? Or better yet, green! Next year, at soccer registration, I will demand that he be placed on a team whose uniform is a color more suitable to a child who spends more time on the ground than standing up.

Jessie appears at the door to the garage and smiles sweetly at me. "Can I spend the night at McKenna's house tonight?" she asks in a pleasantly soft voice.

Again, I match her volume. "Thank you for coming to

me and asking me nicely," I say. "Is this something that McKenna's mom knows about?"

"Like, duh, Mom," my daughter says, rolling her eyes. "We're going to rehearse for the play."

Apparently, McKenna's an Oompa-Loompa, too. And after seeing her in the talent show last year singing "Tomorrow" like Harvey Fierstein in *Torch Song Trilogy*, I can understand why. She may be the only student in the entire elementary school who makes Jessie sound like Julie Andrews.

"Well, I'll just give McKenna's mom a call to make sure."

"What, you don't believe me?" Jessie glares at me.

"Of course she believes you, sweetheart." Jonah jumps in. "But moms and dads have to check with each other, just to be sure."

Jessie looks over at Jonah and scrunches her nose. "Yuck, Daddy, put on a shirt!"

I couldn't agree more.

"What if I go call McKenna right now and you can talk to her mom?"

"Fine."

Jessie skips off to the kitchen. I heave a sigh of frustration as I finally surrender to the stain and toss the jersey into the washing machine. I crank the knob to the On position and dump in some laundry detergent, then turn to see my husband standing next to me holding out his muscle shirt.

"I am *not* touching that," I tell him.

"Come on," he says, rolling his eyes. (I seem to be on the receiving end of numerous eye rolls this morning.) "You're doing a load of whites. Just throw this in."

My first thought is that I don't want his disgusting shirt swishing around the washing machine with, and possibly contaminating, my son's precious uniform. My second thought is that Jonah's battery-acid-like sweat might be just the thing to remove the stain. In the end I scrunch my own nose and say, "Throw it in yourself. I wouldn't touch that thing with a ten-foot pole."

"Pussy," he whispers, grinning broadly, and I can't stifle my own amusement.

Suddenly, Matthew's screech reverberates through the house and reaches the garage. *"MOOOOOM! WHERE ARE MY SHIN GUARDS?"*

Anticipating my response, Jonah instantly covers his ears.

I make a face at him. "Pussy."

I barely have time to make myself look decent before heading out to Matthew's first soccer game, a fact that nags at me all the way to the field. It's not that anyone in particular will be there, no, not because of that. It's because for the past two weeks, I have been making an effort to look good. I have taken pride in my appearance for the first time in several years, and I am starting to feel pretty good about it. Jonah has noticed it, too, although he is keeping mum on the subject. It's almost as though my efforts are a threat to him in some way. I can't help but find it ironic that he has no problem showering me with compliments when I feel like a hag, but now that I'm looking trimmer and have a healthy glow (not to mention some delicately applied cosmetic enhancements), he's become as mute as friggin' Marcel Marceau.

He glances over at me from the driver's seat and I can feel him surveying my appearance.

I turn to face him. "What?"

"Are those new jeans?" His tone is suspicious, as though I've just gone over my spending allowance, like I ever had one.

"They're from the back of my closet."

"Oh." He returns his attention to the road and his message is clear. Subject closed.

A needle of anger jabs at me. Subject *not* closed. "I haven't fit into them for a while."

"Hmmmm," is his response. The needle grows to ice-pick proportions.

"Size eight," I say smugly.

"Jessie! Stop kicking my seat," he admonishes, completely ignoring my comment.

I fold my arms across my chest and stare through the windshield.

I wallow in my annoyance almost all the way to the field until I hear the trembling voice of my son from the backseat.

"I hope I don't embarrass myself too much."

My heart does a little wrench-thing. My poor Matthew. I yank at my seat belt and wedge myself between the minivan's front seats so that I can look him in the eye.

"The most important thing is that you have fun, Matty." I realize that I haven't called him that since he was five, but he suddenly looks so small. "Seriously," I say. "It's supposed to be fun. Do you think you can do that?"

He stares at me for a long moment, as though considering my words. Then he nods almost imperceptibly.

"Good." I smile. "If you can do that, then the rest is just icing on the cupcake."

Too bad the glaring grass stain on his shirt will embarrass him before the game even starts.

The soccer field is crowded and alive with the U10 players and their families. After circling for a full five minutes, Jonah manages to snag a spot almost a mile away from the action. As I get out of the car, I grumble that if he was going to park in Outer Mongolia, he could have had the decency to drop us all off first. He shrugs as if he has no idea what nonsense I'm sputtering, then hauls our three portable chairs and our cooler from the back of the minivan. I herd Connor, Jessie, and a resolved Matthew from the car and usher them toward the field. Matthew is repeating the chant, "Have fun, have fun" like Rain Man, and, not for the first time, I wonder about his mental health. He glances at me and I give him a thumbs-up. He shakes his head doubtfully and rolls his eyes at me. This makes Connor the only member of my family who has *not* rolled his eyes at me this morning, but I'm sure it is only a matter of time.

"I'm going to hang with Jeff," Connor says as we approach the green.

"Aren't you going to watch Matthew's game?" I ask.

And sure enough, I get the eye roll from my twelve-year-old. (See? I told you.) I plant my hands firmly on my hips and glare at him. He hangs his head and gives me an apologetic smile.

"I'm gonna watch it," he says. "From over there." He points to the far side of the field, where a group of tweens has gathered.

"Fine. But I want you to check in." He is about to roll his eyes again, I can feel it, but he manages to stifle the reflex before it happens.

"Okay, Mom," he relents, then grins at me hopefully. "Can I have some money for the snack bar?"

"For a kiss," I challenge him.

He looks at me like I've just asked him for a kidney. Kiss his mom in front of his friends? Yuck! Before he can decide either way, Jonah steps in and hands him a five, for which he receives a knuckle bump.

"Thanks, Dad."

"Yeah. Thanks, *Dad*," I say tersely.

"You should be ashamed of yourself, trying to bribe affection from your son."

I want to give Jonah the finger, but the soccer field is decidedly G-rated, and there is no way to do it surreptitiously. Instead, I pointedly turn my back to him, put an arm each around Jessie and Matthew, and steer them toward Matthew's awaiting team. As we are walking, I feel a slight thump against my back, and then Connor slings his tanned arm around my neck and nudges Matthew out of the way so he can lean in to me.

"Love you, Mom," he says. It is barely a whisper, and before I can respond, he tears away from me and races to his waiting friends. It is a covert display of affection from a twelve-year-old boy, and therefore should probably be placed in the "little things" category. But to sappy old Ellen, it is a big thing. I have a twelve-year-old son who tells me he loves me in public, albeit on the down low. I can't help but feel aglow with pride, at least for a moment. It's not often that mothers are given any confirmation that they are doing something right. I'll take it where I can get it.

The Polar Bears (of the white jersey fame) are playing the Yellow Jackets today on Field 2. The teams and spectators have congregated on either side, and we make our way to where the Polar Bear banner stands. Matthew spies the rest of his team in a huddle with his coach and slowly makes his way over to them. His coach pats him on the back as he continues to pump up the players. I notice that Liam is there, hunched over, hands on his thighs, listening intently to the coach's advice.

I surreptitiously glance around and see Ben Campbell standing next to the bleachers, his arm around a boy of about seven, chatting with Gary Sinclair, Dave Holmes, and a couple of other dads. My stomach does an involuntary flip-flop at the sight of him, and I force myself to keep an ambivalent expression on my face. I quickly scan the bleachers for the notorious Linda, but since I've never met her, I don't know who to look for. There are several people I don't recognize amid the group of regulars, but none of them wears a shirt that says *Greenpeace*, so I have no idea if she's even here.

Jonah comes alongside me and drops the gear, and I jerk my eyes from the crowd. Together, with Jessie trying to help yet not helping one iota, we set up the chairs and place them parallel to the bleachers. Jonah insists on bringing these damn chairs even though there's always plenty of space on the bleachers. He claims the aluminum benches make his ass fall asleep and he ends up walking funny for an hour. I can't vouch for the butt slumber, but he does look remarkably like the Elephant Man whenever he sits on the bleachers for an extended period of time.

Jonah spots his buddies, Gary and Dave, and heads in their direction. Like Jonah, the two men are in sales and they love to spend the entirety of the soccer games discussing their LinkedIn profiles (a far cry from their wives' composting conversations). As Jessie flops into one of the chairs, my eyes follow Jonah as he reaches the group. He exuberantly greets Dave and Gary, and a couple of high fives are exchanged (even though high fives are so passé), then turns to Ben as the others introduce him. He smiles broadly and shakes Ben's hand, and a few pleasantries pass between them.

My insides are churning at the idea of Jonah and Ben conversing, and I recognize the pressing weight of guilt bearing down on me. The rational part of my brain recognizes the absurdity of this response. I have done nothing to feel guilty about. I have not even allowed myself to fantasize about Ben Campbell except for the *Australia* wet-torso thing, but I cut that off pretty damn fast, if I do say so myself. Ben and I have enjoyed a handful of conversations. It's not like we've been secretly meeting at the Motel 6 for afternoons of debauchery. So why am I suddenly sweating like a pig?

A moment later, Ben looks past Jonah and spots me. He cocks his head and smiles at me, gives me a little wave, and the warmth that spreads through me is instantaneous and surprising. I am aware that I am blushing, and thankful that Ben will not be able to see the color of my cheeks from where he stands.

"Mom, your face is red."

I look down. Jessie is staring up at me, an expression of childlike concern on her pretty face. I can't very well tell my eight-year-old that I'm having a hot flash, now can I?

"It's hot out here," I say instead.

"It's not *that* hot," she replies.

When I return my attention to the soccer dads, I notice that a blond woman in jeans and a *Save the Humans* shirt has walked over to the group. She taps Ben on the shoulder, then bends down and hands the boy next to him a bottle of water. The boy smiles up at her and she ruffles his hair.

So this must be Linda of the Wetlands.

Before I can look away, Jonah turns and gestures for me to join him. I don't want to, *really* don't want to go over there. I haven't spent much time imagining what Ben's wife might be like, but now that I think about it, I kind of don't want to know. Even from here, I can tell she is attractive in an earthy way—how appropriate—and probably wears a size six. I know that she is brilliant and well respected and accomplished. She probably cooks like Julia Child and fucks like Linda Lovelace. But if she is genuinely nice and friendly and accessible, I will have to hate her on principle. Women who have husbands like Ben Campbell shouldn't be allowed to be perfect and all-around amazing. That just wouldn't be fair to the rest of us. Of course, there is no way to know what someone is like behind closed doors, so I can hold on to the fact that even if she comes across as perfect to the rest of the world, she may be a closet sociopath with pierced labia who tortures small animals for fun.

Jonah gestures for me again, more urgently this time, and I make my way over to him. Ben Campbell is less than three feet away, and I pray that my face has returned to its normal color. I say hello to Dave and Gary, then throw a "Hi" to Chip Malloy and Paul Reyburn. The next face I see is Ben's.

"Hey, Ellen," he says. A jolt passes through me and I realize that this is the first time he has called me by name.

"Hi," is all I can manage.

Jonah puts his arm around me. "You know Ben, right?"

"Yes," I tell Jonah. I look back at Ben and say "Hi" for the *second* time. Uh-oh. Mentally deficient Ellen is making an appearance.

The little boy beside him has an arm wound tightly around his leg. Ben leans over and chucks him under the chin.

"Evan, say hello to Matthew's mom and dad."

Wide brown eyes the color of his dad's stare up at us. "I'm going to be eight in June," he says defiantly.

"Wow," I say, nodding solemnly. "Eight is a great age. Matthew's little sister is eight. She's sitting right over there." I point to Jessie, and Evan strains his neck to see her. She is amusing herself by pulling on her wad of gum, stretching it out twelve inches in front of her mouth. I give myself a mental forehead slap.

"Maybe you'd like to go over and say hi," I suggest, and am treated to yet another eye roll. And this time from a kid I've just met. God, it must be a new record. Ben grins as Evan quickly retreats to the safety of his mother's side.

Meanwhile, Linda has turned her attention to the center of the soccer field where the players have gathered. Ben reaches a hand out and touches her on the arm.

"Lin. Hey. This is Ellen." A little jolt again at the sound of my name on his lips. What is the deal with that? Is it possible that I am going through puberty again?

Linda turns her head ever so slightly and gives me a close-mouthed smile that doesn't quite reach her eyes. She has high cheekbones and flawless skin, and her blond mane is twisted back into a clip, managing to look careless and stylish at the same time. She stands about five-six, with long legs and an athletic, trim body. She is not a knockout, but she definitely has that "I am attractive without even trying, and I know it" kind of vibe.

"Nice to meet you," she says, then quickly looks back at the field.

"You, too."

"I see you didn't get that grass stain out of Matthew's shirt," comes Rita Halpern's raspy voice from the bleachers behind me. She cackles merrily as I blush yet again.

"Oh, is *that* your son?" asks Linda, eyebrows raised. Her disapproval is heavily disguised under a layer of friendly curiosity, but I catch it nonetheless. I'll bet her résumé includes *Great stain remover* under her list of accomplishments.

"Yup, that's my Matthew," I say. *And if you think that stain's offensive, just wait till you see him play.*

"We still have to get Liam and Matthew together," Ben jumps in. "For that *un*–play date."

"Yeah, we should."

"Oh, they'll get along like a house afire," Jonah offers.

"Absolutely." Ben nods and smiles. For a split second, he gives me that look, and I have the strangest sensation that there is more to his smile than simple acquaintance-like af-fability. He seems to be looking *into* me, and furthermore, he seems to like what he sees there. My arms prickle with goose-flesh at the intensity of his gaze, and a thought flits through my brain that my husband is standing right beside me, my *husband*, who is supposed to be the closest person in the world to me, and he is totally oblivious to what's transpiring between Ben and me.

The shrill cry of a referee's whistle tears through the air, abruptly ending the connection, or whatever it was, and all eyes, including Ben's and mine, turn toward the field.

"All right, Polar Bears!" Jonah cheers, clapping his hands enthusiastically.

I glance at Ben, who is now focused on the soccer field. I watch as he places a hand on the small of his wife's back, let-ting it rest there, and I catch the almost imperceptible way she shies away from his touch, then instantly bends over to say something to Evan. It makes me wonder about their rela-tionship, if they are happy, how his hand would feel on the small of my back and just what he might have been thinking a few seconds earlier when he looked at me.

It was nothing, I tell myself. *It must have been an acid flashback.* (Except that, unfortunately, I never did acid.) *I was imagining things.* But a part of me doesn't believe it. True, I have been out of the game for a long, *long* while, and the last time a man whose first language was English showed any interest in me, there were no such things as Facebook, J-Date, or Brangelina. But I do remember what it was like, that spark, that intangible sensation you get when you con-nect with someone. (I can recall it the same way I sometimes recall a particularly decadent dessert and then find myself practically salivating at the memory.) And what happened a moment ago between Ben and me was a connection. I'm certain of it. There's no doubt in my mind. Not even a shadow of a doubt.

Of course, there's always the possibility he was looking at some hot babe standing right behind me. Come to think of it, that actually makes a lot more sense.

Just as the game officially starts, Dave nudges Jonah and holds up his iPhone for Jonah to inspect. At the sight of modern technology, it's as if Jonah has been sucked into the Matrix. The boys might as well be playing soccer on the moon.

"Nice." Jonah's voice is a reverent whisper.

"The resolution is outstanding," Dave says, bobbing his head up and down. He runs his index finger along the screen, then displays it once more. "My new LinkedIn profile picture."

Now it's my turn to roll my eyes, but no one is paying any attention so I don't bother.

"Hey, Ellen, are you on Facebook yet?" Gary asks, punching something into his own phone.

"I'm trying to get her on," Jonah says. "She's stuck in the year 2000."

Not a bad year, I think. It was before the twin towers fell and before my boobs reached my navel when I went braless.

Dave shakes his head in dismay. "You have to join, Ellen. Maddy reconnected with all her high school friends. She even meets up with them once a month."

"Oh, man, you gotta see what Ken Frankel just posted on his wall!" Gary sputters, drawing Jonah's attention away from Dave. Geez. Facebook.

"I'm going back," I say to Jonah. Without even looking in my direction, he gives me an absentminded wave. I take a step away from the dads and am heading toward Jessie when

I see Rita Halpern climbing down onto the asphalt from the second bleacher. I shake my head and purse my lips at her.

"Thanks for pointing out the stain, Rita."

She puts her arm around me and draws me to her. "There's a lot worse things than grass stains, Ellen. Believe me. Now, if you'll excuse me, I gotta go to the can."

Nine

Y ou have two thousand hits!"

It's Jill and she's shrieking into the phone and hyper-ventilating and I have absolutely no idea what she's talking about.

"Just since last night!"

I pull my cell phone away from my ear as Jonah jerks his head in my direction. I answer his questioning look with a shrug.

"There are a lot of comments, too! Wait till you see them! Some of them hate you, but most of them are totally positive. Here's one. It says 'You f-u-c-k-i-n-g rock!'"

"Jill!" I yell over her. "What the hell are you talking about?"

"Mom said *hell*," Jessie says on a giggle.

"Jessie." Jonah's voice is as threatening as the glare he gives me. The back of the minivan is instantly silent.

"*Heck*," I say, then stick my tongue out at Jonah. "What the *heck* are you talking about?"

"Your blog, Ellen! Wait, here's another one. 'Can't wait to read your next post!' This is so cool!"

My blog. Oh s-h-i-t. I haven't thought about it all day, haven't had a chance, really, since all my thought processes were otherwise engaged in dissecting the split-second eye lock with Ben Campbell, which may or may not have been transcendent. I glance at the clock on the dashboard. Four eighteen. I have exactly seven hours and forty-two minutes to come up with a post.

"So, what's next?" Jill asks.

"I have no idea," I admit. "I'll talk to you later."

I disconnect the call and stare straight ahead. If Jonah is curious about the conversation, he keeps it to himself. Jill and I talk four times a day, at least, and if he asked about the subject of our phone calls every time, we would spend the whole of our marriage discussing my cousin. He likes Jill, loves her even, but finds it easier to do so from a distance.

We reach our driveway, and I hear myself making the requisite proclamations about the soccer game. ("You played terrific!" and "Great game!" and "Well done!") In fact, Matthew did have a banner game, which translates to: he did not fall on his face once. He even managed an assist, kicking the ball to Liam, who effortlessly sent it into the goal. I'm pretty sure that I am the only one who knows Matthew was really aiming for Peter Halpern, but I'll never breathe a word.

Jessie is heading over to McKenna's house and Connor is going to hang with his friend Jason, whose parents have recently separated. According to Connor, Jason is caught in the middle and having a rough time with it. For all of Connor's twelve-year-old bravado and false antipathy, he is a compassionate kid with a really good heart. If we can judge our parenting by whether we would want to be friends with our children, Connor would do me proud. (Although the jury is still out on Jessie and Matthew.) Is it possible that the whole "Jason not dealing with his parents' imminent divorce" thing is a cover for the fact that my son and his friend are going to smoke pot for the first time? Sure, it's possible. But until I detect that telltale whiff of weed on his sweatshirt, I am choosing to think positively.

Matthew is stuck at home with the 'rents and Jonah has challenged him to a rousing game of Wii bowling before dinner, most likely to take his mind off the fact that he is stuck at home with the 'rents. I briefly consider calling up Ben to see what Liam is up to and if he'd like to come over and hang out with Matthew for a while. The first problem is that I don't have the Campbells' phone number since they joined the team late and are not listed on the soccer registry. The second problem is that it is a completely boneheaded idea.

By now, after having mulled it over all afternoon, ad nauseam, I am convinced that I was hallucinating at the soccer field. Ben Campbell and I were *not* having a moment. It was all in my mind. And I fear I made a fool of myself, standing there wide-eyed and slack-jawed, gaping at him like a stroke victim because I actually thought he was looking *into* me. Like it was *Some Enchanted Fucking Evening at the Soccer Game*.

So now, if I were to ascertain his phone number by whatever means are at my disposal—like, for example, the phone book or the online white pages, or my cousin Jill (which I would never do), or even a private detective—and then actually call him, he would take one look at the Caller ID, which of course would say *Ivers*, and let the call go straight to voice mail. He would then turn to his wetlands-loving wife and explain that it was *that Ellen woman* from soccer. He would shake his head with dismay. *She comes across as normal at times*, he'd say, *but after the game today, and the way she looked at me, I don't know, I really think there's something wrong with her.* To which stain-fighting aficionado wifey would reply, *You know, I got that feeling, too, honey; let's go have sex!*

"Oh, for God's sake!" I explode at the frozen lasagna on the kitchen counter in front of me. "Get a grip!"

I toss the entrée into the preheated oven and stomp over to my computer; yank out the chair, which scrapes across the tile floor; and sit down with a *harrumph*. Jonah's laughter and cries of protest and Matthew's delighted yelps float into the kitchen from the living room. Apparently, their Wii bowling battle has begun. The lasagna cooks for approximately sixty minutes. Okay, an uninterrupted hour in front of my computer. I take a deep breath and log on to my blog.

The tracking number at the bottom of the screen tells me there have been exactly 2,649 hits on my blog. My heart does a sudden *thump-thwack* in my chest as I consider that almost three *thousand* people have read my blog. Jill was right; most of the comments are positive. I scan them quickly, stopping to read a few. Clairabelle49 writes: *I sure wish I had checked all the ingredients before I got married! Maybe my cheese balls will turn out better!* And GotUpAndWent1 says: *You are SO right! Except cheese balls actually taste GOOD!* And Hihohiho17 comments: *Thought ur blog would be cheesy ;) but u really make a good comparison. Looking forward to ur next post.* ☺

Excitement builds within me, and I feel laughter bubbling up from my stomach. How crazy is this? Yesterday I was a mere housewife hiding from her family on the toilet, and today I am a full-fledged blogger with the hits and comments to prove it. I look down at Sally, who has parked at my feet, and say to her, "How cool am I?" Her reaction is a less than enthusiastic chuff, followed by a snort and a heavy sigh, but I know she is elated on the inside.

My own elation and self-aggrandizing last only about ten seconds, however, before panic sets in. What now? What am I supposed to follow the Cheeseballs with? *Women are Cream Puffs?* Might not win me too many fans from the *Ladies Living-Well Journal*. Some other food/people comparison? Perhaps I should think outside my own box and write about inanimate objects. Like my mother-in-law. Or my hatred of cell phones, or how I secretly play the Wii when the house is empty.

I feel my stomach muscles tighten, and I consider shutting down my computer and logging a couple of miles on the treadmill, just to clear my mind. But I quickly reject that course of action, because I know that if I don't come up with some idea, any idea, I'll be out of the competition. It's not as if I am harboring any delusions about winning, but this blog contest is my "something new," the foundation on which my entire reinvention has come to rest. I have been on a roll, feeling good about myself (except for the whole Ben Campbell/ soccer debacle) and if I don't work something up in the next, oh, six hours and fifty-two minutes, my momentum will come screeching to a halt. My treadmill time will dwindle, my cosmetics will go untouched for so long they'll start to get that funky smell, and I'll be back to eating Pop-Tarts by Monday.

Wait! I desperately try to corral my thoughts before they crash through the barn. *Inhale. Good. Exhale. Better.* I have always been aware that my inner monologue is like an express train in the New York City subway system, but at this moment I am forced to acknowledge that the mental masturbation has gotten completely out of control. Just this afternoon alone I must have jerked off at least a million brain cells. And I cannot afford to lose them, especially when I'm looking at thirteen blog posts in thirteen days.

Okay. I did it yesterday. I can do it again. *Just relax, Ellen, and write. Just put your fingers on the keys, like you did yesterday. Remember how good it felt? Yes. Just like that.*

My fingers are poised above the keyboard and just as I am about to type my first word into the text box, Jonah pokes his head through the doorway.

"Hey," he says.

I do my best to mask my annoyance at the interruption. Jonah has no idea what I'm doing, and I have no intention of telling him. It would open up another one of those marital cans of worms that are better left sealed. He would want to know why I am blogging for the first time, and I would have to explain the whole reinvention thing to him, and he would then pepper me with questions about why I feel the need to reinvent myself and what could possibly be missing from my life that I need to fill with such drivel, and I would have to lie and say "Nothing's missing, Jonah," and he would be somewhat mollified but would still want to read my blog, just to be "supportive," and I would have to let him, and then when he actually got around to reading it, he wouldn't get past the title before all hell would break loose.

"Dinner'll be ready in about an hour," I answer before he can ask.

"Great." He peers at the computer, but fortunately, with his forty-five-year-old eyes, he cannot make out what is on the screen. "Are you finally doing your Facebook profile?"

A synapse fires inside my brain.

"Hello?" he says, since I haven't answered him.

"Yeah. That's it. My Facebook profile. Doing it right now."

"Excellent!" he beams. "Friend me when you finish."

"Can husbands and wives be friends?" I ask innocently. Jonah is about to reply when he realizes I'm kidding.

"Dad!" Matthew calls. "I'm gonna unpause the game!"

"Coming!" he replies, loudly. Then to me, he says, "I was going to let him win to boost his confidence, but I think it's better for his development if I teach him how to accept being completely slaughtered." He winks.

"*OC Parenting* just called. They're giving you a medal for father of the year."

He laughs heartily, a familiar and comforting sound to my ears. He blows me a kiss, then disappears. A moment later, the muted sound of the Wii resumes.

I turn back to the computer and within seconds I am swept away.

. . . .

Second Post: March 17, 2012
SomethingNewAt42

I HATE FACEBOOK

Call me a traitor to my generation, but it's true. I hate Facebook. I know there are others out there like me, they just don't have the guts to admit it. But there is something very liberating about being able to admit it, and not just in the covert confines of a confessional at church. If I didn't think my husband would instantly have me committed to the local psychiatric ward, I would run outside, stand in the middle of the street, and shout at the top of my lungs, I HATE FACEBOOK.

My husband is the one who has been pushing me for months to join. He thinks it will spruce up my dreary social life. (Thanks so much, babe!) My strident refusal pains him, causes him to question our marriage, and even inspired him to buy me a book on how to cope with menopause. But the truth is, I have absolutely no desire to reconnect with any of my high school compatriots. I attempted to do that at my twenty-five-year reunion only to discover that the past should stay in the past where it belongs and that, for the most part, young assholes simply grow up to be old assholes. The friends I have kept from Ralph Springdale High are still my friends because our bonds go way beyond that gray brick institution I couldn't wait to be released from.

And then there's this business about "confirming" and "ignoring" friend requests, which, in my opinion, instantly transports all Facebook members back to high school anyway. It's like a giant online clique. I imagine that one ignored friend request might result in suicidal thoughts by a less than self-assured person. "Why didn't she confirm me?" one might ask. "What's wrong with me?" And out come the sleeping pills. And then there are those friend requests from people you've never heard of before, like Bandookhi Gimlakhi from India. What do you do with Bandookhi? He could be an ax murderer who, unless confirmed, will hunt you down, ascertain the easiest way to gain entrance to your home, and stand over your bed while you sleep, knife in hand, shrieking, "*I will not be ignored!*"

Not to mention the whole "my friend list is bigger than your friend list" thing. That pesky relative of mine, who continues to remain nameless, has 573 friends. 573! She is friends with everyone from her gynecologist to the janitor at her kids' school. I mean, come on! I like my gynecologist. I even like Mr. Jimmy, who refers to himself as the Cleanup Commando. But I do *not* want to know what either of them had for breakfast.

And that's another thing. Who cares what you had for breakfast or that your infant just upchucked all over your new L. L. Bean Parka or that you just had a Brazilian? Maybe, instead of posting about every little occurrence in your life, you should just go out and *get* a life. Really. Turn off the computer. Put your Internet-capable phone in its charger and go outside. Breathe some fresh air. Take a walk. I dare all of you to do this. Then, when you start to get the shakes from being away from your silicon blankie and megabyte breast, you can come back and post on your wall, to the amazement of all of your Facebook friends, that you just did the most extraordinary thing! You freed yourself from the WWW and became a part of the real world, if only for a moment. You can do it! Good luck!

Not three seconds after I finish polishing the post, the oven timer goes off. I am suddenly, acutely, aware of my surroundings: of the savory aroma of lasagna permeating the air, the way the light has dimmed in the kitchen from the onset of dusk, the muted silence that fills the house. I feel as if I have awakened from a glorious fit of creativity and my senses are more alive than they have been for a long time.

I click the Publish button, then stand and stretch and head for the oven. The cheese on the lasagna is golden brown and bubbling as I set the pan on the granite counter. Wandering through the shadowed house, I turn on lights, taking in the warm homey feel of each room as it becomes bathed in light. At the archway between the dining and living rooms, I pause and lean against the doorjamb. Jonah and Matthew are both sprawled on the couch, side by side, heads flung back against the cushions, hands clutching the Wii remotes, fast asleep. I stare at them, memorizing the moment with my mind's camera. I don't need my Nikon. This image will be emblazoned in my brain forever.

I have many such moments like this. And as I watch their chests rising and falling in unison, I realize that when I rummage through the memories of my life with my family, most of the images that rise to the surface are not of the big events or the milestones. The images that come to mind are ones like these. Simple and pure and so wonderfully real that my heart aches with gladness. I love my husband and my children. I love my life. I even love the fact that both Jonah and Matthew are drooling onto my favorite sage green suede couch.

Well, that last part maybe not so much.

Ten

Of course, all that gooey love business can evaporate in an instant. The next few days are a flurry of meltdowns, arguments, tantrums, and overall discontent in the Ivers household. The only good thing to come out of this block of time is that I have plenty of material for my blog. Bridget Jones, that contemporary literary icon, comes to mind every so often; her philosophy is that when your love life is terrific, everything else in your life falls spectacularly apart. And that is true for me. Only, it's not my love life but my reinvention that's on track.

I am up to four miles a day on the treadmill and am conscious of the way my thighs jiggle less than they did three weeks ago. I have reinstated my nightly Lines-Be-Gone regimen. I am eating healthfully, choosing fresh fruit and vegetables over processed snacks and limiting my carb intake, albeit surreptitiously at dinner, where Jonah seems to be itemizing and calculating my caloric intake as though he is preparing for an anorexia intervention. And I am faithfully writing my blog every day like clockwork, allowing myself fifteen minutes to read my comments before delving into the creation of the new post. (Each day, with each new post, I see that my hits are increasing steadily, and although I still haven't sampled my competitors' posts, I am more than pleased with my efforts.)

But over this next week, my familial relationships are as strained as Israel and Palestine, and, like the United States, I feel powerless to do anything about it. Each subsequent day brings forth a new conflict with a different family member, and by the end of the week, I am ready to dip into my top-secret emergency fund and head for the Mexican border. (My emergency fund is not ample enough to afford me a luxury resort, but as long as the shithole motel I land in has Wi-Fi so that I can write my blog, I'll be good.)

I don't feel the need to recount every detail of every moment of every day, so instead, I am chronicling the specific incidents and subsequent blog posts that made up my week. Right now my blog is the only thing that's keeping me sane, so in deference to the *P* that stands for *post*, I'm writing about piqued progeny, pugilistic partners, and petulant pretties.

Sunday, the official first day of the new week, and the day that God apparently took a union-mandated, much-deserved break, was the start of what I will surely label *My Week from Hell* if ever I get around to writing my memoirs.

I am sitting in the living room, channeling my inner goddess by attempting to mend a hole in one of Matthew's favorite T-shirts. If I were my own mother, I could perform this

task one-handed, blindfolded, in my sleep while simultaneously juggling six dinner plates. But I am me. Therefore, I
have only managed to make the hole bigger and punctured
my left index finger in five places.

I am sucking on said finger when Jessie enters, fresh from
her overnight with McKenna, and informs me that she will
no longer tolerate the consumption of animal products in our
home.

"I'm a vegan," she announces with conviction.

I immediately pull my finger out of my mouth, worried
that she will castigate me for drinking animal blood, even
though it's mine.

"Since when are you a vegan?" I ask.

"Since last night. McKenna's a vegan. And her mom and
brother, too. We had Tofurky and this soy berry ice cream
that totally rocked. And not one living creature had to sacrifice its life or offspring in order to satiate my carnivorous
lust."

My first thought is of Ben Campbell and his wife's pen-
chant for tofu. My second thought is that Jessie is never going
to spend the night at McKenna's again. "Satiate my carnivorous lust?" Do people actually talk like that, and in front of
eight-year-olds?

"So from now on, I'm only eating things that didn't have
to die."

She gives me an earnest look that is well beyond her age.
And this is the moment when I fuck up completely as a mom.
I make the supreme mistake of not giving my daughter even
one iota of validation. Instead, I turn her mandate into a joke.

"Well, you're going to be pretty hungry then, Jess," I say.
"You don't eat what I make, you starve."

Her eyes glisten with unshed tears and she glares at me as
if I, alone, am responsible for shoving grain down the throats

of gaggles of innocent geese to fatten their livers for my personal consumption.

"Fine, then. I'll starve."

....

Third Post: March 18, 2012
SomethingNewAt42

I EAT MEAT

So sue me. Every kind of meat known to the supermarket refrigerated section. (I stop short at *Fear Factor* fare because I have never seen horse intestine featured on a menu at a five-star restaurant.) But I love it. I love masticating on a nice hunk of bloody beef. It confirms my place in the food chain: at the top.

I have never ascribed to the belief that we are what we eat. If that were true I would be known as Prime Rib au Jus with Horseradish Sauce. But what is wrong with enjoying my superiority over the rest of the animal kingdom? We human beings may not be long for this planet, but while we are here, we should definitely exercise our rights. And one of those rights is that we get to eat whatever we goddamned please.

My child, whose name and sex will remain a mystery to you to protect the innocent, told me today that he/she has become a vegan. First of all, what kind of stupid name is that? It sounds like a creature from another planet. Now, someday, our species may have to relocate to another terra firma, and in that case the title *vegan* gets my vote, because I can't imagine there will be too many cattle ranches inhabiting Mars. But here? As long as there's grass for grazing, there will be beef and milk in my fridge. As long as there's corn and grain sprinkled over the dusty pens of the rural farmlands, there will be boneless chicken breasts and dozens of eggs in my fridge. And my child may starve, but he/ she will only be served dishes from a menu that the highest form of intelligence on earth deserves. Meat.

Don't get me wrong. I am not against tofu. Tofu has its place in my world, right there next to enemas and oil changes. Not necessary all the time, but occasionally the need arises. I especially like my tofu deep-fried with a rich and fattening sauce poured over it to mask its lack of flavor. But it should not be consumed regularly. "Experts" wax on about how red meat is bad for your cholesterol, your colon, your heart. But don't be fooled about the miraculous benefits of tofu. No matter what a vegan may tell you, tofu is dangerous. Too much soy can cause five-year-old girls to menstruate and little boys' balls to creep back up into their groins. Does that sound healthy to you? That nameless relative of mine once made a tofu cheesecake for a dinner party, and although I have to admit it tasted fine, the next morning I woke up to find that I had three new coarse black whiskers on my chin.

I'll take the filet mignon cheesecake anytime.

....

Monday hits me with hurricane force. I am a great believer in three-day weekends because frankly, two days is not enough. I know that sounds funny coming from someone who doesn't have a job. But when it comes to raising kids, Saturdays and Sundays are those blissful days when you don't have to get up at five just to make sure your children are clean and fed and combed and brushed and appropriately clothed and have all their belongings, including homework and class projects and items for show-and-tell (which for some reason is now called "share"). Not that I ever truly sleep in on the weekends, but I am able to lie in bed until seven with impunity, knowing that if my children want breakfast before I grace the kitchen with my presence, they can get it themselves. Since it takes a good forty-eight hours to get into a groove doing anything, I think an extra weekend day would be nice, just to be able to fully relax into laziness. But no, Monday comes all too soon and jerks us back to reality.

It is on this Monday morning that Matthew suffers one of the worst meltdowns I have witnessed to date. And it is all because I was not able to mend his favorite shirt and, through a colossal lapse in judgment, deposited it into the trash barrel, which was collected by the smoke-spewing, ear-shattering sanitation truck only moments ago. It is safe to say that as I watch Matthew scream and pace, his scrawny bare chest heaving, clawing at the alternate shirt I provided until I fear he might rip it to shreds, his face a scarlet mask of fury, I consider that a trip to a family therapist might be in order. Or a session with Dr. Phil, which might not do Matthew any good, but would elevate me to TV personality. Maybe I could just casually mention my blog on the air.

"How could you throw it *away*?" he bellows, snot streaming from his nostrils like that girl from *The Blair Witch Project*. "That shirt was . . . was . . . was . . ."

I am afraid he is going to say *my best friend*. I have the urge to put my arms around him and hold him close to me, because whatever the deep-seated reason for this outburst, Matthew is truly feeling pain, and my instincts as a mother far overshadow my incredulity that the loss of a fucking T-shirt can inspire such a cataclysm. However, his rage is currently directed at me and I am aware that he would welcome a hug from me about as much as he might open his arms to a runaway chain saw.

". . . my favorite!" he cries.

The shirt in question was a hand-me-down from my sister's son Luke, now eleven, who Matthew believes saved his life at the beach last summer when the family came for a visit. Luke was learning to boogie-board, and Matthew was showing off his mediocre skills when his foot got looped around the leash of his own board. Luke, sensing my son's distress, leaped into the foaming surf and hauled Matthew out of harm's way before a two-foot wave crashed with ho-hum force against the sand. The fact that Matthew had been in water only ten inches deep escaped his notice, and for the rest of the trip, he followed Luke around like a puppy, waiting on him hand and foot until even Luke grew tired of the attention. But my nephew was gracious enough, on his departure, to award Matthew with a long-sleeved, navy blue, limited-edition cotton shirt with the legend *Surf or Die* emblazoned across the front, which he had finally outgrown due to a sudden preteen growth spurt.

Matthew has worn that shirt twice a week ever since, regardless of its state of cleanliness or lack thereof. When the small hole finally appeared in the armpit, he had to relinquish it to me for healing and safekeeping. And now he is looking at me like I am a traitor, a heretic, an *evildoer* in the worst George W. sense of the word. He is looking at me as though I'd stuffed his cousin Luke into the garbage bin.

"This is the worst thing that's ever happened to me," he proclaims tearfully.

"Jeez," says Connor, taking his seat at the kitchen table and tucking into the nutritious meal of eggs, toast, and melon that I have prepared for him. "Take a chill pill, why don't you."

Matthew wheels around and glares at Connor. "Shut up, Connor!" he snaps.

"Hey!" I yell. "Watch your mouth, Matthew!"

"Or what?" he shoots back. "You'll throw away my favorite sweatshirt and my favorite pants and my sneaks, too?"

I feel a headache coming on.

"Sit down and eat your breakfast, Matthew," I say through clenched teeth

"I will NOT!" he screams. "I want my shirt. I want my *Surf or Die* shirt! I am not going to school without it!"

Just then, Jessie ambles into the kitchen and sits at her place next to Connor. She takes one look at the dish of scrambled eggs and shrieks.

"I *told you* I am a vegan!"

Did I say headache? No. I feel an aneurysm coming on.

Connor grins and holds his hand up in front of his face, his fingers splayed apart down the middle. "Live long and proper, dude," he says.

"It's *prosper, prosper, prosper*!" Matthew corrects him urgently. "Live long and *prosper*, you idiot!"

"Matthew!"

"Whatever," Connor replies.

"It's *vegan*, not Vulcan," Jessie explains.

"Whatever," Connor repeats, taking this crazy morning in stride.

"Matthew," I say again, injecting an icy calm into my voice, "I don't give a crap if you go to school shirtless, but you will sit down and eat your breakfast right now or suffer the consequences."

"He has to wear a shirt, Mom," Connor says around a bite of eggs. "No shirt, no shoes, no education." He winks at me and I thank God at that instant that I have *one* halfway normal child with a good sense of humor.

Matthew has not moved an inch. He fixes me with a laser-like glare reminiscent of that Damien freak in the *Omen* movies. You know, the glare the kid shoots at the unlucky bastard who is about to get decapitated by a renegade sheet of window glass? That's the one.

"I will never forgive you for this," he says in a low guttural voice that I don't recognize.

"I have apologized, Matthew. If you want, I will apologize again. But your shirt is gone, and there's nothing I can do about it." Except haul my ass to the dump and forage through a metric ton of shit to try to find it.

"I hate you!" are his final words as he races out of the kitchen and up the stairs. I hear the door of his room slam shut. Then I watch as my daughter picks up her eggs, stands, saunters over to the sink, opens the cupboard underneath, and chucks the eggs into the trash can, plate and all.

It's definitely time for a faux bowel movement.

....

Fourth Post: March 19, 2012
SomethingNewAt42

RITALIN FOR DUMMIES

Have you ever looked at your kids and wondered, "Where the fuck did you come from?" I apologize for my language, but seriously. You grow these beautiful creatures in your belly, you nurture them and nurse them on your breast, you help them take their first steps, and you're filled with pride by every little accomplishment they make. And then one day you look at them and realize that the amazing little beings you've created have been body-snatched by a tribe of total shitheads.

I have heard the debate about medicating kids, that parents are too quick to introduce Ritalin to their children's brains. But, I ask you, is it such a sin to want even-keeled, socially hospitable, well-mannered offspring? And the truth is, sometimes, for a parent, more specifically, a mom, it's a "lesser of two evils" choice. Like, if I don't medicate Junior, I'll have to make a reservation on the Xanax express myself. And what's the harm in insuring that Junior's first-grade teacher, Mrs. Finklebaum, doesn't get so overwrought by the bipolar behavior of her students that she shows up for class one morning packing a bazooka? Wouldn't that be worse than a wee bit of juvenile pharmaceutical assistance?

My nameless relative is so passionate on the subject of kiddie Prozac that I have told her she ought to run for Congress and use that as her platform. She finds it reprehensible that any parent would voluntarily monkey with her child's synapses or neurons or gray matter, or whatever. She thinks that it's the parents' responsibility to relate to and communicate with their children more effectively and that we wouldn't need any f-u-c-k-i-n-g drugs if there were better parents in this world instead of lazy, disinterested, jack-a-s-s-e-s too wrapped up in themselves to invest the time and energy it takes to raise happy, well-adjusted, confident members of society. Of course, she has the advantage of having three perfect children who are smart, excel at everything, and have self-confidence up the ying-yang.

I myself used to be on the fence about this most heated subject. That was until one of my children turned into a vegan (see post #3) and another one of my children turned into a shirtless spawn of Satan. Yes, folks, after the past two mornings, I have come to think that crushing up an antidepressant and sprinkling it over my kids' Cheerios like sugar might be just the thing.

And if you will excuse me now, it is way past medication time for me!

By Tuesday, two of my children are not speaking to me: Matthew, because I have not made his *Surf or Die* shirt magically reappear, and Jessie because I had the temerity to serve hamburgers for dinner the night before.

"You sort of had it coming," Jill tells me, sipping at her coffee and avoiding my eyes. She has applied a soft, subtle pink shade to her lips, which are uncharacteristically pursed, thereby giving her pretty face a decidedly perturbed vibe.

"Excuse me?" My mug stops halfway to my own lips and I gape at her, stupefied. "How on earth did I 'have it coming'?" I smack my mug on the counter, my coffee as yet undrunk. Droplets splash over the rim of the mug and land on Jill's pristine counter. She quickly grabs a towel from the oven handle, snapping it angrily for effect, and urgently wipes the drops away as if the coffee is molecular acid about to eat through her turquoise-and-gold-flecked charcoal granite. I watch her silently for a moment, then shake my head. "I can't believe you're on their side."

"I'm not on anyone's side," she retorts, tossing the towel into the well-hidden plastic receptacle for kitchen laundry under the sink.

"Bullshit. You're supposed to be on *my* side. Automatically."

"Look, if Jessie wants to be a vegan—"

"She's *eight*!" I hear my voice rise.

"Girls grow up fast these days," Jill says evenly, regaining her practiced composure as an antithesis to my growing ire.

"Since when did you become the authority on girls, Jill? You have three sons!"

"And Matthew, poor guy. Did you ever think maybe he didn't care about a silly little hole in his shirt?"

"This coming from the woman who throws away clothes if they have a thread unraveling from the hem." It's true. The three *D*s never leave the house looking anything less than photo-shoot ready.

"I think you're being selfish, Ellen. They're kids, not robots. You cannot bend them to your will."

This platitude from my cousin stops me cold. I can't remember anyone in my life ever having called me selfish, and it certainly doesn't evoke a pleasant feeling now. My cheeks burn as I sift through the events of the past two days for instances where I was selfish. I can point to several bouts of foolishness, the odd insensitivity, and maybe a couple of moments of outright irrationality. But I honestly don't see how I have been selfish. And I do not want to bend my children to my will. Okay, maybe a little, but what parent doesn't want that? Still, not once have I expected them to be anything other than who they are.

"I do not want to bend them to my will," I say, trying not to sound defensive. "I just want my daughter to eat a hot dog once in a while and my son not to have a nervous breakdown over a T-shirt. If that's selfish, then guilty as charged."

Jill says nothing. She still does not meet my eyes. After years of familial friendship with this woman, I can read her pretty well. "What's wrong?" I ask.

She shrugs, sighs, then shrugs again for good measure.

"C'mon, Jill," I press. "Spill it."

She is silent for a good thirty seconds. "Your blog's doing pretty well, huh?"

Twelve thousand hits as of this morning. I have not yet written today's post, having decided to put it off until after I'd received a little tea and sympathy from my cousin, which turned out to be coffee and lambasting.

"It's doing great, yeah. So? What's up with *you*? Why are you mad at me?"

"I'm not," she replies, but the way she says it, she might as well have said, *Die, bitch.* Well, she would have spelled it out, of course.

"Out of the blue you're defending my kids and calling me selfish. What gives?"

Another thirty seconds. Finally, she gives.

"My kids are not *perfect*, you know."

Oh, shit.

"They have problems, too. And I am not some whack job who pickets the school with anti-Ritalin signs and makes tofu cheesecake. Your 'nameless relative.' You make me sound like a total d-a-m-n weirdo."

I try to decide how best to handle this situation. My track record with my loved ones over the past few days is nothing to write home about, unless "home" is Dear Abby. Jill is my cousin and my best friend and I love her with all my heart, but she can be way too sensitive and she often makes too much out of things that others might find inconsequential. To illustrate this in more detail, I would like to point out that several years ago, between her birthday and Christmas, Jill received four copies of *Don't Sweat the Small Stuff* from various friends and relatives. (All four books are on the bookshelf in her guest room, collecting dust, and, as yet, unread.)

Still, I admit I have not stepped back and considered how my irreverent, and sometimes less than flattering, words might affect her. Each time I sit down to post, I find myself settling into a fugue state, and I can hardly remember the actual writing of my blog. It's not unlike being high. The fact that each post has struck me as amusing is a stroke of good fortune, the fates smiling on me, because it's almost as though someone else is at the computer. And my "nameless relative" has become a *shtick*, a tool, an endearing gimmick that creates continuity with each post. But apparently, the nameless relative is none too happy about it.

I rub my face with my hands and take a deep breath.

"I'm sorry, Jill," I say, because I am, and also because I know she wants to hear it. An apology cements her importance in the world, and I'm all for bolstering one's self-esteem. (I know for a fact her husband has never apologized in the entirety of their marriage.) "It's just a blog," I continue through her silence. "You know? The one you pushed me to write?" I give her a pointed look, willing her green eyes to meet mine. "It's supposed to be interesting, informative, and funny."

One side of her mouth curls up as she finally looks at me. "Well, one out of three isn't bad."

"Exactly!" I agree enthusiastically. "My humor is all I have going for me. You know how much I love you *and* your kids. And I would never want to hurt you intentionally."

"I know," she says, cracking her first smile of the morning. "I'm overreacting, aren't I?"

For a split second, I flash back to the gawky teenager that Jill once was: too skinny, a mouthful of braces, and freckles in the era before they were considered fetching. The boy I liked had called me lard-ass, which was something he'd probably overheard his father call his mother, because, forgive me, but Mrs. Heddy Champlain's rear end was the size of a dirigible. Jill had immediately come to my defense, telling Sonny Champlain that he better get some glasses, because my derriere was perfect, thank you very much, and then she proceeded to sock him in the stomach.

"You're not overreacting," I say. *Not much, anyway.* "And if you want me to leave you out of the rest of them, I will."

She ruminates for a moment, tapping her nails against the

counter in a staccato rhythm. "It *is* anonymous, right? No one knows it's me."

"And no one will," I assure her.

"Until you win. Then everyone will know it's me, but it'll be great because I'll be the 'nameless relative' of a star."

···

Fifth Post: March 20, 2012
SomethingNewAt42

A MOMENT'S REPRIEVE

Dear blog reader, you may have come to expect from me a certain irreverence and a modicum of sarcasm, but I would like to take a moment to ditch the sarcasm, stretch my sincerity muscles, and discuss friendship.

Friendship is a privilege, not a God-given right. It is a precious flower to be nurtured, not an avocado that can be abandoned in the produce drawer of the fridge, forgotten until its already wrinkled skin has fossilized and its flesh has turned grayish brown. It is a blessed gift meant to be placed on an altar and worshipped, not shoved in the closet on a dusty shelf next to those old cassette tapes that you just can't seem to part with even though you no longer own a cassette player.

That "nameless relative" of whom I have spoken in my past four posts is actually more than a relative. She is a friend. She is the kind of friend any of you would be thankful to have, one who sticks up for you even when you are behaving like a horse's ass. The kind of friend who tells you you look great in Lycra even when you both know you should have given it up twenty years ago. The kind of friend who hates your husband when you do and loves him when he treats you right and is deeply offended when anyone makes any untoward comments about your commitment to the PTA even though you know that she knows that you missed the last charity fundraiser because your TiVo was broken and you just couldn't miss the *Lost* series finale.

My nameless relative would walk through fire for me. And she'd do it in four-inch heels and look fabulous. So whatever comments I make about her, or stories I tell about her for the sake of humor, I want you to know that she is just about the best thing since Motrin, and like Motrin, I couldn't live without her.

Eleven

Whoever coined the phrase *Wednesday is hump day* should be shot. I say this because not a Wednesday passes that my husband misses the opportunity to repeat this pithy phrase and wink at me like a Monty Python character, nudge-nudge included. For the past thirteen years, every Wednesday—that would be six hundred seventy-two times—I have endured this same joke with a smile and an obligatory chuckle. So now, on the six hundred seventy-third time, all I can manage to do is raise my eyebrows and groan. And this is the beginning of my uber-fight with Jonah. (Why I didn't just let out a guffaw and get on with it, I still don't know.)

"What's with you?" he asks, pouring out the last of the coffee into his mug.

I have been struggling with today's post since I returned from dropping the kids at school forty-five minutes ago. I had expected Jonah to be gone by the time I got back, but he has decided to work from home for the better part of the morning.

"Nothing's *with* me," I say as the blinking cursor mocks me. "I've just heard that one before." In my mind, I think I am being gentle, but the look on Jonah's face tells me I might as well have zapped him with a verbal taser.

"Got it." Coffee in hand, he stalks from the kitchen.

"Jonah," I call after him, but get no response. I throw my head back and push away from the computer. Sally jumps to her feet expectantly, and her eyes implore me. *Cookie? Cookie?* they say.

"Sorry, girl," I tell her. "Gotta deal with Daddy first."

I head for Jonah's office just off the living room and glance at the mantel over the fireplace, which houses a panoply of family photographs. The images of my children in various stages of their young lives beckon me, as they so often do, but I resist the urge to go to them. I have another matter to address. My husband.

"Jonah," I say, entering the twelve-by-ten-foot space that he has claimed as his own. The kids have nicknamed this room "Dad's Domain" because every single one of his belongings, other than his wardrobe, is crammed into this office. A built-in shelving unit of blond faux wood makes up the far wall. One shelf holds trophies dating back to high school (apparently he kicked ass in shot put), another is filled with his business self-help books that have titles like *You DO Deserve to Be a Millionaire* and *Chitchat for Winners: Small Talk That Makes Friends and Customers out of Anyone!* A third has presents from the kids that Jonah won't throw away because he fears karma (even though *fearing karma* sounds a tad un-Zen). He honestly believes that if he dared to throw away the papier-mâché goat Matthew made when he was five, or Jessie's clay ashtray, which resembles dog poop that was stepped in and then glazed and fired, or the Daddy Voodoo doll that Connor made before he dropped out of Scouts (which I consider one of the creepier projects they were assigned), some terrible tragedy will befall the bearer of the gift. This is a superstition akin to walking under ladders, which Jonah never does.

A few years ago, Matthew's second-grade class made pumpkin turkeys. The kids glued feathers and eyes and a yarn waddle to these apple-sized mini pumpkins and called them decorative. Matthew proudly bestowed his to Jonah, who hemmed and hawed and pretended he didn't notice that the eyes were two different sizes and not in line, that the feathers shot out the back of the pumpkin like projectile diarrhea, and that the wattle was on top of the turkey's head instead of under it. He placed the turkey pumpkin in the prized real estate that was the center of the kids' tchotchke shelf. It sat there for four and a half weeks before it started to rot. Jonah didn't even notice the smell for another week, and even then he didn't equate the stench with one of his children's arts and crafts treasures.

I finally walked in one day to a putrid assault on my nostrils, and, after locating the offending item, which had begun to ooze, quickly and efficiently deposited it into the trash. Jonah was so overwrought that he slept by Matthew's bed for a week and virtually shadowed my son for the whole winter break, convinced that Matthew was about to be impaled by a renegade patio chair or flattened by a meteor. And I won't even mention the tirade he gave me about my lack of appreciation for our children's artistic efforts (which was a load of hooey), and my lack of respect for his space, and my lack of sensitivity to his needs as a parent. In response, I told him he was lacking a few things as well: a sense of smell and his marbles.

Jonah's computer takes center stage on his desk, surrounded by stacks of office-supply catalogs, company brochures, business magazines, and invoices.

At this moment, he is searching through one of the stacks, his face a mask of consternation. He doesn't find what he is looking for and sidesteps over to the rowing machine, where another pile of debris adorns the seat. The pile and a thick layer of dust belie the fact that Jonah has not exercised in a while.

"Jonah," I say again, ignoring that fact that he is ignoring me. "I didn't mean to upset you."

His back is to me now as he crouches next to the machine and fingers through his magazines.

"I'm not upset," he replies in a monotone.

"You're right. It *is* Wednesday. *Hump* day." I have reached a new low today, I realize. Do I honestly believe that regurgitating this stupid joke is going to turn things around with Jonah?

"It's a stupid joke," he says as if reading my mind. "But don't worry. I got the hint."

"Jonah, I love that joke," I lie. Wow, two new lows in the space of thirteen seconds.

"Right," he scoffs. "Just forget it, okay?"

"Look, why are you so upset? I'm sorry. I was trying to concentrate and you kind of interrupted my train of thought."

He pulls a magazine from the bottom of the pile and stands, then turns and smacks it on the desk. "Well, excuse the hell out of me. I sure didn't mean to *interrupt* your train of *thought*." He spits out this last phrase as if it is unimaginable that I actually *do* have a train of thought. "What are you doing on the computer anyway? You're always in front of that damn thing lately, and I know for a fact you haven't joined Facebook. I tried to friend you and it turned out the Ellen Ivers I requested is ninety-two and lives in a nursing home on Long Island."

"I'm writing."

"Writing?" Confusion overtakes his features. "Writing what?"

"Just writing, Jonah. You know, that thing I used to do before we got married and had kids?"

"Why?"

Why? *Why?* The problem with this question is that it brings back some ugly stuff for me, like my resentment toward Jonah for never having taken my writing career seriously. I earned a modest living as a writer, but because I was willing to give it up so readily when we started a family, he assumed either I wasn't any good or I didn't have the motivation to seriously pursue it. Frankly, Jonah wouldn't know whether I was any good because not once has he ever read, nor shown any interest in reading, something I've written. For a long while it irked me, and I would bring it up when I wanted to take an argument to the next level of nasty. But as time went by, and life got crazy, and I saw how hard he was working to support his family, I let it go and gave him a pass on the issue. Until now.

"I'm a writer, that's why." I cross my arms in front of my chest. (Dr. Phil would be disappointed, but fuck him.)

"Writer? Ha! You haven't written anything in fourteen years," he retorts.

"Twelve," I correct him, aware that my pulse is throbbing in my neck. This always happens when I get angry, and right now I am so enraged I finally understand that TV show *Snapped!* In fact, I am contemplating a course of action that will definitely get me my own episode.

"So what is it?" he asks, his voice dripping with condescension. "Your memoirs? A self-help book? Another novel? Don't you remember what happened last time?"

I feel my eyes practically bug out of my head. Jonah's dismissing my writing as frivolous is normal, par for the course. He is not an artistic person. In fact, it is possible that he has no right brain inside his skull at all, though I have never forced an MRI on him to prove my suspicions. He just doesn't understand the whole creative process. But he has never been so hostile about my creative pursuits, or about any other subject, for that matter. I wonder if perhaps I am witnessing a midlife crisis in the offing and he is choosing to explode all over me and my writing because I just happen to be here. Somehow, this possibility doesn't make me feel better.

"Seven chapters, wasn't it?" he continues, riding the wave of derision. "Seven chapters and then, poof! Stowed away in a filing cabinet, never to be worked on again."

"You are being a complete asshole," I seethe, but he isn't even paying attention to me.

"I know, I know, honey, you gave it up for me. But you needed a lot more than seven chapters to be the next Janet Evankovich."

"It's *Evanovich!* And it was *eight* chapters, thank you very much, and if you remember, I stopped working on it because I had a fucking baby!" My voice rises in volume with each word until I am shouting at Jonah across the four feet of space that separate us. Those four feet might as well be a chasm. "And then another baby, and then, because you wouldn't get a fucking vasectomy, another!" I hate myself for throwing out this last bit of venom because I cannot imagine my life without Jessie in it. But after Matthew was born, I was so overwhelmed with the two boys that I was ready to hang up the *No Vacancy* sign and be done with procreating. I asked Jonah on numerous occasions to at least make a consultation with a doctor, but the idea of having a needle in the proximity of his ball sack caused him to practically weep with terror. (He wouldn't last one minute on *Fear Factor.*) I had chosen not to go on the pill because I was still nursing and was afraid birth control hormones would affect my milk or pass through to the baby. I refused to get an IUD, as I had tried it right after we got married and bled like a spigot for six weeks straight until I had the damn thing removed. Jonah promised me that he would not get me pregnant, joked that he was probably out of sperm anyway and that condoms had never failed us before. Famous last freaking words.

"What are you saying? That you wish we didn't have Jessie? You're unbelievable!"

"I didn't say that!"

"Or that it's *her* fault you never got back to your *illustrious* career?"

I start taking huge gulps of air to keep the top of my head from blowing apart. This man in front of me is someone I don't recognize, a stranger. And the suddenness with which he has appeared is alarming. Jonah and I fight, like most married couples, but we usually manage to keep our arguments civil and the outright nastiness to a minimum. He is purposely attacking, belittling, and provoking me, and these are things he rarely does. This is a fight I was not planning on having and will not be able to win. He won't win either, and I think this is just occurring to him.

"I'm sorry," he says suddenly. "You're right. I'm being a jerk."

"I said *asshole*." My voice is stony.

He nods. His mouth is still set in a grim line. "Okay. I'm being an asshole."

"Okay."

Now *this* is typical Jonah, calling a ceasefire before things can get irrevocably out of hand. I am relieved that my husband has returned to his body, but also annoyed that I didn't get a few more zingers in. Plus, I am totally furious at him for the things he said.

"I'm just a little stressed out with work," he tries to explain. "But I have no right to take it out on you. I'm glad you're writing again, I think it's good for you."

I call bullshit. "Mmm-hmm."

He perches his butt on the front of the desk and sighs. "So. What *are* you writing?"

None of your goddamned business, I think. "Nothing important," I say. Then I turn and walk from the room.

. . . .

Sixth Post: March 21, 2012
SomethingNewAt42

WHO INVENTED MARRIAGE?

I think it is safe to say that I would enjoy marriage a lot more if it didn't come with a husband. Or if the obligatory husband lived on another continent. Anyone who blathers and moans and complains about how hard long-distance relationships are is definitely not married and clearly doesn't know how friggin' lucky she is. Marriage is not for the weak. Being married is like being thrown into the Colosseum in ancient Rome. You better hope you're a lion, because if not, more than likely, you're going to get ripped apart.

I have heard women say how wonderful marriage can be if you're with the "right one," and I have listened to many a blushing bride-to-be extol the virtues of matrimony before she has even walked down the aisle, and I have watched with eye-rolling skepticism single friends confessing that all they want is to feel the dreamy, starry-eyed bliss that comes with linking your soul to another's for all of eternity. Oh, please! Get over it.

The problem is that the idea of marriage is so much better than the actuality of marriage. It's like when your child learns to read. The idea of it is amazing, and you are inordinately proud of him (or her) for finally embarking upon this wondrous journey, but you also want to rip your hair out in frustration and boredom because it takes your kid twenty minutes to read the sentence *I do not like it, Sam-I-am.*

And there's also the problem of disillusionment. Because in the beginning, it's all about the idea. The happily-ever-after that is promised to all young girls. You'll notice that all fairy tales end with the wedding or the kiss or the wondrous reunion of the star-crossed lovers. They never show the prince and the princess two years later when Cinderella is having postpartum depression and raging around the castle screaming "What happened to my waist?" and "I'm a freaking milk cow!" and Prince Charming has taken to hitting the singles scene, feeling up every courtier with a decent set of nonlactating breasts. The happily-ever-after ends and the real work of marriage begins and then the rose-colored glasses come off and everything starts to look a little gray.

I often wonder whose idea marriage was. I find it hard to believe that a loving God would create an institution that potentially breeds hatred, mistrust, and insanity. He's a Good Guy, right? Not a Malicious Prankster. I like to think that marriage was invented by a couple of monks sitting up late one night drinking a little too much mead, bitching about the accommodations at the monastery: their six-by-six cell-like rooms, the itchy wool blankets that cause a rash, the growing bald spots on the backs of their heads, and the fact that they aren't ever going to get laid. So they try to figure out the best way to make the rest of the population of the world as miserable as they are. "What if," they say, "we deem that a man and a woman shall have to cleave themselves unto each other, cohabitate, share their meager gain, and only layeth with each other for all of their days?" At this point the monks laugh mischievously. "They shall killeth each other," says one. "Hallelujah!" cries the other. "Let's do it!"

If I sound jaded, you're damn right I am. I have been married for eternity—uh, make that thirteen years. And while I love my husband, and on good days I am convinced that he is the one I'm supposed to be with, and that we are a team, a unified front in this game of life, blah, blah, blah, I sometimes think that human beings should take a lesson from those little grunion fish. My nameless relative loves grunions, by the way. Gets her kids up at three A.M. when those scaly bastards are running and trudges down to the beach to watch their antics. They all flop up onto the beach, the females burrow into the sand and deposit some eggs, the males come in and spray a little sperm over the eggs, and then they all go on their merry way. I know it sounds a little bit like the disco era of the 1970s, but it might be worth a try. You don't see grunion bashing their spouses' heads in with a frying pan or stirring arsenic into their spouses' gin and tonics, now do you?

Oh, gotta go. My husband's home and in need of a cocktail . . .

Twelve

Thursday dawns with the promise of being the best day of my week. I have managed to smooth things over with my two younger children, who I'm sure were just polishing up their letters to the producers of *Wife Swap*. As for Matthew, I was able to find a *Surf or Die* T-shirt on eBay, and although I had to endure a bidding war with someone whose username is shaka14, I won it for $39.95 plus shipping. (Crummy old "softly used" T-shirt: $39.95. Bribing your children for their forgiveness: priceless.)

I catch Matthew as he is rummaging through his dresser drawers for something suitable to wear, showering the room with the cast-offs, which are numerous. I let him know that a new (used) *Surf or Die* shirt is on its way via UPS Ground and will be here in three to five business days. I could have waited until it came and then led him to believe that I did, in fact, forage through smelly and slimy debris at the dump, but

I continually try to convince myself that honesty is the best policy, even if that in itself is a bald-faced lie.

After my heartfelt sermon on how, no, this is not the same shirt, it is exactly *like* the T-shirt his cousin gave him and he can easily transfer all of his warm fuzzy feelings for Luke onto the new T-shirt that, "for your information is a size larger and therefore will fit you for a lot longer than the original would," Matthew seems unimpressed. Until I let slip accidentally on purpose exactly how much I spent on it. At the mention of $39.95 plus shipping, his eyes go wide, as he has never seen that much money in one place at one time, and he proceeds to throw his arms around me and start to cry.

"I didn't mean it when I said I hated you," he reveals. I pat his head and tell him that I knew it all along. Score one for Mom.

At breakfast, I make a point of being totally supportive of my daughter's wacko decision to eradicate animals from her diet. I carefully set a platter of fresh fruit at her place, coupled with a whole-grain cereal and a pitcher of rice milk that I bought at Trader Joe's the day before. When she enters the kitchen her eyes are cast downward and she says not a word. She heads for her seat, frowning, most likely expecting to see sausage or Canadian bacon or a suckling pig on her plate. It takes her a moment to process what is in front of her and I watch as her frown literally turns upside down. She looks up at me, her eyes glistening.

"Thanks, Mommy!"

I merely smile and say, "You're welcome." I do not want to make too much of this, but I'm pretty sure that Jessie stopped calling me Mommy when she was four. My heart is like the Grinch's; I can feel it swelling inside my chest.

I ride this high through the day. It energizes me on the

treadmill, keeps my mood simpatico at Target when a woman whose basket is even more loaded than mine cuts in front of me at checkout, propels me through a painfully boring PTA meeting in which I actually volunteer to co-chair the End of the Year Festival. (What the hell was I thinking?)

By the time the after-school merry-go-round of activities begins, I am still in a good mood, no doubt because of the boost I got when both Jessie and Matthew gave me impromptu hugs right there on the school grounds in front of countless peers, teachers, and moms whose tight smiles betrayed their envy. According to the Ivers rotation, today I am Jessie's spectator at ballet. I drop Connor at baseball, then head for the soccer field where I leave Matthew to Rita Halpern's care. (I can't help but glance around for Ben and Liam, but they have not arrived yet.) Jessie and I are thirty seconds ahead of schedule as we arrive at the Garden Hills Conservatoire du Ballet de Paris é Moscow de Vandermeer. (I swear that is the name.)

Madame Valenchenko stands at the door to the studio like an officer of the gulag, her unibrow furrowed and her deeply set, heavily lidded eyes sizing up each girl who walks through the door. The Madame is four foot ten, is as stout as a barrel, and uses a cane, but if you put her in the ring with Mike Tyson, my money would have to be on the ballet coach. Her stern look alone has reduced grown men to tears.

"I am glat zat you are on time today!" she barks as we push through the glass door. I jerk in surprise, as I always do, at the sound of her voice. She sounds like she has spent the last forty years chain-smoking while chewing on glass. "Qvickly, Jess, to ze barre, to ze barre! Now!" She smacks her cane against the concrete for emphasis and I practically shove Jessie into the studio.

I spend the next forty minutes splitting my focus between

my daughter, in her pink leotard and tights and her shoulder-length hair shellacked to her head because her dictator of an instructor won't allow any student into class with flyaways, and my notepad, where I am making a list of all of the tasks I need to accomplish during spring break, when I will have six days of blissful alone time. Jonah is taking the kids to his parents' house in Arizona so they can bond with their crazy Grandma and Grandpa Ivers.

As Jessie does her barre exercises, I think about the yearly crusade to my in-laws that I used to make with my family, how I endured the six-hour drive of "Are we there yet?" and "I have to pee!" and "I think I'm going to puke" and "Why can't we stop and watch them castrate a bull?" We didn't have the portable DVD player then, the one that straps to the back of the front seat and puts any and every juvenile passenger in the rear of the car into an LCD trance. We had Travel Bingo and Travel Checkers and Travel Backgammon that caused me to vacuum up magnetic playing pieces for months afterward. We had freeway games like the Alphabet Game where you end up stuck on the letters Q and X because license plates weren't allowed. We had songs, like "Row, Row, Row Your Boat" and "Ninety-Nine Bottles of Beer on the Wall" and "Take Me Out to the Ballgame" that were sung so many times I wanted to go into a coma just to escape.

When at last we arrived at Bill and Margaret Ivers's home in the middle of a gigantic wasteland of clay, scrub, and cactus, we'd be ushered into the parlor where the lambasting from my father-in-law would begin.

"What a skinny little string bean you are, Matt-Matt. Doesn't your mom feed you?"

"Hell, Jessie-Bessie, why'd you cut off your hair, you look like a boy!"

"Connor-my-man, you'll never get yourself a girlfriend

if you wear holey pants. Can't your mom sew on some patches?" (We already know that I could not.)

"Helen," he would always call me, though I am certain he knows my name and just does it to piss me off. "I see the old bottom is getting a little wider, huh? Too many bonbons during *General Hospital*?"

With every jibe Bill made, my mother-in-law would merely giggle and say, "William! You're terrible!"

Now, as I watch Jessie do pirouettes across the floor, I am struck by how much she has improved over the last year. She looks over at me when she reaches the other side of the room and I give her a thumbs-up, then safely glance down at my notepad and make an addition to my list. I write it at the top, underline it, and star it because I have to get it done before Jonah and the kids leave: *Get honey for Margaret.*

My mother-in-law is partial to a rose-infused honey that's sold at the local farmer's market in downtown Garden Hills every Friday. Margaret says she uses it for her pound cake, which, I admit, is delicious, but I know for a fact she uses it for other purposes that I am not at liberty to share, except to say that the last time I went to Arizona, rose-infused honey in tow, I happened into the kitchen one late night when I couldn't sleep and witnessed my father-in-law dipping his finger into the jar and dripping some of the golden goo on my mother-in-law's left clavicle. Ewww! Luckily I was able to backtrack undetected, but I have never been able to present Margaret with her prized honey without shuddering. Thank God Jonah now has that task.

I should be honest and say that my in-laws are good people. They are. Good people. Jonah and his two brothers are all responsible, nice men. They make decent livings and none of them has ever spent the night in jail. So William and Margaret have obviously done something right. But William cannot utter a sentence that isn't laden with derision. He thinks that because he accompanies every insult with a wink everyone will know he is just kidding, a jokester extraordinaire. But I don't find anything he says funny. And Margaret comes across as sweet and grandmotherly; she never forgets a birthday or anniversary or any other special occasion, and she is always the first to put our Christmas presents in the mail. But you have to wonder whether she has all her faculties, or whether she is addicted to Lithium, since she truly thinks that William the Terrible walks on water. And when I am with the two of them I always feel like I am under the microscope, and that whatever microorganisms they see on the Ellen slide either are foreign to them or need to be handled with a hazmat suit.

Three years ago, I was excused from the family vaycay because my mom was undergoing surgery and needed me to care for her during her recovery. So what if it was just a face-lift and not some lifesaving operation? And who cares that I begged her to push it up a few months so that it would coincide with the Arizona trip? Forget about the phone conversation during which my sister offered to play nursemaid and I told her to back the hell off. It all worked out for the best as far as I was concerned. For even though I had to unclog Mom's drainage tubes more than a few times, and unpack and repack her bloody gauze, and despite the fact that I had to watch my beloved mother transform into the Creature from the Black Lagoon because of the cataclysmic bruising and swelling that accompany such a procedure, and which her plastic surgeon assured me was perfectly normal, not to have to spend six days with ball-busting Bill was heaven.

The following year, when Jonah broached the subject of

spring break, I hesitated only a millisecond before I told him that I didn't want to make the trip. I expected anger and indignation, but what I got was close to relief. Apparently, the tension between his folks and me always stresses him out, and after six days of playing the peacemaker and diplomat, he would return from his vacation *in need* of a vacation.

I look up from my notepad and see that Jessie's ballet class has concluded. My list has seven mundane items beneath the honey thing, like going through the kids' closets and reorganizing the garage. No prizewinning entries like *take helicopter lessons* or *jump out of a plane* or *track down Hugh Jackman on his movie set*, but at least they are things I have a reasonable chance of accomplishing. That is, if I don't get lazy or distracted or spend too much time with Jill or decide that it is more important to clear my TiVo . . .

Jessie is huddled with a small group of her friends in the corner of the studio near the piano, all of them looking almost as Asian as the Lee twins, with their tight buns on the tops of their heads. One of the girls, Suzette, says something that makes the others giggle. Madame Valenchenko waddles over to them, her cane making a rhythmic racket as she thwacks it against the hardwood floor, scowling as though her students' gaiety is deeply offensive to her. Jessie is now talking animatedly, using her arms like an Italian mama to get her point across. Her friends listen, rapt, until their burly instructor smacks her cane across the piano bench, causing all of the girls to flinch. The group quickly disperses, each girl heading for her respective parent. Madame Valenchenko says something to Jessie that I cannot make out from where I sit and Jessie nods her head. Then the two, an odd couple if ever I saw one, approach me side by side.

"I have overheered zat Jess vud become vegan, da?"

"Yes," I say, pasting a supportive smile on my face. I am expecting the coach to give us a lecture on how important protein is for muscles and that Jessie ought to rethink her choice. Instead, she totally blindsides both my daughter and me.

"Zis is very gud," she says. "Perhaps now she vil get reed of zat horrible gut and not break ze floor wiz her tremendous girth."

My jaw drops to my chest and I have that instant mama-bear rage that makes me want to grab her cane and shove it up her butt.

Jessie puts her hand in mine and looks up at me with glistening eyes. "Can we go now, Mom?" she asks in a small voice I don't recognize.

I give her fingers a squeeze and smile down at her, then flash an if-looks-could-kill glare at Valenchenko. I hold that old Russian bitch's beady eyes for a good ten seconds, then stalk out of the studio, my crushed eight-year-old daughter in tow.

Tonight, Jonah brings home Chinese food. Jessie has been locked in her room since we got home, and when she finally emerges and takes her place at the dining room table, she conspicuously pushes aside the tofu with mixed vegetables, grabs the kung pao beef, and proceeds to empty the entire carton onto her plate. Jonah, to whom I am still not speaking except when necessary, glances at me questioningly. Matthew and Connor also exchange quick looks of surprise. Wordlessly, we all watch my daughter as she shovels the formerly offending animal flesh into her mouth until her plate is clean.

As long as she doesn't go upstairs after dinner and stick her finger down her throat, I'm okay with it.

PEOPLE ARE MEAN

I was going to title this post "Ruskies Go Home" or "Ballet Teachers Suck," but I realized that those titles narrow the margin far too much. My daughter, and I may as well just reveal her sex because I am going to refer to her ballet class and unless you are a fan of the movie *Billy Elliot*, you're going to figure it out anyway, was attacked by her Russian ballet coach today. Not physically. No, the old battle-ax didn't whack my daughter with her cane because she tripped during a *grand jeté*. She called my daughter fat. Now, I know there are obese children all over the world, primarily in the United States if you read the statistics. But my daughter is not even close to being fat. She is neither chunky nor chubby nor slightly plump. She is a normal healthy prepubescent girl. At least she was until Madame Stalin berated her. Now she is eating everything in sight and I fear she might become one of those stats by the end of the week.

But it's not just Russians or ballet teachers. It's all people. We are mean. We can't help ourselves. We learn in childhood the power of a good zinger. Have you ever noticed how especially great little kids are at being bastards? They think they are just being honest when they call someone fat or stupid or weird or a geek. And although we grow and mature and learn to put a filter on our thoughts and manage to be civil to each other most of the time, the underlying fact is that we are mean on the inside, where it counts. We see a homeless guy on the street and we might say, "God bless you," but on the inside, we're thinking, *Damn, you stink! Go take a freaking shower*. One of our peers shows up to a dinner party wearing a particularly unflattering ensemble and we say, "You look fabulous! Where did you get that skirt?" but what we're thinking is, *God, you look like a whale! Didn't you look in the mirror before you left the house?* By some strange accident of evolution, we actually feel better about ourselves when we are putting other people down. How messed up is that?

And just as often, we do give voice to the inner meanie. Words are weapons, but few people are trained enough to wield them safely. It takes diplomacy and tact, and who has time for that? In moments of stress or panic, we hurl words at our enemies. When our inhibitions are lowered (in other words, when we are drunk as skunks or high off our asses), we fling words about without the least bit of concern over the effect they may have. Our mouths open, our tongues twitch, and out they fly. "You're a piece of shit!" "Your meat loaf tastes like cow dung!" "You couldn't get it up with a forklift." "What kind of a moron flunks home ec?" And on and on.

The fact is, being mean is not our fault. It's a part of us, encoded in our DNA all the way back to caveman times where a couple of grunts equaled "Fuck you" and some guttural snorts meant "Damn, you're ugly." And going against our nature can be counterintuitive. Today I was proud of myself for showing remarkable restraint when I didn't allow myself to scream at Madame Wankersky that she was nothing more than an over-the-hill former mediocre ballerina nobody commie with a bad dye job who looks like a bloated beach ball with legs. At the same time, I understand the therapeutic benefits of letting it all out. The whole ride home from the studio, I white-knuckled the steering wheel, nearly got into

two accidents, flipped the bird to an unsuspecting octoge-
narian driver, laid into the postman for not sorting our mail
properly, and screamed at the dog to take a fucking leak before I sent her to the pound. (She is still hiding under my
daughter's bed as I write this post.) So, if I had just gone with
my human instincts and berated the person who deserved it,
I would not have put my children's lives in jeopardy or alien-
ated our mailman or given my poor dog the mother of all
anxiety attacks.

Now, I know we should try to rise above our genet-
ics and be good to each other. We should adhere to the
old adage *If you can't say something nice, don't say anything at all.* But then again, whoever said that was probably
just a stupid bitch anyway.

Thirteen

TGIF. Yeah, right. Today is the capper on my week. In the end, it turned out to be pretty great, but I'll get to that later. First things first. The major downer. The end of my innocence. The disillusionment of a mother about her twelve-year-old son. Cue tragic music and grab a hankie.

"Mrs. Ivers?" comes the nasal voice through the phone line. "Ms. Rodriguez requests that you come to the school as soon as possible."

My heart skips a beat but I manage to keep my words even. "Is Connor all right?"

"In terms of his physical well-being, your son is fine."

"Then what is this about?" I demand. This is Connor we're talking about. Straight-A student, terrific athlete, popular with peers and faculty, tells his mom he loves her, all-around great guy.

"I am not at liberty to say," the voice drones.

I resist the urge to ask if my son needs a lawyer and merely tell the woman I will be there shortly. On the drive to James Meriwether Middle School, I briefly consider calling Jonah but decide against it. I don't want to bring our current marital discord into the principal's office, where it will only pull focus from the matter at hand. Whatever that matter may be. For the life of me, I cannot imagine what Connor has done to warrant a visit from his mother. Maybe someone made a mistake. That must be it. Someone got the wrong kid. It happens all the time, right? By the time I pull into the parking lot, I am all but convinced that Connor is innocent.

Until I see his face. *Guilty guilty guilty*, it says when he looks up at me as I enter the office. He is seated in a blue plastic chair outside Ms. Rodriguez's office, his hands folded in his lap. His face is covered with splotchy scarlet angst, his eyes pleading.

"Sorry, Mom," he says immediately.

Mrs. Frawley, a gray-haired biddy with the mandatory pencil stuck behind her ear, stands on the other side of the counter giving me a harsh look. "Mrs. Ivers."

"Mrs. Frawley," I return, trying for pleasant but falling short of the mark. The sight of Connor has suddenly sideswiped me and I feel tension shoot up my spine.

"Ms. Rodriguez is waiting for you," she says solemnly. Jesus, what the hell did he do?

"I'd like to talk to my son for a minute," I tell her, but she briskly shakes her head.

"You'll have plenty of time for that later, since Mr. Ivers will not be returning to school today."

"What?" I am instantly indignant. But my anger is cut off by the appearance of Herr Rodriguez, as the kids call her. She opens her door and stands in the doorway, narrowing her eyes first on Connor and then on me. She is tall, probably six feet, with striking Latina features that she does her best to disguise. Her hair is bleached blond and perfectly coiffed, and her skin is like coffee with a hefty serving of half-and-half. Her eyes are the perfect shade of sky blue, clearly fake, as are her breasts. She wears a tailored black suit over a charcoal blouse and a pair of black, sensibly heeled pumps. I peg her for midthirties, but she may well be my age, just surgically enhanced.

"Thank you for coming, Mrs. Ivers." Her voice is steel, her gaze cold and piercing, and I have no trouble understanding why her students are scared shitless of her. This is the first time I've had to deal with her on this level, and I can feel my underarms dampen as I withstand her unwavering stare.

However, I have been out of middle school for more years than I care to admit, and I am not some simpering mom who will wither and submit to Herr Rodriguez's idea of intimidation. I throw my shoulders back and say, "I would like to know what's going on. Right now."

Ms. Rodriguez squints at me, perhaps wondering if I am really an alpha female or just putting on a show. I'm actually not sure of the answer to that one myself.

"Please come into my office," she commands.

I give Connor's shoulder a quick squeeze, then follow the principal into her lair.

She directs me to one of the two chairs facing her desk, and as I sit, I notice that her office is sparse and unadorned. None of the usual picture frames holding photos of a smiling family or grinning toothless children, no plants, no coffee mug with the legend *World's Best Principal* or *Is It Five o'Clock Yet?* The walls are a drab shade of beige and the only color accents are from the school flyers tacked to a cork board on one side of the room. Her desk contains a stack of file folders on the left, a notepad on the right, and an open file folder right in the middle, which she peers at as soon as she is seated.

She traces a long acrylic-nailed finger down the top page of the file, reading carefully, her face betraying nothing. After a full thirty seconds I start to get antsy, but I recognize this as another attempt to intimidate, so I merely sit there and continue to wait. Finally, she looks up and meets my eyes and all I can think about is how ridiculous her blue contact lenses look. Joanna Rodriguez, as her nameplate announces, could be a stunner if she weren't trying so hard to stamp out all traces of her heritage. For some reason, this gives me a boost, and not in the "people are mean" kind of way. More in the "this woman must be as insecure as the rest of us" kind of way, which puts us on even footing.

"You may or may not know," she begins slowly, "that here at James Meriwether Middle School we have a zero-tolerance policy."

"I read the parent handbook," I say, and although I say it casually, she reacts as if it is a challenge.

"Then you are aware that any form of contraband is strictly forbidden."

Contraband? What the hell does that mean? I envision Connor in the big house, stuffing chewing gum and comic books under his mattress. This is no laughing matter, however, and I bite the inside of my cheek to keep from grinning.

"We do random locker checks here, every week," Rodriguez continues. "For the protection of our students."

Okay, so I know that in this day and age, i.e., the era of Columbine and bully-provoked suicide, schools have to go overboard in order to cover their asses, but something about this edict strikes me as unfair. Yes, I want my kids to be safe, and I know we are talking about twelve-year-olds, but shouldn't they have some rights, too? Before I can go further with this train of thought, Joanna Rodriguez reaches into her drawer, withdraws a couple of magazines, and slaps them onto the desktop. Suddenly, I am staring at a set of triple-D breasts and a completely shaven twat. *Oh dear Jesus.*

"These were found in Connor's locker this morning," Rodriguez informs me with just the barest hint of a feral smile.

I struggle to come up with a reply, but I cannot tear my eyes away from the naked woman on the desk. Her legs are splayed wide and her index finger is pointing to her promised land and her boobs are so large and high they almost obscure her face. I can just make out two cherry red lips and heavily made-up cat eyes behind the enormous manmade mounds of flesh.

"Mrs. Ivers?"

My head snaps up and I look at Rodriguez. She wears a knowing expression that says it all: *You're not the first mom whose world I have totally shattered. God, I love my job!*

I have the burning desire to smack that look off her face, but at the moment I am completely paralyzed.

"That's not all, Mrs. Ivers," she says, watching me as though I am a caged animal.

I feel my pulse quicken. Oh shit, there's more? What the hell can it be? Condoms? A joint? A Sig Sauer?

Once again, Rodriguez opens her drawer and pulls something out. It is a single sheet of unlined paper. She peers at it distastefully, then holds it out to me and I feel myself flinch as though it has been tainted with anthrax. I force my hand not to shake as I reach up and take the sheet from Rodriguez's clawlike grasp, then bring it to my lap and look down.

What I see unleashes a bastion of conflicting emotions: horror, disillusionment, maternal pride, art appreciation, disbelief. It is a pencil drawing of a naked girl lying on a bed, the sheets around her rumpled and entwined with her bare legs, her arms stretched lazily over her head. She appears to be roughly Connor's age; her face has that innocent and carefree look of youth and her body is thin, her curves as yet unrealized, her breasts mere buds. I recognize Connor's style at once, although his usual subject matter until now has been superheroes, supervillains, and supermonsters. And while the sketch shocks me as much as the *Hustler* magazine on Rodriguez's desk, I can't help but admire the raw (or should I say *naked*) talent of the artist. I realize that Connor has a gift, and I will do everything in my power to nurture that gift. Right after I ground him for the rest of his life.

"In case you were wondering," Rodriguez says, interrupting my thoughts, "this girl is also a student at Meriwether. This kind of thing is considered bullying."

I give her an incredulous look. "Bullying?"

"What would you call it, Mrs. Ivers?"

"Art?" I say lightly, but she is not amused. I get the feeling that this woman wouldn't appreciate the Venus de Milo if it fell on her head.

"Do you think this is a joke?" she asks pointedly.

"No, of course not!" I retort. "But I don't think it's bullying either. It's not like Connor drew handcuffs or a mustache on her. It's actually a very good rendering."

"It's *pornographic*!" The principal's voice is contained, but her nostrils flare angrily. "That girl is twelve years old. Imagine the damage that 'rendering' would have done to her psyche had it been circulated throughout the student body."

Personally, I think that if a drawing like that of me had circulated through *my* middle school, I wouldn't have been lacking for dates to the school dance.

"I understand your point," I say in a conciliatory tone,

knowing I have to be very diplomatic. Rodriguez could kick Connor out of school for this. The alternatives to James Meriwether Middle School are either a twenty-five-minute commute each way to the public school in the next district or a private school that costs about a zillion dollars a year.

"So what happens now?" I ask, all humble and beseeching.

She makes a steeple with her fingers, although the fiery red nail polish makes it look more like the roof of a brothel than the top of a church. She appears to be scrutinizing me, is probably considering the depth of my parental concern. I struggle to look appropriately contrite.

"Connor is an exemplary student," she says, then unhinges the steeple and taps a fingernail against the top page of his file. "He has never been in any kind of trouble before today."

I nod in agreement but remain silent for fear that anything I say might be misconstrued.

"I can't overlook this infraction, *obviously*. But perhaps we can be lenient this one time. In view of his record."

"If you think that's fair," I agree, then repeat her words. "In view of his record . . ."

"I will have to suspend him for the rest of the day, however. This will give him time to do some hard soul-searching"—is she kidding?—"about the kind of person he wants to grow up to become."

I decide not to share with her that Connor wants to be a professional baseball player and if he succeeds he will no longer have to look at magazines or draw pictures of naked women because he'll be swimming in the real thing after every game.

"And I trust we won't be finding any more of *these*"—she gestures first to the magazines, then to the sketch—"among his possessions in the future."

"Absolutely," I say. "And I can assure you, his father and I will give him a stern talking-to."

"I suggest that *more* than a stern talking-to is in order."

What does she want me to do? Beat him senseless? Throw away his Wii? (That cost me over two hundred bucks, thank you very much. It is *not* going in the trash.) Humiliate him and force him to betray his prepubescent urges? At this moment I am confronted with the fact that I have absolutely no idea how I am going to handle this or what I am going to say to Connor. It's one of those sticky parental situations that requires subtlety and levelheadedness. Fuck, why didn't I call Jonah?

I realize that Ms. Rodriguez is glowering at me, and I give her my attention.

"I will be keeping an eye on your son from now on, Mrs. Ivers. One more infraction and the consequences will be severe."

I get to my feet and, grasping the sketch in my right hand, I reach out for the magazines with my left. Before I can grab them, Rodriguez slaps her palm down on the *Hustler*, her bony fingers partially obscuring the money shot.

"*I* will see that these are disposed of properly." As she scoops them back into her desk drawer, I swear I see a gleam in her fake blue eyes, and I can't help but wonder if she might be planning to take the magazines home for an evening of *la vida loca* and a little self-love. Ah, well. Live and let live.

She slams the drawer, then flips Connor's file folder shut with finality. This meeting is definitely over.

During the car ride home I am as silent as death. Connor sits beside me rather than in the back of the minivan because, by God, anyone who has (or had) porn magazines in his possession is damn well old enough to sit in the front seat. I can feel his eyes dart to me every so often as though he is expecting me to strike at any moment. He is assuming my silence means I am furious, but he is wrong. To describe my state of mind, I must borrow a word I frequently heard spoken by the grandmother of my childhood best friend, Susan Stein: *verklempt*. The turbulent thoughts swirling around in my brain are making it impossible for me to form sentences. I give myself credit for remaining calm in Herr Rodriguez's office, but now I am suffering from a kind of posttraumatic stress syndrome.

I have never harbored illusions that my children are perfect, or that they would somehow remain innocent until they were, say, twenty-five. But I honestly thought I had a few more years with Connor before he made that leap into pseudo-manhood. Although Jonah had *The Talk* with him when he turned eleven (and explained to Connor that, no, *vagina* is not a city in Italy), I didn't expect to be confronted with his biologically fueled urges so soon. He's twelve, for crying out loud.

The other thing that's bothering me is that I know how bright Connor is. He is aware of the locker checks at school. How could he be so stupid as to leave such damning evidence where there is a good chance it will be found? It's not on the same level as Clinton and Monica-gate, but still! Did my son just assume it would never happen to him? Or was he so attached to the magazines that he thought it was worth the risk? And what does that say about him? Is he some kind of perv in the making because he can't, just *can't* bring himself to dump the twat magazines into the trash?

I steal a glance at him, and although his posture is defeated—shoulders slouched over and chin resting against his chest—he still looks just like my Connor.

He catches my glance and turns to face me. "Mom?" His voice is soft and unsure. I return my focus to the road.

"I'm not ready to talk about this, Connor," I say.

"But—"

"Seriously."

My cell phone chirps. Connor quickly bends over and grabs it from my purse then hands it to me. I have no hands-free device—Jonah gave me a Bluetooth once, but it never fit right, and it is *not* because my ears are misshapen—so I pull over to the curb and punch on my flashers. I check the Caller ID and see Jonah's name.

"Hi."

"Hey, babe," comes his excited voice. "You are never going to guess what I got from one of my clients."

Lice? Herpes? Diphtheria? "What?" I ask.

"Tickets to the *Blue Man Group*!" he says excitedly. "For tonight! Do you believe it? The guy's wife and kids came down with food poisoning from Grandma's pork loin, or something. So he can't use them." He's talking in a rush, not giving me time to interject. "The one snafu is that there are only four tickets. But I know how much you hate the Blue Man Group."

Loathe would be a better word. I saw the show years ago during a trip to New York and I honestly cannot understand the appeal. All I could think of while watching their painted, shaven heads was *blue balls*.

"So I thought I could take the kids. You know, give you the night off."

"There's a slight problem with that," I say. "Connor is grounded."

"Come again?"

"As we speak, I am on my way home from school with him after having a charming conversation with his principal."

"Herr Rodriguez?"

"The very same." Again, I can feel Connor's eyes on me, but I won't give him the satisfaction of looking at him.

"Is this a joke?" Jonah asks, perplexed. "Connor?"

"It seems your son has taken up a new hobby. Pornographic magazines."

"What?!"

"Well, *Hustler* for sure. I'm not certain what the second one was. I never saw the cover." At this point I do look at my son. He all but shrinks into the seat as I glare at him expectantly.

"*Shaved.*" His voice is practically inaudible.

"*Shaved,*" I report to Jonah.

There is a long moment of silence, and I can almost see Jonah's face. Knowing him as well as I do, I have no doubt that he has a grin on his face and is thinking *Atta boy!* to himself. The boys' club strikes again. As long as it's not guy-on-guy action, he's okay with it. He will not, however, admit this to me.

"That sounds pretty serious," he says.

"He also made a drawing of one of his . . . classmates?"

Connor nods. "Becka."

"Becka," I repeat into the phone. "*Naked* Becka, I should say."

"Is it any good?"

"As a matter of fact, yes," I reply, knowing that Connor could not hear the question.

"I know this is serious, Elle, but . . ."

"It *is* serious," I say for Connor's benefit.

"Maybe we could suspend the punishment until tomorrow. I mean, it is *Blue Man Group.* Connor's been dying to see it. How often do they come to the Garden Hills Performing Arts Center?"

"Never," I admit, knowing that I am going to give in. I can feel it already, and I am annoyed with myself for caving so easily.

"I'd hate for him to miss it. What do you say I come home early and have a talk with him? I'll get there before you leave to pick up Matthew and Jessie. He and I can have a good heart-to-heart."

I take a deep breath and sigh. If Ms. Rodriguez knew that instead of locking Connor in the basement without food or water, we were taking him to a show he's always wanted to see, she'd probably call up the department of child and family services to have him removed from our care. Still, Jonah and I have done our best to instill solid values in our children. At some point, they will have to make their own choices as to the kind of people they want to be. I just pray the foundation we have provided inspires them to make the right decisions . . . and keeps them out of jail.

"Fine," I say into the phone, then hang up.

I turn and face Connor, watching him as he nervously plays with an errant thread on his shirt. He is my baby, my firstborn. When the second and third children come along, life becomes so chaotic that specific events and milestones become hazy, memories fold over each other and become impossible to differentiate. With Matthew, and then Jessie, I cannot recall with clarity when they spoke their first words (although I do know *what* their first words were: *help* in Matthew's case and *mine* in Jessie's). I don't remember the specific date that each took their first steps or cut their first tooth or pooped on the toilet for the first time. But Connor is different. I had him all to myself for almost two years. We were a team, and my memories of holding him in my arms, of nursing him, of carrying him through the aisles of Target in his front-facing carrier so he could see all of the bright colors, of lying on the daybed next to his crib, my fingers intertwined with his through the crib slats, are crystal clear.

But he is no longer a child. I have to accept that fact, no matter how difficult and painful it is for me. He is growing up. A part of me mourns that little boy who couldn't fall asleep without me lying by his side. I suppose a part of me always will.

"Hey," I call to him, willing him to look at me. When he does, I can almost see the handsome man he will someday be. I hope he keeps his hair short so that his beautiful green eyes will always stand out. Those green eyes of his are sure to melt many hearts.

"Yes, Mom?"

"The sketch," I say solemnly. "Did you actually see Becka naked?"

He swallows hard, his Adam's apple bobbing up and down, then forcefully shakes his head. "No, Mom. I just sort of imagined it."

"Good," I say with an emphatic nod. "Let's keep it that way for a few years, okay?"

. . . .

Eighth Post: March 23, 2012
SomethingNewAt42

BOYS TO MEN

I am not a boy. I have never been a boy—and you'll just have to trust me on that. So I cannot begin to imagine what it's like to have this three-inch piece of flesh dangling between my legs that, for all intents and purposes, dictates (no pun intended) just about every aspect of my life. It's like a prank, another one of God's little jokes. I mean, when He

was busy creating us, why did He bother to put a brain inside a man's skull when He was going to put another one
down there that would end up overriding every decision the
skull-brain makes?

Now I know the same could be said of women and
their hormones, that we are frequently driven by them, but,
in our defense, our brains are never completely taken over
by hormonal surges. We are consciously aware of it when
it happens, like *I am sobbing over a Maytag commercial
because I am about to get my period* or *I am throwing away
every single pair of underwear in my drawer because I
am perimenopausal*. Though the action is absurd, rational
thought prevails.

Men are different. When the penis-brain takes over (and
let's be frank, the penis-brain has only one thing in mind),
the skull brain simply shuts down. You have to kind of feel
sorry for the guys. I mean, let's take a look at the statistics.
If a healthy man has about twenty erections a day, and erections can last anywhere from ten seconds to thirty minutes,
by the time he's forty, the average male has lost days, even
weeks, of his life. "Where were you on the night of Sep-
tember 18?" "I have no recollection." Erection. "What are
you doing home in the middle of the workday?" "I have no
idea." Erection. "Honey, where is the remote control?" "I
don't know." You better believe that if he doesn't know
where the remote control is, it's due to an erection.

I was up very late one night putting the finishing touches
on one of my children's school projects. My husband was
in his office getting some work done, or so I thought. When
I finally trudged into the bedroom, I found him fully clothed
on top of the comforter, his fly open, and his hand resting on his thigh. When I asked him what he was doing, he

looked at me with glassy eyes and shrugged. When I questioned him as to why he hadn't gotten into his pajamas or brushed his teeth or turned down the bed, he merely shrugged a second time and said, "I really don't remember. I don't even know how I got here."

My nameless relative, heaven help her, is surrounded by testosterone, with a husband and three sons. I often wonder how she deals with it. (She once brought home a female dog in an attempt to balance out the estrogen level in her home, but within six months, little Fifi was humping everything in sight.) She explains to me that she treats her four boys as though there are eight of them. She can always tell which brain is controlling the body, and her response is based on that knowledge. If the skull-brain is in charge, she uses her reasoning and carefully chosen words to defuse an untoward situation. If the penis-brain is calling the shots, she screams like a Neanderthal and lets fly a properly placed, and never forceful, spanking, in hopes, she says, of shocking the penis-brain into relinquishing control back to the skull-brain, at which point she can fall back on logic. (I should add that my nameless relative majored in anthropology, and clearly, this serves her well in a house full of men.)

The preoccupation with the little brain starts early, in case you hadn't noticed. From the time baby boys begin flexing their fingers, their first destination is always their pants. "Oooh. What's this? Fun!" It's all over for them before their lives even get going. And the fixation continues to grow until they are, haha, erecting shrines to their penises. You see them everywhere: skyscrapers and rocket ships and those color-changing columns that greet you at LAX.

Not that I am putting down the penis, Lord no. I love the little guy. He comes in handy quite often. And I love men, too. At least, I love them when they're not busy being total jerks. I just think it must be hard—uh, difficult—to be a man. I feel sorry for them, actually. Here you have a being on the face of the planet who is so deluded as to think he is in control of his own destiny, when in fact he is ruled by a small squishy creature that looks like an oversized flesh-toned amoeba. God help them, every one.

Fourteen

I thread my way through the heavy foot traffic that crowds Center Street on this unseasonably warm March evening. The Garden Hills Friday Night Farmer's Market is in full swing, and all of the stalls that line the main thoroughfare are jammed with customers looking for the perfect organic tomato or hemp handbag or Indian scarf. I myself am in search of the rose-infused honey, which I've left to the last minute to acquire. Jonah and the kids are leaving on Sunday, so if I don't find it tonight, Margaret is shit out of luck in the honey department. I could have come a couple of Fridays ago, or last week before book club, but I rationalized that I wanted to give Margaret the freshest batch available. I wouldn't want my father-in-law to get a rash, now would I?

My farmer's market friend, Masood, has apparently moved his stall because it is not where it was the last time I was here, before Christmas. I used to come to the market frequently, just to wander, and occasionally, on a whim, I would buy something. Like the organic beets that ended up rotting in my fridge. But as life got busier, my visits became less frequent, and now it seems I only come four times a year for the honey. It's my go-to gift for my mother-in-law: Christmas, her birthday, Mother's Day, and the spring break trip. I know it's not original, and it takes no thought at all on my part, but she loves it. And if you find something your mother-in-law loves, my advice is to stick with it.

I am still energized from my time on the treadmill, can still feel the endorphins coursing through my veins. When Connor and I got home, I sent him to his room to think about his actions, then carefully tucked the sketch of Naked Becka in a file folder in Jonah's office. I spent the rest of the early afternoon writing my blog and finished just before Jonah got home, and the two of us were able to communicate like the adults we claim to be as we rehashed the Connor situation. I finally managed to get my exercise in while the rest of the family excitedly got themselves ready for their night out.

And how I needed it. All week, I'd felt as though I were riding on an emotional roller coaster. I'd been working so hard to stay on an even keel, fighting to maintain my precarious grip on the steering wheel of the familial vehicle in order to keep it from crashing into the side of a mountain. My blog was helping a lot and I'd definitely been using it as therapy (and was heartened to see my hits numbering close to thirty thousand), but there is a finite amount of angst and rage that can be defused through the written word, so I cranked up the resistance on the treadmill and poured the rest of my pent-up emotions into my workout.

With each inhalation and exhalation, I told myself that I had an evening of freedom ahead. While I was conflicted about letting Connor off the hook so easily, I knew that a timeout from my family was exactly what I needed.

By the time I hit the shower, I was blissfully alone in my home, and therefore, I had no one to brag to when I donned my favorite pair of jeans and found that I needed a belt to keep them from falling off.

So just about now, I am feeling good. It's a beautiful night. My ass is tighter than it's been in years. I don't have to cook or do dishes. I made it through a hellish week marginally unscathed. And I am, for the next five hours, free.

And that's when I see him.

I am just walking past the nut stand when I catch a glimpse of Ben Campbell through the throngs of people who are standing around listening to a street performer waffle on his acoustic guitar. Ben stands among them, his arms folded across his chest, his head bobbing to the rhythm of the song. As if sensing my presence, he turns his head and sees me. Our eyes lock, and suddenly I feel like I have been sucked into a Rogers and Hammerstein musical. A sly grin spreads across his face as he uncrosses his arms and slowly moves toward me.

"Hi," he says.

"Hi back," I return. I pray he can't see my pulse throbbing in my neck. The evening light is waning so I'm pretty sure I'm safe.

"We have to stop meeting like this."

I suppress a juvenile giggle and manage to turn it into a throaty laugh. "You're right, we do." I make a show of looking around, even though his wife and kids are conspicuously absent. "Where's the rest of your clan?"

"The boys are home. . . ." He makes a face. "We got a sitter for tonight, thought we'd check out Center Street, have dinner, you know. A real grown-up date. But she, uh, got tied up at the office. Gonna be there late. So, I thought, what the hell? We already had the sitter. Might as well take advantage of it."

"Oh, yeah, well, you wouldn't want to alienate a good sitter by canceling at the last minute either. Good sitters are hard to find."

"Really? I hadn't thought of that."

"I can't find a sitter who doesn't have *Enjoys animal sacrifice* on her résumé."

He laughs at that, a hearty resonating sound that tickles me from head to toe. "What about you? What are you doing here?"

"My quarterly honey run," I answer and receive a puzzled look. "For my mother-in-law. It's rose-infused." As if that's an explanation.

"Does she cook with it?"

"Among other things."

His brow furrows once more. "I don't want to know, do I?"

"Definitely not." I peer past him down the long line of stalls. "Only, I can't find it. My man, Masood, is not where he should be."

"That sounds like a problem. What do you say I help you find him?"

"Oh no," I protest, shaking my head. "Enjoy your evening, do what you were going to do . . ."

"Hey, I am enjoying my evening. And you know what? It just got a little better."

His brown eyes are twinkling with mirth, yet at the same time serious, and I fear that if I look into them too long, I will melt into them and float away.

"Unless you'd rather . . . not . . . have company. . . ."

"No, I . . ." I take a breath then let it out on a chuckle. "Masood's about five feet tall, and almost as wide, with a beard down to his nipples."

"So, in other words, hard to miss." He grins, then holds out his arm, gesturing me forward. We walk side by side down Center Street, in search of a short fat hairy Persian man with the best damn honey on the West Coast.

Five minutes later, Ben spots him at the end of the aisle of stalls, situated in front of Yogurtland, prime real estate by farmer's market standards. As I step beneath the caramel-colored canopy, the beefy Persian greets me with a magnanimous smile.

"Ah, Miss Ellen! You found me! I knew tonight you would not disappoint me with your absence!"

He clasps both of his enormous hands over mine and gives them an emphatic shake.

"Nice spot," I tell him, hooking a thumb toward the yogurt shop.

"Ah, yes. Allah smiles on those with pure hearts." He winks at me. "Well, those with pure *products* at least. I have your precious nectar right here." He waddles over to one of the display tables and gingerly picks up a glass jar filled with the rose-infused honey. He hands it to me as though it is a priceless relic, then glances at Ben, who is perusing the rest of his merchandise with interest.

"I see you have brought Mr. Ellen with you this fine evening!"

I glance at Ben, feeling myself flush as he grins back at me. But instead of correcting Masood, he steps forward and puts out his hand.

"I'm Ben," he says simply.

The two men shake hands and then Ben compliments Masood on his offerings, which include an assortment of both regular and infused honey, many different kinds of fruit preserved in spiced syrup, dried dates and figs and other fruits I don't recognize, and a variety of sweet and savory chutneylike spreads. Masood beams and gives Ben an earful about each item, and Ben graciously listens, nodding and asking questions.

After Masood finishes his discourse, I pay him and receive a bear hug in return. Ben and I wander back out to the middle of Center Street and stop. He shoves his hands into the back pockets of his jeans and I glance around, unlike Masood, at a sudden loss for words.

"Hey, any good sushi restaurants around here?" Ben asks out of the blue. "I'm having a craving. Linda won't eat it, so now seems like a good time."

"Is it the vegan thing?"

"No, the brain worm thing."

I laugh. "Yeah, I read about that once. I try not to think about it."

"It's good to live on the edge."

"Says the man who belongs to the three-mile-high club."

He cocks his head at me and smiles with such boyish sincerity that I feel warmth spread through my chest. I clear my throat and glance down the street, not wanting him to see the effect he is having on me. (But if he's even a halfway decent detective, it's a good bet he already knows.)

"There's, uh, Sushi Yummy," I say, pointing to a building in the middle of the next block that houses my favorite procurer of raw fish.

"Sushi *Yummy*?" he repeats doubtfully. "I don't know about the name."

"It's ridiculous, I know. But, trust me, the fish is the freshest in Garden Hills and their special rolls are orgas—" I stop myself and bite my bottom lip in embarrassment.

He raises his eyebrows and suppresses an amused grin. "You were saying? Their rolls are . . . ?"

"Very . . . yummy," I finish.

He shakes his head. "That's not what you were going to say. You know, I am a trained officer of the law. I could get it out of you. So, what was it?"

I remain mute.

"Chicken," he teases and I can't help but laugh. I also can't help but wonder what kind of interrogation techniques he had in mind. A few are zipping merrily through my brain right about now. Like handcuffs and wax and feathers and . . . oh shit. *Stop, Ellen!*

"So, you heading home to the family?"

Lie, Ellen, I tell myself. *Say "Yes, I am going home to my husband and children."*

"Actually, Jonah's taking the kids to see the Blue Man Group tonight, so I'm on my own."

"Those guys with the shaved heads and the blue body makeup, who make a huge mess on stage and call it theater?"

"The very same."

He shudders. "So why aren't you going?"

"Not enough tickets."

"I can see you're really broken up about it. Not that I blame you. I can't stand those guys."

"I thought all men loved the Blue Man Group."

"I think you have them confused with the Three Stooges."

"Oh, yeah. That's right."

We both chuckle, and then the sound dies away, and there we stand, in the middle of the carless street, people passing between us and by us, neither of us moving.

"Why don't you—"

"Well, it was—"

We both start to speak at the same time, then go silent in unison. We laugh again. I look at him expectantly, allowing him to go first.

"Why don't you come grab some raw fish with me."

I open my mouth, but nothing comes out. My brain is on high speed, like a 33-rpm record being played at 78. *Don't, Ellen, no you can't, but it's totally innocent, it's never totally innocent, remember* When Harry Met Sally, *men and women cannot be friends, but I want to and it's just dinner, and what if one of your friends sees you or one of Jonah's buddies, it's just sushi for God's sake not a suite at the Ritz, don't even think about it, you slut, nothing is going to happen, you floozy, just say no and go buy a pint of Ben and Jerry's and masturbate.*

"That sounds great," I finally manage to say.

As soon as the words are out of my mouth, an image of Jonah skirts through my mind. I am still upset with him, but, as is usual in married life, my anger has lost its intensity and become tangential. I have been carrying it with me for the past few days, but it has remained on the periphery of our normal routine. I tell myself that accepting Ben's invitation has nothing to do with Jonah and our squabble, but I wonder if I would have given the same answer if Jonah and I were on good terms.

"Great." Ben smiles. He doesn't reach to take my hand, although I have the strangest sensation that he wants to, wants to reach out and touch me in some way. But he doesn't. This isn't a date. We are not two giddy teenagers caught up in some adolescent fantasy. We are two married adults who can certainly spend time together without it becoming something untoward or deceitful. This is no big deal. It's perfectly innocent. Whether there is an attraction between us or not, we are adults. We are mature enough to behave like the rational *married* people we are. We are just going to have some sushi, and that will be the end of it.

Of course, that was before the sake bombs.

"So there I am, crouched down with my pants down around my ankles, trying to . . . uh . . . you know, *make*, and all of the sudden I look up and there's like twenty-five Indian Princesses staring down at me, tomahawks at the ready."

Ben is in the middle of a story about a camping trip he and his college buddies took and I am laughing so hard I am afraid Sapporo is going to shoot out my nose.

"Talk about shrinkage!" he cries. "For Christ's sake, I told my buddy Paul I wasn't ever going camping again unless the place had outhouses."

"Those poor girls!" I exclaim. "They must have had the shock of their lives."

"Poor girls? What are you talking about? They were armed! I was *literally* scared shitless!"

I groan at him and shake my head, then laugh with him some more. I watch as he half fills my empty beer glass with a fresh bottle of Sapporo, then grabs the pitcher of sake and pours some into the white porcelain cup in front of me. He repeats the procedure with his own, lifts the sake cup and holds it over his beer mug and treats me to one of his trademark grins.

"Bombs away!" he cries, then drops the porcelain cup into his beer glass and raises the glass to his lips. I notice his throat working as he rhythmically swallows the beer/sake concoction, and for some absurd reason this turns me on.

He finishes and places the empty down on the sushi bar, and the porcelain cup drops to the bottom of the beer glass with an alarming clank.

"Your turn," he challenges.

"I haven't done sake bombs since college."

"It's just like riding a bike," he encourages.

I mimic his every step, wincing as the combination of hot sake and cold beer hits my mouth, but I manage to drink it down with only one brief pause. I pull the sake cup out of the glass with two fingers and set them side by side next to my soy sauce dish. The warmth of the double dose of alcohol spreads through me, and for the first time in a few days, I feel myself relax, feel the tension draining from my shoulders.

"Wow."

"See? No problem," Ben says with a smile.

"This is great. I really needed this tonight."

"Long week?" he asks.

"An endless series of family dramas," I explain.

"Ah, yes." He gives me a knowing look. "Those suck."

The sushi chef, a slight Asian man with the incongruous name *Pierre* stitched into his uniform, sets a plate in front of Ben on which sits a gorgeous, delectable-looking roll with eel and uni and some kind of sauce on top that has been flash-broiled to bubbly. At my place, Pierre places a tray of salmon sashimi drizzled with ponzu and garnished with bonita flakes. Using his chopsticks, Ben expertly picks up a section of his roll and pops it into his mouth. His eyes immediately roll back in his head and he moans loudly, and rather unself-consciously, to the amusement of the couple seated on the other side of him.

"Oh my God. Oh my God! That is *so* good. Oh God." He scrunches up his face. "I feel like Meg Ryan in *When Harry*

Met Sally. Oh GOD. YES!!" Suddenly, he turns to me and deadpans. "That sounded gay, didn't it?"

"I was just thinking about that movie," I tell him. "And, yes, it did sound a little bit gay."

He straightens up and puffs out his chest satirically, his voice deep and overflowing with bravado. "I *did* see that movie on a date with a *chick* who promised to *put out* afterward."

"Will you stop?" I plead as I erupt in more laughter. "I cannot eat and laugh at the same time, and this sashimi is really good and I really want to eat it."

"No no no no no." He slashes at my chopsticks before they can grab some salmon. "You *have* to try this." He jabs at his roll. "Seriously. You have to. You will go out of your mind. You'll have one of those things you can't say out loud!"

"No, that's yours. I am not going to take it away from you."

He shakes his head and grabs one of the sections of his roll with his chopsticks and lifts it toward me. I see it in slow motion, heading for my mouth. I look past the sushi and meet his eyes and for a split second, all the humor has drained away, replaced by a hunger that has nothing to do with raw fish.

He wants me, I think, and intuitively, I know it's true. My heart thumps crazily in my chest as the world around us completely clouds over. Because I know he must see the same hunger reflected back at him from my eyes.

But before I can confirm my suspicion, his eyes snap back to the piece of Yummy roll suspended in the air mere inches from my lips.

"Open wide!" he commands, the irreverent twinkle once again in his gaze. "And don't make me hold your nose, young lady."

I obey him and allow him to place the roll in my mouth, and it is amazing, like nothing I have ever eaten, but I suspect it tastes even better because of the way it was fed to me. I give him a closed-lip smile as the flavors explode over my tongue.

Ben is watching me closely. "What, no orgasm?"

I have swallowed just in time to keep from giving him an eel-and-uni shower.

"It's really good," I report.

"That's all? Just 'really good'?"

"Really, *really* good."

"Oh, c'mon!" he jokes. "You can do better than that! Where's the moaning and writhing in ecstasy?"

"I'm moaning and writhing on the inside, where it counts."

He laughs at that, then signals to the waitress to bring us another round. I shake my head in protest.

"I can't drink any more, Ben."

He turns suddenly to look at me. "I like the way you say my name."

"Well, maybe just one more round."

By the time we leave the restaurant, the farmer's market crowd has thinned and most of the merchants are beginning to close down their stalls. The outdoor seating of the many restaurants on Center Street has filled up proportionally as shoppers have given in to their hunger and thirst. Friday night energy abounds; laughter and chatter permeate the air, with people having a good time in that "I don't have to work tomorrow" kind of way.

I myself am feeling no pain—in fact, I am almost giddy— but it has less to do with the revelers around me than with the sake and the Yummy roll that was fed to me by a yummy man who wears Levi's better than anyone I have ever seen.

Ben glances at his watch and I am surprised by the pang of disappointment I feel. I don't want this evening to end. It has been so long since I have felt attractive to a man other than my husband, an eon since I have had that easy repartee that is coupled with sexual tension. It is an exquisite sensation. I am me, but I am someone else, too. Not merely Jonah's wife, or Connor, Matthew, and Jessie's mom. I am the me *before* the family and the me *after*. Ellen revisited and Ellen 2.0 at the same time. Tomorrow I will wake up and recognize myself when I look in the mirror, but earlier tonight, when I went to the restroom at the sushi bar, I saw a different person staring back at me. Someone whose cheeks were flushed with excitement and whose eyes were sparkling with . . . something new. I am loath to climb into my Flex and drive back to my house, where I will once again just be me.

And also, I am drunk.

"It's early," Ben says, and my heart skips a beat. "Just after eight."

"That is early for a . . . Friday night."

He peers at me with those gorgeous brown eyes. "Don't you just love sake bombs?"

"I do."

"I'm a little buzzed myself. You?"

I shake my head. "Nope. Not me. I'm perfectly fine."

He smiles at me, and I notice for the first time that his bottom teeth are slightly crooked. I find this downright sexy.

"What do you say we grab a Starbucks and sober up?"

Yes, oh yes, I really want to do that but I'm afraid that I'm going to do something stupid like jump you at the wrought-iron table outside the coffeehouse.

"I should get home," I say aloud.

"Yes, you should, but only when it's safe for you to drive. I am an officer of the law, remember. It's my duty to protect and serve."

I squint at him. "I thought that motto was strictly for uniformed officers. You know, like it says on the side of their cars. You're a detective."

"And what do you know about the hierarchy of the police force?"

"Only what I see on TV," I admit and he laughs.

"Really. Come on. Your family won't be back for a few hours. Blue Man Group is just starting. Have some coffee with me, we'll sober up, and then we'll both be okay to drive."

Call a cab, Ellen! my mind screams at me. *Do not have coffee with Ben Campbell. It's been fun, but it's time to go. End this evening while you can still look your husband in the eye.*

Three minutes later, we are sitting in the back corner of the Starbucks on Center Street. Ben is drinking the house blend and I have opted for a latte with no foam. The after-dinner crowd has not yet materialized, and we are alone in this part of the cafe, save for a bespectacled twenty-something seated a few tables over, laboriously plunking away on his laptop.

Our conversation has transitioned from the raucous and rollicking superficial subjects we discussed at the sushi bar to more serious fare, and although the mood is decidedly more somber, I find it no less satisfying.

"Sometimes it's tough," Ben is saying, his eyes focused on the lid of his beverage. "It sounds cliché, but you really do see people at their worst."

"I can't imagine," I respond, my voice sincere. "I don't know how you do it. How do you . . . deal with . . . I don't know, dead bodies? I mean, the only dead body I ever saw was my Grandma Phyllis, and that was after the mortician stuffed her and did her makeup." I smack my forehead. "I'm sorry. I shouldn't be joking about it."

"Actually, a sense of humor is what keeps most of us sane. But the truth is, the bodies are nothing compared to seeing what people are capable of doing to each other." He rubs his face with his hands. "I'm the one who should be sorry. I should never start talking about work. It's a total downer."

"No," I tell him, wanting to reach out to him. "It's what you do. And it's important. I'm glad you talked to me about it."

My hands are cupping my latte when Ben slides his right hand across the table and covers my fingers with his. It is such a minimal gesture and yet so intimate. A torrent of emotions races through my brain, fear and exhilaration topping the list, while at the same time, a completely physical electrical charge zaps through me, seeming to fire off every nerve ending throughout my body. If I were standing, I would have fallen to the floor in a heap of jellied, sizzle-fried limbs.

"Thanks, Ellen. You're a good listener."

My first instinct is to jerk my hand away, but Ben, perhaps sensing my distress, removes his hand before I am able to.

"I'm sorry," he says. "I'm really sorry. I shouldn't . . . It must be the sake."

My hands are suddenly cold, despite the fact that they are gripping my latte for dear life. I want to rewind ten seconds and feel his touch again, to experience that rush of warmth and electricity that has been absent from my life lately.

"It's okay, really." I laugh, trying to lighten the tension that hangs between us. "It's not like you reached out and grabbed my breast." *Oh my God. Did I just say that?*

But Ben lets out a hearty chuckle. "No. I would never grab anyone's breast in a Starbucks."

When his laughter dies away, an uneasy silence descends over us. He inspects his empty cup, then meets my eyes and I see that he is serious again.

"Ellen. This is weird."

My stomach flips over, not at the words themselves, but at the underlying message they convey.

He shrugs. "I haven't felt this comfortable with anyone for a long time."

"Me, too," I whisper because although I shouldn't admit it, it's true. He holds me in his chocolate gaze for a timeless moment, then takes a deep breath. He is about to say something, and I feel myself tense with anticipation.

And that's when my cell phone rings. Ben wordlessly exhales and with that breath, whatever he was going to confess disintegrates like steam in the air. I curse myself for remembering my cell phone, then remind myself why I'd made sure to bring it with me. In case my husband calls.

My husband. I remember him. The guy whose hands are the only ones I'm allowed to hold.

I reach into my pocket and pull out the damned intrusive device, then spy Jill's name in the Caller ID.

"Sorry," I say to Ben, then punch the Talk button. "Hi, Jill."

"Where are you? I called the house, but you didn't answer. I got worried that maybe you were the victim of a home invasion or something."

"I'm still downtown."

Ben leans back in his chair and casually looks around the coffeehouse.

"What? I thought you went over at five."

"I did. I'm still here. I, uh, decided to grab some dinner." I catch the grin on Ben's face and my cheeks go hot.

"Okay," she says slowly, suspiciously, because she knows

me so well. I have never been the kind of woman who likes to dine alone or go to the movies alone or take a trip to Barbados alone. Not because I worry about the pitying looks from fellow diners or filmgoers or tourists, but merely because it is less interesting. If I take a particularly delectable bite of seared foie gras, or watch a heart-pounding action flick, or gaze across at a perfect expanse of beach, I prefer to share it with someone. Plus, if you say aloud "That is amazing goose liver!" to an empty chair in a crowded restaurant, the maître d' might think you need a psychiatrist and eighty-six you from the place.

"Tell her I said hi," Ben calls as he gets up from his chair. He gestures to his coffee cup and then points to mine questioningly. I nod my head.

"Thanks."

"Who's that?" Jill pounces.

"Funnily enough, I ran into your next-door neighbor on Center Street."

"My what? My he-of-the-tight-buns next-door neighbor?"

"Exactly," I reply, trying not to look at his aforementioned ass as he deposits our empty paper cups into a trash can.

"His wife, too?"

"No. Just him."

"What the f-u-c-k is going on?" she nearly shouts, and I have to pull the phone away from my ear. Ben heads toward the table slowly, hands in his front pockets. Just the sight of his approaching visage makes my insides do a crazy happy dance. I feel lightheaded and giddy, am grinning stupidly, and have an overwhelming urge to cross my legs. Jesus, I'm fifteen again.

"Ellen? Are you there?"

"I'm here."

"Okay. Detroit has a morning game; he has to be on the

field by eight forty-five, so Greg and the boys will be out of here by eight thirty. You, *cousin*, are coming for coffee. Am I making myself clear?"

"I'll see if I can."

"Oh, nooo. You will be here at eight thirty-five. Not one d-a-m-n minute later. Yes?"

"Sounds great," I say into the phone, and end the call before she can ask any more questions or make any more demands.

Ben looks down at me. His placid face belies any intensity that might have sprung up between us only moments ago, as though it is already forgotten or has been deliberately suppressed. Whatever he was going to say to me is now lost forever. D-a-m-n Jill and her f-u-c-k-i-n-g timing.

"Think you can drive?" he asks me, and I nod quickly.

"For sure. In fact, after that latte, I'll probably be up all night."

"Me, too." It is a casual comeback, but I detect subliminal meaning. I get to my feet, clutching the bag of honey, and find myself face to face with him. We look at each other for a moment, another one of those damn romance-novel gazes that makes me want to throw my arms around his neck and suck his face for about twelve days.

"I'll walk you to your car," he says, quickly averting his eyes, then wordlessly escorts me out of the coffeehouse.

It is just after ten when we reach my car, parked on a side street at a meter that I didn't bother to refill, having temporarily been rendered brain-dead by a chocolate-eyed detective. I am greeted by the sight of a parking ticket in the form of a curled-up piece of paper trapped under my windshield wiper. Ben sees it at the same instant I do and automatically reaches for it.

"I completely forgot about the meter," I say dumbly.

"I'll take care of it."

I want to protest, but his jaw is set in a firm line. "Thanks," I say. "Gotta love those perks."

He nods and a small grin tugs at the corners of his mouth.

If we were single and twenty-two, this would be the point where I would hope he would ask for my phone number, or I would say something inane like, *This was great, let's do it again sometime*. Or he would lean into me tentatively and press his lips against mine. But twenty-two is a lifetime ago, and my wedding band weighs heavily on my finger, practically pulling my left hand to the ground. Still, I don't want to end this magical evening with just a *See you around* or *Catch you later*.

"So, I'll see you tomorrow," he says, and I give him a questioning look even as my heart bangs against my chest plate. "At the soccer game."

Duh, I think. "Right. Eleven o'clock."

"Well." He takes a step back. "You were right about the sushi. Thanks for keeping me company."

"My pleasure. It was fun." I watch him retreat, backing away so that he can continue to look at me even as the space between us widens. I know that this night has been a happy accident, a fluke, brought about by circumstances that will not be repeated, and for some reason that I don't quite understand, but which I'm certain I will contemplate later, I want the last thing he hears from me to have some meaning. *My pleasure, it was fun* just doesn't cut it.

As he is turning toward Center Street, I call to him. "Ben." Immediately he reverses direction and moves toward me. He cocks his head to the side and stares at me, waiting.

"Yes?"

I take a deep breath. "I really have to thank you."

"Hey, you introduced me to a great restaurant; the least I could do is pay."

"No, not for that," I say. "I mean, yes, thanks for the sushi, but that's not what I was talking about. Last week at Trader Joe's you said something that . . . struck a chord in me, I guess . . . and it inspired me. . . ."

He grins. "Wait. I said something inspiring? This has to be a first."

His self-effacing humor makes me smile, but I am not finished yet. "You were talking about trying new things. How important that is. And I realized that I haven't done that in a long time. Because of you, what you said, I, uh, did something I've never done before. Something new."

"What? Tell me."

I shake my head. "No. I'm not going to tell you. But I just wanted to say thanks."

"Oh, come on. You have to. You can't leave me hanging like this." His grin morphs into a lascivious smile. "Is it, you know, dirty?" He pronounces *dirty* with an Irish brogue and I laugh, shaking my head. "It's women, right? You tried women?"

"I said it was something *new*."

He cracks up at that. "*Really.*"

"Hey, all college girls experiment. They should offer a class in it. Girl-on-Girl 101." Suddenly self-conscious, I look down at my feet, at the pavement, at the parking meter, at the dry cleaners across the street. Anywhere but at him. "Anyway, it's not that exciting. It's not jumping out of a plane, or climbing Mount Everest, or anything. But it was new to me, and it felt good. Still does. So thanks."

My focus is now on a couple of teenagers hanging out on the corner fifty feet away, so I am surprised when Ben takes my hand in his. His touch is no less jarring than it was in Starbucks, and I watch as if in a dream as he raises my hand to his lips and kisses it softly.

"I appreciate you sharing that with me, Ellen," he says quietly.

Slowly, he lowers my hand and releases his grip. His gaze is penetrating and sears through me and in that split second, a series of images run through my head, a montage of Ben-and-Ellen fantasies that flash onto the movie screen of my brain so rapidly that they are indistinguishable from each other. And just as quickly, the screen goes dark.

I watch Ben walk away, this time facing Center Street instead of me, and this time, he does not look back.

Fifteen

When the key turns in the lock at eleven fifteen, I'm on the couch, Sally at my feet, staring blindly at the big-screen TV, which is playing an old Adam Sandler movie I've never seen. I have absolutely no idea what's going on because my brain has been busy processing the evening, reliving and dissecting every moment from when I first laid eyes on Ben as he listened to the street performer to watching him slowly retreat from my car.

Connor, Matthew, and Jessie appear at the archway into the living room, trailed by Jonah. My three children look tired yet energized by their evening out.

"Okay, guys, kiss Mom, and then straight to bed. It's late."

One by one, they come over to me and give me kisses. Jessie's eyes are already at half mast and I know she will be asleep within seconds of hitting her pillow. Matthew yawns right in the middle of kissing me, and I am treated to a sample of his ten-year-old pre-tooth-brushing breath. Connor bends over and gives me a hug, then kisses my forehead.

"How was it?" I ask.

"Awesome!" Connor exclaims.

"Totally," Matthew chimes in.

"Those guys are really silly," Jessie says with a giggle.

"You can give me all the details tomorrow," I say. "Right now, get some sleep." I pat Matthew on the behind as he turns away from me. "You've got a game in the morning, partner."

"I know," he returns in a weary voice.

Connor lingers as Jessie and Matthew make their way to the stairs.

"Thanks for letting me go," he whispers. I smile and ruffle his hair, then nudge him toward his siblings.

"Teeth," I order, watching the three of them as they trudge up the stairs.

"Yes, Mom," they say in unison. Jonah remains in the archway, also following their ascent with his eyes, then steps into the living room and heads in my direction. He glances at the TV, then squints at me.

"I thought you hated Adam Sandler."

"I liked *Wedding Singer*," I point out.

"This is *Happy Gilmore*."

"Right," I reply. "It's not too bad."

He perches next to me on the arm of the sofa as I grab the remote and pause the movie.

"The kids loved it, huh?"

"Oh, yeah. We had great seats. Three rows back, center. We missed you."

"I missed you guys, too." *Liar, liar, pants on fire.*

"Did you get the honey for Mom?"

"Yeah, it's in the kitchen."

"Great, thanks. So, you had a nice evening to yourself?"

"Mmm-hmm." I can't bring myself to look my husband in the eye, even though I have decided, after careful consideration, that I have nothing to feel guilty about. Ben and I behaved innocently, despite what might have gone through either of our minds. Despite what went through *my* mind. If there was a definite attraction between us, and at this point that is no longer an *if*, we resisted, ignored, and suppressed it, just like two honorable, respectable, moral people should.

So he kissed my hand, I tell myself for the tenth time. *It's not like he fondled my clitoris in the back of Starbucks.*

"Good."

"What?"

"Good. I'm glad you had a nice evening."

He sits quietly for a moment, gazing at the frozen image of Adam Sandler swinging a fist at Bob Barker. Then he returns his attention to me. I, on the other hand, am staring at the coffee table, my inner debate with myself continuing at full volume.

If he had tried to fondle my clitoris in the back of Starbucks, would I have let him?

That is the $64,000 question.

"We're okay, right?"

I turn toward Jonah but say nothing.

"I was a total shit the other day," he says, taking my hand in his. His hands are larger than Ben's, and rougher. I instantly put a stop to the comparison. It will lead to tragedy, I'm certain.

"I really am sorry. I know I said it before." This is to remind me that he is now apologizing for a *second* time, and I should be intensely grateful. And I am. Unlike many men, Jonah is great about apologizing.

"We're okay," I tell him, because, let's face it, after my

spending the evening in the company of another man, seriously flirting and indulging in luscious, albeit brief, fantasies, Jonah's behaving like a jerk kind of pales in comparison.

"I'm glad," he says. He bends over and kisses my cheek, and I feel the familiar and comforting chafe of his five o'clock shadow. "I didn't want to leave on Sunday without us resolving things."

"Consider them resolved," I assure him, and give his hand a squeeze.

"So." He glances back at the TV. "Are you going to watch all of this or come up?"

"I think I'll give it a few more minutes. Want to join me?" I ask this last because I know he wants me to; it serves as a confirmation that things really are back to normal. Of course, in reality, things are as far from normal as they ever have been within the construct of our marriage.

"It's tempting. You know how I love Adam Sandler. And this is a classic."

I pat the cushion next to me, but Jonah shakes his head. "I think I'll go check on the kids." Which is code for *As soon as I'm sure they're down, I'm going to crash*. I nod to him. "Don't stay up too late?" he adds.

"I won't." Just long enough to rehash my evening with Ben one more time, in an effort to defuse its power over me.

He releases my hand, stands, and makes a beeline for the stairs, turning back to me when he reaches the bottom. "Love you."

"Love you, too," I reply.

And then, the most unexpected thing happens. My cell phone, which I actually remembered to plug into its charger in the kitchen, makes a pinging sound that I have heard only once before when I accidentally accessed the ring tone menu.

"That's your phone," Jonah says as he steps onto the first riser. He stops and gives me a quizzical look. "When did you start texting?"

"I didn't." I set down the remote, push myself off the couch, and head for the kitchen. The phone's red light flashes conspicuously at me from the computer station and I move toward it as though it is a beacon. My fingers close around the phone and I think, *Could it be?*

I stare at the device, not lost in thought, but rather trying to figure out how to receive a text, since I have never done it before. When Jonah gave me the phone the previous Christmas, he treated me to a long and stupor-inducing dissertation on the infinite number of apps this particular model possessed. I had subsequently made it clear that I had no intention of texting anyone, *ever.* This led to an argument about the indisputable benefits of cell phones. How could I not be rapt with elation over possessing such an amazing piece of technology? Jonah even sank so low as to call me a dinosaur, which, since I hadn't really been paying close attention to his whole diatribe, offended me no end. I told him that he might as well have called me an elephant or a hippo or a cow, to which he responded that *dinosaur* was a comment not on my girth but on my archaic sensibilities.

Speaking of archaic sensibilities, I have to say that I am not enamored of my cell phone at all. In fact, I pretty much hate it. Of course this is something I dare not profess out loud, lest someone hear me and call the nearest insane asylum to alert them that there is a loony tune on the loose.

I remember a particular PTA meeting a few years back at which I confessed to Lila Bonaventura that I had accidentally left my cell phone at home. The PTA room went thunderously silent and all eyes turned toward me. Sixty faces regarded me wearing expressions of complete disbelief as though I'd just been caught fornicating in church or I had voted to let Susan Smith out of jail free. A moment later, when the moms returned to their tittering, Lila whispered to me, "Next time you should just say you dropped it in the toilet." As if I ever would take my cell phone into the bathroom with me. Jesus.

I know that they are great for emergencies, but I just don't understand why it is so imperative that we feel the need to be *reachable* every hour of every day. As far as I'm concerned, cell phones have changed our society for the worse. They allow people to ignore their own children and be unfailingly rude to cashiers and servers. I've read they cause brain tumors, to boot.

"Need any help?"

I jump at the sound of Jonah's voice.

"No," I lie. "I got it."

He watches me from the doorway as I follow the prompts on the screen and actually manage to get to my texts. Or, *text*. I do not recognize the phone number at the top of the box, but then, that's no surprise. Anyone who knows me knows not to text. I press the Select button and a message of only four words appears on my screen. My heart skips a beat and I tighten my jaw muscles to keep from smiling. Donning a mask of casual indifference, I look up at Jonah.

"It's one of those spam texts," I tell him. "I'm supposed to delete it, right?"

"Oh yeah. You can delete those. You know how to delete, right?"

I smirk at him and stick out my tongue. "Yes, I know how to *delete*."

"It's a miracle. See you upstairs." He disappears from view and I listen to his footsteps on the stairs. Once the floorboard of the second-floor landing creaks, I return my attention to my phone, ignoring the fact that I have just officially lied to my husband.

Thanks for tonight. B.

My hand is shaking as I depress the Menu button and choose Reply. A blank rectangle appears on my screen and I stare at it for a moment, considering my words. As I type, my fingers hit several wrong keys, and the resulting message is a garbled sentence that might mean something to an alien visitor. After backspacing to the beginning, I carefully reenter my reply, check it twice, then hit Send. It is a question: *How did you get my cell number?*

Not thirty seconds later, the cell vibrates against my palm and pings so loudly, I'm afraid Jonah can hear it from upstairs. I look down, a bubble of excitement bursting through me. *I'm a detective, remember?* I read, and, God help me, I giggle like a teenager. I only make a couple of mistakes the second time around: *How could I forget?* Thirty seconds later, *ping!* He writes: *The soccer team contact list.* I want to slap my forehead. Instead, I write back: *Duh. Must be the sake.*

He doesn't reply right away, and after a few minutes of standing in the kitchen staring dumbly at my phone, I pull out the chair at the computer desk and sit down. Another couple of minutes pass and I set my cell aside, trying not to wonder about his abrupt silence. Instead of allowing my mind to loop around that unanswerable question, I congratulate myself for diving into the texting world so quickly and easily. Of course, when properly motivated, I can pretty much do anything.

A full ten minutes stretch by, during which time I boot up my computer. I start up my browser and type in my blog's address. I had no intention of posting tonight, or even logging in to see the number of hits I've had or to read people's comments, but I am suddenly wide awake. I almost have myself convinced that I am *not* staying up in case Ben texts me again, but I probably wouldn't pass a lie detector test on that subject. Yet as I scroll through the comments left by a gaggle of readers, most of whom are supportive and complimentary, and see that I have almost a hundred thousand hits, I am overtaken by an emotion as powerful as the one I felt when Ben Campbell kissed my hand tonight. (Okay, maybe not *quite* as powerful, but close—and yes, that does say a lot about my life.)

Ellen Ivers has done something to be proud of, something she can point to and say without modesty, *I did that!* I know that for a woman, children are a great source of pride, and I am exceedingly proud of my children, but I have to share that success with Jonah. And really, I have always believed that being a good mom isn't something you should be proud of, it's just something you should *do*. But this blog is all me, and that fills me with a sense of validation and purpose that I thought I'd lost somewhere between diapers and Big Wheels and projectile vomit from a four-year-old's overindulgence in corn dogs.

I am a realist, so I am not blind to the fact that the *Ladies Living-Well Journal* has a readership in the millions, which makes my blog's hundred thousand hits proportionally low. Still, I am going to allow myself to feel like hot shit for a little while. It beats brooding over Ben Campbell and feeling guilty about Jonah.

I have just finished reading a touching comment about my meat-eating post from a reader who calls herself Cow-Lover when my cell phone pings. (I was prepared for the comment to be a scathing dressing-down on the perils of ingesting flesh, but apparently, CowLover is enamored of plate-sized portions of bloody beef and she wrote that if I am ever in Des Moines, she knows of a great steakhouse that serves forty-eight-ounce servings of prime rib and she would love for me to be her guest.)

I grab the phone and press the Menu button and the screen comes to life.

Sorry. Had to take a call.

No problem. Was just (I think for a minute) *revisiting that something new I told you about.*

My curiosity is getting the better of me. Not to mention my imagination.

It's not that exciting, I promise. You'd be disappointed.

Maybe someday you'll trust me enough to tell me about it. See you tomorrow.

Bye.

I read through our conversation, then plug the phone into its charger and set it next to the computer. I stare at my blog as thoughts both weighty and feather-light move through my mind. They tumble and turn over each other, threatening to give me a migraine. As if on autopilot, I scroll up to the menu bar of the blog and click the New Post tab. If my blog has become therapy for me, I desperately need some right about now.

. . . .

Ninth Post: March 24, 2012
SomethingNewAt42

THE FLIRTATION FACTOR

My nameless relative said something to me not long ago, and it went like this: "A little flirtation with someone who is not my husband is sometimes the only thing that gets me through the day." I think I am going to put that on a bumper sticker.

Experts say (and by experts, I mean *Cosmo*, of course) that flirting is healthy, something that all women should actively experience regardless of their marital status. It is as natural as breathing and as necessary to one's mental health as air is to one's staying alive. (I don't know if I believe this last, but who am I to question *Cosmo*?) For married women especially, flirting, and being flirted with, does wonders for our self-esteem. It lets us know that we are still desirable despite the sweat-sock fuzz between our toes that has replaced pedicure foam. Flirting is our God-given right to be completely ourselves instead of someone's wife or mother. And we must remind ourselves of who we are every once in a while or we may eventually be swallowed up by anonymity, never to be heard from again.

And the bottom line is that flirting is harmless. Or is it? The act of flirtation itself is harmless. Placing the emphasis on certain words, throaty laughter, witty replies, double entendres: very stimulating, yes. But where is the demarcation line between innocent flirting and adulterous betrayal? It's somewhere between batting your eyelashes at the male in question and mounting him in the back of a Starbucks. (I am speaking hypothetically, of course.) But the line is fuzzy and easily overlooked. You might not even be aware that you are crossing it, and then what do you do? Double back? Suppress the side of you that has just begun to make you feel whole and desired and good about yourself again? Life is so short, a roller coaster ride that is over before you can decide whether you've enjoyed it, and it is often devoid of surprises (particularly for marrieds). It just doesn't seem right to deny ourselves that small modicum of pleasure that doesn't cost us anything. Except when it does.

Let's take me, for example. For a long time, I thought my inner coquette had taken a permanent vaycay to the south of France, where her talents would come in handy, but I found out recently that she isn't gone at all; she's just been imprisoned deep within me. The thing is, when she reared her fabulous and perfectly coiffed head, perhaps I should have just pushed her back into the tiny cell I've been holding her in and thrown away the key. That sexy bitch is dangerous! She could get me in a lot of trouble. Now I have to figure out if there is a way I can use her for good instead of evil.

For a few weeks now, I have been involved in a flirtatious sparring match with someone who is not my husband and who is a bona fide hottie. Our repartee has renewed me. But I have begun to question just what the hell I am doing. When it began, it took me by surprise. I even questioned whether he was really flirting with me or was I simply making an ass out of myself. But it has now become clear that ours is a two-way tango, and I fear I might be starting something that I have no control over. There has been nothing untoward, no stolen kisses, no breathless whispers in each other's ears. But the idea of such things has bloomed in my head. It says somewhere in the Bible, don't ask me where, that the thought is as bad as the deed. If that is the case, I am pretty well screwed, especially since the Good Book also says *Thou shalt not commit adultery.* I have a sneaking suspicion that Jesus is not very happy with me right now.

The problem is I don't want to give it up. At the same time, I fancy myself a Good Wife, never having considered being unfaithful. And I am just obtuse enough to think that even now, I would never be unfaithful. But perhaps the flirtation factor opens the mind to the possibilities, and those who are weak cannot resist them. Knowing myself, and the ease with which I can fall prey to a carton of Ben and Jerry's

or a two-for-one special at Target, I should probably hand-
cuff the flirt and send her back where she belongs. My
nameless relative may be able to flirt with impunity and not
be in danger of crossing the line. Most women may be able
to do it, but I don't think I am one of them.

Damn. It was fun while it lasted. And that inner vixen of
mine is really going to be pissed when I slap the cuffs back
on her.

Almost groggy with fatigue, I rub my eyes, then click the
Publish button. I have no idea if the blog will make any sense
to anyone, but it doesn't matter. It makes sense to me, and
writing it has helped me realize what I have to do.

Starting tomorrow, I must keep my distance from Ben
Campbell. I have made my choices in life, and although I
didn't obsess over it at the time, when I got married, I promised to love, honor, and cherish Jonah. Flirting with other
men doesn't fit into any of those categories. Although it has
been innocent up to now, something changed inside me tonight when Ben kissed my hand. It became more real. I know
Jonah flirts with the girls at the office, customers, waitresses.
But he honestly isn't aware of it. And although many women
have sworn their mates would never cheat on them only to be
sorely disillusioned, I just don't think Jonah has it in him. It's
not so much his taking a moral or ethical stance as it is a matter of pride. He wants to be the eighty-year-old man in the
nursing home who is able to brag to his cronies that he never
cheated on his wife. Besides, Jonah is not good with duplicity, even on a minor scale. He once lied to me about finishing
off my Death by Chocolate cake, which I'd been looking
forward to all day. He pretended that one of the children ate

it. Not only did his face turn lobster red, but he tossed and turned all night, woke up in a cold sweat, and confessed to me at three o'clock in the morning. This is not a man who would do well at adultery.

I think about a line from *Titanic*. *A woman's heart is a deep ocean of secrets.* Yes, I know. You cannot get more cheesy. But it also strikes me as very true. There are many things, ideas, memories, feelings that I have never shared, nor ever will share with Jonah. They don't affect our relationship, but they make me realize that no woman is ever really *known* by her husband or partner. We *feel* things on every level of our existence and we connect to our feelings. Sometimes they are normal, sometimes overwhelming, and sometimes downright insane. But we own them. Men cannot understand these feelings, these interwoven connections we have to each other and the world around us. So it is better not to share them with the men in our lives. Men's thinking is more simplistic, linear. The past is the past. *Want food? Kill deer. Want sex? Club woman over head.* They don't tie emotions in to every situation and circumstance as women do.

Anyway, this *thing* with Ben, whatever it is, will go the way of my other secrets, wedged into one of the few remaining empty compartments of my heart. I will be able to pull it out from time to time, dust it off, and relive the way it made me feel, but only for a short while before I place it back where it belongs. Hidden.

I glance at my cell phone dispassionately, pick it up, and carefully delete each of Ben's texts. My phone pings as each text is swallowed into the vortex, and I force myself to feel good about my decision. It's the only sensible thing to do. It's the right thing to do. Stop it before it has the potential to become more than a *thing*.

My eyelids seem weighted with bricks, and when I close them, I instantly see a pair of warm chocolate brown eyes gazing at me. I want to melt into them, to be swept away . . .

No!

I open my eyes and see the faces of Jonah and the kids on my screen saver, smiling up at me. But even they, the most important people in my life, cannot overtake the image of Ben's gaze, which is now burned into my brain.

I quickly shut down and push away from the computer and make my way through a house full of shadows. Navigating blindly, I climb the stairs and move quietly down the hallway, stopping and looking in on my children, all of whom are clearly deep in REM sleep. Pushing through the door of the master bedroom, I hear Jonah's snore, which is softer than usual tonight. I wonder if he, too, is dreaming, and what images might be floating through his slumbering mind.

I head for the bathroom to do my ablutions.

Three minutes later, I pull back the covers and nudge at my husband, not caring that it is well past midnight. He can sleep when he's dead, right? He mumbles something that sounds like "I'll check the tuna cage" but I can't be sure. I give up nudging at him and slide my hand down his stomach, then slip it beneath his boxer shorts.

"*Wha?*" he croaks, and then his eyes open partway. "Hi there." His voice is a low rumble, heavy with sleep, but his cock is rock hard. "What're you up to?"

In answer, I mount him and ride him to within an inch of his life.

· Sixteen ·

There is nothing going on."

My words ring hollow in Jill's kitchen. I am seated at the counter with my cousin standing across from me, staring down at me like an interrogator from the CIA. I pray she doesn't have waterboarding in mind.

"*Really*," she says slowly.

"It was totally innocent." The defensive edge to my voice makes me cringe, and I take a deep breath. "We ran into each other. We were both free for the evening. We grabbed a bite to eat."

"Sushi," she states triumphantly. I shrug up at her. "Raw fish is a well-known aphrodisiac!"

"You're right!" I spout sarcastically. "That's why we ended up humping on a side of mackerel!"

"Ha ha."

"Jill, there was no humping or making out or anything else that I need to confess to you or anyone else."

She levels me with a knowing look. "Come on, Ellen. Something's going on. Look at you. It's eight forty-five in the morning and you're not wearing sweat pants, you have makeup on, and your hair doesn't look like you just went a round in the clothes dryer. This is not you!"

I detect a bout of indignation rising from within. I try to suppress it but without success. "Haven't you been paying attention? I am trying to reinvent myself. I am trying to look decent at all hours of the day. I've jogged off eight pounds! I've been making smarter food choices. I'm blogging every friggin' day! Why does any of this have to do with your next-door neighbor?" As the words pour out of me, I realize that I am talking to myself as much as to my cousin.

Jill looks appropriately chastised and taps a pink-lacquered nail on her coffee mug. "I'm sorry. You're right. You're look-ing great and feeling great and being creative."

"Thank you."

"But . . ."

I roll my eyes. "Oh, here we go!"

"No, seriously," she says. "In all the years that you've been married to Jonah, have you ever had dinner alone with another man? Someone not related to you?"

I don't even have to think about it. "No."

She crosses her arms over her chest and regards me accus-ingly. "I read your blog this morning."

I lean back against the hard wood of the stool and release a sigh.

"You say that nothing's going on, but you devoted an en-tire post to the fact that you've been flirting with this man for, what, two weeks now? And you never mentioned it to me? I'm not just your cousin. I'm your best friend. Why didn't you say anything?"

A few seconds pass before I answer her, and she waits

patiently. "I didn't mention it because I didn't want to make it into a big deal. I didn't even know we were flirting. I thought he was just being nice."

"But you know now."

I laugh. "Yeah. It was something about the way he fed me a piece of Yummy roll."

Her eyes go wide. "Oh my God!" she says.

"And he kissed my hand," I add, more for effect than anything else.

"Holy s-h-i-t!"

I can't decipher her expression. Consternation? Shock? Disillusionment? I expect her to launch into a lecture about how terrible I am and how I need to get myself together because this whole thing is just wrong, wrong, wrong. For Jill, the moral dilemma of adultery is overshadowed by the idea of the chaos it would unleash, like opening the door to anarchy and disorder, things she despises. She would never have an affair because she is not tolerant or capable of handling anything so messy. I am expecting a reprimand, deserving of one, even. But my cousin surprises me.

"I'm so jealous," she admits with a grin.

"Jill!"

"I *am*! Do you know what I'd give to have an attractive man feed me sushi? Hell, I'd be happy if my *husband* fed me sushi. Or anything, for that matter."

"Oh, cuz . . ."

"So what are you going to do?" Having now been let in to my confidence, Jill is bubbling with excitement and curiosity. I guess disorder and chaos are okay with her as long as they're relegated to *my* life.

"Nothing," I tell her, then quickly amend. "That's not true. I am going to keep as far away from Ben Campbell as possible."

She frowns. "Wow. Just when it was starting to get interesting. I thought I was going to be able to live vicariously through you for a while."

"Sorry to disappoint you, but it's the right decision."

"Yes, it is," she says. "But the right decision isn't always the *best* decision."

"What does that mean?"

Her face is thoughtful. "It's like you wrote in your blog. Life is short. And sometimes the *wrong* decisions can make the ride a lot more fun."

When I emerge from Jill's house twenty minutes later, I move purposely to my Flex, not even allowing myself to glance at the house next door. Just as I reach the driver's side, I hear a child's laughter and I can't help but look over. In the driveway of the Campbell home, Liam is pitching softballs to his little brother, Evan. Evan wears an adult-sized glove that is almost as big as he is, yet he manages to maneuver well enough to catch Liam's lobbed balls.

I watch the two for a moment, scrutinizing their features for signs of their father. Liam definitely favors Ben, and Evan his mom. I fleetingly wonder what Ben was like as a child, then quickly banish the thought from my mind.

"I'm gonna play for the Dodgers!" Evan yells at full kid volume.

"You are not," Liam chides. "You gotta be able to *hit*, you know."

"I can hit!" Evan shrieks.

"Can *not*," Liam fires back.

"I can hit *you*!" And true to his word, the boy makes a mad dash for Liam and tackles him to the ground, then starts swinging.

"Liam! Evan!" The sound of Linda's voice propels me into my car, and I just catch a glimpse of long blond hair as I stamp on the accelerator and head down the street.

Jonah, bless him, has made breakfast for the kids, and because of a slight culinary disability, breakfast means toaster waffles, a dish he only recently mastered. (I told him there were some microwave sausages in the freezer that I keep for emergencies, but he opted out, joking that he was considering becoming a vegan.) When I return from Jill's at nine thirty, the kids are fed and clothed, and Matthew is already wearing his soccer uniform. All three of them are safely ensconced in the living room for their Saturday morning allotment of Wii. I wave to them, then head for the kitchen, where I kiss Jonah and hand him a thank-you cup of 7-Eleven coffee. (I know he prefers Starbucks, but I am planning to avoid all Starbucks stores for the next, oh, twenty or thirty years.) He is grateful for caffeine in any form and returns my kiss enthusiastically.

"Thanks for taking the morning shift," I say sincerely.

He raises his eyebrows a couple of times and grins at me. "I should be thanking *you*. For last night?" He glances around to make sure none of the kids are within earshot. "You were a wild woman!" He sets his coffee on the counter, slips his arms around my waist, and peers down at me. "You were hot," he purrs.

"And you are to be commended for *rising* to the occasion even though you were dead to the world."

He winks down at me. "Anything for you, baby."

Suddenly, as I rest my head against Jonah's shoulder and feel him run his hands slowly up and down my back, I am filled with a sense of contentment. This is the Jonah and Ellen of old: flirty and sexy and *connected*. Whether this reappearance stems from my vow to abstain from Ben Campbell, or the fact that last night Jonah and I fucked like we were eighteen years old, I don't know. But I'll take it no matter the reason.

However, since life is, well, *life*, contentment lasts only so long. In *this* case it lasts about fifteen seconds.

"I have to go to the warehouse this morning," he says, giving my ass a double pat. As I pull away, Jonah drops his arms to his sides.

"You're not going to soccer?" I ask.

"Can't, Elle. One of my drivers screwed up a delivery and I have to go make it right. It's Fluor Corp., babe."

"Jonah, we talked about this . . ." And we had, at length. When Jonah first started with the company, he'd been working 24/7 in order to secure his position. He'd given up precious family time on the weekends to please his superiors and to show his customers how invaluable he was. In the beginning, he'd maintained that as soon as he was on stable ground, he would reclaim his weekends as his own. But after two years, he was still in absentia at the Ivers home on most Saturdays and quite a few Sundays, too. The kids were older then, and noticed how Daddy never made it to softball or soccer or tennis and could never volunteer for Scout camping trips. And I was starting to feel like a single mom. So I finally put my foot down.

I had tried for a civil discussion, but a heated argument ensued that prompted me to pull the kids out of school and take them for a spontaneous trip to my mother's house in Northern California. After three days, Jonah, having been haunted by the echoes of an empty house, called and apologized, asking me to come home and telling me that he'd realized just how much he was missing out on. He went on to promise me that he would make sure that weekends were sacred family time and he'd simply get his lowly assistant to handle Saturday and Sunday emergencies, because, by God, that's what they were paying him for.

"Why can't you get Shane to handle it?" I ask now. Shane of the high-top sneakers, bow tie, and Poindexter glasses fame who'd been to dinner once and was so flabbergasted by the frenetic energy of my three kids that he has never returned despite numerous invitations.

"Shane can't handle it. It's a corporate account," he reminds me for the thousandth time. "You know, the kind of account that allows you *not* to work?"

"I don't work?"

"You know what I mean."

"No, no, that's right. You go out to the coal mines every day, and I sit around and eat bonbons."

"Ellen. That is not what I meant. I know how hard you work running this household and raising our kids. It's the toughest job in the world."

All the right words are coming out of his mouth and in the proper order, but they sound more like a speech he's reading from a teleprompter. I cross my arms over my chest in response.

"But I work hard, too," he is saying. "I bust my butt to keep us in this five-bedroom house and I—"

"You want to move?" I snipe at him.

"Elle, you're missing the point! *My* job is what supports this family and we can't afford to jeopardize it."

"You're telling me that if you don't go to the warehouse this morning you're going to get fired?"

"It's a precarious time right now. You know what the economy is like . . . well, maybe you don't."

I snicker. "Because I don't listen to NPR?"

"Because you're not interested in anything going on in the world outside your home."

I feel my face go slack with disbelief. Jonah doesn't notice, just keeps charging ahead. "Times are tough and if my accounts aren't serviced properly, they'll give their business to our competitors."

"Fine." I try to infuse that one syllable with as much ire as I can.

"Look, it's *one* Saturday," Jonah says, placating, but I am still stunned by his earlier comment. Since when am I not interested in the outside world? *You should have seen me last night, Jonah, then you would have seen for yourself just how interested I am in things outside my home.* But, seriously, his biting words have cut me to the quick. This is the second time in the last week that he has purposefully been nasty to me. Since when did I become such an object of disdain to my husband?

My mother's words ring in my ears. "Familiarity breeds contempt, dear," she always says. Which is why, since she and my father divorced after twenty years of marriage, she has never allowed a relationship to extend past six months. (She is currently involved with her dentist, a nice man in his late fifties who happens to think the sun rises and sets with my mother's smile—which is quite wonderful. He has no idea that in about three and a half weeks, his world will be completely destroyed.) But Mom has no compunction about her choices. She wants to make sure that she is never on the receiving end of the loathsome epithets that people who are supposed to be in love tend to sling at each other. And now, I can finally see her point.

"I'll try to make it quick so we can have family time this afternoon," he adds.

"Whatever."

"Maybe I can take us out to dinner tonight."

"Okay."

I turn away from him and head for the sink where the dirty breakfast dishes stare up at me from their sudsy soak. Instead of loading them into the dishwasher, I begin to wash them by hand, hoping that the mundane task will calm me.

"You're pissed, I get it," he says from across the kitchen. I don't answer, not even with a one-word sentence. Because I am more than pissed. I am hurt.

"Look," he begins. I am expecting an apology, but he doesn't offer one. "I think you're being unreasonable, Ellen. I'm taking all of next week off to take the kids to Arizona." I snort derisively and Jonah responds with his own brand of antagonism. "Just because *you* don't want to come doesn't mean it isn't 'family time.'"

I keep my back to him, cannot bear the thought of looking at him. I slide the soapy sponge over a plate, then hold it under the faucet and watch the water rinse it clean. I set it in the dish drain and pick up another. I resist the impulse to turn around and fling the syrup-stained ceramic plate at my husband. He doesn't deserve such a dramatic display of emotion. He doesn't deserve a goddamn thing from me.

As I finish the last of the dishes, I consider tomorrow's blog post. This charming interlude with my supposed "life mate" has inspired a couple of choices for titles: *I Hate Jonah* or *Husbands Suck Ass*. Catchy, huh?

Regardless of the many untoward circumstances and seemingly earth-shattering occurrences that often plague us, like recognizing that deep down, your husband thinks you're an insipid freeloader, life marches on. Including soccer games. I have struggled to cast off the negative effects of my fight with Jonah for the benefit of my kids. I manage to keep from exploding all over Matthew for misplacing his cleats for the

fortieth time, stay calm when Jessie breaks my favorite brace-
let after insisting on putting it on my wrist, and merely shrug
when Connor tells me he'd rather go to Jason's house to
watch videos than go to the game.

It's as though I am on autopilot. Jonah's words are taking
center stage in my head, and everything I am doing is by
rote. Get kids in car, drop Connor at Jason's, park at soccer
field, unload kids and folding chairs, walk Matthew to his
team. By the time Jessie and I have set up our seats next to the
bleachers, I have the beginnings of a headache. Absently, I
wonder if eleven in the morning is too early to start drinking
and why didn't I load my thermos with vodka?

And then I see Ben. He is standing against the low fence
between the spectators and the field, listening to Nina Montrose, who is talking candidly about God knows what, her
fake tits nearly bursting from her low-cut sweater as she ges-
ticulates like a thespian. A surge of jealousy sweeps through
me, surprising me with its ferocity. Nina and her husband,
George, are separated and are apparently in the process of
splitting up their assets. (Rumor has it that George is demanding to get her tits in the settlement since he paid top
dollar for them.) For the past few months, Nina has been
flirting shamelessly with any person in a ten-mile radius who
happens to own a penis. (Yes, according to Jill, even women
with vibrators in their bedside drawers will do.) And now she
is casting her plastic, coquettish spell on my Ben.

My thoughts screech to a halt. *He is not* my *Ben*, I tell
myself. *He is* Linda's *Ben*. Linda, who I discover as I furtively
glance around, is nowhere to be seen. I direct my attention to
the field where the Polar Bears and their opponents, the Fire
Ants, are doing warm-up exercises. Jessie sits beside me,
completely engrossed in a Junie B. Jones book that she found
on Matthew's bookshelf (although he denies that a Junie B.

Jones book has ever been in his possession). I keep my gaze fixed on the field, willing myself not to glance over at Ben and Nina. However, like the T-rex whose eyes are drawn to movement, I cannot help but look over when, out of the corner of my eye, I catch Nina making a wide-sweeping gesture with her left hand that concludes with said hand landing on Ben's shoulder. She leans into him as he says something, and then she erupts into a fit of laughter, throwing her head back so violently I fear she might snap a vertebra.

My insides do another jealous dance as my fingers white-knuckle the armrests of my chair. I am feeling profoundly—and yes, irrationally—angry with Ben for allowing Nina Montrose to touch him. (And also having criminal thoughts about detaching Nina Montrose's hand from her bony arm with a machete—despite the fact that I don't own one.)

Ellen! my thoughts shriek. *Stop this nonsense.* I proceed to remind myself, yet again, that I am an almost-forty-three-year-old woman, not a high school freshman, and that even though I currently dislike my husband with the white-hot intensity of a thousand burning suns, I must stick to the decision I made last night. To steer clear of Ben Campbell. Who he flirts with is none of my business. Hell, he can screw half the soccer moms right there on the bleachers, and it will be none of my concern.

Just as I am about to yank my attention back to the field, Ben turns away from Nina and his eyes find mine. A smile of secret pleasure spreads across his face. Nina is chatting away, unaware of her prey's divided attention. Ben surreptitiously gives me an eye roll, then mouths the word *Help.*

Despite all of my good intentions, I feel my resolve start to slip. I bite my lower lip to keep from returning his smile and quickly turn my attention to the field.

As the players get into position for the starting kick, I steal a quick look at Ben. Nina is touching his arm again. I tell myself that this is not my problem and shift in my chair so that the two of them are out of my line of vision. A moment later, the whistle sounds and the Polar Bears face off against the Fire Ants, the field becoming a sea of thrashing ten-year-olds. And a moment after that, I feel the pocket of my jacket vibrate.

I withdraw my cell phone and gaze at the screen. A text awaits me. I glance at Ben and discover that he is now holding his cell in one hand while Nina continues to babble, probably about something like how great divorce is for your complexion.

Don't look at it, I tell myself firmly. *You know who it's from. Just put your phone back in your pocket and ignore it.*

Oh, who am I kidding? If curiosity kills the cat, then I am about to be buried in kitty litter. No matter how much I try to stop myself, I can't seem to keep from pressing the Retrieve button on my cell. I peer at the screen and read: *Who the hell is this woman?*

I laugh, but on the inside so as not to arouse suspicion. And before I have a chance to contemplate the fact that I am about to throw my resolution into the waste can, I reply.

Be careful of her. She's extremely dangerous.

With my peripheral vision, I see Ben peer down at his cell. A grin tugs at the corners of his mouth. He nods absently to the oblivious Nina as he nimbly types on his keypad. It takes a nanosecond for the message to reach my phone.

That's OK. I'm armed.

At this, I can't help but laugh out loud.

"What are you doing?"

I turn to see my daughter staring at me with an expression

of horror on her face. Feeling caught in this covert exchange by my eight-year-old, my throat goes dry and I am at a loss for a reply.

"Mom, you're *texting*!" She says this in the same manner in which she might say *Mom, your* head *just fell off!* or *Mom, you're growing another* boob!

"Yes, I am," I say nonchalantly as my pulse begins to even out.

"Since when do you know how to text?"

Since about eleven thirty last night?

"I know how to text," I tell her. "It's pretty easy once you get the hang of it."

"But you said you would *never* text," she says suspiciously, as though she might be addressing an alien creature who has invaded her mother's body. "Never *ever*, you said."

"Well, I am now." I smile at her and place a finger under her chin, hoping to dispel her fear that I am no longer her mother but an intergalactic being intent on taking over the planet. "I figured that if my children knew how to do it, then I should learn, too."

She squints at me, probably considering the truth of my words, then smiles back and gives me a thumbs-up. "Good for you, Mom. You're really doing it. I'm proud of you."

She wouldn't be proud if she knew exactly why, and with whom, I am texting.

"Is that Daddy?" she asks as if on cue. Not waiting for a reply, she says, "Tell him I love him."

As she returns her attention to Junie B., I think, ruefully, *Tell him yourself, Jessie.* Because I have no intention of ever speaking to her father again.

My cell phone vibrates in my hand and I glance at Jessie before retrieving the text. Satisfied that she is immersed in her book, I read the message.

Do me a favor. As inconspicuously as you can, call me. Please.

My heart skips a beat and I suddenly feel like Angelina Jolie in *Salt* (albeit with a bit more poundage and a lot less collagen) having been drafted for a covert op. I wrestle with myself for a mere three-point-five seconds about the fool-hardiness of granting Ben's request, but by the fourth second, I rationalize that I am simply doing a favor for a friend in need. I don't have to get close to him to answer his cry for help. I can maintain my distance and still do my altruistic duty.

Donning a casual expression, I slowly stand and stretch, then quickly peer at Ben. Nina has him backed against the fence, leaning into him with a decidedly voracious expression on her face. I yank my eyes off them and look down at Jessie.

"Want anything from the snack bar?" I ask and notice that my voice sounds unusually shrill. I clear my throat and try again. "Popcorn? Soda? Snickers?"

She squints at me. "Seriously?"

"Sure, why not?" I reply.

"Because you never let us have candy before noon and it's not even eleven thirty."

"Well, I can buy it now and you can wait a half an hour to eat it."

"O-kaaay," she says doubtfully. "Snickers. Please."

I nod and, clutching my cell phone tightly in my hand, head for the snack bar. Ten yards from my daughter, I punch in Ben's number and hit Send.

He answers before the first ring ends. "Ben Campbell."

"Hello, Ben. This is animal control calling. We hear you are currently being attacked by a hungry and dangerous cougar." Where did that come from? All I had to do was make the call, hang up, and let him take care of himself. But no, I have to go and make some cutesy comment. I mentally slap my forehead, but I do not hang up.

"Yes. That's affirmative," he says very seriously.

"Will a tranq gun be sufficient?" *Jesus, Ellen, just stop!*

"Um, that's a negative. The situation may require more force."

I hear a muffled sound, then Ben's faraway voice. "Sorry, Nina. I have to take this. See you later."

Relief surges through me as I end the call and pocket my cell phone. I helped Ben out and now I can go back to avoiding him. I reach the snack bar and make a show of perusing the offerings while at least a dozen kids elbow and shove at each other to get the cashier's attention. I stand well away from them, not wanting to get bruised and battered by their pressing need for hydrogenated fat, simple carbs, and Red Dye Number Forty. I glance up at the menu and realize that there is nothing for sale that even remotely fits in with my food regimen.

I feel his presence before he opens his mouth, and my whole body reacts as though I am a tuning fork that has just been tapped. I turn around and there he is, taking his place in line behind me.

"Thanks," he says, grinning crookedly. "She's, uh, tenacious. I thought I might have to draw down."

"You're welcome," I say, my voice neutral even though my insides are churning at his proximity. "Just doing my civic duty."

"You'd make a great secret agent," he jokes as he scans the menu. "What's her story anyway?"

"Soon to be divorced. Lonely. Horny." God, did I just say *horny* out loud? I quickly glance around to make sure the kids didn't hear me. But they are far too busy buying junk food to notice our conversation.

Ben is smiling at me. As if reading my thoughts, he says, "I think they all know what the word means."

"I just don't want them to think *I* know what the word means."

"But you do, don't you?"

Oh shit. Danger, danger, Will Robinson.

"I have heard it used on occasion," I say, returning my attention to the menu, where it belongs.

Ben takes a step closer to me and I can feel the heat of his body. If I were to lean back a couple of inches, I would be pressed against his chest. I don't move, don't flinch, but I realize with crystal clarity just how much I am craving contact with this man. I step forward a few inches, pretending interest in the display case, but Ben closes the distance with a step of his own. I keep my eyes glued on the snack bar.

"Last night was fun," he says in a low voice only meant for my ears. I nod, but don't turn to him. I am suddenly worried about the inquiring minds of all of the people around me: friends, acquaintances, fellow soccer parents, even the children. Anyone looking at us, at this moment, would simply see two grown-ups standing in line chatting. But there is more to it than that, and I am afraid that if I smile too much or make a familiar gesture toward Ben, everyone will know what's going on.

But nothing is going on, I remind myself. And I'd believe it, too, if it weren't for the fact that I am suddenly perspiring and feel the need to clamp my thighs together because of Ben's proximity.

"Come on, guys!" the older woman behind the counter barks. "You have ten seconds to decide! There are other people waiting!"

This is Doris, the snack bar empress, a petite yet overbearing sixty-something who has made it her life's work to send Little Leaguers and soccer players down the road to juvenile diabetes. At her coarse command, the kids quickly make up their minds and hand over their parents' cash for their desired treats. A few seconds later, they disperse, leaving Ben and me alone in front of the counter. Doris stares at us expectantly.

"What'll it be?" she demands.

Ben ushers me forward and I step up to the counter.

"One Snickers."

"It's so satisfying," Ben singsongs.

"For Jessie," I qualify, feeling the need to make it clear that junk food never passes my lips. "And a bag of M&Ms. For Matthew."

"What about for you?" Ben asks, sidling up to the counter.

"I'm good," I tell him as I withdraw a couple of singles from my pocket.

"I know you are," he says with a smile, and I can feel Doris's speculative gaze on the two of us as she lays my bounty on the counter.

"I'll take some Corn Nuts and a Diet Coke, please," he says to her, bestowing upon her one of his most ingratiating smiles. She doesn't look impressed by either his smile or his manners, but merely scowls at us. "And just add all of it together."

"No, no," I say, proffering up my bills.

"It's the least I can do. You saved me from a most unpleasant experience." He places a five on the counter, which Doris snatches up, then hands me my candy and grabs his Coke and Corn Nuts. We move away from the snack bar as a new herd of children scrambles toward it.

"Thanks."

"No problem," he replies.

We walk slowly toward the field, and I realize that every

time I attempt to put space between us, someone passes on either side of us or we have to narrow the gap to avoid an obstacle like a trash can or bicycle or a soccer bag. It feels like we are magnetized to each other, and I am powerless to fight it. Okay, that's a fib. *Unwilling* to fight it. As we maneuver through a crowd of players listening to their coach, Ben's free hand brushes against mine and I can't help but recall the way he kissed it last night.

"Where's your husband? Jonah, right?" His question is casual, but it makes me tense nonetheless.

"He had to work."

"Sore subject?"

I hadn't meant to sound curt or angry, but apparently my ire has seeped through.

"Um, a little. Where's Linda?"

"At home with Evan. He says he has a sore throat."

"You don't believe him?"

"There's a new episode of *Imagination Movers* on today." I nod knowingly. "Ah."

"*I think what the situation needs is some imagination!*" he sings loudly enough to make a group of parents in the parking lot turn and gape at him. "Don't worry, folks, I'm all right," he calls to them, and I have to laugh.

We stop at the outside edge of the field and I check to make sure Jessie is where I left her. There she is, curled up in her red chair, nose in her book. I see that the game is in progress and we have made it back just in time to catch Matthew successfully (if uncharacteristically) pass the soccer ball to Liam.

"All right, Matthew!" I cheer, then watch as my son trips over his own feet and takes a flying header onto the grass. Liam, who has already scored, trots over to Matthew and helps him up, then slaps him on the back enthusiastically and holds up his fist for a knuckle bump. I read Liam's lips well enough to ascertain that he is complimenting Matthew on his pass. Matthew, whose face is bright red with embarrassment from his fall, allows himself to smile and return Liam's knuckle bump.

"You have a nice boy there," I tell Ben, meaning it.

"Yeah, he's a good kid," he replies, then takes a long swallow of his Diet Coke. We stand in companionable silence for a few minutes watching the game. Our arms are inches apart, and I swear the hair on mine is sticking straight out as though I'm in the middle of an electric storm.

"So what are you doing for the break?" he asks, tossing his spent Coke into the nearby trash can. "Anything fun?"

"I have a very detailed agenda," I say. "Starting with the upstairs closets and moving down to the garage."

"Sounds exciting," he teases.

"It's spring," I remark. "You know? Spring cleaning. Plus, it's the only time of the year that I can throw out my kids' junk without them knowing."

I glance up at him to see that he is peering at me speculatively.

"Jonah's taking the kids to his parents' in Arizona," I explain. "They leave tomorrow."

"A week on your own!" He laughs. "How will you ever manage?"

"Six days, but who's counting?"

A whistle sounds and the players march to either side of the field for halftime. I catch sight of Matthew scanning the crowd for me and I raise my hand to wave at him. He smiles as though he is genuinely enjoying himself, and I feel something pluck at my heart strings. Thanks to Liam's generous spirit, Matthew finally feels like he belongs on the soccer field. I give him a thumbs-up and he returns it, then hurries over to the huddle, wedging himself next to Liam, who immediately moves to give him space.

"What about you?" I ask. "Is your family doing anything for the break?"

"Actually, I'm kind of in the same boat as you. Linda's parents offered to take the boys to San Diego for a few days. Sea World, the zoo, Balboa Park. They'll be so overstimulated by the time they get back, we'll have to put them on Ritalin."

"Wow. A couple of days without your kids. Sounds romantic."

I regret my words as soon as I see the look on his face.

"If only," is all he says.

A question about the state of his marriage is on the tip of my tongue, but I bite it back.

Stop, Ellen. It's none of your business.

"Anyway, I do have something fun planned for me. It's, uh, *something new*." He looks at me for a second too long, and my legs threaten to morph into Silly Putty. "You said last night that doing something you've never done before felt really good."

A thrill races through me as he recounts my words from the previous evening. Knowing that someone—especially an attractive man—has really listened to you and remembered what you said is pretty exciting. I can't recall the last time I was certain that Jonah was actually listening to me. Years ago, maybe. And, truth be told, I was probably deluding myself back then, because every single time we had one of those deep, meaningful conversations that lasted for hours, we ended up having sex. Looking back now, I realize that Jonah could have been faking it, pretending to give good ear, in order to get laid. Well, I occasionally fake orgasms, so I guess it serves me right.

"What do you say?" Ben asks, pulling me back to the present. I guess I'm not such a great listener myself.

"I'm sorry. What was the question?"

He laughs. "I was asking if you'd like to try something new with me."

The entirety of the Kama Sutra does a sprint through my brain, and I shake my head to clear it.

"No, huh?" Ben says, mistaking my head shake for a negative. I should let him think that I'm saying no. Because whatever it is, whatever "something new" he has in mind—and I know it's not related to sex or he would never have asked—I shouldn't, should *not* do it. No way, never, not a chance, in that order.

"What is the something new?" I really need to buy myself a muzzle.

"I'm going to learn to surf," he declares proudly.

I give him a wide-eyed stare. "Surf."

"Yup."

"I'm surprised you don't know how already."

"Hey, I grew up in the Midwest. The only waves in Indiana are the—"

"Waves of grain," I finish for him, and he smiles.

"You're quick," he says, tipping an imaginary hat toward me. "I've always wanted to learn. There's something about it that seems so, I don't know. Freeing, I guess."

"A surfing detective." I grin. "Sounds like a movie I saw once."

He matches my grin. "*Point Break*. Only they were feds. I saw that movie about twelve times. Of course, if you repeat that to anyone, I'll have to kill you. My wife doesn't even know that about me."

A tendril of pleasure uncurls in my stomach and I have to suppress a giggle. "Your secret is safe with me." I don't mention that I also watched *Point Break* more times than I can count, having had a huge crush on Keanu Reeves at the time.

"I'm going to start with stand-up paddleboarding," he continues. "It's the latest thing, apparently. One of my new co-workers told me about this place in the marina that rents all the gear."

"Well, good luck to you."

"You don't want to try it?"

"Uh, no," I answer.

"You should. You look like you have good balance. I bet you'd be great." His eyes sweep over me, and I shiver involuntarily.

"You do know it's March," I say quickly, rubbing the gooseflesh that has popped up on my arms. "The Pacific Ocean is freezing this time of year."

"Nothing a little wet suit can't fix."

Yes, I think. *Problem is, my wet suit wouldn't be* little. *Plus, I'd have to shave my legs, unless I wore the kind that goes to your ankles. Then I could get away with just shaving my feet. I would definitely have to get a pedicure. . . .*

"Be-en!" comes a woman's siren call from somewhere to our right. Nina Montrose nearly falls out of the bleachers in her haste to get to him, smacking Rita Halpern so hard in the right eye with her pointy breasts that I fear Rita might be rendered blind.

"Jesus ever-loving Christ!" cries Rita. "Those goddamn tits are dangerous!"

"Rita! There are children present," Tina Sinclair admonishes from the front row.

"Well, keep them away from Nurse Ratched!" Rita fires back. "Someone could lose an eye!"

Nina is totally oblivious to her less-than-graceful bleacher dismount. Breathless, shameless, she stalks right over to Ben, who is looking at me with an expression one might wear when heading to the firing squad. I smile sweetly at him and watch as he paints on a pleasant face.

"Oh, hi, Ellen." Nina acknowledges my presence with a quick turn of her head, but her attention is unabashedly on Ben. "Is everything okay with work?" she asks him in a throaty, conspiratorial whisper.

"Yes, fine, Nina, thanks," he replies, his smile glued in place.

"So where is the little woman?" Nina asks without a hint of self-consciousness.

"Home," is all Ben offers.

"You know, that's how my marriage fell apart." Her voice is steeped with false regret. "My soon-to-be-ex-husband stopped coming to all of the games, then all the school functions. I thought he was working, but he just didn't have any interest anymore. Not in the kids, and not in me." Her lower lip starts to tremble and I suddenly feel like I am about to puke. "Anyway," she sighs. "I'm sure your marriage is just fine."

To his credit, Ben doesn't take the bait, merely crosses his arms over his chest and peers out to the soccer field. "Marriage can be tough," he says noncommittally.

"Amen," I agree under my breath, but Ben catches it, and I feel his speculative gaze turn toward me.

"Excuse me," I say quickly, sidestepping away from the two of them. "I have to deliver a candy bar before my daughter goes hypoglycemic on me."

Nina's eyebrows slam together in puzzlement, battling with her Botox, and I realize I have just used a five-syllable word in front of a woman who can barely spell her own name. Oops. I shrug and head over to Jessie, leaving Nina to slobber all over Ben.

"Stand-up paddleboarding," Ben calls to me, and I give him a two-finger wave without turning back.

I reach Jessie and lower myself into my seat, absently handing over the Snickers. Her eyes go wide at the sight of it.

"King size!" she exclaims reverently. "But, Mom, it's only like eleven thirty-five." She clutches the candy bar to her chest like a precious gift. When Doris had laid it on the counter, I hadn't noticed that this particular Snickers bar was the size of an SUV. I contemplate taking it back from my daughter. Surely it will lead to a sugar high of rehab proportions, but instead I merely shrug.

"It won't kill you to eat it before noon," I tell her, and she smiles beatifically.

"Thanks, Mom."

Watching the two teams jog to their places for the start of the third quarter, I hear the crinkling of the candy wrapper as Jessie strips the Snickers bar naked and takes a huge bite.

My eyes are on the field, but my thoughts are roiling and bubbling like a pot of stew on high heat. Why, oh why, didn't I stick with my resolution to stay away from Ben Campbell? Now look what's happened. He has just given me a bona fide invitation. Not a lewd and indecent suggestion that I meet him at the Motel 6 on Steinway, mind you, but an invitation nonetheless. Our meetings up to this point have been the result of random encounters, fate having its way with us. But an invitation is different. It is premeditated, an assignation, a—dare I say it?—a date. This is not running into each other at Ikea and grabbing a soda.

True, I did decline his offer, but before I go and pat myself on the back for my restraint, I must consider the fact that I have absolutely no desire to go stand-up paddle surfing (except, of course, to see Ben Campbell in a skintight wet suit). But how, I now ask myself, would I have responded if he had suggested something that *did* interest me, like, say, a day at a swanky spa or a trip to a vineyard for a wine tasting? I'd like to think my answer would have been the same. But if I am completely honest with myself, I'll admit I am not sure.

I have always considered myself a good person. Not Mother Teresa or Joan of Arc, maybe, but a decent woman with solid ethics and a sound moral compass. I always make the right decisions on the big stuff. And I know that this is part of my appeal as a wife, mother, friend, and person. Good old dependable Ellen. But the bottom line is that I have never had a moral dilemma shoved so squarely into my face before now. It's easy to say *I would never take a life* when you've never had someone threatening to harm your children. It's easy to say *I would never knock over a liquor store* when you've never been a slave to crystal meth. And it's a no-brainer to declare *I would never cheat on my husband* when you've never had a complete hunka-hunka show a heart-stopping amount of interest in your bod.

I would have thought that at the ripe old age of almost forty-three, this situation couldn't possibly crop up. Back in my thirties, maybe, when my waist was a bit smaller and the skin on my neck hadn't yet started its downward journey. I honestly believed that once I hit the big 4-0 I'd be immune to this kind of temptation, if for no other reason than the fact that men in their forties and fifties who are having a mid-life crisis or looking to stray tend to do so with twenty-somethings whose tits point skyward and who don't know the meaning of the word *Reaganomics*. And forget about getting propositioned by a younger man when you're in your forties, unless he happens to be European or you happen to be Demi Moore. So, really, I thought I had safely made it past this particular situation.

I hazard a glance over my shoulder and am surprised to

see Ben laughing at something Nina is saying. And his laughter appears natural, not forced or phony. Immediately, I feel my hackles rise, then subsequently chide myself for my stupidity at having ruminated so dramatically over something that probably isn't even valid. Ben Campbell isn't after me. How could he be? I mean, seriously. Look at me. If this handsome, charming hunk of burning passion were looking to cheat on his wife, and that's a big *if*, he wouldn't set his sights on a perfect candidate for *Extreme Makeover*. He'd be more likely to choose someone like Nina. And who could blame him? She's not twenty-four, but her boobs definitely face the stars. And from what I've seen of her, Nina has no moral compass whatsoever. She'd drop and spread 'em without hesitation. That kind of characteristic goes a long way in the *Cheating Husband's Handbook*. In fact, he's probably inviting *her* to stand-up paddle surf at this very moment. The skinny bitch. And the superficial adulterous cad.

Wait! Here I go again, letting my thoughts run wild. They ought to have a support group for people who are addicted to creating wild scenarios in their heads and mentally dissecting every last nuance of every single moment, like I've been doing since I met Ben Campbell. They could call it the Walter Mitty Clinic for Delusionals and Serial Overthinkers. I could be their first patient, with the caveat that I simply must be treated with Class A drugs.

I steal another look at Ben and Nina, and now they are both watching the game, side by side, casually conversing like two soccer parents. They are not copulating against the back of the bleachers, much as Nina would like to be. Ben is simply being nice to her, just as he has been nice to me this whole time. Because he is a nice man. Not because he has ulterior motives. Nor does he harbor any lascivious underpinnings. The sushi feeding was due to the sake. The hand-kissing was due to old-fashioned chivalry (and probably the remnants of the sake). The invitation to stand-up paddle surf was just that, nothing more.

As the soccer game plays out in front of me, and my daughter chews her Snickers bar enthusiastically beside me, I try to put a name to the emotion washing through me. Relief. Yes, that's it. Although the realization that I am not the object of someone's desire is a blow to my ego, I have to admit that safety has its rewards. I don't have to worry about making a tough choice. I don't have to worry about smashing my own moral compass. I don't have to think about the consequences of doing something extraordinarily stupid. On paper, it sounds exciting, like the perfect antidote to the crushing boredom I've been experiencing lately. But in reality, it is far too complex an issue for me to contemplate. Especially since I suspect that given the chance, I might just blow my reputation as the good girl straight to hell.

"Want some?" Jessie asks me, holding out the mammoth chocolate bar.

I am suddenly ravenous for something that is bad for me. I grab the Snickers, break off a chunk, shove it into my mouth, and laboriously chew, anticipating the sensual contentment that chocolate promises.

Okay. It's *not* so satisfying. But at the moment, it's all I've got.

· Seventeen ·

Jonah's master plan was to be on the road by five A.M. in order to reach his parents' house in time for lunch. But by six twenty-two, he is still scrambling to get his shit together. Having fulfilled my motherly obligations the night before, making sure Connor had his nasal spray (which staves off his nosebleeds in the dry Arizona climate) and Matthew had his clean underwear (which he always forgets to pack) and Jessie had her matching Hannah Montana shirt, jacket, and socks ensemble (which she can't go anywhere without), I am now seated at the kitchen table, leisurely drinking my first cup of coffee, listening to the *thump thump thump* of my husband stalking through the second floor in search of all of the necessary items for his six-day sojourn. Normally, I would be helping him, cutting his prep time in half, as I know where everything is. But since he did not offer me an apology for yesterday morning's noteworthy display of animosity and disdain, I have not offered him one iota of assistance.

A half hour later, I stand in the driveway, faithful Sally sitting beside me, mournfully gazing up at me with her watery brown eyes as though wondering where her family is going and why are they going without her. My groggy children take turns kissing and hugging me good-bye as Jonah waits by the driver's door of my Flex, which is packed to bursting. He impatiently glances at his watch, and instead of hurrying the kids along, I leisurely grab each of them and give them a second hug, telling them to be on their best behavior for Grandma and Grandpa. Then I watch as they all climb into the car and take a few minutes to get situated.

Jonah looks at me, and I can tell he is waiting for me to give him some kind of sign that I want to kiss and hug him as well. Usually, no matter what state of conflict the two of us are currently embroiled in, we make a point of kissing good-bye and telling each other *I love you*—just in case, you know, one of us gets hit by a truck or struck by a bolt of lightning during our separation. But not this time. I fold my arms over my chest and glare at him.

"I'll call you when we get there," he says.

"Fine."

He gives me a curt nod, then gets behind the wheel and closes the door. I fleetingly wonder if Jonah and I have reached a crossroads in our marriage and whether we'll be able to find each other again, to actually *like* each other again. It doesn't feel like it right now, but I also know that marriages float on a changing tide, sometimes a lazy current that brings you safely into harbor, and sometimes a violent wave that catapults you straight into a rocky bed and pulverizes you. I can't help but question which way the tide is turning for us.

A sudden stab of regret slices through me as I watch Jonah tug at the safety belt and buckle himself in. What if he *does* get struck by lightning? What if this is the last time I ever see him alive? What would his last thoughts of me be just before he drifts off into the light?

As he starts the engine, I walk over to the driver's window and softly rap my knuckles against the glass. He looks up, surprised, then lowers the window.

"Have a good trip," I say, then bend down and give him a light peck on the cheek.

"Thanks." He doesn't smile, but I can tell he is relieved by my paltry offerings. "Go easy on the Lexus, okay?"

"What, no drag races?"

"Just keep the hairpin turns to a minimum."

I allow myself to grin, and Jonah follows suit.

"I love you," he says, and I know he thinks he means it, just as most people in their second decade of marriage believe they mean the words that automatically tumble out of their mouths.

"Love you, too," I return, because although I'm not feeling it right now, somewhere deep down inside me, it must be true. At least, I hope to God it is.

By eight thirty, I have done four miles on the treadmill; taken a leisurely shower, during which I actually shaved my legs from my toes to my thighs (little do I know I will be inordinately happy about this in roughly six hours); have brewed an entire pot of coffee for my own consumption (how decadent is that?); have roamed through each and every room of my blissfully empty house; and am now seated in front of my computer, waiting for it to boot up.

I already know what today's post will be about, having decided upon it the moment my Flex turned off our block and my six days of Me Time officially began. When I log on to my blog, I bypass the dashboard and immediately begin typing in the new post, not bothering to see how many hits I've garnered or to scan the comments posted by readers. These things make no difference to me anymore. I couldn't care less whether I win the damn competition. The process itself has become the thing. The rhythm of my writing, the consistency of my words, the discipline of creating a new piece of prose every day, no matter how sophomoric it may seem to me. These things are what matter to me now. I have recaptured a part of myself that I thought was lost. No matter what Jonah thinks, I am a writer. By trying something new, I have rediscovered something old. Something, I realize, that has been dying to be set free.

I have no idea where this literary reincarnation will lead; whether I will be an amateur blogger for the rest of my days, or finish my novel, or get a job on the local paper. But I do know that I will keep writing, just for me.

As I write, I am basking in the knowledge that I am alone in my house. No one will pop his or her head into the kitchen asking for a snack. I won't be summoned to break up any fights. I won't be interrupted by my shrieking daughter as she searches for her missing Silly Bandz or by Matthew wailing about his dead goldfish, or by Connor demanding more time on the Wii. For six full days, no husband will ask if I picked up his shirts from the dry cleaner or noisily rifle through the fridge for leftovers. This state of being is as close to heaven as it gets. And it is exactly what informs my blog.

Tenth Post: March 25, 2012
SomethingNewAt42

THE EMPTY NEST

Everyone has heard the term *empty nest*. Books have been written on the subject. It's been the focus of *48 Hours* segments, sitcoms, and those Hallmark movies starring middle-aged B-list actresses that my nameless relative absolutely adores. A lot of time and energy is spent on understanding and dealing with this particular phase of a parent's life. And I have one question in response to all the hoopla: Why?

Okay, I haven't yet experienced it firsthand. My kids are all still under my roof, and will be for the next ten years, so it might be that I am, as my friend Mia would put it, talking out of my ass. But speaking as someone who treasures every single moment of preternatural quiet that is so graciously bestowed upon me every time my husband and children leave the house, I just can't understand the problem. I look forward to my children growing up and getting the hell out of my house. I just wish there were some way, when they do, that they could take my husband with them.

It's not that I don't love them with all my heart, I do. And it's not that I won't miss them, in that Stockholm syndrome kind of way, because I will. But I will have no problem finding other ways to fill my time besides being a maidservant to the whims of three needy, egocentric midgets. I am not being nasty here, just stating a fact. Children are by nature self-involved, as they should be at this time in their lives, before they are forced to learn the definitions of words like *responsibility* and *independence*. And I am not complaining about a mother's 24/7 subservience, either. I am happy to be a servant, as became my obligation the moment my husband's sperm burrowed its way into my egg. I am just saying that when this whole slave labor thing is over, I won't shed too many tears about it.

I have a couple of friends whose children have gone away to college and, although they have read the books and, in one case, even undergone therapy, they still can't come to terms with the fact that they are no longer needed on a moment-to-moment basis. They complain about the echoing silence that bounces off the walls of their empty houses as they wander aimlessly through their days. I would like to offer them the following advice: Turn on the TV—you get to watch whatever you want, girl! Crank up the stereo with that 80s pop music that your kids thought was crap! Dance naked through your living room—yes, naked! Make a dinner that consists only of pâté and smelly cheese! You can do it! You have the freedom to do anything you want now! Grasp that freedom with both hands and run with it.

Oh, and by the way, your kids still need you. You'll see them every weekend when they bring home four sacks of laundry and a raging appetite. (Unless they've moved to another state, in which case they'll call you to send them money for books—yeah, books, right!) I don't think we ever stop needing our parents. Even at my age, my mother always gives me the best advice, the best support, the best encouragement of anyone in my life. A few years ago, I even recorded her talking, just in case something happened to her, so that I would always be able to hear her voice when I needed it. So stop pacing your empty house and bemoaning your children's absence. They still love and need you; they just do so from the lovely distance of their own, grown-up lives. Stop crying and go do something! Get a job.

And by the way, according to a recent census, a great number of children are returning home after college, so, probably, by the time you have settled into your new life of emancipation, they'll be knocking on your door with their suitcases at their feet, calling you Mommy even though they are now the proud bearers of university diplomas.

My own kids are on a trip with their dad for six whole days. It's not a permanent situation, but I intend to milk it for every dancing-naked, stereo-cranking, favorite-show-watching moment it's worth. When they return, I will welcome them with open arms and celebrate their presence in my house, but within days, when the sounds of screaming and fighting swirl around me, and the mounds of laundry pile up, and I am told on a weekly basis that I am hated for one transgression or another, when I am spread so thin from racing from one activity to another that I wish I had a couple of clones, a small part of me will mentally count the months, weeks, days, and hours before I get to send them on their way again.

Empty-nesters, you don't know how lucky you are.

. . . .

After posting my blog, I spend the rest of the morning ransacking my closet, the first job on my list because it is the hardest for me to tackle. It is far easier to go through my children's closets with a garbage bag, mindlessly chucking out anything I haven't seen them use/wear/play with for the last year. But my own closet is a different story. How many times have I withdrawn that size six pair of Calvin Klein jeans I wore on my honeymoon and set them on the pile meant for Goodwill, only to return them to a hanger and place them between the size six cocktail dress I wore to my wedding rehearsal dinner and the size four capri pants I fit into just after a particularly nasty bout of salmonella? For me, letting go of those jeans, and the dress and the capris, signifies letting go of the woman I used to be and accepting the fact that I will never be that woman again. I liked her. She was recklessly optimistic about life and its possibilities. She knew what she wanted and wasn't afraid to do whatever it took to get it. She was sure of herself and secure with her place in the world. She was young.

With my hands on my (size eight) hips, I stand and gaze upon these items that have had an almost magical hold on me. For a long time, I believed that if I could fit into those clothes, I would be *that* Ellen again; by buttoning up the fly, or easing the zipper into place, I would suddenly cast off the ravages of time and be transformed. Slowly, as I run my fingers over the familiar fabric, it dawns on me that my beliefs were merely illusions birthed by a woman who had lost herself and wasn't sure whether she would actually like herself if she was ever found.

One by one, I ease the capris, the cocktail dress, and the Calvins off their hangers, carefully fold them, and set them into a half-filled box labeled *Goodwill*. I wait a moment, anticipating that twinge of regret that will cause me to grab the clothes and return them to the safety of my closet, but I find that I have no urge to rescue them this time. It is not because I have let go of ever becoming that woman again, but because I now realize that I *am* that woman. Older, certainly more rounded, a few battle scars here and there, but the same woman nonetheless. The wrinkles and pounds may blur the image, but they do not erase the person at the core. I now know that being optimistic, having self-confidence, knowing what you want and getting it are choices that we have to make every single day.

My reinvention, I finally understand, is not about becoming someone new. It's about taking the Ellen of yesterday and the Ellen of today and blending them, so that the Ellen of tomorrow will be the best of both. This knowledge doesn't slam into me like an epiphany, just eases through me like an IV drip. As I lift up the box, my eyes find my reflection in the mirror on the back of the closet door, and to my delight, I like the woman I see staring back at me. She looks confident. She looks strong. She looks like me.

It may well be that this new round of self-assurance and self-love is the result of endorphins, but what the hell? I'll take it where I can get it. Besides, endorphins are a lot cheaper than Lexapro.

Just as I start down the stairs with the Goodwill box in tow, I hear a familiar voice call out from the entry hall.

"Hell-ooo! I'm home!"

I reach the landing just in time to see Mia, a vision in purple, disappear into the kitchen, singing an old blues number with her rich contralto pipes. Her arrival is not unexpected, even though we have not had so much as a phone conversation since book club last Friday. Every year, from my first boycott of the Arizona trip, she drops in around noon on the day my family leaves with a picnic basket full of grown-up food and chilled wine. I am glad that I finished my closet and did my run already, as I will be useless by the time she leaves.

I set the box by the front door, then follow the smooth sound of my friend's song into the kitchen. I stop for a moment at the doorway, watching her as she unloads her bounty from the wicker basket onto my kitchen table: a loaf of

French bread, a triangle of Brie, a container of paté, some olives, and, of course, the Chablis.

"*'Cause any place I hang my hat is home,'*" she sings. Mia's voice is butter-rich, sultry, and mesmerizing, and I have often told her that she could have been a star. To which she always replies that being a star would have meant starving herself, and she likes her fat ass just fine, thank you very much.

The ass in question is currently enrobed in a muumuu the color of a Pleione orchid, which actually makes it look larger than normal. Mia is a big woman, almost six feet tall, and carries around about sixty extra pounds. But she is more secure with her body than any woman I know. She doesn't even mind that her husband is always on her case about losing weight, which would inspire nervous breakdowns and relationship implosions with any other couple.

"Oh, that's just him," she says, defending her man. "If I did go and join Jenny Craig and turned into some skinny bitch, he'd just find something else to harp on me about. That is, as they say, married life, girl. Still, he doesn't complain at all in the sack, no. I give him a good whole lotta to hold on to, know what I mean?"

She turns to me now and smiles that teeth-whitening-commercial smile of hers. "There you are!" she says, rushing over to me with open arms. "Congratulations, girl. You're free!"

We embrace like we haven't seen each other in years, as that is Mia's way. She embraces everything, for better or for worse, but good friends especially. She releases her hold on me and steps back, her smile suddenly absent, replaced by a pensive expression.

"Damn. You look *good*, Elle."

I feel my cheeks flush at her praise. "Thanks."

"No, really. I thought you looked different at book club, but you look even better now. Okay, girl, level with me. You go under the knife?"

"No!" I exclaim, shocked.

"It's Mia, baby. Come on. Give it up. A little nip here, a little suck and tuck there. Right?"

"I swear to you, Mia. I'm just making healthier choices, that's all. Treadmill. Low fat. Face creams. Like that."

"Damn," she repeats. "Well, it's all working." She glances over at the table and frowns. "You better not tell me you're bowing out of this fine picnic," she says sternly.

"Hell, no," I assure her, because fighting with Mia is a losing proposition. "What's life without a little cheating?"

She smiles, relieved, and ushers me to the table where we begin to feast.

We are a third of the way through the bottle of wine, a quarter of the way through the duck liver, and midway through a story about Mia's college-aged daughter and her first serious relationship when my cell phone rings. I almost let the call go to voice mail, as Mia has me in stitches with her retelling of how Lettie reacted when her new boyfriend farted for the first time in front of her and she almost broke up with him on the spot. But I assume it's Jonah calling to let me know he and the kids arrived safely, so I reluctantly push back from the table and head for the counter, telling Mia to hold that thought.

I glance at the clock. It's not yet one o'clock and unless Jonah drove like Mario Andretti, there's no way he can be at his parents' by now. I pick up my cell and glance at the Caller ID, and my breath catches in my throat. My hands tremble so much as I fumble to answer the call that I almost drop the phone into the sink. "Hello?"

"Hi. Ellen?"

"Yes. Hi."

"It's Ben. Ben Campbell?"

"Yes. I know."

"Is this a bad time?"

Yes. "No. It's fine. How are you?"

"I'm good," he says, then chuckles. "The kids just got whisked off by their grandparents. Linda's at work. I'm just, sort of, basking in the silence of the house."

"I did that all morning," I confess. I can feel Mia's eyes on me and I put up one finger. *Just a minute,* I am telling her. *Jonah?* she mouths, and I shake my head. She narrows her eyes at me, then cuts into the Brie and slathers a huge chunk over a piece of bread.

"When did they leave?" he asks.

"About seven."

"So you've been basking for what, six hours already?"

"I'll have you know that I've been very productive," I say.

"Spring cleaning, huh?"

"Exactly."

For a moment, neither of us speaks. Finally, his voice breaks through the quiet of the phone line.

"So, I, uh, I'm heading over to the marina in about an hour."

"Stand-up paddleboarding," I say.

"Right." He hesitates for just a second. "Are you sure you don't want to come? I mean, you seemed pretty definitive yesterday, but it is something new."

"Just for future reference, the *something new* I tried did not require me to even leave the house."

His throaty chuckle makes my knees go weak. "That sounds fun."

"And," I cut him off before he can do further damage, "it didn't require me to wear a wet suit."

"You only need a wet suit if you fall in the water," he jokes, and I laugh. In my peripheral vision, I see Mia lumber out of her chair and head in my direction. She makes a show of grabbing a glass out of the cupboard and filling it with water, all the while giving me the fish eye.

"Thanks for the invite," I tell him. "But I can't."

He is silent for another moment. "Okay. But if you change your mind, I'll be at the kids' beach next to Pier Three."

"Have fun," I say, then quickly disconnect the call. As I set the phone on the counter, I hear Mia clear her throat. Loudly.

"Okay, Miz Thang. What in the hell was that? Or should I say, *who*?"

I wave my hand dismissively at her and head for my seat at the table. "No one."

"No one, huh? That's why your face is the color of a burst pomegranate seed?"

Without thinking, I raise my hand to my cheek and find it warm to the touch.

"You *will* tell Mama Mia what's going on, girl."

I glance over at her and see her dark brown eyes boring into me, her left eyebrow raised in a question.

"He's this . . . soccer dad I know and we keep running into each other. He's just a nice man."

"Nice."

"Yeah. He's nice to everyone."

"And he calls everyone on their cell phones?" Her left eyebrow descends just as her right eyebrow rockets upward.

"I don't know. Maybe." I think of Nina Montrose and mentally cross my fingers that Ben is not, at this moment, calling her as a consolation prize. Then I find myself hoping that *I* was not the consolation after a prior phone call to Nina.

"Oh sure," Mia says sarcastically. "He calls all the soccer moms and makes them laugh and blush and cross their legs."

I look down to see that, sure enough, my legs are crossed. I quickly raise my head and shrug my shoulders casually.

"Maybe he does."

"Bullshit," she counters, then sighs. "Good looking?"

"Uh, yeah," I answer slowly. Mia would sniff it out if I lie to her.

"He text you?"

I open my mouth to answer, but cannot expel the word. I nod a yes.

"Oh, girl. You in a world of trouble."

We sit at the kitchen table and finish the bottle of wine while I recount the story of Ben Campbell. Mia doesn't interrupt, just listens, rapt. As I tell her, I worry that I am giving the situation too much power, that I am making a big deal out of nothing, that I have created this imaginary precipice in my mind and that even if it were real, there is no way I would jump off.

I finish with his invitation to go paddle surfing, then sit back against my chair and drain my wineglass. Mia is no longer looking at me but instead at a spot just over my head. Her expression is contemplative, and I suspect she is trying to choose her words carefully, just as she does with a student who has been sent to her office. If anyone is going to give me a lambasting, it's Mia. She adores Jonah and is very protective of family values, having witnessed as a social worker far too many families destroyed.

"It's nothing," I insist before she can start in on me. Because, honestly, if you look hard at the facts, it *is* nothing. Everyone, at one point or another in their lives, has to decide exactly what constitutes cheating for them. Some people would say holding hands. Others might say swapping spit. And there are those (men mostly) who insist that everything up to penetration could be considered platonic ("It was just a friendly blow job, honey, didn't mean a thing"). At some point in my twenties, I decided that touching tongues was an adulterous act because it required effort. Anything before that could be written off as mindless flirting. So, yes, I am guilty of flirtation, but according to my personal cheat-o-meter, I am innocent of the big *A*.

"I cheated on Sidney," Mia says. Her voice is so soft and her admission so implausible that I think I have misheard her. I have to concentrate to keep my jaw from hitting the table.

"What? When?"

I have known Mia for seven years now, and our friendship was instantaneous, like the immediate reaction you get when you pour baking soda into a bottle of Coke. A mutual friend of ours, Julia Simpson, had started a book club and had invited us both to attend. From the moment we found ourselves seated next to each other, and discovered that we both were bored to tears by *Pride and Prejudice*, a bond was forged. After a couple of meetings, Julia informed the group that she was joining AA and would no longer be serving alcohol. At which point, Mia and I seceded and formed our own book club faster than you can say *twelve steps*.

She has never mentioned an affair to me before, not even the time we drank too many margaritas and shared our fantasies about the perfect seduction scene, substituting fetching men we knew for our husbands.

"A long time ago," she murmurs. "Before I knew you."

She takes a sip of her wine, sets it down and runs a finger around the lip.

I am so stunned by this revelation that I am hardly able to speak. "Wh-who . . . who was it?"

Her eyes fog over with memories and for a moment, I

think she may not answer my question. Then she takes a deep breath and sighs heavily. "His name was Peter Stormcloud."

I cover my mouth with my hand to keep from laughing because I can tell by Mia's expression that this is no joke. She catches the gesture and furrows her brow, reprimanding me with a frown. Then she shakes her head and the corners of her lips curl up into a grin.

"I kid you not. That was his name. Actually, I think his full name was Peter Gathers Mighty Stormcloud, or something like that. We worked together at family services in San Bernadino. He handled most of the Native American cases. He was . . . he was a beauty." She looks past me again, a dreamy expression washing over her face as if Peter Stormcloud were standing right behind me. So vivid are the memories surfacing for her at the moment, so intense is the look of rapture those memories are painting on her face, that I almost turn to see if he is really there.

"Six-six," she says reverently. "Two fifty. Solid as a rock. My kind of man."

This also surprises me, coming from a woman who is married to a bean pole.

"It just happened. We were working together on a particularly nasty case, some drugs, some abuse. We just got done removing the kids and placing them in protective custody, and we decided to go out and get ourselves blind drunk. One thing led to another, you know? I rationalized at the time that we were using each other to forget the horror we had to deal with on a daily basis, and that was the truth. But we also wanted each other. Bad."

Her eyes focus on me again and she shrugs. "Anyway, it only lasted a little while, and Sidney never found out."

"You ended it?"

She nods, and when she speaks, her tone is bittersweet. "I'll always regret what I did."

"Because of the guilt?" I ask knowingly.

But she shakes her head and gives me a pointed look. "No, girl. Because until the first time Peter Stormcloud kissed me, I didn't know what I was missing."

· Eighteen ·

I sit in the driver's seat of Jonah's Lexus, my hands gripping the steering wheel even though the car is in park, and stare out at the blue water of Sea Garden Marina. I know Mia's story was a cautionary tale meant to dissuade me from following in her fuchsia-leather-encased footsteps, but it has had the opposite effect on me. Of course, I assured her that I had no intention of meeting Ben Campbell here today, or any day, for that matter. But by the time I closed the door behind her, I had already decided I would come. And not because of the wine, either—unfortunately, right now I'm as sober as a judge.

I am still in that sketchy state of denial where I have myself convinced that I am not going to do anything I will regret. I have sworn to myself up one side and down the other that I am only here on a reconnaissance mission, to find out exactly what the hell is going on. I am not going to sleep with

Ben Campbell. I just want to find out if he wants to sleep with me.

And if he says yes? my inner voice asks me. *What then?* But I don't have an answer.

I can still leave and no one will be the wiser. Not Ben, whose Land Rover is parked a few spaces over from me. Not Jonah, who called just as I was raiding my newly organized closet for something appropriate to wear to the marina in the middle of March, to tell me that he and the kids had arrived in Arizona safely. Not Jill, who caught me on my cell as I was pulling out of my driveway to invite me over for dinner because she can't imagine that anyone could enjoy being alone in an empty house. No one would know that I had almost stepped out of the car and into a situation that might dramatically alter the shape of my life. Except me. I would always know that I had come this far, only to turn around and hightail it back to the safety of my comfortable complacent existence.

I could live with that. It would be far simpler to know that I am a coward than to live with the knowledge that I have done whatever it is I might do if I step outside this car.

Just as I am turning the key in the ignition, there is a *tap-tap* on the passenger window. I glance over and behold Ben Campbell peering in at me, a smile of such radiance on his face that I almost have to squint in its glare.

"You came." His voice is muffled through the safety glass, but even so, the pleasure that infuses his words is loud and clear.

I quickly roll down the window and he braces himself against the frame, gazing at me expectantly.

"I'm not staying," I tell him, and watch his delighted expression deflate.

"Why?"

There are about a thousand reasons why, but looking into Ben's eyes, I can't grasp a single one. I just sit there, helpless, white-knuckling the steering wheel. He sighs, then pulls open the car door and folds himself into the passenger seat. He is wearing his Levi's and a faded hunter green T-shirt with the legend *Death Row Iguanas* silk-screened across the front. He closes the door and turns to me, and suddenly the interior of the Lexus shrinks to the size of a Smart car. We have been this close, at the sushi bar, but never enclosed, and I can almost feel the air being sucked out through the vents.

"Why did you come?" he asks quietly.

Because I currently hate my husband and the feeling is mutual? Because I am tired of my boring life? Because I am sick of always making the right choice and doing the right thing? Because I feel like I could float away in your eyes every time I look into them?

Because I wanted to come.

"I don't know," I say aloud.

He nods slowly, thoughtfully. Then he reaches over, gently uncurls my fingers from the steering wheel, and encases my right hand in his left. There is no explosion of light at his touch, but rather a subtle, comforting warmth that slowly eases through my entire body.

We sit there in silence for a long moment, mindless of the world outside the car. After a while, Ben pulls my hand up and rests it against his chest, and I can feel his heartbeat through his shirt, strong and steady. Then he lifts it to his lips and kisses it tenderly, turns it over and kisses each of my fingertips, then my palm. For a split second, I cannot draw breath, cannot see, cannot feel any other part of my body but the hand he is kissing. I try to recall how long it's been since my husband engaged in such an intimate act with me, then I quickly banish the thought. Jonah does not belong here in this moment. Even if this is his car.

When Ben relaxes his grip and releases my hand, an arctic cold sweeps through me. He grasps the door handle and pushes the door open, stretches his long, lean leg toward the pavement. I watch him get out of the Lexus, my heart suddenly pounding in my ears.

Without saying good-bye, he closes the door and starts to walk away from me, toward the marina, toward *his* something new.

Before I can think twice, I swing open the driver's door with such force I am afraid it will snap off its hinges, and I jump out of the car.

"I don't have a wet suit," I call to him.

Ben stops in his tracks and slowly turns to me, a grin spreading across his face like the genesis of a brush fire. He places his hands on his hips and cocks his head to the side.

"That's okay. I brought a spare. Just in case."

I stand in the public bathroom of Pier Three, staring into the full-length faux mirror which looks suspiciously like aluminum foil. My fun house–like reflection is not a pretty sight, as I strongly resemble a giant deformed penguin, shiny black middle protruding over short stumpy legs.

It was no easy feat squeezing myself into the wet suit, which clearly reads *Women's Size 8* but must have been mismarked because, fuck, it's tight. I had thought, while squishing down my upper thigh with one hand and yanking up the suit with the other, then sucking in my stomach until I almost passed out in order to coax the stubborn zipper over my abdomen, that the wet suit might have some kind of magical slimming effect on me, that I might even want to invest in one of my own to wear as a kind of industrial Spanx. However, one look in the mirror, distorted as it may be, dispels me of such a ridiculous notion.

I have a sudden urge to flee but know it would be impossible. Ben had said he'd meet me right outside the bathroom after he finished getting his own wet suit on, and I can hear him already, on the other side of the door, humming an old Eagles tune softly to himself.

I glance behind me at the far end of the bathroom. Just past the last stall is a window, roughly five feet off the ground. Unfortunately, it is only twelve inches square. Perhaps if I slathered this goddamned wet suit with lard I could manage to squeeze through. But barring the whole grease-and-slide maneuver, I am pretty well stuck. Where the hell is a vat of Crisco when you need it?

Ah well, I think, squaring my shoulders. Surely I don't look as bad as the distorted image in front of me would suggest. And anyway, if Ben Campbell finds my body repulsive, it will probably be a blessing in disguise. If he finds me repulsive, he won't want to touch me or sleep with me or be interested in me on any level. And then I won't have to make a decision that could ruin my marriage and force me to take a good hard look at my own character.

God, I hope I don't look that *bad.*

I grab my shoulder bag from where it hangs on the paper towel crank and pull the bathroom door open. Stepping out, I turn to my right and see Ben leaning against the building, one knee bent, the sole of his foot planted firmly on the wall, beach towel in hand. His wet suit is unzipped and folded over at his waist so that his entire upper body is naked as a newborn. When I say that the sight of this man's torso causes me to take a step backward, I am not exaggerating.

And I am lucky it was only *one* step, otherwise, I would have ended up in the marina. His chest is golden brown and taut, with a smattering of curly hair that thins out as it makes its way down to those amazing six-pack abs, the ones his white T-shirt only hinted at the day we met.

At this moment, I wish I were a superhero with the ability to freeze time so that I could reach out and brush my fingertips along the ridges of his stomach, the slight swell of his chest, the ropy curve of his biceps. He is not ripped like a weight lifter, but perfectly proportioned, sinewy and strong, a man who is in shape because he chases bad guys and jumps out of planes, not because he spends hours in a gym. This fact makes him even more appealing.

Mia's words ring in my ears. *Oh, girl. You in a world of trouble.*

He turns to me, his eyes hidden behind sunglasses, and smiles inscrutably. I am painfully self-conscious as he inspects my decidedly unsinewy body.

"Nina Montrose would look a lot better in this," I say, trying for humor to cover my insecurity.

He frowns at me as he pushes himself away from the wall. "If you like that kind of thing, I guess." He reaches out and touches me on the shoulder, and I can feel the heat of his fingertips through the eighth of an inch of black neoprene. "You look great," he says. "Come on."

After pulling the wet suit over his arms and torso, he guides me back toward the parking lot, then down a sandy path to the kids' beach, a small alcove of sheltered shore smack-dab in the middle of the marina, where children can play without worrying about waves. There are only about a dozen other people there: a young bronzed couple catching whatever rays the March sun has to offer; a Hispanic mom and dad holding a toddler by the hand between them, lowering her inch by inch until her toes hit the water and she squeals with delight; some teenagers trying their hands, or feet, at stand-up paddleboarding, though they appear to have consumed a few too many beers to really make a go of it. From where I stand I can see that their teeth are chattering despite their wet suits. Not a good sign.

I follow Ben down the sand to the edge of the water that abuts the pier. There, a skinny, shaggy-haired youth stands waiting for us. He wears happy-face board shorts that ride low along his hips, revealing a striking tan line that makes me think of a black-and-white cookie. On the wooden planking next to him sit two oversized surfboards, one turquoise, the other white, each with a rectangular strip of rubber matting in the center. Leaning against an open crate filled with life preservers are a couple of long paddles.

"Eric," Ben calls out as we approach. "This is Ellen."

The kid, whom I expect to shrug and mumble *Dude*, stretches out his hand to me. "Nice to meet you, Ellen."

"You, too," I reply, shaking his hand.

"Have you ever paddle surfed before?" he asks.

"Uh, no."

"You're going to love it. It's a good day for it, too." He glances up at the sun, which is on its downward journey toward the horizon. "A little cool, but no wind at all."

As I watch, the two men haul the boards from the pier to the shallow water. I drop my bag next to Ben's beach towel and take a step forward, submerging my feet into the freezing surf. *Holy shit, it's cold*, I think as I retreat to the safety of the dry sand. *No way. No way, no way.*

Eric holds the white board steady against the lazy tide while Ben pushes the turquoise board in my direction. I shake my head slightly as Eric begins to explain the basic concept of paddleboarding.

"It's easy peasy lemon-squeezy," he says, and I can't help but wonder how recently he graduated from kindergarten. "You just crouch down," he continues, climbing onto the board to demonstrate, "get your bearings, then stand up." He springs to his feet with minimal effort, maintaining a light grip on the long paddle as he does.

"I might have left my bearings at home," I say, and receive a toothy grin from Ben. Eric looks confused, but he shrugs good-naturedly, then gives us a lesson on how to use the paddle to maneuver.

"Ladies first," Ben says, gesturing to the turquoise board.

This time, there can be no mistaking my head shake, as I probably resemble one of those fembots from *The Six Million Dollar Man* when they malfunctioned and started to smoke.

"Maybe I'll just watch you for a little while." *Which would be even more fun if you pulled your wet suit back down!*

"You don't go, I don't go," he threatens, but I cross my arms over my chest, unconvinced.

"This is *your* thing," I say defiantly. "Not mine."

He regards me for a few seconds. "You really don't want to try this."

"I've been trying to tell you that all along," I retort, but I am smiling. "Oh, for God's sake!" I take a deep breath and stomp toward the turquoise board that Ben holds, ignoring the fact that the water feels like a Slurpee and my innate sense of balance has not been tested for three decades, since I placed second in the balance beam competition at the Grady Junior High Gymnastics Meet. I was so excited to have won a silver medal that I did a spontaneous back handspring into the wooden bleachers that lined the gymnasium and tore my rotator cuff. I didn't even know what a rotator cuff was, aside from the fact that it hurt like a son of a bitch, but I did know that it was the end of my dreams of becoming the next Nadia Comaneci, which was actually just fine with me because I was allowed to start eating dessert again.

The water reaches my knees as I drag the board away from Ben and set myself gingerly upon it. It rocks to one side, then the other before I can steady it. Not for the first time in the past five minutes, I wonder what the hell I am doing here. I could be home watching a movie on the big screen, or playing the Wii (I love the tennis game), or drinking a dirty vodka martini with the bleu cheese–stuffed olives I keep hidden in the outside fridge. Instead, I am lying on a polyurethane-and-fiberglass harbinger of doom, about to make an ass of myself.

Much to my relief, Ben is not watching me as I try to keep the board level enough to get into a crouch. He has waded over to his board and has begun the arduous process of getting to his own feet. And although he starts a few seconds after me, when I glance at him, he is already standing. I give myself a little pep talk, then manage to push myself to my feet. The board wobbles beneath me for a precarious moment, and I am certain I am about to plunge into the frigid sea, but I quickly compensate, and I realize that if I tighten my thighs, and glutes, and calves, and my feet and toes, I can keep the board static. (I won't be able to walk tomorrow for all the stress I am putting on my legs, but at least I won't freeze my ass off.) Carefully, I reach down and pick up the paddle, just as Ben makes his way over to me.

"Not too hard, huh?" he asks. The gleeful smile that radiates from his handsome face instantly erases the lines of tension around his eyes and mouth and makes him look about twelve.

"Not at all," I reply. *As long as I keep every muscle from my ass to my toenails clenched tighter than a drum.*

"Hey," Eric calls to us. I turn my head and forget to stay

taut, causing my board to dip to the right. I immediately squeeze my butt cheeks together and regain control. But I don't make the mistake of turning back to Eric again. He'll just have to talk to the back of my head. Which he does.

"Don't go past the buoys," he instructs. "Not too many boats coming and going right now, but there's a few. The wake's not too good for beginners."

Since I am not facing him, I can't be sure, but it sounds like he is grinning when he says this. Once again, not a good sign.

I spend a few minutes getting the feel of the board and the paddle in my hands, slicing the oar through the water, first on my left, then on my right, noting that now my upper body is getting in on the action, from my hands all the way up my arms and to my chest. I won't be able to move *at all* tomorrow, which is fine, because my kids' closets can wait one more day. As I start to pick up speed, I discover that Eric was right. It is, indeed, easy peasy lemon-squeezy. Ben is a few yards ahead of me, looking as though he has been doing this his whole life, making powerful cuts in the water that thrust his board forward at a hasty clip. He turns back to me, smiling.

"This is good, right?" he says, and I laugh my response. Because it *is* good. I am doing something I have never dreamed of doing; I'm standing on a surfboard in the marina, my whole body straining, feeling wonderfully alive and in the moment. My thoughts have taken a breather, and the only work my brain is doing is sending messages to all of my muscle groups, telling them what they need to do to keep me upright and on the board. It is such a peaceful state, so Zen-like, and so unfamiliar to me that I want to bottle it and store it up for some future overthinking emergency.

Ben gestures with his head toward the other side of the

small cove, where the marina is lined with million-dollar houses built so close together that you can shake hands with your neighbor through your kitchen windows. I nod and follow him.

The board glides over the water, the sun shimmers on the surface, an ever-changing pattern of light on the dark turquoise quilt. My heart pounds and my muscles strain with each stroke. I am exhilarated. A single image flashes briefly across the blank canvas of my mind, of me gazing at my reflection this morning. I liked the woman I saw. And although, at this moment, I have no mirror to look into, I like her even more now.

Ten yards from the private docks on the far side of the cove, Ben stops paddling and waits for me to slide up beside him. I plunge my oar into the water and rotate it, expertly bringing my board to a stop. Feeling triumphant, I glance at Ben to find him watching me.

"You're awesome," he says, and I am excessively pleased by his praise. *Take* that, *Nina Montrose!*

"This is actually pretty great," I admit. It would be better in the Bahamas where the water temperature is like eighty-seven degrees, but as long as I stay afloat, I like it just fine.

"Race you back?" he asks, deftly swinging the nose of the board around with one fluid stroke of the paddle.

"Nah," I answer, then follow his example, cranking the oar until I am facing Pier Three. I have no desire to compete with this man, and moreover, I don't want to lose this sense of tranquillity by adding a challenge to the mix.

"Me either," he says, as if he knows what I'm thinking, what I'm feeling. And maybe he does.

Our return journey is slow and languid and, for the most part, we remain side by side. We are able to chat, but do so only minimally; occasionally one of us will point to a boat with a humorous name like *The Happy Hookers* (fisherman joke) or a house designed to look like it belongs in the Swiss Alps (why?) or a pelican dive-bombing for his afternoon snack. Pier Three grows larger as we approach, but it is not until I hear the rev of a boat engine that I realize we have drifted farther out than we should have. The buoys bob up and down a mere ten feet from where we are.

Ben notices the sound of the motorboat at the same time I do, and he jabs an elbow toward the shoreline. As we both put our muscles into our strokes, a twenty-five-foot cabin cruiser tears past at a speed that far exceeds the posted limit, just beyond the buoys. I glance over my shoulder and see the foamy wake moving toward us, and even though the ridge of water isn't even big enough to qualify as a wave, it might as well be a tsunami.

On his board beside me, Ben starts laughing. I turn to him, still furiously paddling, trying to outrun fate.

"What's so funny?" I holler.

"We're toast," he cries, laughing harder still. And suddenly, I am laughing with him. I draw up my paddle in surrender as the first crest of the wake pushes at my board. I desperately try to compensate, squeezing my muscles tight as the unrelenting water rocks me back and forth, back and forth like a seesaw. I go with it, alternately bending my knees and using my paddle for balance. And for a glorious instant, I think I am going to make it, am just about to congratulate myself for my newly acquired skill, when the last and most powerful part of the wake slams into my board and sends me ass over teakettle into the frigid sea. My only consolation is the sight of Ben hurling toward the water a split second after I do, laughing all the way.

———————

Eric is waiting for us, and he quickly guides us to the shore. Ben and I lay the paddles down on the boards and hop into the shallow water. My teeth are chattering and I am having trouble feeling my hands and feet, which is why I immediately trip and fall face first into the wet sand. Ben grasps my elbow and hauls me to my feet, then herds me up to dry land where his beach towel and my bag lie. With numb fingers, I dig through my bag for my towel, then fumble to draw the inadequate rectangle of terry cloth around myself. Ben shakes the sand off his own and dons it.

I don't know exactly what time it is, but the sun is low enough in the sky that it offers no warmth whatsoever. I pull my towel more tightly around my shoulders, wishing it were a battery-operated electric blanket.

"Thanks, Eric," Ben manages to say through lips that look disturbingly blue. I would like to say *Thank you* as well, but can't seem to form the words, so I settle for a quick wave in Eric's general direction.

"Come on," Ben says, placing an arm casually around my shoulder and guiding me toward the pier.

By the time we reach the bathrooms, I am shaking so violently, I am afraid I am going to have a seizure. Before I push through the door, I claw at the zipper on my wet suit, but my fingers will not cooperate. Ben notices my struggle and comes to my rescue. He reaches up and clasps the tongue of my zipper, then slowly eases it downward. If I weren't so cold, this would be a very sensual experience. But I cannot enjoy it, because, aside from worrying about burst brain vessels and hypothermia, I am now self-conscious about the too-low position of my breasts and my upper arm jiggle.

As he slides the zipper down, exposing the top half of my black-and-red one-piece that I nabbed from a clearance rack at Target, Ben looks at my face. I assume that he is being chivalrous, averting his gaze from my newly exposed flesh, or that he is horrified by the sight of an extra ten (okay, fifteen) pounds of flesh, but when I look into his liquid eyes, I see that they are suddenly smoldering, even though the rest of his body is akin to a Popsicle.

"Th-th-thanks," I say, although now I am not sure whether I am trembling from the cold or from the feel of his fingers so near to my navel.

He quickly drops his hands and steps back.

"You're welcome. Hurry and get dressed before you catch pneumonia." His tone is a little gruff, which surprises me, even hurts me a little, and I flee into the safety of the women's room.

Pulling off the wet suit is not much easier than putting it on, and I find myself thinking of that vat of Crisco again. I think about the fact that if I hadn't shaved, the hair on my legs might be keeping me warm, like a fur coat, at this very moment. I think about the boat in the marina with the funny name. I think about all of these things so that I won't think about the tenor of Ben's voice.

I strip naked, my body racked with uncontrollable tremors, and do my best to dry myself off with my sodden towel. I can hear the hinges of the men's room door squeak, signaling that Ben has already finished dressing. A thought flashes through my brain, a fantasy maybe, of Ben throwing open the door, catching me naked and ravaging me against one of the stalls, but on second thought, the idea of gettin' jiggy in a dreary pier bathroom that smells of urine and sea life and has a mirror made of aluminum foil leaves a lot to be desired.

I shimmy into my jeans and T-shirt, then stuff my wet bathing suit and towel into a plastic grocery bag I keep in my purse (all prepared mothers carry one for emergencies). I gather the wet suit and my belongings, step into my shoes, and hustle out of the bathroom, expecting to find Ben waiting for me. But he is nowhere in sight.

I look left and right, but the pier is deserted. Still shivering but starting to regain feeling in my extremities, I head away from the water and toward the parking lot. When I reach the place where the wooden planks give way to asphalt, I see Ben at his Land Rover, the back hatch gaping open. I move toward him as he stows his duffel bag in the cargo area and reaches up to close the hatch.

"Hey," I call to him, holding out the wet suit. He turns to me, his face a mask of ambivalence, and gives me a curt nod. When I am a few feet from him, he reaches out and grabs the wet suit from my hands.

"Thanks," he says briskly, then tosses the suit in with his bag. "So, thanks for coming."

"Yeah, it was great," I say awkwardly. His sudden coldness has nothing to do with the arctic temperature of the ocean, and it confounds me. Less than a half an hour ago we were having a great time, albeit freezing our asses off, flailing around, trying to get back on our boards, poking fun at each other, and laughing so hard we both nearly choked on the salt water. Now he is treating me like he owes me money, like he can't get away from me fast enough.

He slams the hatch shut with resounding force and places his hands on his hips, trying for studied casual.

"Well, I'll, uh, see you at soccer. . . ."

I nod and offer him a smile. "Or Trader Joe's."

His chuckle is forced. "Yeah."

"Thanks a lot," I say softly, taking a step back. I want to say something to him to bring back the fun, charming, irresistible Ben, but I have no idea what the right words would be. Instead, I give him a casual wave, then turn and head for my car, forcing myself not to run.

Nineteen

It's close to five o'clock by the time I enter my empty house. Shadows envelop the downstairs, but I do not switch on the lights as I wander through the foyer to the kitchen and absently open the back door to let Sally out. I stand in the dark, waiting for her to do her business, then fill her bowl with dog chow, take a minute to give her some love, then head for the stairs. On legs that feel like lead, I climb to the second floor, finally flipping a switch when I reach the landing. I am still scratching at the mental bug bite that is my last five minutes with Ben Campbell at the marina.

In true female fashion, I lay the blame squarely on my own shoulders. It must have been something I did, something I said, something about *me*. Maybe it was the angry-looking scar on my upper arm that has never faded even though I got it when I was nineteen, or the unflattering swimsuit that bulges at the belly line, or my breath, which probably smelled like a sea anemone. Or maybe it *was* my gravity-challenged boobs.

I do remember the way he'd looked at me, have called up the image of his heated gaze several hundred times since getting into my car, yet I realize that I must have misinterpreted what I saw. Perhaps it's been so long since a man has looked at me with unadulterated lust that I simply don't recognize it anymore. It's possible that Ben's expression was one of disgust or derision. Or that I was projecting my own desire onto him.

Stop it, Ellen. You know what you saw. He wanted you.

I tell myself it doesn't matter what I saw as I drop my tote on the bed. The plastic bag with my wet gear spills out onto the bedspread, and I grab it up, tear open the top and dump the contents into the laundry basket by the bathroom. I should take the towel and suit downstairs to the washing machine and rinse them out, but I simply don't have the energy. My muscles are already starting to make their displeasure known at the workout they were given earlier. And although I have stopped shivering, I feel a bone-deep chill that the Lexus's heater could not dispel no matter how high I cranked it.

I strip off my damp jeans and T-shirt, pile them on top of the hamper, then head straight for the bathtub. I twist the hot handle as far over as it will go, turn the cold handle just far enough that I won't give myself third-degree burns, then squeeze some of my favorite bubble bath under the gushing stream and climb in.

As soon as the blissfully steamy water reaches my chest, I hear the phone ring. I briefly consider getting out of the tub, even scoot up into a sitting position, but think better of it and allow myself to slide back into the foamy tub. A few minutes later, the muffled, electronic ring of my cell phone sounds from the bottom of my bag. Again, I ignore it, this time by submerging my head.

I stay under for as long as I can hold my breath, then bob up and wipe the bubbles from my eyes. I lie against the hot porcelain and struggle to regain that peaceful state I experienced at the marina. Of course, *struggling* to be Zen is an oxymoron, so my failure to clear my mind doesn't come as a shock.

The bottom line is that Ben Campbell's sudden cold shoulder was for the best. Today, on that board, I felt an emotion that has eluded me for years. I felt free. But it was only an illusion. And the illusion of freedom is seductive. It makes you forget that you are married with children. It makes you forget your responsibilities and the promises you have made. It makes it easy to say *Hell, yes!* when what you should be saying is *No, thanks.* I know now that I am not strong enough to say *No, thanks* to something that feels so great.

I will always have this afternoon, and I will carry it with me like a talisman. I will be able access the memory of trying something new with someone terrific. I will be able to remember the way Ben looked at me, and I will not bastardize it by pretending it wasn't what it was. And the knowledge that someone actually wanted me, even if it was only for a moment, will perpetually fill the gas tank of my ego. But I won't have done anything I'd certainly regret or that would inspire that gnawing rodent of guilt.

The water in the tub grows tepid, and one glance at my wrinkled-prune fingertips tells me it's time to get out. I stand and grasp at the towel on the rack beside me, quickly dry myself, and pull the drain plug.

Feeling better and warmer, wearing my favorite pair of

sweats and an oversized T-shirt with my husband's company logo on the front, I walk into the bedroom to find Sally lying on the bed. Jonah is vehemently opposed to dogs being allowed on the furniture, and Sally is usually very obedient about this, but somehow she knows that she is safe for the time being. I plop down next to her and stroke her soft fur, for which I receive a few enthusiastic licks, then reach for the remote. My brain is as weary as my muscles, having been on overdrive for the past hour, and I figure a little television will give it the rest it sorely deserves. I click through the channels until I come to an airing of *Titanic*. Since it's water-themed, I interpret this as a sign and, of course, the ship sinks, which is a perfect metaphor for the way things ended with Ben today. I drop the remote, lie back against the pillows, and let the James Cameron epic sweep me away.

I awaken to the now familiar *ping* of my cell phone. I glance at the clock, which reads 9:07, and realize that I have been asleep for more than two hours. On the television, Kate Winslet is just prying her fingers loose from Leonardo DiCaprio's icicle digits, and down he goes into the murky depths.

Fumbling for my bag on the end of the bed, I overturn it and grab my cell. In the dim light of my bedroom, I cannot read anything on the screen, so I lumber to the side of the bed and switch on the lamp. I read the information on the LCD and suddenly I am wide awake. Ben has sent me a text. It reads: *Are you awake?*

"I am now," I say to no one in particular.

I wait a full two minutes before I text back, watching as Kate, sorry, *Rose*, hides from her cad of a fiancé. Then I text back the letter: *Y.* According to my eight-year-old, you no longer need to type out whole words anymore, and when she told me this, I wondered whether the technological advances of our generation are in effect creating a society of illiterate mutes. But in this case, I kind of want to be curt, and you can't get more curt than a single letter. A *ping* sounds on the heels of my text, as if he has already written his and was just waiting for an affirmative from me to send it. It reads: *Can I call you?*

I put the cell down and haul myself off the bed, then pace around my bedroom. *Can I call you?* Fuck! *Can I call you?* I should tell him no. I should say I'm busy or I'm on the landline with my husband or I should not even respond at all. But this is what I do instead, because for some reason, when it comes to Ben Campbell, I turn into a jellyfish: I pick up my phone and type the single letter *Y.*

The cell rings in my hand so fast I almost drop it. I force myself to hesitate, take a deep calming breath, then answer.

"Hello?" Casual. No big deal. *Who is this, anyway?*

"Hi. It's Ben." His voice is low and soft, like he's trying not to be heard.

"Hi." I give the word two syllables, bending up the second with a question mark. Like, *And what is it you want?*

"Look, Ellen, I'm sorry to bother you. I just had to call to apologize for the way I was this afternoon. I don't know what came over me."

I do, I think. *You came down with a sudden case of manitude.*

"Actually, that's not true," he corrects. "I do know what came over me, but it's hard to explain."

"Don't worry about it," I say. Nonchalant. Carefree. *Nothing bothers me, big boy.*

"It's just that I think you think it was one thing, when in fact it was just the opposite."

"Ben, it's okay, really." This time I'm sincere. He might as well be speaking in tongues for all the good his explanation is doing. But if his earlier actions are causing him this much distress, I am fine with letting him off the hook. "I had a great time paddle surfing. I really did. I might even do it again someday. You know, in the summertime?"

I don't receive even the barest hint of amusement from his end of the line. "You being there made it better," he says quietly.

A knot of tension curls like a fist in my stomach. His admission is not a declaration of lust, nor a proposal for a bump-and-grind session in the back of his Land Rover. It is far more intimate than those would be, and therefore far more disturbing. I can think of no appropriate reply and keep my mouth firmly closed.

"Can I ask you a question?" he says, disrupting the silence. *No, please don't.* "Sure."

"What would *your* something new be?" He waits a beat. "I mean, paddle surfing was mine. What would you like to try?"

"I've never flown in a helicopter." This is the first thing that comes to mind, and it's something I have always wanted to do. When Jonah and I went to New York a few years back for a grown-up vacation, we booked one of the helicopter tours to take us around Manhattan. When we arrived at the downtown heliport, we were greeted by a harried clerk who informed us that there was an issue with the main rotor head on their chopper, which meant nothing to us but apparently is one of the causes of helicopter crashes. Although other tours with different lines were available, we took it as a sign not to go up in the air that day and ended up blowing our refund on an amazing lunch at Daniel.

"I highly recommend it," Ben tells me. "It's a rush."

"Says the man who 'highly recommends' jumping out of planes."

He chuckles at this. "Well, it's not quite the same rush, but it's pretty good."

Again, neither one of us speaks. Again, it is Ben who breaks the silence. "So, are we okay?"

I have no idea how to interpret this question. I'm sitting on the bed I share with my husband talking to a man I am exceedingly attracted to while my family is out of town. Am I okay? Not really. Is Ben okay? Maybe. But who is this *we* he is talking about?

"We're friends, right?" he asks when I don't answer him.

"Are we?" I can't help myself. Definitions are almost as important to me as words. And I can't help but feel like I am missing something, something important.

"I hope so," he replies, his voice low. "I feel connected to you, Ellen. I know that sounds strange, but it's true. And that doesn't happen to me very often."

I let out a sigh and rub my forehead with my free hand. "I feel the same—"

"Great! That's perfect. I'll let you know," he says hurriedly. Then the phone goes dead in my hand.

I glance up at the TV and see that the old woman looks like she's about to hurl herself into the ocean. She doesn't, I know. She throws the necklace in instead. But if *I* were standing at the side of a ship right now, I'd *jump*.

Two seconds later, the cell rings. I hit the Talk button. "Is everything okay?"

"I was going to ask you the same thing." It's Jonah. Of course. I realize with horror that I could have said something like, "Hi, Ben" or "Are you all right, *Ben*?" or "Come on over and climb on top of me, *Ben*." Beads of sweat pop out on my upper lip.

"Everything's fine," I say evenly. "Why?"

"I called the house earlier and got no answer, so I called your cell and got no answer on that, and you still hadn't called me back, so I started to worry."

With good reason, I think. *Just not the* right *reason*.

"I was in the bath when you called," I tell him, glad that this is the truth. "And I fell asleep without even checking my voice mail."

"You fell asleep at seven o'clock?" he asks skeptically.

"Mia came over today, you know, her annual send-off? I might have had a bit too much wine."

"Oh. Well, it's good to know you're having a grand old time without us." He is using the same tone Ben used at the marina, and it's enough to make me want to scream.

"What would you like, Jonah?" I ask icily. "That I curl up into a fetal position and spend the next six days bawling my eyes out?"

"It would just be nice to know that you missed us."

You just left! He sounds so petty and juvenile that I can't resist telling him the truth. "I miss the kids a lot."

"The kids, huh? But not me, right?"

"Jonah, your behavior of late hardly inspires me to pine away for you."

That shuts him up for ten whole seconds. "Okay," he concedes. "But just for the record, I don't miss you either."

"Give the kids my love," I say through clenched teeth. Then I disconnect the call and fling the phone across the room. Sally looks up quickly, snorts, then falls back against the pillows.

Eleventh Post: March 26, 2012
SomethingNewAt42

MEN ARE SCHIZO

Enough said.

Hanging around. Nothing to do but frown.
Rainy days and Mondays always get me down.
Monday, Monday. Can't stop that day.
It's just another manic Monday, I wish I could run day . . .

A constant string of Monday songs echoes through my brain as I sit on the floor of Connor's closet and proceed to go through every single pair of shoes he owns. In terms of mental stimulation, this job ranks about a one-point-two, whereas in terms of the smell factor, it rates a solid nine. My son, God love him, has stinky feet. I gave up on handing down Connor's shoes to Matthew before Connor turned eight because of the offensive odor that emanated from his sneakers even though he'd worn them on only a handful of occasions. And I should note that Connor is a very clean young man. He showers every day and is positively anal about grooming, a trait he inherited, obviously, from Jonah. But put his feet in a pair of socks and entomb them in anything other than sandals and you have a recipe for a stench that could knock out a stadium full of people.

The house phone rings. My stiff muscles protest as I push

myself off the floor and head for my bedroom to answer it. I pray that it won't be Jonah. I have already spoken to my children this morning. Jessie called from her father's cell, since her grandparents don't let the kids use their phone because of the "outlandish long distance rates, by God." She spent five minutes telling me about a lizard she spied this morning that was as big as a cat before handing off the phone to her brothers. Connor and Matthew had little to say other than to bemoan the fact that Grandma and Grandpa don't have a Wii and only have basic cable and won't let them use the computer to play games and what the heck are they going to do for the next five days? When Connor asks me if I want to speak to Jonah, I give him the excuse I always do when I want to avoid speaking to my husband: that I have to make number two.

I don't expect it to be Jonah on the line, but just in case, I answer with a chilly "Yes."

"'Yes?'" Jill echoes. "Is that your new way of answering the phone?"

"I thought you might be Jonah."

"Ah, the one-syllable tactic," she says. "I take it things are still a little rocky with hubby."

"If the fact that I can't stand the sight or sound of him equals things being a little rocky, then yes."

"You know," she says, "you could just answer the phone *Prick*."

Oh my God! "Oh my God!" I say aloud. "Jill, you just said *prick*! I mean, you actually said it! You didn't spell it! What the h-e-l-l is going on? Did you check in to swear-word-spelling rehab?"

"Ha ha," she says, amused. "For your information, *prick* is not actually a swear word. 'If you prick us, do we not bleed?'"

Since when does Jill quote *The Merchant of Venice*? Something is definitely up.

"What is up, cuz?" I ask.

"I don't know what you mean," she says coyly, and I think she knows exactly what I mean.

"You just quoted Shakespeare."

"So? I love Shakespeare. I could compare Shakespeare to a summer's day."

"Are you high?" This is the only possible explanation I can come up with.

"I am high on life," she says. "And on the fact that I had the most incredible sex of my entire life last night."

"With who?"

She laughs. "With Greg, of course. You know, my husband?"

"Since when are you having the most incredible sex of your life with your husband?" I can't help but ask.

"Since last night," she replies. "Since I told him that if he didn't start treating me like the desirable woman I am, I was going to divorce him."

I sit down on my bed, shocked at my cousin's brass balls. I've always known she has balls, but I just assumed they were made of something softer, like Knox Blox.

"Wow," is all I can say.

"Wow is right," she agrees. "Do you know that he actually cried when I threatened divorce? Said he couldn't imagine his life without me in it. And I told him that he better start proving it to me because I was almost done."

"Jill, you are the *man*!"

She giggles effervescently and I realize that I haven't heard her sound this happy for a very long time. The cynic in me wonders how long Greg's renewed attentions will last, but I don't give voice to this question. I don't want to spoil her mood. And maybe, just maybe, this is the kick in the ass he needed to change his ways for good. I pray for this with all my heart because my cousin deserves it.

"So I read your blog this morning," she says breezily. "Were you in a hurry or something?"

Actually, I wrote the blog last night after throwing my cell phone across the room. I went downstairs to make myself a sandwich, then sat in front of the computer, intending to write a long and laborious treatment on how men are schizophrenic and multiple-personalitied and bipolar and just plain psychotic (and those are the *good* ones) as an addendum to my first post, *Men Are Cheeseballs*. My hope was that writing it would be therapeutic for me and I would be able to release some of my tension over Jonah and Ben. But after coming up with the title, I realized that no amount of description or detail was necessary. I sat for a long moment, debating as to whether I should expound, wondering if I was copping out. I even began several paragraphs. But everything I wrote ended up taking away from my main point, so I scheduled it for today's publication and shut the computer down.

"You didn't like it?" I joke. "I thought it was brilliant."

"Apparently, so do a lot of readers," she says. "You got more comments for today's blog post than any of your others. And every single one agrees with you!"

I laugh. "Simplicity is key," I say.

"So, what's on your agenda for today?"

A sigh escapes my lips because I know that as soon as we end this conversation I will have to return to smell central. "Finish going through Connor's closet, start on Matthew's. I don't know if I'll get to Jessie's today. I think I should pace myself."

"Gee, you really know how to live," Jill says.

"What about you?"

"Well, I'm going to bask in the afterglow of my magnificent lovemaking for at least another hour. Then I promised the boys I'd take them to the movies. The Pixar one that came out on Friday. Want to join us? That is, if you can tear yourself away from your closets."

I contemplate a theater full of popcorn-munching, sugar-frenzied, vociferous preteens and decide, in true Jack Nicholson fashion, that I'd rather stick needles in my eyes.

"Thanks anyway," I tell her. "I really want to get these chores finished."

"Okay. But let's do a girls' lunch later this week. Just you and me. I'll get Patty down the street to take the boys."

"Sounds great," I say. I put the receiver down, stand up, and head back to Connor's closet, wishing I had some of that ointment that coroners rub under their noses before an autopsy.

· Twenty ·

It's amazing how much you can accomplish when you don't have four people and a dog constantly asking you to do something. (Well, Sally is here, but she is, without a doubt, the most low-maintenance of the bunch.) By four o'clock that afternoon, I have successfully rampaged through my children's closets, leaving them frighteningly neat and organized. I know how the kids will scream and complain when they see the fruits of my labor (*Where's this?* and *What happened to that?*), and I also know that within a month, said closets will be restored to their usual chaotic state, but at this moment, as I pull open the door of the fridge and grab a well-deserved beer, I am feeling very pleased with myself. It's only Monday, after all. If I can get the garage done tomorrow, I will have the rest of the week at my disposal to indulge myself in whatever activity suits my fancy.

I haven't heard from Jonah today, which is fine with me. For the first time in my marriage, I realize that I have absolutely nothing to say to him, with neither love nor anger. I feel as though our marriage is an ocean, and for a long time now, we have both been sitting in separate life rafts, floating aimlessly along on the whim of the tide. Up until now, the currents have been moving in the same direction, but a huge swell has surged between us and is pushing us apart. I don't know whether this comparison was influenced by my aquatic hijinks yesterday, but it seems right on the mark.

I was never one of those women who suffered from the delusion that marriage is forever and that love lasts a lifetime. I come from divorced parents, after all. But I did believe that making it all the way to old age with one person, persevering through troubled times and surviving the unavoidable ups and downs of married life, would give a person a mighty sense of accomplishment, akin to climbing Mount Everest. But my opinion of marriage has changed along with my views on mountain climbing. Both are too damn much work. Just the thought of attempting to have a conversation with Jonah exhausts me.

I take my beer into the living room and park myself on the couch, grabbing the new edition of the *Ladies Living-Well Journal*. I ended up reading Jill's March issue cover to cover, and although the contest isn't over yet, I figure I should familiarize myself with the content. Just on the very way off-chance that I win. Not that I honestly believe that is a possibility, and not, believe me, that I care a great deal about it. But should the impossible become the actual, I want to be prepared.

The April issue has an interview with Sandra Bullock and I skip ahead to that page. I like her, I really do, but when I look at the picture of her next to the article, I think, *Sandy, what have you done to yourself?*

I am squinting down at her image, trying to find a single

wrinkle on her forty-eight-year-old face, when I hear the slam of a car door out front. My first thought is that Jonah has already had too much quality time with his parents and the kids and has come home early. But I quickly dismiss the thought, knowing full well, from my daughter's loquacious ramblings this morning, that Jonah is finally making good on a promise he made to the kids three years ago. He is taking them to see Meteor Crater.

Thinking the car outside must belong to a neighbor's friend or a meter reader, I return my attention to the magazine, only to be interrupted by the doorbell.

Frowning, I get up and head for the door, casting a quick glance out the front window to see a plain black sedan sitting at the curb in front of my house. I don't recognize the car, but when I open the door, I recognize my guest, and I have to swallow the lump that immediately rises to my throat.

Ben Campbell stands on my front porch, dressed in slacks, a sport coat, and a conservative blue-and-gold tie.

"Hi," he says, looking as awkward as I feel. When I say that I am not dressed for visitors, I mean that I suddenly wish an earthquake would hit Garden Hills and tear a gaping crevasse right through the baseboards of my foyer that would swallow me up, tattered painter pants, *Flashdance*-style collarless T-shirt, and all.

"I tried to call your cell," he explains, "but you didn't answer. I thought I'd just come by."

Suddenly I am thankful that our house is situated at the end of the block. There is no one on our right and no one across the street, just my neighbor to our left, Vivienne Dulac, an eighty-seven-year-old woman from France who doesn't hear very well and pretends not to speak English even though she has lived in the States for forty-two years. Even if, perchance, she caught sight of a strange man entering my house,

Jonah would never be the wiser because he doesn't speak French.

"Come in," I say, drawing the door open, but he shakes his head.

"Actually, I was hoping you'd come with me. I have kind of a surprise for you." When I don't respond, his expression falls. "I'm sorry. It's a bad time. I shouldn't have just dropped in on you. How rude. Sorry." He starts to turn away, but before he can reach the steps, I reach out and grasp his sleeve.

"Just give me a minute to change, okay?"

The inside of the sedan is as unremarkable as the outside, if you don't count the shotgun mount between the seats, the squawking CB radio, and the mesh grate that separates the front from the back.

"Nice car," I say with a grin, and Ben winks at me.

"Courtesy of the GHPD." He has relaxed completely since I accepted his invitation, even went so far as to loosen his tie and remove his jacket. I, too, feel relaxed. Although Ben's side of the conversation on the phone last night was cryptic, he did manage to give me clarity on one subject. He thinks of us as friends. Just friends.

Suddenly, Billy Crystal's voice pipes up in my head. *Men and women cannot be friends because the sex always gets in the way.*

I mentally tell Billy to fuck off.

"So where are we going?" I ask, trying to change the course of my thoughts.

"You don't like surprises?"

"No, I do," I assure him. "As long as they don't require me to wear a wet suit."

"Ah, but you had fun!"

"Yes," I agree. "But I'm still trying to warm up."

"I promise, no ocean adventures today."

As he aims the car toward downtown Garden Hills, I gaze out the window, taking in the shops and restaurants and local landmarks as we pass them. I am struck by the odd realization that I am very rarely a passenger in a moving vehicle, and that when I am, it is usually at night, on a date with my husband. It's fun to see the streets of my hometown in broad daylight, and I notice things for the first time, like the way the light posts in the civic section are made to look like gas lamps, or how the top scoop on the sign for the Garden Hills Ice Cream Parlor magically falls off, then reappears seconds later, or that the roof tiles on Casa Mexicana have letters painted on them that spell out *comida buenisima* over and over again. These things are all new to me, and I smile to myself as I drink them in.

When we reach Police Plaza, Ben turns into the parking lot and weaves past several buildings before coming to a stop in a slot designated for civil servants. He opens the door and gets out, and I follow suit, giving him a questioning look over the top of the sedan.

"You're going to give me a guided tour of the jail?" I ask, raising my eyebrows.

He laughs. "No. But I'll let you try out my handcuffs if you'd like."

Gulp. *Just friends. Sure. Yup. Friends say things like that to each other all the time.* Billy Crystal snickers at me in my head.

Ben comes around the back of the car and holds out his hand to me. Without thinking, I grasp it, and he yanks me in to him as though we are doing a tango on *Dancing with the Stars.* A surprised laugh escapes me as he clutches me to him. For a microsecond that seems to last a year, he stares intently into my eyes, and I allow myself to stare back. Then he twirls me out to arm's length and lets go of my hand.

"This way," he says, gesturing toward the redbrick structure in front of us. Instead of heading for the double doors, he gives the entrance a wide berth and heads around the side of the building, and I trot to keep up with his long strides. When we reach the back courtyard, I freeze in my tracks and suck in a quick breath at the sight before me.

A helicopter sits smack-dab in the middle of the helipad adjacent to the courtyard. I feel my jaw drop and my eyes go wide, and I know that I must look like a gaping idiot, but I can't seem to pull my teeth and lips together. Any moment, drool will start to leak out of the corners of my mouth. I glance over at Ben, who is sporting a Cheshire grin. He takes hold of my elbow and ushers me toward the forest green flying machine, talking as we go.

"We share this with two other police departments," he says. "The pilot's a buddy of mine from up north, moved down here a few years ago." As if on cue, a tall, trim man in his late thirties, with close-cropped hair just going silver at the sides, steps out of the helicopter and walks purposely toward us. He grasps Ben's hand and gives it a hearty shake, then smiles at me and puts out his hand.

"This is Sergeant Fred Walker," Ben says. "He'll be our pilot today. Fred, this is Ellen Ivers."

"Nice to meet you," I say as I withdraw my hand from his Wolverine-like grip and flex my fingers open and closed just to make sure they still work.

"She's all fueled up and ready to go," the pilot says with a nod to the helicopter. "Just climb on board and fasten your safety belts. I'll be right there."

He walks over to a small booth where another officer sits.

The officer hands the sergeant a clipboard and a pen, and Walker starts checking things off.

I look at Ben, feeling something close to awe. "You arranged all this?" I pause, then clear my throat. "For me?"

He smiles. "I figured I owed you."

I am so overwhelmed I don't know what to say. No one—not my husband, not my parents, nor any of my friends—has ever executed a surprise as magnificent as this. I am beyond touched. I am undone. This is like a fairy tale or fantasy or a really good romantic comedy. And though I am well aware that there will be no happily-ever-after in this story, at this moment, I don't care a damn. I am going to take this ride, both literally and metaphorically, and if I crash and burn, so be it.

"Thank you," I say quietly, and the intensity of my gaze causes Ben to look suddenly serious. He glances past me, I assume to make sure the two officers are not looking in our direction, then slowly bends down and kisses me tenderly on the lips.

I am thirteen, and Sean Goldman is awkwardly grasping my shoulders and pulling me toward him as my knees turn to spaghetti. I am seventeen, and Kyle Krauss is revealing his newfound talent for French kissing behind the gym during fourth period. I am twenty-three, and David Carlson is clutching my hair with his fingers as he presses his lips against mine, leaving me breathless and inspiring in me a yearning that persists long after he breaks my heart. I am twenty-eight, and Jonah is hungrily crushing his mouth over mine, demanding my tongue, sending heat all the way to my groin.

It lasts only for an instant, but Ben's kiss will now be archived among my greatest hits.

"You're welcome," he says, his face an inch from mine. He

lingers a second or two, then straightens up, takes my hand, and leads me to my seat.

My seat in a fucking helicopter.

There are four seats in the chopper, two in the cockpit and two behind. Ben and I sit in the second row and strap ourselves in with safety belts so cumbersome and complicated that it takes me a few minutes to get mine in place. Sergeant Walker leans in, eyeing my belt to make sure I am tightly restrained, then climbs in and takes his seat in front of the console, donning a large white headset. He punches some buttons, and immediately the helicopter comes to life. A low hum sounds, slowly gaining volume and coupled with a deep vibration that shudders through the aircraft.

My heart beats crazily in my chest, and I feel like I am a child about to take her first ride at Disneyland. Ben looks over at me, and his grin falters.

"You okay?" he asks, and I realize I must look scared shitless instead of what I really am, which is so excited I might not need an aircraft to take off.

I shake my head. "I'm *not* okay. I am fantastic!"

He smiles, relieved. "This is a Eurocopter EC 120 Colibri," he explains. "The wide cabin design makes it perfect for law enforcement, and the tail rotor makes it fairly quiet in comparison to other types of choppers."

As the rotor blade starts to churn, I realize that *fairly quiet* is a subjective phrase. A high-pitched, rhythmic whine fills the cabin as the blade picks up speed. I watch Sergeant Walker flick a few switches and depress several buttons before reaching for the joystick. The helicopter lurches slightly, and then I feel the kick as we ascend, a few feet only, then higher and higher until we are hovering about thirty feet over the helipad. Sergeant Walker is speaking into his mike, his words unintelligible from where I sit. He glances back at Ben and me and nods, and five seconds later we are airborne, hurling toward the Pacific Ocean.

I feel like I am going to burst through my own skin. Never before have I experienced such sheer exhilaration, all of my senses on hyperdrive. We sail over the long stretch of beach, right along the shore, and from our perspective the deep blue-green water sparkles with a million sun-made diamonds. From the height of an airplane, the ground seems disconnected, and when I fly, I always feel detached from life below. But from the far closer vantage point of a helicopter, I feel completely connected to, almost reverential toward, the vista below me.

Conversation is made difficult by the buzz of the blade and the wind whipping through the open window, but I wouldn't want to speak anyway. I just stare, wide-eyed, as we move inland along the nature preserve, wind up over the cobbled streets of downtown, past the huge expanse of Garden Hills Buffalo Park, where half a dozen dancers in colorful garb are giving some kind of performance on the grassy knoll. We zoom over the soccer field, empty today save for a few kids breezily kicking around a ball, then up we go, the helicopter picking up speed along with my racing heart, and head for the reservoir. Along the concrete planes of the faux river, Sergeant Walker seems to put his pedal to the metal (yes, I know there is no gas pedal) and we whoosh back toward the ocean.

I have been so focused on the sights below me that I have almost forgotten that Ben is seated beside me. When I feel his fingers intertwine with mine, I snap my head around and flash him a smile of sheer joy. He smiles back and rests our interlocked hands on my thigh. I don't pull away, have no desire to. I expect a voice in my head to whisper a warning, or an angel to appear on my shoulder and tell me to be good. But perhaps both the voice and the angel are on vaycay. Perhaps they realize that I am too content at this moment to pay them any heed. Perhaps they are well aware of the fact that I would tell them both to get lost. For the rest of the ride, down the river, south along the coast and back to Police Plaza, our hands remain there, and only when the feet of the chopper hit concrete does Ben finally release me.

Back at my house, Ben kneels on the floor of my kitchen, good-naturedly allowing Sally to smother him with dog kisses. His sport coat and tie are slung over the back of a chair and he has unbuttoned his shirt far enough to reveal his white undershirt.

"You're a good girl," he coos as he strokes her fur and scratches behind her ears. Sally looks like she has died and gone to doggie heaven, and I think, *I know what you mean, girl.*

I am trembling slightly as I pop the tops off a couple of beers, not because of Ben's presence in my kitchen, but because I am still reeling from the helicopter ride. It's as though all of the endorphins produced by a triathlon were injected into my veins at once and the euphoria has yet to evaporate.

"Would you like a glass?" I ask, Miss Manners that I am.

"No, thanks, the bottle's fine." He stands and walks over to the sink, much to Sally's chagrin. She follows him, watery eyes pleading for more love, tail thumping back and forth. I set Ben's beer on the counter next to him as he washes his hands, and then I grab a dog bone from the bag next to the fridge to offer Sally. She considers it an unworthy substitute for Ben's affections, but reluctantly takes it from me and carries it to her dog bed.

Ben dries his hands on the dish towel next to the sink as I try desperately not to think about the fact that that very towel was a gift from Jonah's mother. Then he reaches for his beer. He turns to face me, and our eyes lock. There we stand, beers in hand, saying nothing for what feels like an eon, an eon I spend trying to resist the magnetic pull of his gaze. Honestly, his eyes are like two tractor beams and I am a mere star fighter whose thrusters are down. I take a step toward him, then another, and he closes the distance by taking a step of his own.

He's going to kiss me, I think. *He's going to kiss me in my kitchen.*

I break the stare first, look down at my beer, at the floor, at Sally, at anything other than his hypnotic brown eyes.

Ben sets his beer down, undrunk, and pulls mine from my grasp, returning it to the counter. Then he cups my chin in his hand and raises my face so that I can't help but look at him. And now I am trembling because of him, because of the heat of his fingertips on my skin, because of the fact that this is the line, the point of no return, and as he lowers his head toward me, that inner voice suddenly comes to life with THX force, screaming, *No, Ellen! Stop, Ellen! DON'T, ELLEN!*

His lips touch mine, tentatively at first, so soft and delicious, and the decibel level of the voice in my brain must be what causes people to go postal with machine guns, and I can literally feel the shocked glares of my husband and children from the photographs affixed to the fridge behind me, but I cannot stop myself, cannot pull away. Ben cocks his head ever so slightly to the right, then covers my mouth with his and claims it completely, crushing against me as the metaphorical dam bursts. And suddenly, everything goes silent in my mind.

He presses me against the counter, his strong arms encircling my waist, his hands sliding across the small of my back as he kisses me hungrily, his tongue seeking out mine. And I kiss him back, yes, with reckless abandon, my arms reaching around his neck and clutching him fiercely as I feel every corpuscle in my entire body turn to molten heat. And I can't breathe, and I don't care because it feels so good, so goddamn fucking amazing that I don't think I will ever stop kissing him, even if the Big One hits, even if my kids or Jonah walk into this room right now, because if I spent the rest of my life sucking face with this man I would die happy.

"Ellen." A guttural whisper in my ear. One word, two syllables that make me instantly wet, and he grazes my neck with kisses, then begins to suck at the tender skin on the side of my throat, and it feels incredible, but his lips are no longer on mine, and I miss them already, so I grab his face and guide his mouth back to my mouth and experience that same inner explosion when our tongues meet again. And then I realize, with ever mounting anticipation, that I can feel his erection through both of our clothes, rock hard against my abdomen. Without thinking, I reach down and place my hand over it, tracing its outline with my fingers, my pulse throbbing in my throat as I detect *his* pulse throbbing in my palm.

A gasp escapes him and when I look up at him, I see that his eyes are practically rolling back in his head. I walk my fingers up to the clasp of his trousers, and quickly, urgently, undo it, then tug on the zipper. So frantic am I to free him that I barely notice the small vibration coming from the pocket of his pants. Just as I reveal the cotton fabric of his underwear (boxer-briefs, for the record), his cell phone blasts me with a rendition of "Ballroom Blitz." I immediately recoil as though the cell phone has see-through vision and at this moment is recording the fact that my hand is on its owner's crotch.

Ben moans, then says "Shit" under his breath as I disengage myself from his grasp and head for the sink. In a hasty move I'm certain he's perfected at countless urinals, Ben restores his fly to its upright position, then reaches into his pocket and pulls out his cell. His brow furrows as he reads the Caller ID, and he glances at me apologetically.

"I have to take this," he says quietly, and I nod, not trusting my voice to come out sounding remotely normal.

He leaves the kitchen in a hurry, stopping at the foyer long enough to answer the call, then continues through to the darkened living room.

As much as I'd like to follow him and eavesdrop, I don't. Instead, I open the tap at the sink and splash my burning cheeks and forehead with cold water, then reach for a glass in the dish drain and pour myself a healthy belt. I gulp it down, then refill the glass and sip it slowly as I stare out the kitchen window toward the park.

For the second time today I am waiting for the remorse, the guilt, the voice in my head to call me a sleazy no-good hoochie mama. But none of that comes. I am still glowing from the inside out. Everything in the room is vibrant and alive to my eyes, the tap water tastes like Evian, and my skin, from my forehead to the tips of my fingers, is buzzing with sensation. I have no doubt that the guilt will soon make an appearance, but at least I am getting a slight reprieve to bask in that long-forgotten glow of a transcendent first kiss. (Yes, *kiss*. The other doesn't count because there were two layers of fabric between us.)

I turn to face Ben as he walks back into the kitchen, pocketing his cell phone, an ambivalent look on his face.

"Timing's everything," I say, trying for humor, remembering what happened at the marina yesterday when he merely unzipped my wet suit. God only knows what his reaction might be today. But as soon as he looks at me, he smiles, all ambivalence gone.

"I'm so sorry. I have to go."

"I know," I say, because I do. "I understand. It's probably for the best anyway."

"Look, Ellen . . . I'm really sorry about *that*. I shouldn't have. . . . I'm sorry. . . ."

"Well, I'm not." He looks surprised by my words. "I haven't been kissed that way in over a decade, Ben. So, thanks."

He does not come over to me, and I am glad for it. If he were to move any closer, neither one of us would be able to resist a good-bye kiss, and that would be dangerous, would lead to more kissing and then to the same place we were before, only this time, he wouldn't be able to leave, despite the consequences. So he stays where he is, safe from the magnetic pull.

"I don't want you to think that I do this—"

"I don't," I reply, cutting him off. "I don't."

I watch as he gathers his coat and tie from the kitchen chair and strides toward the foyer. At the archway, he stops and turns to me, but says nothing.

"Thanks for the surprise," I tell him and he smiles warmly before walking out of my kitchen and out of my house.

Twenty-one

The garage door is open, letting in the fresh air and morning sun on this glorious March day. It's the kind of spring morning that makes you want to go Rollerblading along the coast, or take a bike ride down the river, or a hike through Buffalo Park. It is not the kind of day you want to spend holed up in your garage sifting through ten years' worth of accumulated junk. But that is exactly what I am doing at this moment, and I actually welcome the job. It is mindless and meditative, and since I read somewhere that purging is good for the soul, I can only hope that I have enough crap within these walls to wipe my proverbial slate clean.

The guilt finally claimed me last night as I was talking on the phone with my kids. I had been anticipating it for hours, like you do when you feel that first stomach rumble after eating something that doesn't taste quite right. But it didn't take hold of me until the middle of Matthew's soliloquy about Meteor Crater, which he described as *totally boss* and *way cool* and *completely awesome*. My heart started pounding and my chest constricted to the point where I could barely draw breath and I realized I was about to have a full-blown anxiety attack. I struggled to calm myself, sucking in air slowly and rhythmically through my teeth as my oblivious son passed the phone to Jessie, who proceeded to repeat the exact same story, although with slightly different descriptive adjectives. By the time Connor got on the line, my heart rate had evened out, but I was drenched with sweat and could not hear a word he said because of the roaring in my ears.

I managed to make the appropriate noises while Connor spoke, oohing and ahhing in all the right places, though I did make a giant faux pas when I said, "That's great, honey," in response to his telling me that one of his grandparents' rabbits had mysteriously vanished. I quickly covered my mistake by murmuring that rabbits are very resourceful and at least Grandma and Grandpa had twelve more where that one came from.

When Jonah took the phone, the roar in my ears had subsided, but I was feeling nauseated. And I couldn't help but second-guess everything I said to him. I worried that "It sounds like the kids had a great time today" would come out as "I sucked face with another man in our kitchen." Jonah seemed vaguely suspicious, but I realized that this was because I was being nice to him, which, quite frankly, I felt was my duty as a floozy. However, I did force myself to become chillier toward him as the conversation progressed, just to maintain our status quo. Wouldn't want him to suspect me of adulterous behavior just because I was being civil to him.

After I hung up the phone, I paced around my bedroom for a full five minutes, waiting to see whether I would actually throw up (I didn't). But as the night wore on, and the conversation with my family became more distant, and the bottle of wine I had opened magically emptied, my shame and regret dissipated into the air like ether. And when I fell into bed at ten thirty, the last thing that went through my mind was a replay of my five blissful minutes with Ben.

This morning, I awoke before dawn and dragged my ass out of the house for an actual street run, taking a confused and utterly disinterested Sally with me. It was odd to be pounding the pavement, not listening to music or watching TV. The asphalt was hell on my joints, and my knees ached within the first ten minutes, but in an odd way, I felt like this was penance. My head was full of conflicting thoughts and emotions: the guilt, the pleasure, my children, Ben's wife, Ben's crotch, Jonah's face, my name whispered on a sultry breath in my ear. Forty minutes later, when I returned to the safety of my kitchen, my clothes were drenched with sweat and my head was still full of noise.

Knowing I could not possibly face my blog yet, I quickly showered, ate half of a whole-wheat bagel, and headed for the garage.

So here I sit, surrounded by piles of old scooters (two Iron Man, one Batman, two generic Razors, and a pretty pink princess Razor with the faces of all the Disney princesses along the bottom, which Jessie refuses to ride because she doesn't want to step all over Cinderella and Jasmine), roller skates, skateboards, helmets, and other assorted paraphernalia disgorged by the huge toy bin next to the garage door. Add that to the rusted tools from the interior shed to my right and the corroded camping equipment and long-forgotten sporting goods hauled out of the steamer trunk to my left. What I would like to do is dump everything into the recycling barrel, but my upper-middle-class guilt keeps me from doing so, and I mull over the fact that I am probably more guilt ridden about the prospect of throwing away not-so-gently-used toys than I am over making out with Ben Campbell in my kitchen.

Do not go there, Ellen, I warn myself, as it is only ten A.M. and I am already mentally exhausted. The point of garage purging, aside from my desire to create enough room to park the Flex next to Jonah's Lexus, is to clear my mind. *Breathe in, breathe out. Goodwill for this Razor, recycling bin for this helmet. Breathe in, breathe out.*

I hear the engine of an approaching car and I clutch Jessie's old Elmo kneepads to my chest as though they will protect me from whatever temptation might be headed my way. (*Hahahahahahaha, today, boys and girls, we're going to talk about* adultery. *Can you say that?* A-dul-tery. *Hahahaha. Oh, it's Mr. Noodle!*) When Jill's champagne-colored Chrysler Town and Country pulls into my driveway, I sigh with relief. I had forgotten her promise to bring the boys by to see if there was anything they might like to salvage from my garage. She pops out from behind the wheel, cardboard carry carton with two paper cups in hand, just as the back door mechanically slides open with nary a sound. The three *D*s jump out of the minivan and follow their mom up to the garage, eyes wide with the promise of discovering buried treasure.

"Hi-yo, Elle-belle," says Decatur.

"Hi-*yo* yourself," I return as I push myself off the garage floor to the musical accompaniment of popping joints.

Denver and Detroit each toss a "Hi" in my general direction as all three immediately begin to pilfer through the junk. Jill is wearing cream slacks and a mint green pullover sweater, and she looks around with alarm at the piles of dirt and dust-encrusted crap. I should have advised her to wear a hazmat suit. She gingerly steps over to me and hands me a coffee. I try not to think of Ben as I peer at the Starbucks logo emblazoned on the side.

"Thanks," I say, brushing off my tattered jeans and taking the cup from her.

"So, how's it going?" she asks, still surveying the wreckage of my garage.

"Life is an accumulation of crap," I say.

"Check it out!" exclaims Decatur as he unearths a blue-and-rust (yes, actual rust) pogo stick from one of the piles. His younger brothers ooh and ahh and the three of them trot to the driveway to test it out. I pray their tetanus shots are current.

"You need your own Dumpster," Jill offers, and I frown at her. "What are you going to do with this stuff?"

I take a sip of coffee and set the cup down on the tool bench. "Some of it's going to Goodwill, some I'm just going to dump, and the rest—"

"Oh my *God*! What the h-e-l-l is that??"

She is staring at me with something like horror on her face. Or, I should say, she is staring at my neck with horror. Reflexively, my hand shoots up to my throat.

"What?" My first thought is *bug*. Yikes! "What is it? What?" I start swatting at myself like I'm demon-possessed as phantom insects creepy-crawl over my skin.

"It's not a *bug*!" Jill states as she leans in to get a closer look. "It's a d-a-m-n hickey, that's what it is." Her words come out in a strangled whisper so the boys won't hear. My hand freezes midswat and I feel my mouth form an O of surprise. And apparently, my left temporal lobe is on a union break because I suddenly can't remember how to speak.

Jill straightens up and arches a brow at me. "And just what have you been up to, sugar?" she asks, sounding exactly like Scarlett O'Hara. "If you tell me that's from the curling iron,

I will club you to death with that Justice League baseball bat over there."

I clear my throat violently, hoping to startle my vocal chords to life. "I, uh, I . . ."

She bites her lip, trying to stifle a grin. "Ben, right?"

I nod.

"Oh my Lord." She shakes her head, then narrows her eyes at me. "Why didn't you tell me?"

"It happened last night!" My voice has returned, but I keep the volume turned way down. "What was I supposed to do? Interrupt your freaking sex-fest to tell you I made out with Ben Campbell in my kitchen? I thought it could wait till this morning."

Actually, I hadn't thought about Jill at all. I was too consumed by my own guilt/euphoria to consider calling my cousin.

"Okay, fine," she relinquishes. "So . . . you made out? Is that all? Just, what, kissing, and neck sucking?"

"That about covers it," I say. "Isn't that enough?"

"It's not enough to get you into h-e-l-l." Her grin slowly slides from her face and she regards me seriously. "But it is enough to get you booted out of a marriage."

"Oh, Jill!" I rub my eyes, which is a mistake since my fingernails are full of grime. "Don't say that."

"If you found out that Jonah made out with that chick from his sales territory, you know, the one with the death's-head moth tattoo between her shoulder blades, you'd go completely ballistic. You would kick his sorry a-s-s out of the house faster than you can say *Silence of the Lambs*."

Her words are like a glass of ice water dumped over my head. She is absolutely right. Before this moment, I hadn't considered how I would feel if the situation were reversed. I may not harbor any fondness for my husband at this juncture of our marriage. I may even be subconsciously hoping that some kind of natural disaster sweeps him away or a freak accident befalls him. But the idea of him making out with another woman behind my back makes me seriously queasy.

"I hadn't thought of that."

"Obviously."

"Look," I whine. "It's not going to happen again." Jill's gaze remains steady, as though she is sizing up my words. "Really," I add for emphasis. "It was a mistake. And anyway, we stopped before it got out of hand." I don't mention the phone call, or the fact that if Ben's wife (because who else could it have been?) hadn't interrupted us, it would definitely have gotten out of hand. But even as I am assuring her of my contrition, I can feel my skin grow hot at the memory of Ben's touch.

Whoops of laughter from the sidewalk catch our attention and we both turn to see Detroit bouncing on the pogo stick like Tigger on methamphetamines while his brothers applaud him. Jill and I laugh along with the boys, and then she returns her attention to me as her smile fades.

"I'm your cousin, Ellen, and your best friend, and I love you." I groan inwardly and prepare myself for one of Jill's sermons, which in my experience, could land her a gig as an evangelist on Sunday morning TV. The only thing that keeps me from sticking a wide swath of duct tape across her mouth is the knowledge that she really does have my best interests in mind. So I obediently listen to her.

"I know things with Jonah aren't so hot right now. And I know you've been focusing on *you*. And you really are looking great, and I can tell you're feeling great. And you've started writing again, and that is amazing. Your blog seriously kicks a-s-s. But at this point in your life, you have to be practical. You are not twenty-three, when life was fun and exciting. You're almost forty-three, and life, well, it's just life."

She stops to take a breath and I catch the subtle slump of her shoulders, notice the slight shimmer of her green eyes as though tears are threatening.

"We make choices, and we have to stick with them. We have responsibilities and commitments, and we have to live up to them, even when they practically crush us."

It dawns on me that her words are meant as much for herself as they are for me. I reach out and place a hand on her arm.

"We are where we are," she says finally. "And we just have to deal with it."

"Jill."

She looks at me, and I see the regret etched into the faint lines around her eyes and mouth.

"But the other night, you told Greg you'd divorce him if he didn't start treating you right."

She flashes a sad smile. "It was a gamble," she admits, then sighs. "I'll never divorce him, Ellen. What would I do?" She laughs without humor. "At my age? A single mother? Please. It's not an option I want to consider. Do you?" I remain silent, and she shrugs dispassionately. "All we can do is just make the best of it."

Make the best of it? *Make the best of it?* This sentence rattles through my skull like a bowling ball, knocking out all other thoughts.

"Anyway," Jill says, casting off her gloom as though she is a molting snake. "This thing with Ben . . . Oh my. How am I ever going to look him in the eye again?" She giggles, and the sound is so at odds with her mood just seconds ago that it makes me cringe. "It's not like he was ever going to sweep you off your feet and take you away from all this, right?" She makes a point of looking around the garage.

I swallow. "No, of course not."

"It was a nice distraction, that's all. A little ego boost. And that's perfect! Just what you needed! Now you can get back to your life."

I nod acquiescently.

"Great!" she says brightly. "So, how can I help you with this *other* mess?"

For a woman who takes pride in the fact that she is one of the few people on planet earth, not including those in third world countries, who is not a slave to her cell phone, I am ashamed to admit that I have been carrying mine around with me all day, tucked into the back pocket of my jeans. It's not as though I believe Ben will call, or that I want him to call. I may not even answer the phone if he *does* call. But *if* he does, I want the option of answering. All day long, while immersed in Operation Clean Garage, I have subconsciously been anticipating that slight vibration against my butt cheek that precedes the ring.

Of course, my cell phone finally does vibrate just as I am pulling down my pants to pee. The ring tone assaults me and I jerk to my feet, yanking my jeans up so violently that the phone pops out of my back pocket and lands right smack-dab in the toilet bowl with a *kerplunk*! Three thoughts piggyback through my brain almost simultaneously. The first is that Jonah is going to be pissed. The second is that the PTA ladies will be immensely proud of me for bringing my cell phone into the bathroom. And the third is that it's a good thing it fell in *before* I peed because what woman wants to touch her own urine, unless she's just been stung on the hand by a jellyfish?

I quickly reach into the toilet and withdraw the phone, then cover it with a towel in a vain attempt to save it. When I stare down at it, the light on the screen is fading, like the man-machine's glowing red eyes at the end of *Terminator*. Going, going, gone. Dead in my hand. And I didn't even have a chance to see who called. Fuck.

It was probably Jonah or the kids, I tell myself. They'll try the house phone next. But as I wander out of the bathroom, unevacuated—as I have suddenly lost the urge to pee— the landline remains silent.

I know there is a way to retrieve messages from my cell from any phone, but I resist the urge. First, it would require me to find the instruction manual, which is probably buried somewhere under the debris in Jonah's office, and *second*, I am reading the whole cell-phone-as-Jacques-Cousteau de- bacle as a sign from God. If it *was* Ben who called, I should ignore it. But after pacing my house for a half an hour, which included a brief tour of my garage to admire the fruits of my labor (I give Jill no credit, because although she did stay, hers was more of a supervisory position which included saying things like "Dump" or "Recycle" or "What the h-e-l-l does *that* do?" while keeping her cream trousers dust-free), I am literally going out of my gourd. I just want to know who called, I tell myself. That's all. Knowing who called requires no reciprocal action, but at least I won't be driving myself crazy with curiosity.

I head for Jonah's office and begin rifling through the piles of papers and magazines on his desk. With my hus- band's deep-seated adoration for his cell phone, I would have thought he'd erected a shrine to the BlackBerry gods, but the his-and-hers tomes of technological elucidation are nowhere to be found. I pull out the top drawer, find only the requisite *p*s: pens, pencils, paper clips, and Post-its. I move down to the side drawers, come up empty on the first and second, then hit pay dirt on the third. I reach down and close my fingers around the manual, which has more pages than an Encyclopedia Britannica, because, let's face it, it's important to print the instructions in Swahili. Then my eye is caught by a small envelope the pale pink of early-morning clouds, tucked into the bottom crevice of the drawer.

I grasp the envelope and tug it free, then slowly turn it over in my hands. There is nothing written on the outside, and for a brief moment, I consider shoving it back into the drawer unopened. But who am I kidding, right? As I lift the flap and withdraw the note card from within, I realize that my heart is doing a tap dance against my chest plate. I have been with Jonah for fourteen years and have never given him a card even remotely like this.

I unfold the card and read the inscription and practically fall onto my ass on the office floor. I read it a second time. Short, sweet, to the point:

J–

Thanks for everything. You really saved me. Let me know how I can repay you.

T.

Okay. Okay. Okay. That one word flip-flops over and over again in my mind as the tap dance turns into the River-dance, twenty-four wooden clogs stomping around my chest in unison. I read the note again, trying to discern the deeper meaning. It is fairly innocent, I conclude, even though I am now sweating like Seabiscuit charging for the finish line. It doesn't say anything like *Thanks for the hot night of wax, handcuffs, anal stimulation, and vaginal penetration. Love and flowery kisses.* But the *J* and the *T* somehow make it more intimate. *We are not only on a first-name basis, we are on an initial basis. Hi, J. How are you? Great, T. You look terrific in that cashmere sweater that shows off your double Ds.*

Okay, again. I take a deep breath. Maybe I am overreacting. Perhaps I am reading into the whole pink stationery/initial-using circumstances. But a needling question remains: Why didn't Jonah say anything about it? If the whole thing is innocent, and Jonah, brave shining knight that he wishes he were, helped someone through a crisis, like someone's dog getting hit by a car or the rupturing of an appendix, or the disposal of a dismembered corpse—a situation that warranted a thank-you card—my husband never mentioned it to me. You would think that if it *were* innocent, he would have said something, at least in passing, brushing it off in that humble Jonah way, "Oh, it was nothing, I was just glad to help out." But not a word.

And, come to think of it, just who the fuck is *T*? I scan my mental rolodex for all of Jonah's work colleagues but the only *T*s are men: Tom, Tony, Tariq. So unless Jonah is actually gay and Tony, a New Jersey transplant who is always saying "fogeddabowdit," or Tariq, who is an ex-linebacker for the Redskins, or Tom, a twenty-two-year-old rookie with a new wife and baby, has taken to using flowing cursive on pale pink note cards, *T* is not one of his co-workers. Unless . . .

Death's-Head Moth Girl's name is Patricia. *Oh my God! Tricia.* It could be her. Since she was hired last year, Jonah has talked about her frequently. Nothing blatant, not *I'd like her to mount me during our ride-along.* Just that kind of off-hand chatter that speaks volumes. *Oh, Patricia did this crazy thing today at our meeting with Office Max.* Or *You should have seen Patricia's face when the Geico guy stapled his tie to our contract.* Little things. Inconsequential. Meaningless. Right up until you find a pink note card tucked into the side of your husband's desk drawer.

I sit for another few minutes, afraid that if I stand too quickly I'll fall back down again. Then I heave myself up with a grunt, still clutching the card in my clammy hand. I watch myself tuck the pink envelope back in the drawer, slide the drawer shut, and lean against the side of the desk. What now? What now *what now*? I feel dizzy and nauseated and yet a bubble of crazed lunacy in the form of the giggles is churning inside me. The irony of this find is not lost on me. Here I've been, flirting with disaster, paddleboarding and helicoptering and sucking face with a man in my kitchen, and it just might be that Jonah has beaten me to the extramarital shag.

Well, this is certainly Something New.

I give in to the giggles, and within seconds, they turn to full-blown, belly-cramping gales of laughter, and just when I think I am going to puke on Jonah's carpet, the laughter turns to tears and I am sobbing and retching and gasping for air.

Either I am in the middle of some kind of breakdown or I am a drama queen of the first order. I can't decide which bothers me more, and that conundrum alone helps me pull myself together. If I am wondering about the nature of this crying jag, I mustn't be completely out of my head. Then I start to question just what it is I am crying about. Is it because my husband is possibly having an affair? Is it because I might have an affair? Is it because, despite my recent skepticism regarding the institution of marriage, the eight-year-old girl who lives inside me, who lives inside every woman through the age of a hundred, desperately wants to believe in happily ever after? We want to believe, *I* want to believe, that the choices we've made were the right ones. And how can we ever really know?

I glance at the floor and spy the cell phone instruction manual, lying open, as fate would have it, on the call retrieval page. If that's not a sign from God, I don't know what is. I reach for the booklet and grasp it like a lifeline, then bolt out of the office and head for the kitchen.

Hi. It's me. Ben. If you get this message, give me a call back. If you want to.

Oh, yes. I want to.

....

Twelfth Post: March 27, 2012
SomethingNewAt42

ADULTERY FOR BEGINNERS

What do you do when sweet temptation thrusts its clamoring fingers at you and draws you into its lair? What do you do when you find that the touch of someone who is not your spouse turns your insides to hot jelly and makes you feel the way you haven't felt for twenty years? What do you do when you find something that may or may not prove that your spouse has already been unfaithful to you? Do you move forward with your own plans for duplicity? Do you grind your extramarital activities to a screeching halt in order to play the martyr while you tell yourself, "Well, at least *I* didn't cheat." And, in the end, what good does that do anyway? Does it change what has already transpired, erasing it into nonexistence?

From the dawn of man, people have been cheating. Sure, there are some who are like swans and mate for life, holding fast to their monogamy and chortling about how superior they are to the rest of the population because they have been able to deny their primal inclination to hump anything and everything that moves. In today's society in puritanical America, however, adultery is regarded as a sin. (Not in France, of course. In France, men parade their mistresses around as though for a panel of judges: *I gif Monsieur Bertrand's mistress a* neuf *point* quatre.) But here in the States, it's not so simple.

So what does it take to successfully cheat? A preternatural talent for scheduling comes to mind. Especially if you and your adulterous intended both have families. Hard to juggle, but doable if you've got Outlook on your computer. (Just don't forget to use a secret code with those reminders unless you want your spouse to see the pop up alarm with the words: *Meet lover for good schtupping.* He/she might suspect something's up.)

It also takes the ability to lie to others with ease. Example #1: Spouse: What are you doing tonight? You: I'm exhausted from spring cleaning. I'm going to crash early. Spouse: Then I shouldn't call later? You: No, I'll be asleep by eight. (Phone tucked in the crook of your neck while you rampage through your closet looking for just the right ensemble for your late-night rendezvous.) Example #2: Nameless Relative: You really need to put an end to things before they explode in your face. You: You're right. It was a mistake. I won't let it happen again. It was wrong wrong wrong. (Crossing your fingers behind your back while checking to make sure your cell phone battery hasn't died.)

You also must be able to lie to yourself convincingly, which is harder than it sounds, but once you're successful at the small stuff, it starts to get easier. Example #3: You: It's nothing. Just flirting. It doesn't mean anything. You: It was just one kiss. That's not cheating. You: I'm going to stop right now. You: I will not meet up with him/her ever again. You: It's just one drink. I can control myself. You: I have no intention of letting things go too far. You: This will be the very last time, I swear.

(By the way, lies of omission count, like not telling your spouse about a situation that inspires a cryptic thank-you note using only initials.)

To be successful at adultery, you must also carry in your arsenal one or more of the following character traits: selfishness; recklessness; the ability to douse the angel on your shoulder with kerosene and light it up like a tiki torch; an overwhelming sense of entitlement that encourages the phrases *I deserve some happiness*, *I deserve to feel good*, *I deserve to be desired*; and a hefty dose of denial, i.e., *What's the harm? No one will ever find out.*

So, if you possess the proper traits, can lie to yourself and others, and have no problem bending your own moral code (which is perhaps simpler if you're Catholic because a few Hail Marys release you from a world of hurt), then my advice to you is to go forth and fornicate. (But make certain you have an orgasm, so that if it does blow up in your face and your world comes crumbling down around you, at least you have that thirty seconds of pleasure to look back on.)

Sorry. Gotta go now. I have a date.

Twenty-two

The T Bar is more crowded than I would have expected on a weekday, but apparently Two-fer Tuesday is a draw. Most of the wooden tables are taken and the T-shaped bar (surprise) has few open seats. Votive candles decorate the tables and bar top, and a muted TV playing an NBA game is mounted just behind the bar, offering minimal illumination to the room. The stage in the far corner, which is simply a six-by-four-foot platform, has a single spotlight shining down on an abandoned microphone. An old Harry Connick Jr. song drifts softly from the speakers.

I stop at the doorway just long enough to catch my breath and scan the bar stools. Ben sits at the far end of the bar, surrounded by shadows, light from the flame of the nearest candle dancing over his features. Just the sight of him causes a swarm of butterflies to flutter through my stomach. He looks up and his eyes find mine, and I watch him sit back and smile at me. He reaches out and lifts the beer bottle in front of him, tips it toward me in a toasting gesture.

As if in a dream, I make my way toward him, all thoughts, inner voices, and not-so-subtle warnings temporarily silent. On the way here tonight, inside my husband's Lexus, I had a full-blown debate with myself that would make any presidential hopeful proud. I actually pulled the car over at one point and spoke aloud to my reflection in the rearview mirror. The argument circled around my reason for coming to meet Ben tonight. I needed that reason to be perfectly clear to me.

My discovery in Jonah's office propelled me to retrieve my cell phone message, but I did not want my decision to be based on my suspicions of Jonah's infidelity. I didn't want this to be about vengeance. I wanted to meet Ben tonight simply because I *wanted* to. And here I am.

I am an almost-forty-three-year-old woman who wants something just for me. And that *something* is sitting right there.

As I approach, Ben stands and pulls out the empty stool next to him. I am touched by the chivalrous gesture, and as I stare at him, I am once again taken by how handsome he is; the strong line of his jaw, the chiseled cheekbones, the warmth of his brown eyes, the supple red lips that are turned up in that trademark grin.

"Hi," he says quietly.

"Hi," I return as I place a steadying hand on the back of the stool.

"You came."

I nod, a bit puzzled. "I said I would."

"I know. But you sounded, I don't know. A little unsure."

That's because, at the time, I was in the grips of another panic attack over the decision/mistake I was about to make.

I got dressed and undressed three times, applied makeup and then scrubbed it off so violently with my Clinique cleanser I must have taken off the top two layers of my skin, started the car only to turn it off, get out, and march back into the garage. (Indecision, thy name is Ellen.) And then, when I managed to actually pull out of the driveway and head for downtown, the internal debate about the *why* began. But at this moment, as I gaze at Ben, remembering yesterday in my kitchen, recalling the last three weeks and how I have felt every time I've been in his presence, I am utterly calm.

"I'm here."

He smiles and takes my hand, giving it a gentle squeeze. "I'm glad."

Is it warm in here?

When he releases my hand, I peel off my sweater and tuck it over the back of the stool and sit as Ben eases me toward the bar. He takes his own seat and raises a hand to the bartender, then looks at me.

"What would you like?"

Multiple orgasms would be nice.

"Vodka soda, please," I answer instead.

He repeats my request and we sit in silence for the three minutes it takes the bartender to fill my order. Then we each raise our drink to each other.

"To Tuesday nights," Ben says.

I laugh, then take a long swallow of the highball. For thirty seconds neither of us says anything, and I am suddenly overcome with awkwardness. What on earth are we supposed to talk about? Basketball stats? Obama's health care plan? The global economic crisis? The cheater's new online mecca, AshleyMadison.com? Thankfully, Ben comes to my rescue.

"How's the spring cleaning going?"

"Great," I say. "It's very therapeutic, getting rid of stuff. It's amazing the things we hold on to."

"Life is an accumulation of crap," Ben says, and I look at him with surprise. He raises his eyebrows at me. "What?"

"I said that very thing today. Word for word."

"Great minds think alike." He laughs, then scoots his stool closer to mine to allow the bartender to pass behind him. Our thighs touch, and I can feel his heat through both layers of denim, his jeans and my skirt. I clear my throat and take another sip of my drink.

"Are your kids back from San Diego?" I ask him and he nods.

"Got back this morning. Bright and early. I swear, Linda's parents must have left at the crack of dawn. I think they have a canasta tournament at the senior center today. Couldn't miss that."

"God, no." I laugh. "Did they have fun?"

"Oh, yeah. Got lots of souvenirs. Shamu bobble heads and stuffed lions and a couple of T-shirts with elephants on them that say *Keep On Trunking*. Nanni and Poo-pop can't resist those little guys." He says this without rancor, and his fondness for his kids shines in his eyes. "They had a great time. Totally wiped out. They were asleep by seven thirty, which is miraculous in my house."

I let the warmth of his words drift through me, yet I can't help but circle back to one word in particular. I squint at him. "Poo-pop?"

"I know. How *Grandpa* became *Poo-pop* I have no idea. But it stuck. He's a good sport about it. Doesn't seem to mind. I even call him that. Not to his face, of course."

I chuckle, but my thoughts turn serious. We are talking about his in-laws. The parents of his *wife*. The grandparents of his *kids*.

What the hell am I doing on this bar stool?

"Can I ask you a question, Ben?"

His eyes are hooded as he turns to face me. His voice is low and sultry. "I like it when you say my name. Say it again."

My breath catches in my throat, but I manage to whisper his name. "Ben."

He reaches down and places his palm on my leg, and I instinctively want to slam my thighs together. Not as a defensive move to imply I will remain chaste, but because this simple gesture on his part, this infinitesimal contact makes a surge of moisture shoot to my crotch. (God, I am *so* easy.) I try not to stare at the thick gold band decorating his ring finger.

"Ask me anything."

"Where does Linda think you are right now?"

He looks down at his hand on my thigh but doesn't remove it.

"She thinks I'm doing surveillance . . . you know, a stakeout," he admits, raising his eyes to mine. "It happens sometimes in the middle of the night. And I do have one, tomorrow. I just fudged the time a little."

"Oh."

He lifts his hand from my thigh and rests it on the bar, his gaze falling on his half-empty beer bottle. "Ellen . . . I have never done anything like this before. But I . . . I just want . . . I just, I think about you . . . I want to be with you . . ." his voice trails off as he thoughtfully fingers the label of his beer.

Oddly enough, his words, spoken haltingly and in a sincere boyish manner, do not fill me with warm fuzzies. Instead, I am immediately suspicious. I am suddenly ten years old, standing on the playground of Kellerman Elementary School, and Noel Zimmer, the most popular boy in the fifth grade, is asking me to go to the Emerald Dance with him. I can't believe my good fortune, and because I am a cynic, even at such an early age, I immediately accuse him of ulterior motives, like being put up to the whole thing by his bully friends. *But why?* I'd asked Noel. *Why me?*

"Why me?" My voice is not that of a grown woman but of a little girl, the one who found out that Noel Zimmer's invitation was, in fact, a prank. I feel foolish, wish I could take the question back. *Of course you want me! I am woman, hear me roar. I am smart and funny and beautiful and . . . why me?*

"Ellen." I turn to see his chocolate fondue eyes on me. "Are you seriously asking me that?"

"Sorry. This is my first time, too."

What is the proper etiquette for officially embarking upon an affair? Is there some ribbon-cutting ceremony? Undie cutting? Does someone fire a gun, and off we go? (Ben's armed, we can use his.) Is there a whistle or a horn or a guy waving a flag? Inexplicably, I cannot go further with this whole *thing* until I know Ben's reasons. I know my own, regardless of the fact that they are all, every single one of them, rationalizations of the highest degree. But now, I need to know *his* why.

He leans in to me, reaching for my hand and pulling it to his chest. "I don't know why."

Oh crap. Time to go, I think.

"We've known each other, what," he continues, "three weeks? A month? We don't really know each other at all."

Uh-oh. Check please.

"But I feel like, God, this is going to sound cheesy as hell . . ."

That's okay. I like cheesy. Go on.

"I feel like I've known you a lot longer." He shrugs and blows out a breath. "I feel comfortable with you. I'm *drawn* to you." He shrugs again and shakes his head. "I like being with you. You're quick and funny. And you make me feel *interesting* again. Like I matter. Like I'm . . ." He laughs. "Like I'm cool. I haven't felt that way in a long time."

"But you could have your pick of women," I hear myself say, and want to cringe at how wretched it sounds aloud.

He chuckles and shakes his head. "Yeah. I do. Sure, hell, I get fake boobs and plastic faces and friggin' designer booty thrown at me all the time. I'm a cop. Women think I'm god-damned Bruce Willis. But those women don't really know me. And they don't really like me, either."

"What about Linda? Does she like you?"

His smile fades. "Does that make a difference?"

I think about his question for a moment, my eyes never leaving his. "Not really," I answer finally. "I was just wondering."

"With Linda, it depends on the day."

"I understand." I try to remember the last day I actually liked Jonah. Monday? Tuesday? It's been a while. *But that's not why you're here, Ellen*, I remind myself.

No. I am here because of the way Ben is looking at me right now, like he wants to run his hands over my entire body.

"What about you, Ellen?" he asks throatily. "Do you like me?"

Thank God the bar is as dark as a catacomb, because I can practically feel my cheeks flame scarlet. "More than I should," I whisper.

"I like you, too. You're beautiful." He presses his index finger against my lips, then traces a line down to my throat. I shiver involuntarily. "You felt so good yesterday." He moves nearer to me and I can feel his breath on my cheek.

"For the record," I say, trying not to gasp as he tenderly kisses my temple, "I've never had a thing for Bruce Willis."

He pulls back and grins, his hand still holding mine hostage. Gently, I pull away and carefully raise myself off the stool. He frowns and gives me a confused look, like he thinks I'm about to leave.

"I'm going to the ladies' room," I say. And before my mind processes the action, I reach up and run my hand through his hair, smoothing it behind his ear. It is such an intimate gesture that it surprises both of us.

"Mmm," he purrs. "That's nice."

My hand lingers for another few seconds, then I turn and head for the corridor on the other side of the room. My steps are slow and measured, and I feel almost drunk, although I know it has nothing to do with the vodka. I am tipsy on lust.

There are two bathrooms, both unisex, as is the new trend. I test the doorknob of the first, find it unlocked, and push the door open. There are no stalls, merely a single toilet, a sink set in a vanity, and a worn upholstered chair in the far corner. The walls are a tired shade of yellow and the air smells of faux pine.

I lean back against the door as it clicks shut and stare sightlessly at the wall. My head is swimming. I don't really need to pee. What I need is to get away from Ben Campbell for a few minutes to gather my thoughts. Because until two minutes ago, a part of me didn't actually believe that anything was going to happen or that I was going to be able to go through with it. A part of me thought I was going to meet Ben for a drink and we were going to talk about yesterday and what a mistake it had been and that we should remain soccer acquaintances. I knew that putting the brakes on things would be difficult, yet it would be infinitely easier than starting an illicit affair. But he wants to. And I want to. There is no question about that.

You can still leave, Ellen. Sneak out the back or march right up to him and tell him that this isn't a good idea, that

you've thought better of it, that you've come to your senses,
that you don't want to hurt anyone, least of all your children,
or his children, that it's been great getting to know him and
blah blah blah, but you're just not cut out for this type of
intrigue.

Yes. That is exactly what I should do. That is exactly what
I am *going* to do. But as long as I'm here, I might as well pee.

Just as I reach down to engage the lock, the knob turns in
my hand and the door sweeps open on its hinges. I look up
to see Ben standing in the doorway, gazing at me hungrily.

He charges into the bathroom, simultaneously grabbing
for me and kicking the door closed with his foot. He swings
me around and pins me against the door, fumbles at the lock,
then slams his mouth against mine, crushing my lips with
his. I reach up and encircle his neck, all thoughts of escaping
to the safety of my boring life gone. Because his kiss is all-
consuming, ravenous, oh-so-fucking-amazing I can't think
at all, can only feel. Feel his tongue dart into my mouth and
entwine with mine, as they do their slick and sumptuous
dance that sends fire down to my loins. Feel his hands move
down to my waist as he tugs at my sweater, yanking it free of
my skirt; feel them slide back up again, over the tingling skin
of my stomach, my sides, my back, oh, God, his hands are
everywhere, and our mouths are still locked as he sneaks his
fingers up under my bra and rakes them over my breasts, rubs
his thumbs over my nipples and I shudder with desire, my
back arching and my toes curling inside my leather boots.

"Ellen," he rasps, as he grasps my shoulders and whirls
me from the door to the vanity and lifts me so that I am
perched on the counter next to the sink. He lowers his mouth
to mine again, treats me to another blistering kiss, then tears
himself away from my swollen lips and moves down, biting
at my sweater just where it stretches over my breasts. He

pushes the fabric up, past my waist, over my chest, then roughly rips at the silk of my bra, jerking it down and exposing my nipples, which are hard as pebbles, to the cold air.

He flicks his tongue across my right areola then closes his mouth around it and sucks, nibbles, bites, and I feel my insides quake with wanton desire. My hands snake down to the waistband of his jeans (*What are you doing?* screams the one rational brain cell I have left) and I grasp, tug, claw at his fly until I manage to yank it open, then shove my fingers beneath his boxer-briefs to the rock-hard erection that twitches at my touch. I graze the smooth head of his penis with my index finger, hear Ben gasp, then run my hand along the entire length of him.

Ben grabs my skirt and pushes it up, up to my waist, then I feel his own hand inside my undies, seeking, lightly brushing against my pubic hair, and continuing until his fingers find my folds, and he parts them, gently at first, his touch so soft, like a whisper. I squeeze my eyes shut and moan as a wellspring erupts, *down there*, washing over his fingers as he pushes them deep within me. A primal cry escapes me and I reflexively contract both the muscles in my groin and the muscles in my right hand, which is currently clutching Ben's shaft.

But the shriek of ecstasy that originates in my own vocal cords serves to cut through the animal frenzy I am submitting to. When I open my eyes, the first thing that comes into focus is the cracked toilet and the useless shriveled air freshener sitting on the back of the tank. The fog of passion lifts faster than you can say *Glade*, and I quickly pull my hand out from the heat of Ben's briefs and gently place it on his hand, stopping him from further plunder.

"Not here," I gasp, sucking in a few gulps of artificially scented air. I'll be damned if I am going to consummate this affair in a unisex bathroom in a bar downtown. It would be like winning the Miss America title in a bowling alley.

I try to stay his stream of endless kisses by gently nudging him. When that doesn't work, I use a bit more force, pushing at his chest until he has no choice but to break free. His eyes, which are practically glazed over, take a few seconds to clear, and when they do, they roam over my face suspiciously.

"What?" he asks in that annoyed, coitus interruptus kind of way.

"Is there someplace . . . ? Can we go somewhere . . . else . . . ?"

He looks around and seems to realize for the first time where he is. His sweeping scan takes less than a second (a skill learned as a cop, I assume) but he clearly registers the cracked toilet, the peeling paint, the ancient vinyl flooring, the deodorizer.

"I'm sorry," he whispers, and looks truly mortified. "I just . . . I couldn't help myself. I want you, Ellen."

The force of his words slams into me with the impact of a freight train. It's not that his actions have left any doubt in the matter, but hearing the words aloud are even more powerful, and for a crazy instant, I want to grab him by his beautiful and noteworthy body part and help him shove it deep inside me and let him fuck me until I go blind.

"I want you, too," I tell him, resolutely resisting the temptation. Because if I am going to throw caution, common sense, all of my morals, and possibly my marriage to the wind, you can bet it will be in surroundings more dignified than this place. The Four Seasons? Absolutely. The back of Ben's Land Rover? If need be. But not here.

He raises a finger and traces the O of my lips. "The GHPD has an apartment, on La Croix. They keep it for undercovers, or witness protection. More than a few of the guys have bunked there when their wives kicked them out. It's empty tonight . . ."

I nod. That sounds more like it.

"We could go there," he suggests, his finger lightly mapping out the contours of my chin, the hollow of my throat, my clavicles. This feather-light touch is almost as good as the hot raunchy frenzied heavy petting of a moment ago. In fact, it is even better.

"Let's go there," he says.

"Okay." One word. Two syllables that seal my fate. If I hadn't yet crossed the line by shoving my hand down this man's pants (and who are we trying to fool anyway?), I have just taken a giant step over to the dark side by agreeing to go to the PD's apartment. I try not to think about it. I know the guilt will get me; I do not exist in a vacuum, after all. But since I know I will eventually experience the retroactive regret, I refuse to feel it now. (Do you see what kind of bullshit you can sell yourself because a hunk with a great ass finds you beautiful even at the ripe old age of almost forty-three?)

"Just give me a minute." I glance at the toilet to my left.

He chuckles softly, lowering his hand to his side and stepping back. "I didn't give you a chance to pee, did I? How rude of me."

"I forgive you." I grin at him and bite my lower lip. "You might want to, uh, wash your hands."

He cocks his head to the side, then seems to realize what I am talking about. He smiles as I turn on the faucet and squeeze some soap from the wall-mounted dispenser. Side by side, hands interwoven beneath the spray of water, we take a quiet moment to scrub each other off our fingers. Then we dry our hands and do our best to make ourselves presentable, which causes us both to break into laughter.

When we're as good as we are going to get, he grazes my cheek with a kiss and says, "See you out there."

I lock the door behind him and press my forehead against the cool metal door. My pulse is still racing, and I can't seem to wipe the stupid smile off my face. I don't have to look in the mirror to see it, I can feel it, plastered to my face with Click Bond. It is the "cat that ate the canary" smile, the "I have a secret" smile, the "I just got down and dirty in the bathroom of a bar with a hot guy and am going back for more" smile. The kind of smile that gives you away, the one you never want to allow yourself to reveal to the jury lest they vote to hang your serial-killing ass. I try to rub it off with my hand, try to force the corners of my mouth down, but it will not budge, and I absently wonder, as I wash my hands for a second time—post-pee—if I will ever be able to frown again.

As it turns out, the answer is yes, and the *when* is three and a half minutes later when I make my way back into the main room, glance past the tables to the corner of the bar where Ben stands, and see that he is flanked on his left by none other than Nina Montrose.

What the fuck?

If you had told me that DNA testing revealed that I was related to Catherine the Great, I would not have been more shocked. *What the hell is Nina Montrose doing here?* Trolling, of course.

I stand at the archway of the corridor, frozen in place, sifting through my options with the speed and urgency of John McClane in *Die Hard*. What to do? What to do? My sweater is hanging on the back of the very stool that Nina Montrose is perched against, her hands grasping the lip of the bar top, her arms straight at the elbows and squeezed together in order to create an eye-popping tableau of her expensive breasts. To his credit, Ben is studiously avoiding looking at her; his eyes are glued to his beer bottle as she rattles on about something.

Okay. So these are the facts. I need my sweater. And I need to get the hell out of here without the plastic queen of Southern Cal putting two and two together. If only I *were* John McClane and had a little C-4 I could create a diversion, like blowing up the stage in the corner, microphone and all, thereby giving me an opportunity to snag my sweater unnoticed. But I am me. And, alas, I have no C-4.

I make a decision, wait a moment until the bartender crosses to the other side of the T, and saunter toward the bar, donning a distracted expression. I sidle up to the counter and make a show of waiting to catch the bartender's attention. Not three seconds later, I hear the high-pitched keen of my new nemesis.

"Oh my God! Would you look at who it is? Ellen!"

I glance to my right and see Nina waving frantically at me while Ben empties his beer with one long swallow. He sets the bottle down and looks at me, shaking his head almost imperceptibly.

"Ellen! Ellen! Come over here!"

I paste on a surprised smile and move toward them.

"Oh my God!" Nina cries again as if the three of us being in the same place at the same time is comparable to George W., Osama bin Laden, and Saddam Hussein having a tea party together. "This is unbelievable! It's like old home week. All we need are a couple of balls!" She turns to Ben and snorts with laughter. "*Soccer* balls, that is." She snorts some more and I can tell she's a few vodkas short of a Russian militia.

"Ben," she coos, "you know Ellen! From soccer!"

I manage to nudge my way between them, placing myself behind my former bar stool, my sweater just out of reach. Ben gives me a guarded smile.

"You're Matthew's mom, right?"

Now call me crazy, but Ben's pretense of not knowing me makes me suddenly furious.

That's right, I think. *Matthew's mom! The one whose vagina you were just inspecting!*

"Yes," I say through gritted teeth. Two can play at this game. "And you're Liam's dad."

"Right." Cool as a cucumber.

"What are you doing here?" Nina asks me. "I didn't know you liked music." As if I am some kind of tone-deaf mutant who doesn't own an iPod.

"I was supposed to meet my cousin. But she just called to tell me she can't make it." Forget that my cell phone is drying out on a rag on my kitchen counter. The lie slides effortlessly out of my mouth.

"Oh, too bad!" Nina says. "Well, you should stay and have a drink with us, right, Ben? The kids are with my ex, the bastard, so I'm free all night." She leans in to Ben and jabs him with her bony elbow. I take the opportunity to quickly snatch my sweater from the bar stool and covertly tie it around my waist, giving silent thanks that Nina didn't see it. Then I step back and watch her hail the bartender with a coy "Yoo-hoo!"

As the barman moves toward us, Nina seems to notice my drink for the first time. "Whose is this?" she asks Ben suspiciously. *Oops.*

"It was there when I got here," he quickly assures her, and once again, I feel a stab of anger toward him. Nina pushes the drink out of her way and smiles at the bartender.

"I'll have a Cosmo and he'll have another Heinie." She laughs at herself, then turns to me. "What are you having, Ellen?"

"I'm going to go," I say, hoping that Ben will follow suit and beg off the *Heinie*.

"Oh, come on," Nina pleads. "Just one?"

Say something, I telepathically urge Ben. *Thanks, anyway, Nina, but I've got to be going, too. That was my last beer. Got a stakeout tomorrow, can't drink too much, blah blah blah.* But Ben says nothing.

"Thanks anyway," I hear myself say.

"Well, if you *have* to go." I detect a note of relief in her words, a hint of victory, as in *I have him all to myself!* I wait a fraction of a moment longer for Ben to make some kind of an excuse, but he remains where he is as the bartender hustles off to mix Nina's Cosmo.

"Good to see you," I tell Nina, and as she turns and watches the bartender shake up her drink, my eyes find Ben's. I am expecting to see regret or frustration or irritation or a glimmer of the desire he expressed five minutes ago, but his expression is flat.

"Bye."

With that single syllable, I turn on my heel and march to the door of the T Bar. I am about to glance back, want to give Ben one last opportunity to communicate something to me, *anything*, but I don't. Instead, I push through the door and wander aimlessly into the night.

Twenty-three

The drive back to my neighborhood is a blur of sensory recall. I can still see the lust shimmering in Ben's eyes as he pushed me against the bathroom door, can taste his tongue, can feel his lips on my breasts, his fingers probing my core. I can hear Nina Montrose's drunken cackle and her conspiratorially whispered words, "I guess it's just the two of us," upon my departure. I am so immersed in these thoughts that I don't remember how I came to be leaning against the counter of the 7-Eleven.

I want to disappear. I want to shrivel up into nothingness and be carried away on the ocean breeze. I want to be a character in *Eternal Sunshine of the Spotless Mind* and have all memories of the last three weeks erased from my brain. Hell, I'll even settle for a lobotomy. But since none of the above is an option, I will have to make do with being comforted by the only two men I have always been able to count on for solace. Ben and Jerry.

When I arrive home, Sally greets me at the door and I allow her to trot to the front lawn to do her business. Once properly drained, she follows me up the stairs, sniffing at the brown bag in my hand, and jumps onto my bed for a better view of my striptease. I set the bag on the night table, then tear off my clothes and shove them straight into the trash. I root around in my dresser drawer for my most conservative flannel nightie, pull it over my head, and collapse onto the bed next to my faithful dog. I should take a shower. I should brush my teeth and wash my face and apply my gaggle of creams and magic tonics. What I do instead is turn on the TV, pull the pint of New York Super Fudge Chunk out of the bag, along with a plastic spoon, and dig in.

I consider my reinvention, all of my recent hard work that has made me feel so good about myself. I think of my stomach, which has flattened considerably. This pint of ice cream will set me back four hours on the treadmill at least.

But who the fuck cares?

They say that chocolate is a perfect substitute for sex. Once again, *they* are full of shit.

The phone rings at twenty after twelve, and I groggily reach past the empty carton of ice cream for the receiver on the nightstand. My head feels like it's full of cotton, my mouth feels tacky, and my stomach feels like I swallowed a vat of guppies. Can you say *Ben and Jerry's hangover*? I knew you could.

"Hello?" I croak.

"Hi."

Jerk cretin bastard motherfucker!

"Hi."

"I'm so sorry."

There is an unwritten rule about apologizing. If a man apologizes to you more than once in any given week, you should realize that there is a problem with your relationship. Jonah averages about twice a month. Ben has apologized to me every single day for the past three days, more than once. But apologies from men are akin to stays of execution. We women are so grateful for them, so surprised to hear the words *I'm sorry* uttered from the mouth of someone with testosterone, that we tend to overlook the underlying reasons for said apology. For example, it doesn't matter that he beat me unconscious and broke three of my ribs. He *apologized*! I am not that kind of woman, mind you. I won't be taken in by two simple words of remorse. I need more. . . .

"I'm really sorry."

Sigh. Well, he didn't just say he was sorry. He said he was *really* sorry.

"It's not your fault," I say.

"That woman! Someone needs to put her out of her misery."

"And everyone else's," I mutter, hoisting myself into a sitting position.

"I'm sorry about calling your landline, too." Uh-oh. Apology number three in the same conversation. *Warning!* "I tried your cell a couple of times, but you didn't answer."

"It's fine," I tell him, and in truth, I am relieved to hear his voice. Despite his protestations about annoying, surgically enhanced women, I had an irrational fear that he would use Nina Montrose as a replacement—the "Love the One You're With Syndrome," I call it. I did my best to swallow this fear with every creamy chunky chocolate spoonful, but neverthe-less, it lingered. "I'm glad you called," I admit.

"I was kind of worried about you," he says solemnly.

Worried? About what? That I would drive my car into a cinderblock wall over sexual frustration? That I would empty a fifth of Jack Daniels down my gullet because I didn't get to have an orgasm? Nope. Ben and Jerry's for me. Equally dan-gerous, but far less permanent.

"I'm a big girl, Ben," I say. Bigger now that the pint is gone. All four million calories have settled on my thighs, hips, and abdomen.

"I know you are." He is quiet for a moment and I have a strong sense that he is about to invite me to meet him, right now. And if he does, I suspect that I will say yes, although if I do anything even remotely strenuous in the near future, I will almost certainly puke Ben and Jerry's all over anything and everything within close proximity to my person.

But he doesn't ask. Instead, he says, "Look. I have that surveillance thing tomorrow. And it's going to be a long day. But maybe we could meet on Thursday. At the, uh, PD's apartment. . . ."

I am nodding to my empty bedroom. Thursday. Good. I can work off the ice cream between now and then.

"If everything goes well tomorrow, I'll be off. Linda's working from home, uh, so she'll be with the boys. We'd have all day. . . ."

I don't say anything because I am busy rooting through the nightstand drawer for something to write with. Ben mis-takes my silence for hesitation.

"Maybe it's a bad idea," I hear him say as my hand closes around a pen.

"Give me the address," I say.

Thirteenth Post: March 28, 2012
SomethingNewAt42

CHOCOLATE DOESN'T WORK

Take it from me.

Let's say, for example, and by this, my nameless relative, I mean *hypothetically*, that you find yourself in the grips of a passionate encounter in a place you consider unsuitable for such debauchery, for instance in the bathroom of a bar. Unless you want to be sexually frustrated for days afterward, you had better relax your standards and just get it on amid the cracked toilet and empty paper towel dispenser. If you don't, if you demand to be ravished in more appropriate surroundings, and then something occurs that forces you to abandon your anticipation of multiple orgasms, and you end up downing a carton of chocolate chunk ice cream in the hopes of quelling your need for climax, you will be, as the expression goes, shit out of luck.

Not only will you have to do five miles on the treadmill the next day just to purge the previous night's butter-fat binge through your system, you will still be horny. And then, you will forage through your kitchen in search of more chocolate—at ten A.M., mind you— because you have been told that chocolate equals sex. But here's what *they* never told you. Chocolate may be a substitute for sex, but it is *not* a substitute for an orgasm. In fact, so lugubrious and sensual does chocolate taste in your mouth that it will only heighten your desire for a happy ending. You will take one bite, feel it melt on your tongue, and spend the next hour pacing around your house, fantasizing about the detachable shower head and cursing the fact that you've run out of AA batteries. I'm telling you, the cucumbers in your refrigerator are not safe.

I am only writing this blog as a cautionary tale to my fellow women. Because it becomes a vicious circle. We become sexually frustrated and we turn to chocolate to soothe us. And like an alcoholic or drug abuser, looking for a high with just one more sip or hit, we eat more, hoping that those neurons in our brains will get that chemical reaction that will cool our loins. And we eat more and more chocolate. And pretty soon, we are carrying around an extra twenty-two pounds of sexually frustrated chocolate consumption, and carrying around an extra twenty-two pounds makes it far less likely that we will be sexually fulfilled the good old-fashioned way. Because who wants to have sex with a chocolate-addicted fatty?

So my advice to you is this: When it comes to sex, get it when you can, wherever you can, and if at all possible, carry it through until you, um, strike oil, so to speak. When it comes to chocolate, do not use it as a placebo for your libido. Enjoy it for its own delicious, delectable sake, in moderation. And if you find my advice is impossible to follow, you can always just give up both.

But in my opinion, life without sex and chocolate just isn't worth living at all. Don't you agree?

Twenty-four

Iblame my cousin Jill for ruining my life. Or saving my life. It pretty much depends on my mood. I will let you draw your own conclusions. But for now, I will just tell the tale with as much objectivity as possible.

Jill has punctuality down to a science. She could give symposiums on it. She could be the punctuality ambassador to any country on the planet. If she says she will be somewhere at a certain time, you can bet your last dollar she will be there. And if *you* say you will be somewhere at a certain time, and you're not—regardless of the reason, like a tsunami wiping out your house or your arm falling off because of flesh-eating bacteria—Jill will boycott you for a month only after she's given you a scathing verbal reprimand. Which is why I am more than a little surprised to be sitting in the Lexus in front of her house five minutes after our designated meeting. Her car is nowhere to be seen, and my knock on her door, thirty seconds before "go time," was greeted by echoing silence.

I would call her cell phone if mine weren't the equivalent of six feet under. I consider, as I sit, inconceivably waiting for my cousin, how attached I have grown to my cell phone. After my futile attempt to blow-dry the little bugger, I realized it was a goner and I immediately called up our phone store to ask about getting a replacement. I was informed that not only am I *not* due for a replacement, but the local outlet is out of stock on my particular model and it will be at least forty-eight hours before the shipment comes in. I was then asked if I would I like to try a different model. (*Are you kidding?* I practically screamed. *It took me a decade to figure out the one I've got!*) The poor operator had to suffer through my hostility and disdain, which I admit was over the top. But in my defense, being sexually frustrated, concerned about the possibility of spending all eternity in hell, and cut off from instant communication with the very person who is the reason I might be going to hell had me in a bit of a snit. I hung up the landline (what good is *that* anyway?) and went in search of more chocolate.

It is now twelve fifteen, a full fifteen minutes past target. I am about to turn the key in the ignition so that I can go home and use the *landline* to call Jill when I see Linda Campbell frantically storm out of her house dragging a completely sodden rug in one hand and holding a lamp with the other. Her face is set in a grimace as she drops her things on the front lawn and runs back into the house. Ten seconds later, she hurries out with a small side table. Liam and Evan trail her, soaking wet from their hair to their sneakers, and giggling in direct opposition to their mother's distress. She scowls at them as she sets the table down, then clambers back into the house.

Now, a normal person would immediately jump out of the car and rush over to offer assistance. But a normal person probably isn't having an *almost*-affair with the husband of the person presently in need. Plus, for one crazy moment, my usual empathetic and do-gooder tendencies take a backseat to the voyeuristic thrill of watching someone who has no idea she is being watched undergo a situation of obviously calamitous proportions. Still, when I see Linda at the front door, trying to lug a dripping, formerly-plush easy chair through the doorway, I spring into action.

"Can I help you?" I ask, trotting up the front steps of Ben's house.

She looks up at me sharply, and there is no sign of recognition on her face, only doubt. Under these circumstances, which I have yet to discern, her pretty features are obscured. She looks angry, weathered, and beaten.

"I'm Matthew's mom, Ellen. From soccer?"

"Oh," she grunts, trying to support the weight of the chair on her thighs. "Hi. Yeah, thanks."

I cross to the door and bend at the waist, grabbing the underside of the chair. Together, Linda and I manage to haul the piece of furniture out to the driveway and set it down on the concrete. Briefly, I think of the first time I met Ben, the day his family moved in, when the direction of the furniture was reversed.

"I can't believe this!" she hisses between gritted teeth. "I just can't *believe* this! It's just . . . *unbelievable*!" For a smarty-pants environmental lawyer, her vocabulary sure is lacking. She stomps back up to the house and disappears through the front door. I look at Liam and Evan, who evidently have realized the severity of the situation in their own seven- and ten-year-old ways, as they are no longer smiling.

"What happened?" I ask them.

Liam shrugs and remains stoic, but Evan cannot suppress a sudden grin. "Waterfall."

Confused, I leave them on the lawn and make my way up to the house and step inside. As soon as I reach the foyer, I hear what sounds suspiciously like the water show at the Bellagio sans the musical accompaniment. Turning to my right, I gaze through the den toward the sliding glass door on the far side of the room and my jaw drops. Water gushes from the second floor, cascading over the open doorway like Little Niagara. Linda stands a few feet back from the spray, surveying it, hands on hips, temporarily paralyzed.

"That bastard! God damn him. God *damn* him! He said he'd fix it. He told me he'd get to it!"

I take a step toward her as she continues to vent angrily. I don't think she even realizes that I've entered the house.

"And now where is he, huh? Surveillance, my ass! He's probably with his goddamned *girlfriend*!"

I freeze in place, and I mean literally. An arctic chill sweeps through every fiber of my being. Linda suddenly senses my presence and turns to see me standing there, like an ice sculpture, unable to move or speak. For a split second, her venom is directed at me. Not because she knows I was dry-humping her husband in a bar last night, but because I am the only one here. But I imagine that she knows and it fills me with dread.

Snap out of it, Ellen! I tell myself as the water continues to rush into the room, soaking everything in its path. Linda is shaking her head and flapping her arms like a mental patient, clearly overwhelmed and without a clue as to how to deal with the situation. I manage to break free of my own paralysis and reach out to grasp Linda's arm.

"We need to shut the water off."

She stops shaking her head long enough to give me a perplexed look, as though I'm speaking in a foreign language.

"Do you have a wrench?" I ask the question slowly, emphasizing each word.

After a beat, she nods and races from the den, disappearing down the hallway past the foyer. I glance at the waterfall one last time because I may never see something like it again, then head outside and trot to the Lexus. I pop the trunk and grab the crowbar, which is exactly where it should be, on the far right tucked behind Jonah's emergency road kit and Jonah's emergency overnight bag.

Crowbar in hand, I move back toward Ben's house, scanning the sidewalk for the main water line for his house. When I find it, I wedge the crowbar beneath the concrete cover and, putting all my weight into it, lift it and push it away with a grunt. In my peripheral vision, I see Liam and Evan scamper up to the house. A moment later, Linda races past them, waving a crescent wrench in the air like a victory flag. She hands it off to me as she crouches beside me, and silently watches me reach into the hole to turn off the line. I try not to think about the herd of black widow spiders that are lurking below, probably waiting for a nice fleshy hand to appear on which they can feast. I locate the valve and give it half a dozen forceful turns with the wrench until I can turn it no more.

"Bye-bye, waterfall," says Evan from the foyer, looking forlorn as he gazes into the den.

Linda sits back on her haunches and blows out a heavy sigh, releasing most of her tension. She looks up at me and gives me a wry smile.

"Thank you so much," she says. She laughs with little humor. "I'm usually good in stressful situations, but when it comes to . . . I don't know . . . what do you call it? Being handy? I suck."

I only know about the main water valve because a few

years back, one of Matthew's Bakugans rolled down the driveway and fell through the small slot in the cover, and my son wouldn't stop yammering about it until I rescued the damn thing. Before then, I just assumed that the water magically appeared when I turned on the faucets, brought into the house by little water elves who lived in the pipes. I don't tell Linda this lest I shatter her belief that I am cool.

"Anyway, I'm really grateful for your help. Can I make you a cup of coffee?" she asks.

"Actually, no." She is surprised by my refusal and I allow myself to grin. "You can't make me a cup of coffee," I tell her. "You have no water."

A sly smile plays on her lips. "That's okay. I have a Keurig."

The Keurig is the best invention since Spanx. I want one. For Mother's Day, I am going to demand that my kids pool all of their piggy bank savings and get me one, and if they don't, I'm putting them up for adoption. It's a coffee machine that makes one cup at a time using these little things called pods, enclosed plastic cups with the exact amount of gourmet grounds for a single serving. Every cup of coffee comes out just the right temperature and perfectly delicious. No mere mortal can make a cup of coffee this good, which is why, if you're getting married, make sure a Keurig is on your bridal registry. Because your husband-to-be might end up being a total schmuck who leaves you for a younger, higher-breasted chick, but your Keurig will never let you down.

I am sitting at the kitchen counter sipping my heavenly brew while Linda piles dishes in a water-free sink. Liam and Evan frolic in the empty wading pool that used to be the patio outside the den.

"Can I get you anything to eat? Are you hungry?"

All of a sudden, I remember: *lunch with Jill.* I ask to use the phone. Jill's cell rings only once before she picks up.

"Hello?"

"It's me."

"Where the h-e-l-l are you? I've been calling your cell for forty-five minutes!"

"I'm at your next-door neighbors'. Where are *you*?"

"Oh my gosh," she breathes. "Emergency at the salon this morning. You would not believe."

She's right. I would *not* believe. It's hard to imagine any cataclysmic event happening at the salon. But then, I don't spend much time there, so who am I to say?

"Kiki got the color wrong on my roots; they were Day-Glo orange! I think she's hungover." She whispers this last in the same way you might say *She has can-cer,* which is probably on the same level as *hung-over* since Kiki is an *al-co-hol-ic.* "So she had to start all over again—"

There is dead silence on the line for five full seconds. Then: "What the h-e-l-l are you doing next door?"

"We had a bit of an emergency here, too," I say as Linda sets a tray of crackers and cheese on the counter in front of me. "I'll tell you about it later. So, no lunch?"

"We're at the home stretch," she says. "Shouldn't be more than a half hour. I have to pick the kids up from Patty at three, but that'll give us time. We need to talk."

Her implied meaning is transparent, but she clarifies anyway. "I read your blog today."

"Uh-huh."

"*Uh-huh,*" she mocks. "I get it. I'll see you soon."

She rings off and I set the phone down in its cradle. Linda is looking at me speculatively, like she might be privy to my inner thoughts and is about to charge into her bedroom and get Ben's off-duty weapon (because every cop on TV has one) and come back in and shoot the crap out of me. But perhaps I am projecting.

"I'm sorry," she says, surprising me. "About earlier." She lowers her gaze to the counter. "What I said." She chuckles softly. "Well, screamed, actually. About my husband."

"Don't worry about—"

"That thing about his girlfriend . . ." She tucks a loose strand of blond hair behind her ear. "Ben's a great guy."

Don't I know it, I think, then immediately feel ashamed.

"But, you know. Marriage."

"Yeah, marriage." I laugh, but it sounds forced and unnatural, more like someone trying to hack up phlegm.

Linda fingers a cracker, absently moving it around on the plate. "He, um, Ben . . . He had an affair a couple of years ago."

My mouth goes dry and when I swallow, my throat feels as though it is full of sand.

I've never done anything like this before. . . .

"It didn't last long, you know? And we were going through a tough time."

I can tell that this is hard for her, a kitchen confession to a virtual stranger, but one she feels compelled to give. And if I weren't so consumed with my own torrent of conflicting thoughts and emotions, I would be able to offer her some comfort. I try to paint my face with an open and empathetic expression, but the effort is exhausting.

"I thought about leaving him, but, you know. The kids . . . Not just the kids, me too. I'm a lawyer. I see what divorce does. So I stuck it out, and I'm glad. But it never really goes away, you know?"

I've counted four *you knows* in Linda's last several sentences and I recognize that the structured writer in me is seizing on something tangible to think about in order to avoid thinking about what I absolutely do not *want* to think about.

I've never done anything like this before.

"Anyway," she says. "I don't know why I'm telling you this. I just didn't want you to think . . ."

"It's okay," I assure her, resisting the urge to lower my head into my hands and weep. Because it's about as far from okay as it could be.

The rest of the day passes in a haze, including my lunch with Jill, during which she alternated between grilling me on the lurid details of my bathroom encounter and chastising me for the lurid details of my bathroom encounter. She seemed almost disappointed by Nina Montrose's interruption of what surely would have been a night to remember, then proceeded to wax philosophic about how it was for the best and ultimately Nina Montrose had unwittingly saved my marriage. I related to her the tale of the Campbells' water disaster but kept Linda's revelation about Ben to myself. I also chose not to mention tomorrow's planned rendezvous because right now, I am confused to the point where I wonder if there will even *be* a tomorrow. (Melodramatic, I know. But now I understand why soap operas are so popular.) And although, under ordinary circumstances, Jill would be the first person (the *only* person, actually) I would tell about Jonah's love letter, I inexplicably omitted that lovely little anecdote from our conversation.

I spend the afternoon going through every single drawer of my monolithic-sized dresser. This task is not on my spring cleaning list, and there is little to purge, but it is mindless and meditative. When I finish, only having thought about Ben and Linda a total of four thousand, seven hundred and sixty-two times, I move on to my computer desk and sort through every scrap of paper, take-out menu, magazine, and kid's homework assignment that managed to get tucked inside. Thoughts of Ben: two thousand, three hundred and six. Since the desk takes less time than my dresser, I guess the lower number doesn't count. I move on to the bathrooms, scrubbing the toilets and counters and mirrors to clean-room proportions, but it is impossible not to think of Ben while performing this job, and I have to stop several times, mid-scour, when I am overcome by images of Ben and me at the T Bar.

I have never done anything like this before.

Bastard. Liar. Gorgeous sexy hunk of man that I still want to ride like a stallion despite the fact that you lied to my face, because when it comes down to it, who the fuck really cares what you've done before now?

I do.

Fuck me.

At four o'clock, I lace up my sneakers and take Sally to the park adjacent to the house and spend thirty minutes trying to get her to chase a tennis ball. I beg. I plead. I entreat her with snacks waved in front of her nose, at which point she promptly lies down on the grass and rolls over for a belly scratch.

"I know, girl," I surrender, kneeling beside her and raking my fingernails through the fur of her stomach until she gives me bicycle leg. "We could all use a little belly scratch, couldn't we?"

She thumps her tail as if in agreement.

When we return home, Sally finally accepts the cookies from my pocket and carries them to her dog bed where she munches away on them—loudly. I check voice mail, but there are no messages, and I realize that Jonah has not called at all today. A whisper of unease skitters through me, but I shake it off. Jonah and the kids are a thousand miles away. They are probably spending the day watching Grandpa shoot at desert rats with his own father's army rifle, which he loves to show off. (Thankfully, he has terrible aim, and as far as I remember, he has managed to hit one only once, and only because he tripped on a rock at the same time that he pulled the trigger.)

I pick up the phone again and dial my in-laws' phone number. Their machine picks up after the second ring, and a hollow anonymous voice asks me to leave a message.

"Hi . . . It's Ellen. I haven't heard from the kids today. Just wanted to say hi. Tell them I miss them. Hope you're having fun."

I replace the phone to its cradle and stare at the counter, realizing with surprising intensity that I do miss my kids. Jonah? Not on your life. But Connor's sunny smile, Matthew's constant look of concern, and Jessie's off-key singing? I miss them all.

The evening stretches out before me. On a whim, I decide that I am going to cook a lavish meal for myself. I have been so strict with everything that has passed my lips of late—well, excluding Ben's tongue and the Ben and Jerry's tangent, but neither of those counts as eating, merely lapses in judgment. I feel like Linda Campbell unknowingly sucker-punched me in the brain, not to mention the heart. Which is not to say that I am in love with Ben Campbell or that I am harboring any fantasies about the two of us running away together. I am neither sixteen nor delusional. But I have fallen in love with the *idea* of Ben Campbell, with the notion of being his lover, with the thought of being wanted by someone with whom I have no other ties. It is exhilarating and liberating in a duplicitous and clandestine kind of way. But I don't know if I can go forward with someone who has purposefully deceived me. I still have my integrity. Sort of.

And to add to all of that, my husband may well be having an affair. Which equally infuriates me and makes me jealous. Not, mind you, in the healthy "my husband's cheating, I'll kill him" kind of way but in the foot-stamping "he's already cheated and I haven't gotten to yet and now I might *never* get to!" kind of way. Needless to say, I am feeling vulnerable and unsure of myself and utterly lost. And what better comfort is there than good food?

Unfortunately, my refrigerator will not comply. It has a host of items fit for a family of five, meaning food so bland in taste and texture, it will not offend a single person in the house. Frozen dinners and ground beef and a fryer chicken that would take three days to thaw out, plus all of the leftovers from the previous week, which are quickly gaining momentum in the smell department, and a drawer full of dejected-looking veggies. If I am going to have a gourmet meal, it isn't coming out of this kitchen. I consider ordering Chinese, quickly change my mind, and head for the stairs.

Forty minutes later I am seated at a lovely table for two in the chichi Garden Hills restaurant Flowers. While I usually shy away from eating out alone, tonight I feel almost smug with my own independence.

I gaze around the richly appointed dining room. Flowers's claim to fame is that the executive chef, Joey Winter, was challenged to a throwdown by Bobby Flay over his famous *pommes frites*, which are amazing, redolent with roasted garlic and shaved Parmesan. Unfortunately, Joey got his ass kicked as Bobby showed up with a deep-fryer the size of a Jacuzzi, killer Cajun spices, and an aioli dipping sauce that was, apparently, *trés magnifique*. Still, Joey's French fries—

that's what they are—rock, and the rest of his food is delicious as well. The prices are extortionate, but worth it, and since I am alone, I am free to order the most expensive thing on the menu without compunction. I glance at the placard posted next to the wine bar and read the market price of the lobster. . . . uh, maybe not. Maybe I'll just settle for the beef Wellington, which, as I remember from my one and only previous visit with Jonah on our tenth anniversary, was melt-in-your-mouth scrumptious.

A waiter with slicked-back brown hair and an indulgent smile approaches my table and leans toward me expectantly.

"Good evening," he intones with an accent that is a cross between Cockney English, French, and Count Chocula. "Would madame like something to drink while waiting for your dinner companion?"

I blink at him a few times, processing his question. "Uh, uh," I stammer.

"Perhaps you would like to wait for your company," he suggests, backing away from me as though I have bubonic plague.

"No, I—" But he is already gone, striding briskly to a table in the far corner.

Now, this is the new millennium. People eat by themselves all the time. So I am surprised by the waiter's assumption that I am meeting someone. Apparently, people don't dine solo in Flowers. I look around the room, and sure enough, there is not a single *single* person in the restaurant save for me. I glance at the empty place across from me, the vacant chair, and I feel my pulse start to race. My heart thuds in my chest and my throat goes dry. I reach for the water glass on the table in front of me and am alarmed to see my hand shake. I yank it back and place it in my lap, with my other shaking appendage, where it can do no harm.

And then, a deliriously funny thing happens. And when I say funny, I mean that every inmate of every sanitarium across the country would be in straitjacketed stitches over it. I have a vision. Yes, right there in the dining room of the most luxurious restaurant in Garden Hills. *I am waking up in my bed, alone; the space next to me that is usually inhabited by my husband is barren. I am sitting at my dinner table with my three sullen children. Jonah's chair is gone. I am driving in the minivan, the passenger seat empty, the kids arguing behind me while I slowly go mad. I am watching a high school graduation, maybe Connor's. I look around at all the proud parents, holding hands and resting their heads against each other's shoulders, but Jonah is conspicuously absent. I am sitting in a glamorous restaurant, by myself amid a sea of couples and groups. . . .* Oh wait, that's really happening.

I bolt out of my seat, almost knocking it over, grab my purse, and head for the door as fast as my wobbly legs will take me. My waiter catches a glimpse of my hasty departure and hurries after me, probably riled about being denied a tip for his thirty seconds of service.

"Is everything all right with madame?" he inquires solicitously, pawing at my sleeve as I reach the hostess stand. I have the sudden urge to swat him with my purse and tell him to pick a country whose dialect he can master.

"Everything is fine with *madame*," I tell him. "My husband is stuck at work, so I won't be staying."

"Ah," he nods, removing his fingers from my blouse. "How regrettable. Well, next time."

I push through the door and make a beeline for the Lexus, which I had the sense to park on the street rather than with the valet service, which is free only if you don't count the traditional and *expected* five-dollar tip. I start the ignition and race toward home, the radio blasting at full volume with me singing along to Collective Soul at the top of my lungs. I stop only once, at the McDonald's drive-through, where I purchase an Angus wrap and a small fries. This is the fast-food version of beef Wellington and *pommes frites*, and it is not what I anticipated when I left home earlier tonight, but hell. A girl's got to eat. Even an almost-forty-three-year-old girl.

When the gods of foresight sent their vision to me at the swanky Flowers, they probably did not anticipate that I would glean the wrong lesson from it. I am certain they intended for me to appreciate the perils of being a divorcée, which seems, at best, unappealing, and at worst, downright tragic. But I took from my vision an entirely different lesson: I do not want to stay in a marriage because I am afraid of the alternative. I don't want to remain in a complacent union out of fear. I don't want to be with someone I don't love and who doesn't love me simply because I don't want to be alone. And these realizations raise the question: Do Jonah and I love each other any more?

None of this has anything to do with Ben. Still, the million-dollar question remains, and it has been lurking in the back of my mind all day. Will I meet him tomorrow morning or won't I? And the answer to that question leads to more questions. If I go, mindless of Ben's deception, mindful of his forgiving wife and my own possibly two-timing husband, will it be the experience I want it to be? I don't mean the sex. I know the sex will be phenomenal, apocalyptic, mind-blowing. But will it give me what I need, right now, in my life? Seeing as how *I'm* not even sure what I need, it's a tough one. And if I don't go, will I be not going for the right reasons? Will I be not going in order to preserve a marriage that I suspect camouflages the reality of two people living together with nothing in common aside from their children? Will I be not going so that I can feel morally and ethically sound? And just where will that get me? To heaven? Last time I checked, God takes sinners and saints both. And by not going, will I be missing out on something that could bring me extraordinary pleasure, not just physically, but emotionally as well? Will I regret not going for the rest of my life because I do, in fact, know what I'll be missing?

Another thing is plaguing me as well, doing a do-si-do in my brain alongside thoughts of Ben and thoughts of Jonah, and that is my blog. Tomorrow is the last day of the competition, my last post for the *Ladies Living-Well Journal*. I have no idea what my final post will be, but that's not my main worry since I have managed to conjure up complete posts out of thin air and bullshit. And I am not attached to the outcome, whether I'll win or lose, because what are the odds, really? I am a good writer, but there must be at least one blogger out of the thousands of entries who is as good as me, and who probably writes about more important and socially relevant subjects than men's resemblance to cheese balls. What concerns me is the day *after* tomorrow. Without the motivation of the competition, will I actually sit my fat ass down at my computer and compose? If I want to continue blogging, I will have to set up my own site, buy a domain name, come up with some kind of coherent theme, then map out a stringent daily schedule of writing for no other reason than I want to. As inspired as I was a week ago, I am beginning to feel my resolve slip. And what does that say about my reinvention? First goes the writing, then goes the treadmill, then goes the healthy eating, the glowing skin, and I'll be right back where I was a month ago.

I really need to find an Overthinkers Anonymous meet-

ing, I tell myself as I stare at the ceiling of my bedroom. When my mental masturbation hits Defcon One, and I feel like my eyes are going to burst out of my sockets for all of the gray-matter activity pressing against them, I roll over and reach into my nightstand drawer for my last resort, my little ally for that one activity that can actually clear my mind. The batteries are low, and therefore the vibration comes in fits and starts, but it will have to do.

I don't fantasize about Ben, and of course not Jonah, but instead envision a steamy scenario with a tropical setting starring Hugh Jackman. But, in the end, Hugh only takes me halfway there before I fall, exhausted, fast asleep.

Twenty-five

On the drive to the Garden Hills Police Department's safe haven for witnesses and errant husbands, I find myself thinking about something Jill said. Not yesterday at lunch, because, honestly, I was in such a state at the time that I can barely recall anything that was said, by her or me, but something she said in my garage on Tuesday. Several things she said, actually.

We make choices, and we have to stick with them. We have responsibilities and commitments, and we have to live up to them, even when they practically crush us. All we can do is just make the best of it.

When I awoke this morning, I had already made up my mind to meet Ben. There was no thought behind this decision, no mulling it over or obsessing about it or yanking my hair out in frustration. I simply knew I had to go. But now, as I weave through the sunny streets of my city, I realize that

Jill's words have inspired me, although, as with the gods of foresight, not in the way she meant them.

All we can do is just make the best of it.

This notion is not only depressing, it is ludicrous. Seriously, what are we supposed to do? Just sit around, mentally crossing off the days, ambling in a haze of ambivalence through the rest of our lives, accepting our sorry lot, until, when death finally comes for us, it is a merciful relief? Jesus! I don't want to *amble*. I want to charge! I want to suck every ounce of life out of this sorry state of existence right up until I'm so old that I have to use a straw! If that includes making mistakes of gigantic proportions, so be it. I will embrace my mistakes. I will celebrate them, if for no other reason than because they keep me from drowning in a sea of apathy.

When I turn onto La Croix, a parking spot magically opens up right in front of the designated building, and I take this as a sign. I pull into the space left vacant by a dented Chevy Blazer with a couple of surfboards on the top rack that roars in the direction of the beach in a trail of fumes. I turn off the ignition and sit for a few moments, staring sightlessly through the windshield, sucking in a dozen calming breaths. Then I get out of the Lexus and gaze up at the two-story apartment house.

The complex is unremarkable for this area, with a brown-and-beige wood-sided façade and simple landscaping that includes the indigenous succulent ground cover, flowering hedges, and several obligatory palm trees. I follow the concrete path up to a breezeway, walk past twelve metal mailboxes and a bulletin board that holds a cornucopia of multicolored flyers hawking everything from a cheap sofa to discount personal training. The staircase looms ahead. With each ascending step, my heart beats more furiously in my chest, and it's not solely from the exertion.

The door to apartment eight opens a microsecond after I ring the bell. Ben stands before me, a vision in unbuttoned jeans, no shirt, a towel slung around his neck, his hair just-showered wet, and an eighth of an inch of beard growth peppering his chin. He smiles warmly at me and a single thought steamrolls over all other thoughts in my brain.

I want this man.

He steps aside wordlessly to let me pass, but I stand frozen for moment. Never in my life has a man actually taken my breath away, at least not one who wasn't being projected onto a movie screen. I want to hurl myself at him and wrap myself around him and rocket to the stars at the speed of light.

"Come in," he urges.

I walk into the apartment. The interior is what you would expect from a dwelling that is home to no one. The walls are bare, the furniture is clearly an amalgamation of thrift store purchases, and there are no personal effects or items of interest decorating the room. The plus side is that two walls in the living room are made up of floor-to-ceiling windows, through which the sunshine blazes, cheering the otherwise drab surroundings. At least it's better than a dingy bathroom in a bar.

"Can I get you something?" Ben asks, coming up beside me and gingerly placing his hand on the small of my back. "Coffee?"

I shake my head. My heart is still pounding, and I fear that adding caffeine to my body chemistry would give me a coronary.

He nods, then leans in and kisses me softly on the cheek.

I turn toward him and his lips slide to mine, never breaking contact with my skin. My first instinct is to pull away. He and I should talk first, and I fear that once we get started with the touching and kissing and, uh, the rest, there will be no stopping us until we are a sweaty, sated, horizontal mass. But Ben breaks off the kiss first and takes a step back.

"Are you . . . okay?" He is looking at me intently, as if reading my mind.

"I'm fine," I assure him.

"Sit, sit," he says, gesturing to the worn gray-green couch. "I'm sorry about my ensemble." He chuckles as he crosses the room and grabs a white oxford shirt hanging over the back of a chair. He quickly puts it on, tossing aside the towel, and all I can think is, *Oh, please, no! Don't cover those spectacular pecs.*

"So, how did your surveillance thing go?" I ask him.

"Good," he answers, taking a seat next to me and relaxing back against the cushions. "I can't really talk about it." He grins, embarrassed. "Ongoing case. But we got what we needed. Thanks for asking." He reaches over and brushes his fingertips against my cheek. "I heard there was some excitement at my house yesterday," he says, pulling his hand back and raking it through his wet hair.

"Yeah. You could say that."

"Thanks for your help. Linda is a wunderkind at litigation, but she's not great with exploding pipes. Anyway, the plumber came out and fixed it, and everything's drying out nicely, including the boys."

We sit in awkward silence for a moment. Then he cocks his head at me. "This is kind of weird, huh?"

I exhale, possibly for the first time since I entered the apartment. "Yeah. It is. Kind of."

"Yeah, well, I thought, maybe. I don't know what I thought. . . . I'm not really, uh, well versed at extramarital seduction."

I feel myself go rigid, and Ben notices.

"Sorry. I shouldn't have said that."

I'm silent.

"It's just, this is a first for me," Ben says. "And obviously for you, too. Which makes me feel great, that you'd choose me, that you'd want to. . . . Oh, God, I should just get my jaw wired shut!"

I want to laugh, he is so earnest, but I can't laugh, because he has just lied to me again, *twice*, in the last thirty seconds. I could overlook *one* fib, said over drinks in a bar. But *two*? *Three*, all together? What kind of woman am I, anyway? Have I no standards? *Just don't think about him naked from the waist up and you'll be fine.* I stand and immediately move to the door. I turn back to him but keep my eyes on the floor.

"I'm sorry, Ben."

He bolts off the sofa and takes a few steps toward me. "Wait. Don't go. Ellen, what? What is it?"

Balls, Ellen. Grow some. Right now!

I raise my eyes and stare directly into his. "Linda told me about your affair, Ben."

He looks at me, puzzled, and then slowly, understanding dawns on his face. He leans back against the arm of the couch and blows out a sigh. "Oh. Jesus."

"She was upset. I don't think she even knew what she was saying," I explain, suddenly protective of her.

"No, I . . . I didn't mean . . ."

"So, clearly, this is *not* your first time . . ."

"Wow. You must think I'm . . ." His voice trails off.

A liar? A cheater? A bastard? Check, check, and check. A handsome, sexy, desirable one, but still . . .

"It's true," he admits quietly. "But it was different."

But it was different is right up there in my book with *It didn't mean anything.* I stand there and look directly at him.

"I understand if you want to go, but at least let me explain what happened."

No, I think. *I don't want to hear about it. I don't want you to regale me with your conquest of a twenty-two-year-old hooker with a heart of gold or how you tripped and fell and your dick accidentally landed in your best friend's wife.* What I want, what I wish for with all my heart, is to have the ability to time-travel back to yesterday noon. To have Jill show up on time, so that I wouldn't have had to bear witness to Linda's distress and subsequent revelation. So that I would not be caught in a quagmire of conflict, and would instead be in bed with this man, luxuriating in the feel of him holding me. His dick would probably be inside me by now and there would be nothing accidental about it.

Ben pushes himself to his feet and crosses to me, taking my hands in his. "Please," he says entreatingly. "Come back. Sit down for a few minutes. Then you can go."

Begrudgingly, I allow him to lead me back to the couch. We sit side by side, and after a brief hesitation, he releases my hands and stares down at his own, which he folds in his lap like a contrite schoolboy. My gaze lands on the scarred coffee table in front of us.

"It was a couple of years ago," he begins. "I was working out of L.A. South, which is about a billion miles from here. I was breaking in a new partner. She was straight out of uniform, spent a lot of time with youth services while she was on patrol. Sharp woman, but . . . young." His voice takes on a faraway quality, as though he is caught up in the memory. He doesn't look at me, just continues to inspect his hands. "We'd been working together a couple of weeks when we caught a domestic violence call. It exploded before we got there. Two kids, the mother. I'd been a cop for almost twenty years at that point, and I'd never—It was bad. It was really bad." The way he says *bad*, in a low whisper, causes a chill to course through me. I look at him and see that his eyes are closed and his expression pained, as though he is reliving the scene. I want to reach out to him, but I don't. He opens his eyes and gazes at the coffee table.

"When you see something like that . . ." He clears his throat, swallows, takes a breath. "Your first instinct is to reach out to someone else who's seen the same thing, so you can both try to pretend you didn't see it in the first place. It's like you're trying to prove to each other—to yourself—that the human race actually does have redeeming qualities, despite what we're capable of." He shakes his head regretfully. "It doesn't work. It only gives you a momentary escape. But it happens sometimes."

I think of Mia's dalliance with Peter Stormcloud. *Yes, it does happen.*

Ben scrubs at his face as though trying to wipe the memory away. "Linda blew it out of proportion. Not that she didn't have every right to," he adds quickly. "But it was one night. The night of possibly the worst day of my life."

And now, I do reach out to him, closing my fingers around his. I feel his wedding band digging into my palm, but I don't care.

"Still, it *was* cheating," he says. "But this is different." His eyes find mine. "I feel something for you, Ellen."

"You don't even know me," I say, so softly that I'm not even sure I said the words aloud. But I must have, because Ben counters them.

"At this moment, I probably know you better than anyone else in your life."

I choose my words carefully because he is wrong. There is someone who knows me better than Ben does. That person is *me*.

"I would be lying if I told you that I don't want to be with you," I say. At this, he raises my hand to his lips and kisses it. His beard stubble against my skin sends shivers down my spine. "But," I say, gently withdrawing my hand, "this whole thing, between you and me. It's the same as your . . . one night with your partner. It's an escape. We're drawn together because we're . . . we're new to each other. I feel like I'm the best version of myself when I'm with you."

"Is that such a bad thing?" he asks.

"No," I answer. "It's not. But you don't know anything *about* me. You don't know any of the ugly stuff. The secret stuff. The things that make me who I am. For better or for worse."

"I want to know."

"No, you don't. That's not what affairs are for."

"Ellen."

He suddenly reaches out and pulls me to him and kisses me fiercely. I start to recoil, but when his tongue presses against my lips, demanding access to my mouth, I am unable to resist. We sink against the cushions, fused, as my insides burn. But Ben takes the kiss no further. He retreats, only by inches, and holds my face in his palms.

"I want to know the ugly stuff, too. I want to know all about you. Tell me. Tell me something you've never told anyone before."

I smile at him. "Just one thing?"

"Everything."

"This could take a while."

He chuckles and his breath is sweet. "I'm doing surveillance, remember? I've got all day."

—————

Five hours later, completely drained and in need of a long soak in a hot bath, I pull the Lexus into my driveway. The sun is low in the sky and a faint breeze flutters through the trees, but I am warm, have a surplus of heat flowing through me from my time with Ben.

When I open the front door, I know instantly that something is amiss. There is no sign or telltale sound of Sally. Also, the air feels different, as though it has shifted in the wake of something larger than a dog. My first instinct is *burglar*, and I consider walking out to the front lawn and calling 911. Except for the fact that I can't call 911 from the lawn because my cell phone is currently lying in the bottom left drawer of the kitchen among a veritable buffet of dead batteries that await recycling.

I tentatively tread across the floor of the foyer, my senses on alert, expecting someone to jump out at me, cheap horror-flick style, from any number of hiding places. I stop at the archway and turn toward the living room and let out a frightened screech of deafening proportions.

"Jesus!"

Jonah sits on the couch, staring at me expectantly. He stands up, but doesn't move an inch in my direction.

"Jonah! What are you—shit! You scared me!"

"Sorry," is all he says. He is looking at me like I am a total stranger and my stomach roils with sickening dread.

"Where are the kids?" I ask, trying to keep my voice steady.

"I dropped them at Jill's."

Oh, God. What did my cousin tell him? Did she call him and relay my whole sordid week to him, hickey included? Tell him to get his ass home before things went from worse to downright irreversible? No. Jill wouldn't do that. Would she? No. She wouldn't.

"I guess you parked in the garage," I say dumbly.

"Yup. You did a great job in there." While his words are complimentary, his tone is anything but. I am sweating with guilt and shame and wonder if Jonah can smell the scent of my sins from across the room. He narrows his eyes at me and shoves his hands in his pockets while I stand there, taut with tension, awaiting a verbal firestorm. "What happened to your cell phone?"

It takes me a minute to process his question, since I was expecting a far different one, then quickly think of a few alternatives to the truth. *Stolen by a marauding purse snatcher, crushed beneath an alien spaceship's crash landing, borrowed by MacGyver to avert nuclear holocaust.* Anything to deflect the blame away from my irresponsibility. As if my mishap with my cell phone is the worst thing I've done.

"I dropped it in the toilet," I say finally. At least I can be honest about that.

"I didn't realize you were so attached to your cell that you brought it with you to the bathroom."

"It was in the back pocket of my jeans. I keep it there sometimes."

"Since when?" His voice is laced with sarcasm.

I realize that this conversation is probably not about my cell phone, and if it is, it shouldn't be. Wearily, I drop my purse on the stairs and head into the living room. As I move toward him, Jonah recoils from me as if he were a sea urchin being poked by a stick.

"What are you doing home, Jonah? You weren't supposed to come back till Saturday."

"Yeah. Sorry to disrupt your schedule," he says coldly.

He knows he knows he knows is all I can think. *But how?*

As if in answer, he says, "I read your blog."

My mind reels. *My blog?* I can't access enough words to form a question, but, again, I don't need to. Jonah continues without being prompted.

"My mom showed it to me."

Oh God, of course! My mother-in-law has been an avid reader of the *Ladies Living-Well Journal* since its inception in 1963.

"Drove me crazy about it, actually." Jonah laughs without warmth. "She's been following the competition from the beginning, kept going on about this one blogger, almost as soon as we got there. Said I had to read it. Said all men should read it if they want to know how a woman's mind works."

Well, I'll be goddamned. Margaret likes my blog. Margaret *agrees* with my blog. Margaret and I are like-minded about something. I don't think this has ever happened in the entire course of our thirteen-year relationship. It's a good thing she doesn't know who wrote it, however; otherwise she would not only dismiss it as garbage, but would come after me with her husband's precious rifle because *no one* messes with Margaret's son.

"Obviously, she didn't know you wrote it," he says, his words mirroring my thoughts. "But I figured it out pretty quickly. Imagine my surprise." He glowers at me. "Can you? Can you possibly imagine my surprise?"

I cross my arms over my chest, suddenly furious.

"Actually, I can," I say defiantly. "I *imagine* it was the same way I felt when I found that sweet little love note hidden in your desk drawer. You obviously didn't read my blogs closely enough or you'd know that I found it. Tell me, Jonah. Who is *T*? I figured the *J* part out all by myself. But the *T* kind of stumped me."

The color drains from Jonah's face and his shoulders

slump. He leans back against the arm of the couch, exactly the same way that Ben did earlier. In fact, I am having a vague sense of déjà vu as I wait for Jonah to explain his own extra-curricular activities.

"It's not what you think," he says and I almost want to laugh at the cliché. *Almost.*

"I feel so much better," I snap, not feeling better at all. "Tricia, right?"

He nods but says nothing. A silence stretches between us, and I recognize this moment as a turning point. No cannons firing or cymbals crashing, just a quiet moment between two people whose future is unclear.

Jonah pinches the bridge of his nose between two fingers, then lowers his hand. He has the decency to look up at me as he talks. "Her brother died a few months ago. Car accident. Crazy thing. Fluke. She took it hard. He was all the family she had left. I thought I told you about it."

I shake my head. He shrugs. "Maybe I didn't."

Maybe he did but I wasn't listening. Or maybe he thought he did, but he wasn't really speaking. Such is marital life.

"She asked me to go with her to the funeral, and I ended up taking her home and staying with her. I was afraid to leave her alone. I let her talk through it, get it all out." He looks at me. "I didn't sleep with her."

I can tell by his expression that while he may not have done the nasty, he did more than just listen. But I am not angry. In fact, I suddenly feel like a weight has been lifted from my shoulders. It's not that each of our individual actions serves to cancel the other out. It's because the rug has finally been pulled away, revealing the dust beneath. The dust that accumulates in a marriage. The dust that has to be swept up, whether or not the marriage is going to survive. His secret note and my anonymous blog have opened up fresh wounds in our relationship, but perhaps open wounds are exactly what we need in order to start seeing and hearing each other again. And paying attention to the course of our marriage rather than allowing it to blow whichever way the wind carries it.

"Did you sleep with him?" Jonah asks quietly.

I drop my arms to my sides, no longer defensive, and really look at Jonah for the first time in a long time. He looks tired and sad and hopeful at the same time. He is worried about my answer, but ready to accept it, whatever it is.

"Does it matter?" I say. "I *wanted* to sleep with him. Isn't that enough?"

His eyes focus on my face and I can tell that he is doing exactly the same thing to me as I am doing to him. Seeing me, as if anew. He slowly shakes his head.

I put my hand out to him and he takes it, then gives it a squeeze. A few seconds later, he stands up and opens his arms to me, and I step into them, feeling their strength as they envelop me. I slide my hands around his waist and rest my head against his shoulder, detecting his heartbeat against my cheek. Jonah's hugs have been a constant in my life. He hugs enthusiastically, always has, and his hugs are an infusion of warmth and energy. But today, his embrace feels different. It feels like a safe haven, a calm port in a hurricane, a momentary respite from being alone in a big bad world. Today, his embrace feels like something new.

We stay that way for a long time, neither of us willing to break free. When the living room becomes full of shadows, and we hear the faint scratch of paws on the kitchen door, I lift my head and look up into Jonah's face.

"We better let her in."

He nods and kisses the top of my head. But instead of pulling away, I nestle my cheek upon his chest once more.

"Then," I tell him, in rhythm with his beating heart, "I'd like to go pick up our kids."

....

Fourteenth Post: March 29, 2012
SomethingNewAt42

A LESSON LEARNED

So, my friends, we come to the end of the blog competition and my final post. I must tell you that these past few weeks have been quite an amazing ride, and although you have been privy to only a fraction of my life, doubtless you can understand what I am talking about by what you do know.

I took an hour to read through all my earlier posts and realized that every single title is made up of three words. I didn't plan this, nor did I think about it when I was writing each blog, it just happened. It's kind of funny, though. And as I looked at each title, I thought about those other three words that are perhaps the most used three words in the history of the world, and I do not mean *Give me drugs!* or *I need chocolate!* You know the ones.

I love you.

Those three words are bandied about all the time. Sometimes they are said with true emotion behind them, and sometimes merely spoken in order to get laid. They are whispered to sleeping children in the middle of the night and cheerfully called to canines who have finally mastered scratching on the sliding glass door instead of peeing on the rug. They are said with regret and remorse and tearfully sobbed to lovers on departing trains. They are said by almost-forty-three-year-old women to their mothers over the phone (which are sincere) and to Hugh Jackman on the

TV screen (which—alas—are not *really* sincere). They are said to coffins being lowered into the ground and to inanimate objects (like the Keurig I'm going to get for Mother's Day) and to favorite foods (generally the high-fat, high-caloric kind because who would say *I love you* to a stalk of celery?). They are said all the time in all manners of ways.

But they are rarely said by us to ourselves.

I have learned a great deal about myself in the last month. I have learned that I am not such a moral person as I thought I was. I have learned that I can rationalize with the best of them. I have learned that I have a rash daredevil inside me. I have learned that while I love what exercise does for my body, I loathe my treadmill. I have learned that I easily bend to temptation, but at least I am willing to admit to it.

You know what else I've learned? That despite my lines and limitations, I love me. For better or for worse, the good, bad, and the ugly included. I love me. And I'm going to start telling myself that I love me, aloud, at least once a day. I dare you to join me in this pact. Each morning, when you wake up, go to your mirror. Don't worry about your bedhead or your morning breath or the fact that your boobs are sagging a fraction of an inch lower than they were yesterday. Just look at your reflection and say, "I love you." It may be awkward at first. You may stutter and stammer and grow hot with embarrassment. But say it anyway. Aloud. It will certainly be something new. And eventually, after a while, after a lot of practice, it will end up being Something True.

EPILOGUE

As it turns out, I was the overwhelming favorite of the blog competition, and readers demanded that I win first prize. Everyone, that is, except my mother-in-law, who, when she found out I was the one whose blog she loved, reversed her opinion about my posts, demanded that Jonah divorce me, and started an e-mail crusade to the *Ladies Living-Well Journal* in which she harangued them for awarding $10,000 to a cruel, heartless, adulterous debaucher. She has not spoken to me for months now, even goes as far as hanging up when I answer the phone. Since Jonah and I are making an effort to work on our marriage, I keep my derogatory comments to myself, but I'll have you know that the next time she gets a jar of rose-infused honey from me will be the twelfth of friggin' never. (But to keep Masood happy, I have added dried dates and walnuts to my diet, which give me a boost of energy in the afternoons.)

I am now gainfully employed by the *Ladies Living-Well Journal* as their official blogger, and I also write a column once a month for their print magazine. Both the blog and the column are called—you guessed it—*Something New*. For the sake of literary greatness, or more accurately, pop entertainment, I undertake something new every week and then write about it, in the hopes of inspiring other women to get out and experience all of the wonderful things life has to offer. Not surprisingly, the *Journal* has asked me to tone down my colorful vocabulary, but this is no problem, as I have also set up a personal blog on which I can curse like a truck driver if I so choose.

For the record, since I know what curiosity can do firsthand, and it ain't pretty, I will reveal to you the answer to the question that may be plaguing you. No, Ben and I did not. During our five-plus hours together, we talked until our throats were sore, held hands, laughed, joked, ordered in Chinese, watched a soap opera he claims he is *not* addicted to, talked some more, and even lay together on the bed cuddling. But over the course of our lengthy conversations about everything from our deepest, darkest secrets to the craziest thing we've ever done in public to our opinions on democracy in the Middle East, we got to know each other well enough to mutually decide that we shouldn't go forward with the affair.

It wasn't that we realized we didn't like each other. Quite the opposite, actually. We liked each other even more than before. Sex would ruin it. It would be amazing for about an hour, but ultimately sleeping together would sour us. We agreed to be friends, friends with a delicious memory to revisit whenever we needed to, friends who could call each other to pick up the other's kids in an emergency, who could hang out with spouses present and not squirm with guilt. We also decided that if both of our marriages should mysteriously, spontaneously combust, we'd meet at the Four Seasons before the ink on our divorce papers dried.

I was afraid that the first time I saw him after our rendez-vous would be awkward and uncomfortable, that Ben might ignore me, and that I should probably ignore him, too. But as soon as I reached the soccer field for the Saturday game, accompanied by my kids, their gear, and my husband (who never asked for my would-be lover's identity and was never offered it, although deep down, he must have some idea), Ben waved to me from the fence, hurried over to help with our stuff, shook Jonah's hand, and slung his arm across my shoulder like an old friend. And I suppose that's exactly what we are now. Old friends.

Jill has started her own blog called *Marriage Whoa's* in which she tracks her husband Greg's every movement. (She writes under a pseudonym, of course.) Poor Greg. I almost feel sorry for him. Jill may never divorce him, but there is no end to his wife-inflicted, Web-published torment if he goes even a day without complimenting her in some way. She actually signed him up as a subscriber, along with all of his co-workers to whom she revealed the truth, so that her blog goes straight to the office e-mail for all to see. I have to say that I am very proud of her for being as proactive in her marriage as she is in all other aspects of her life.

My kids were thrilled that I won the competition, but upset that they weren't allowed to read my blog. I requested that the *Ladies Living-Well Journal* remove the old posts from the Web in order to protect the innocent, and the magazine graciously complied. I'm certain that some genius computer hacker could find it somewhere in the vortex of the vast Internet, but I'm pretty confident my kids can't. They are too young to understand it right now, even Connor. Someday, when they are adults, if they ask me about it, I will let them each have a copy of all of the posts, which I printed up right after I won the contest. I'm not worried about what the blog will say about me, or what my grown children will think of me once they've read it. I'll deal with that when the time comes. At some point, we all realize that our parents are not superheroes, but real live human beings. It's natural and healthy. But for now, as long as it lasts, I'll relish being Wonder Woman to my kids.

As for Jonah and me, we are taking every day as it comes. We have had our fair share of arguments over the past few months, but even those have been a welcome change from the ambivalence that's been clouding our marriage for the last few years. We have given each other license to be brutally frank with one another about our feelings, our needs, and our expectations. If you were secretly eavesdropping on one of our conversations with some of Ben's surveillance equipment, you might hear the following phrases: "You are hearing me, but are you actually listening?" or "You're looking at me, but are you really seeing me?" or "Are you at all present in this discussion?"

You also might hear laughter. Because we are getting to know each other again, and learning to make each other laugh like we used to. And while I can't predict the future of our relationship, I can tell you that for the first time in a long time, I have hope. I love Jonah and he loves me and we are both willing to try to rediscover the reasons that we're together. These days, an old Carly Simon song frequently comes to mind. *Don't look at your man in the same old way, take a new picture*, she sings. I am trying to follow that advice. *Something New* might be exciting and invigorating and rejuvenating, but you can take it from a recently-turned-forty-three-year-old woman: finding something new in *Something Old* can be even better.

READERS GUIDE

Something New

QUESTIONS FOR DISCUSSION

1. Ellen describes herself as bored, and her life as a "suburban cliché." Is Ellen is going through a midlife crisis, or does her discomfort stem from something deeper?

2. Ellen says, "At some point between being a good wife and a good mother and always doing the right thing, I have lost me." Does Ellen resent being defined as a wife and mother? How does she want to be defined, and how does she see herself? Do you think she is happy with her life?

3. Jill and Ellen are best friends, although very different. Describe the dynamic of their relationship and why it works. Do you think they would be friends if they weren't related?

4. Ellen struggles at first to find a topic to write about in her blog. If you were starting a blog, what would you write about?

5. Describe Ellen's tone as a narrator. How does her self-deprecating humor shape her story?

6. Along those same lines, why do you think Ellen's blog was so successful with the women who read *Ladies Living Well Journal*?

7. Ben teaches Ellen, "If you stop trying new things, you might as well just stop." Do you agree with this statement? Is it important to try new things all the time?

8. Explain why Mia's cautionary tale of her own affair influences Ellen to continue to pursue her affair with Ben. Shouldn't this revelation have had the opposite effect?

9. The reader is privy to Ellen's constant inner conflict. Why do you think Ellen keeps going back to Ben, even when her inner dialogue tells her not to? Overall, why does Ellen stray?

10. Discuss the theme of reinvention. Is it possible to reinvent yourself? Why or why not?

11. When Ellen finds the love note in Jonah's drawer, does this give her a free pass to cheat on him, in her mind? Describe her emotions surrounding the note, up until the end of the story when she confronts Jonah.

12. Do you believe Ellen's affair with Ben saved her marriage to Jonah? Why or why not?

13. Is Ellen a likable character? Does her ability to laugh at herself make you sympathize with her, or does it just hide her unlikable qualities?

14. Ellen's final blog describes the lesson she learned from the blog contest and the affair: to love herself. Why is this an important lesson for her?

15. What do you think the future holds for Ellen and her family? Can Ellen and Ben truly remain "just friends"? Was the author's ending realistic to you?

16. Is Ellen's "something new" the blog, or the affair, or both? How do those two things influence the other?